A Plain and Simple Truth

Jane Emersson

A Plain and Simple Truth

Copyright © Jane Emerssen 2015
First published in 2015 by JayStone Publications, Bewdeill, Ashtree Avenue,
Keswick, Cumbria, CA12 5PF

www.jane-emerssen.co.uk

Distributed by Gardners Books
1 Whittle Drive, Eastbourne, East Sussex, BN23 6QH
Tel: +44(0)1323 521555 | Fax: +44(0)1323 521666

British Library Cataloguing in Publication Data
A catalogue record for this book is available from the British Library

ISBN 978-0-9574310-1-0

Typeset by Amolibros, Milverton, Somerset
www.amolibros.com
This book production has been managed by Amolibros
Printed and bound by T J International Ltd, Padstow, Cornwall, UK

Acknowledgements

═══════════

My grateful thanks to John Oxley for providing me with a lively account of the life and times of a Northumbrian farmer in the late 1980s and '90s; also to the many members of various reading groups in Cumbria who encouraged me to finish this sequel; and last, but not least to my forbearing Other Half, who has learnt to live with someone who tends to go suddenly AWOL at odd moments during mealtimes when wrestling with wayward characters or an unexpected shift in the plot.

JE, April 2015

═══════════

CHAPTER ONE

November 1988

Tom rolled over onto his back and studied the ceiling. The harsh light from the full moon filtered through the curtains, filling the room with a blue-white glow and impenetrable shadows. Outside, there was the stillness of a frosty night.

How long had he been awake? Too long. It seemed like an eternity of relentless tossing and turning, his pillow an uncomfortable lump, the blankets and sheet in mortal combat with his quilt refusing to respond to any attempt to keep them in order. He was sleepless and exhausted. Two over-generous tumblers of fine malt whisky, consumed in very short order, should have rendered him unconscious until the beep-beep-beeping of the alarm percolated the fog in his head at six-thirty. Instead, his brain was on fire.

He threw off the rebellious quilt and reached out for the bedside clock. The luminous hands informed him it was ten-to-four. Ten-to-four was way, way too early to face what had to be faced – his changed life – his altered state.

Perversely, he knew this required his undivided attention. But not now, and his thoughts kept sliding away, like guilty children avoiding awkward questions. His failure to concentrate was troubling. Instead of focusing, his mind seemed determined to indulge itself, randomly selecting an unrelated topic and pursuing this to extreme lengths. Anything, rather than face the truth.

Barely eighteen hours ago, he had wandered into his mother's silent studio, grief lodged like a lump of lead in his chest. Around him was the abandoned evidence of her artwork, and the students who had occupied the stools and easels three short weeks before. They had gone – and now, so had she.

Sitting alone in the high-backed leather chair behind the old mahogany desk, he had read her letter from the grave: a strange letter, telling him things she could have spoken of when he had been sitting beside her in those final days.

'To my special son:' it began.

'Darling Thomas,

'I'm writing this because there are things I've never talked to you about before.

'After my father died, I became curious to find out more about my family history. You'll find what I discovered written down in the blue ring-binder in the bottom right-hand drawer of my desk, together with the documents and photographs referred to. It proved an emotional journey at the time, until I became able to put things into perspective.

'If I learnt anything from this painful exercise, it was that truth isn't always plain – or simple. Circumstances at the time can prevent people from being entirely honest, and sometimes precious relationships depend on a necessary fiction. But often, whether we like it or not, the truth will come to light in the end.

'I've been extraordinarily lucky, Thomas. I've had three splendid children, and twenty-five happy years with a wonderful, loving man. Please look after him for me – and look after yourself too. I only wish I'd been given longer to see you settled. Sarah is a lovely girl. Don't take too long to decide if you love her enough. Time slips away too quickly. Remember that.

'Your loving Mother'

Underneath, she had added four kisses.

Eighteen hours ago, after reading her letter, it had seemed so easy to make such a promise. He was only sorry she had not asked him to make it when he could have given her his word, and she would have died knowing that he meant to keep it.

Please look after him for me.

Yes, he would, he had vowed. Fate had been unkind. Everyone said so. Robert Moray deserved better.

"He took it hard the first time," folk had said, shaking their heads. "Went south and stayed away for years. Aye, it'll be worse for him the second time around." And Robert's cousin, Ian Robson, over at High Oakbank Farm, who had seen it all before, said they were right. The signs were there. Robert was turning in on himself again, a shadow of the man they had seen in the lambing sheds that spring. He had aged over the summer, his head bowed, his chestnut hair threaded with grey. His mouth had become a tight line, the creases etched more deeply at the corners, his cheeks sunken, and the joy had gone out of his eyes. He would need love, and care – and hope for the future – and Tom had felt no hesitation in making his promise. Beyond his own sense of loss, lay the strong conviction he could be the rock to cling to – unshakable and unshaken.

But that was before – before he had found the notelet box and opened it. Eighteen hours ago. Such a simple act; such profound consequences beyond his imagining.

He had dug out the family history, curious now – although he had never been curious before. And there was so much to read! He had been engrossed: painstaking notes; family trees filled with names, dates and places; photographs carefully annotated; documents and scraps of paper, each telling the story of another time; remote, peopled by folk unknown to him, except for his lovely old great-aunts – Millicent and Sylvia – who had lived in their sprawling Georgian house in Broxley, deep in the heart of the Cheshire countryside. Now they too were gone. He remembered thinking how uncomplicated his own life was compared with those laid bare before him.

He wondered why he had been so incurious. Too absorbed in helping to run the farm at the time, no doubt – but no excuse. His mother's past, he realised, had remained something of a mystery. The distant family connection between Robert and herself – the Douglas Connection – was well-known, but little else. Of her father, James, she had never been forth-coming. Now he knew why.

James Driscoll was long dead, weighed down by shame, and although Tom had learnt long ago that his grandmother

Daphne had always planned a marriage between her nephew Oliver Gorst and her daughter Laura, he had never queried why she harboured such lasting animosity towards Robert Moray. To the end she had remained estranged, bitter and resentful, dying unloved and alone, a chronic alcoholic.

Among his mother's photographs, there was not a single record of this domineering woman, and the only image of her unassuming husband was a black-and-white print of him taken with his daughter 'On the Occasion of her Twenty-First'. This solitary reminder had stood in its neat silver frame on the corner of the desk for as long as Tom could remember, along with the cherished Venetian glass paperweight streaked with crimson, blue and yellow, and the Edwardian silver letter opener with chased ivy leaves on the handle.

Tom's thoughts drifted back to the present. Outside, from one of the ancient oaks behind the farm, the stillness of the night was pierced by the haunting cry of an owl, sending shivers down his spine.

The night of the funeral, he had been out in the barn moving bales of straw, eager to find peace and solitude after so many strangers had demanded his attention. Kindly folk, offering condolences. But he had gone beyond wanting these. Out of nowhere, a ghostly shape had glided past on silent wings, swooping up onto its perch high in the rafters, from where it had surveyed him with dark, unblinking, eyes. Had it been an omen? The coming of knowledge? Superstitious rubbish of course. But the following afternoon he had found the notelet box – and opened it.

Inside the box, the little volume of poetry – *The Rubaiyat of Omar Khayyam* – would have roused little interest beyond a cursory inspection of its well-worn leather binding, and the novelty of the title mimicking an exotic eastern script. On the bookshelves in the sitting room next to Palgrave's *Golden Treasury*, there was a less ornate, but more pristine copy: an unremarkable scholarly work with copious explanatory notes, yellowing pages and a cream cloth-bound cover. But this smaller version, with its evidently well-used appearance, had stirred his curiosity. As he held it, it had opened naturally in several places. From one of the pages, a small deckle-edged black-and-white photograph had fallen to the floor. At first he had thought it nothing more than a bookmark for a favourite poem. And so it was.

> *Ah, fill the Cup: – what boots*
> *it to repeat*
> *How Time is slipping underneath*
> *our Feet:*
> *Unborn To-morrow and dead*
> *Yesterday,*
> *Why fret about them if To-day be*
> *sweet!*

But in the act of retrieving it, he had unintentionally opened a Pandora's Box.

For the rest of his life he would remember that first inconsequential moment: feeling the deckle-edging rough against his finger tips; his mind beginning to concentrate on what he saw; the creeping sense that all was not well; the sudden recognition of the image in his hand. It was a studio portrait of a man not much older than himself: the generous mouth caught in a half-smile; the thick dark hair falling almost carelessly onto the broad brow; the intensity of the expression in the eyes; the strong, straight nose with slightly flared nostrils; and the contours of the face – all familiar because they precisely matched his own.

He could remember the silence inside his head that seemed to expand and swallow him up; the onset of remoteness from everything around him; of becoming a casual observer of himself as he turned over the image and read –

'To Laura from John, with love – February 1963'

He remembered the rising panic.

Outside, the owl was calling out to him again.

Almost five o'clock. Almost time to face a new day pretending to be someone he was not. He was no longer Thomas Moray of Rigg End Farm, the twenty-four year old son of Robert and Laura Moray, elder brother to James and Flora; the heir apparent to ten acres of fine pasture land down by the broad river in the valley bottom, and seventy acres of good grazing up on The Rigg, sheltered from the harsh north winds by the ancient Roman Wall. Nor could he pretend he was Thomas Moray, the intended fiancé of Sarah, younger daughter of Wallace and Mary Armstrong of Rattling Gate Farm, Stanegate. He was someone else.

The moon began to set and the room slipped into pre-dawn darkness.

He remembered the sea of strangers among the family and friends crowding into the house; people in their uniform funereal black; some being introduced, some introducing themselves, their names and faces soon forgotten – art dealers, collectors, reporters – circulating around him like eddies in a stream. Except for one. The man his father had introduced without much ceremony as someone who had a fine collection of his mother's work. Beyond the fleeting notion they might have met somewhere before, Tom had not given him much thought. But the face in the photograph was the same man. Older, of course, but not much changed by time: the hair still thick, a lustrous dark brown, greying slightly at the temples; the broad brow a little more furrowed; but the same curve of the lips and strong straight nose; the eyes, chocolate brown, like his own.

Tom remembered the scent of aftershave, and the man's reaction on being introduced – shock – smothered almost at once by a careful politeness. Remembered the softly-spoken voice; the intensity of gaze; and the tears held back; the lingering handshake, then Robert ushering the man away. The memory grew sharper with every recollection; more painful, leaving behind the nagging question, like an ache in a tooth – why had Robert introduced them? What had spurred him on to say those few simple but potentially devastating words – "Thomas, I'd like you to meet Mr Rufford"? Had he gambled it was better to control what might prove uncontrollable in other circumstances? To keep the meeting brief and simple away from more perceptive eyes? Jamie's – or Flora's? Friends and neighbours? Why else take such a risk?

Questions, questions, questions: questions Tom had found himself too discomfited to ask, even with a generous tumbler of whisky to help him find the words. And even when Robert had asked him that evening in that softly-spoken Scottish burr of his, "Do you want to ask me something, Tom?" he had lacked the courage to demand the truth. All he could muster was the lame response, "What can you tell me about Mr Rufford, Dad?"

And Robert had taken a long, slow draught of whisky, in no hurry to answer as they sat together by the fire. And who could blame him? "We were rivals once," he had said sombrely. "Given time, he would have won her in the end."

And when Tom had tried to press him further asking, "What happened?" Robert had said, almost defiantly, "I stole her from him. He'd played the field before they met. She thought he'd never change. I seized the moment." But his elation had melted away as quickly as it came, and he had sunk back into his melancholic state, staring into the flames, crushed under the weight of an old and terrible knowledge he had held close to his heart for too many years. There had been a long silence, and finally, baring his soul he had confessed, "I'd no illusions, Tom. I knew I was the safe haven she needed at the time. I could never light the spark in her the way he did," adding with a touch of triumph in his voice, "I can't complain – she's left me three wonderful children – and years of loving to remember. That's what I stole from John Rufford."

A log had collapsed into the red-hot core of the blaze, burning down to ashes in a roar of flame, and Tom had sat there, overwhelmed and unable to respond, thinking of his mother and this stranger's deep abiding love for her spanning the years with a silken thread, and her own secret feelings for him, hidden away but harboured nonetheless. Faced with her mortality, had guilt prompted her to write the letter to her 'special son'? – To explain herself, however opaquely, fearing what might lie ahead?

The truth will come to light in the end.

And it had. There was tragedy written in Rufford's face when recognition dawned: the sense of loss and wasted years; of love that might have been and could be no more.

At some point in that painful conversation by the fire, Tom had downed his whisky no longer seeking answers. Did the truth matter? Did it diminish the love Robert had given him? Did it alter the feelings he had for this upright, faithful man? No, he had convinced himself, pouring a second whisky for them both, it did not. He would help Robert through his grief and loss. Shield him from unnecessary pain. Give him hope for the future. Except that now, with the passing of the hours and the coldness of that late November dawn, a feeble light creeping in at the window, the certainties of life had crumbled into dust. And with them, all his sense of being who he was – Thomas Moray – a rock to cling to – solid and dependable – no matter what. He was none of these. He was a weak and feeble straw, easily broken and blown in the wind. An insubstantial nothing.

How could he keep a promise made in ignorance? He no longer knew. He was a cuckoo in the nest, pretending he was not.

The bedside clock clicked suddenly, and beeped into life.

CHAPTER TWO

John reached Lower Chursley just before dark. Too tired to care, he left the car parked on the driveway and stumbled into the house. His image in the hall mirror showed a man visibly the worse for wear. He ran a hand distractedly through his hair disconcerted by his dishevelled state, and for a moment, a younger face looked back at him. He quickly turned away.

The light on the answerphone was blinking. There were several messages – all from Gemma – increasingly anxious. He had no inclination to phone her to explain.

He drew the curtains against the onset of a frosty night, a full moon rising overhead. Showered and changed, he prepared to numb his brain, not with alcohol, but with music. Lying back on his recliner, eyes closed, he let the spine-tingling Puccini aria wash over him. He did not want to think, but his random and chaotic thoughts whirled in his head like dervishes. And they always brought him back to the same point – the moment he had looked into that face and felt the full force of what he saw.

The day before – or was it a lifetime ago? – he had struggled down the rutted farm track to his car and driven away with exaggerated care. Mud from melting snow had splashed up onto the paintwork. It was of little consequence. What mattered most was that he should quit the place with as much dignity as he could muster under the circumstances. In his rear view mirror, he had seen Robert Moray standing sentinel-like, watching him leave.

Out on the lane, he had headed west into an early dusk. To the north, an angry bank of purpled cloud had gathered and spread southwards, blotting out the sinking sun. By the time he had reached the main road, the sky had become a sullen iron-grey wash, and a thin but persistent drizzle had set in with a rising wind behind it. Further on, where the road climbed steadily into open wilderness, curtains of rain had swept in. Soon the rhythm of the wipers had become hypnotic: swish, swish, swishing; beating time with the blood that was pounding in his head.

What had been done, had been done, and could never be undone. *The Moving Finger writes: and having writ, Moves on …*

It had gone dark. In a steady downpour, he had turned southward onto the motorway and travelled twenty miles or so in the wake of articulated lorries throwing up walls of salted spray and obliterating the road ahead. His concentration had flagged. At the next junction he had turned off finding himself on a minor road in the middle of nowhere. He had driven on for a mile or two before pulling into a rough gravel access to a field-gate, and stopped the car.

For a while, he had watched the slanting rain caught in the headlights before he turned them off, closing his eyes and shutting out the world.

He could recall nothing of the journey so far – except the rain. He had driven in this state of mind before, many years ago – on the day that Laura told him they would never meet again. Ever after, he had clung to the hope she might change her mind. But she never did. Now, she never would. She was beyond his reach.

The young man's face leapt into his mind once more.

He should never have gone to her funeral. He should have had the good grace to confine himself to composing a well-penned letter of condolence, and explain perhaps, if this were really necessary, why he had wanted to remain the anonymous purchaser of so much of her work for so many years; expressing regret too that his anonymity had been compromised earlier that year by the unfortunate lapse of concentration on the part of the gallery's temporary assistant.

But from the moment the art dealer had phoned to give him the shattering news that Laura had died, he had felt compelled to meet Moray face-to-face just one last time.

It was a selfish act, surely, to impose his presence on a man mourning the loss of his wife? Why should Moray want to see *him*? – the man she had rejected all those years ago? – a self-confessed obsessive who could not let her go? How could he explain himself?

His mind drifted back to that balmy autumn Sunday afternoon ten years before. He had been sitting on his balcony listening to the sounds of life around him: children playing in the park across the road; laughter from a neighbouring flat; someone's television on too loud. He had been listless and dispirited. A mid-life crisis someone called it later. His prestigious status as Chief Officer of Weaverdale's District Council no longer gave him any satisfaction: he found the duties tedious; the petty Party politics beneath contempt. Mentally adrift, he had been idly leafing through a Sunday supplement when an image in a full-page photograph had leapt out at him and rocked him to the core. In that heart-stopping moment, he had been thrust backwards to another time, to another Sunday afternoon – in January 1963 – when he and Laura had walked hand-in-hand across the frozen fields down to the reed beds fringing Rothwell Mere, and a heron had taken flight. Suddenly, barely touched by time, she was smiling at him once again, as she had done all those years ago when he had photographed her standing by the mere – when he had realised she was someone special, but failed to tell her what he truly felt – that he did not want this brief relationship to end.

Here, in the article beside the photograph, were the details of her life in those lost years without her: her initial artistic success; the adoption of her professional name, 'Laura Douglas', to acknowledge the family history she and her husband shared; and the recognition by many in the art world of the highly-acclaimed courses she had inaugurated and continued to run from her studio at Rigg End Farm. There was a photograph of her at work in her studio, and another showing her with Moray at the opening of her latest exhibition at a gallery somewhere in Edinburgh, his arm protectively around her waist, an image John found hard to bear. There had been a passing reference to their children, Thomas, James and Flora, but no smiling family photograph. Now John knew why.

He had kept the article, although it tortured him to read it, and he had tucked it away in one of his photographic albums, believing this to be its rightful home.

Freed from the expectations of her past and fired by her own determination to succeed, Laura had forged a new beginning for herself, just as she said she would. And that afternoon on his balcony – for a second time – she had changed his life as well. She had shown him the way: he had thrown off his past and started on the road to become the professional photographer he had always wanted to be. He could not claim to have reached her exalted heights of course, but he had made a modest mark, and hoped if she should ever hear of his success, she would recognise the part that she had played in this. A fanciful notion no doubt, but it gave him pleasure to believe it.

The following morning he had handed in his resignation, walked away from his desk and travelled up to Edinburgh, found the gallery and bought the first of her paintings he would buy in years to come – *Snow on Larches*. It reminded him of the little practice pieces she had shown him once. They had been tentative explorations into the colours hidden deep within newly-fallen snow. They had been luminous and exquisitely executed, and in them he had briefly glimpsed her life to come.

Afterwards, waiting for her to join him on the drive at Meeston Lodge, he had come face-to-face with Robert Moray for the first time.

For reasons John could no longer remember, Laura had recounted the sad tale of this lonely widower who worked part-time in the garden at the Lodge, and whose love for a local schoolmistress had fallen foul of village gossip and ultimately come to nothing. In a moment of casual indifference, John had jokingly dubbed him 'The Pale Knight' from Keats' poem 'La Belle Dame Sans Merci'. But the man who had stood squarely in front of him that afternoon on the driveway at Meeston Lodge had been no pale knight, and John had sensed a rival without ever knowing why. There had been something about him, and he could not say what: he was a man slightly older than himself; stocky, with a strong physique; a shock of unruly chestnut hair above an intelligent, taciturn face, and a defiance about him it was impossible to dismiss. Even now, John could remember the close scrutiny of those intensely green eyes, an intensity that had not dimmed with age. But the man John had seen standing outside Rigg End Farm, for all his fierce pride, was a shadow of his former self: greying now, hollow-cheeked, weighed down by loss.

From the hi-fi, the strains of Beethoven's *Pastoral Symphony* filled the room, briefly intruding on John's thoughts.

Then he was in the car again, travelling north. The journey had not been easy, sudden flurries of snow making driving difficult. He had arrived at the crematorium with only minutes to spare. There, outside the red-bricked building with its arched porch, people were gathering in close-knit groups. He had sat in the car, alone, waiting, but at the sight of the hearse, his courage had failed: he could not watch her make that final journey. Later, like a reluctant shadow, he had followed the string of cars winding down the wintry lanes, keeping his distance. When at last they had turned up the track leading to the farm, he had driven on, stopping a little further out of sight.

He had waited, debating the wisdom of being there at all.

Some time later, a Range Rover had driven away and he had thrown caution to the winds, negotiating his way up the rutted track to fill the vacant parking space.

The acrid tang of wood-smoke had drifted on the breeze when he got out of the car, and with it came the sound of cattle lowing in the byres and dogs barking somewhere in the yard. No one had seen him arrive. He could have turned back then, and no one would have known he had ever been there. Instead, he had set off up the track towards the house keeping to the wall, picking his way carefully between the melting snow, mud and slush.

The house itself was set back with a little garden at the front. It was unpretentious in design: a sturdy double-fronted building in rough cream and black stone with grey slab tiling on the roof and solid chimney stacks at either end. There was a stone porch at the front and five neat sash windows facing south across the valley that would capture the sun, even in winter. A fine view. He had turned to look. The fields and farmsteads below were dappled in snow; the broad river, black and undulating, snaked into the distance.

On either side of the house, outbuildings and walls enclosed a yard to the rear. Through a gap in the wall, he had glimpsed a complex of newer barns and sheds set against a backdrop of a small wood. Beyond this, the steeply rising ground and bare hillside dominated the skyline to the north, sheltering the farmstead from the icy winter winds. A pleasant spot then, for all its isolation. Was this why Laura loved it? He had never understood.

The front door had been left ajar, and a hubbub of subdued conversation drifted out into the afternoon. Once inside, he had merged into the crush of people in the hall, indistinguishable from everyone around him in his funereal black. An anxious middle-aged woman with dimpled cheeks had moved cautiously between the groups of mourners with a tray. She had given him nothing more than a fleeting glance as she offered him refreshment. He had taken his cup and found an unobtrusive corner by the stairs, hoping he might see Moray in the crowd, but he could not make him out. He had waited awhile before abandoning his empty cup to manoeuvre his way into the sitting room. Beyond the immediate cluster of people by the door, he had seen a young woman standing by the fireplace and a young man with chestnut hair trying to console her. There had been the likeness of Laura in the girl and the clear resemblance of Moray in the boy.

He had turned away, surprised by his emotional reaction, and come up against a short, well-polished man of middling years with a shiny forehead and rapidly receding hairline, who had introduced himself as Roger Ash, the owner of a small, but well-respected gallery in York, or so he said. From the tenor of his conversation, he had assumed John was a member of the family, and it had been easier to leave him in his ignorance.

Mr Ash had been eager to state the obvious. "Her death is a dreadful tragedy," he had said with a furrowed brow, adding, "Fifty is no age at all these days, is it?" taking care not to mention the Big C. "Devastating for her husband of course." And he had turned to nod in the direction of the man standing by the window, head bent, shoulders hunched in on themselves, listening solemnly to the earnest condolences of an elderly lady patting his arm attentively.

Across that space, in a fleeting moment when no one stood between them, Moray had glanced up, and their eyes had met. In that instant, Moray had straightened perceptibly, and then quietly, but politely disengaged himself. In no hurry, yet with a certain determination, he had advanced across the crowded space between them, pausing occasionally to thank this person or that, until he had stood squarely in front of him as he had done all those years before on the gravel drive outside Meeston Lodge, the old defiance in his eyes. "John," he had said unflinchingly.

"Robert."

"We thought you might come. Would you mind?" And Moray had taken him aside and quietly ushered him away through the hall into the bright, airy room John recognised as Laura's studio.

Behind the closed door, they had been alone, surrounded by her memory, and his brain had turned to mush trying to explain why he had come; why her work had meant so much to him; how she had inspired him; how he had never shaken off his feelings for her. On and on – a disgraceful outpouring of self-pity that he was ashamed to remember.

Moray had been silent at first, evidently deciding what to do with his unwelcome guest. Then, after a long pause, he had said, "I think perhaps there's someone you should meet," and his expression had been carved in stone when he added, "He won't know who you are. Give him your condolences – then leave. I want your word you won't come back or try to keep in touch."

And John had made his promise without knowing why, and Moray had led him back to the sitting room, skirting the people in the hall, and brought him to stand before the young man, head bent, lost in thought.

Moray's voice had cracked under the strain as he said, "Thomas, I'd like you to meet Mr Rufford."

And the young man had looked up.

Nothing in John's life would ever equal the shock of that moment; of suddenly knowing the truth, and wondering afterwards if he had said anything remotely coherent or appropriate under the circumstances. The young man's expression however, had remained locked in grief, his mind too distracted perhaps to notice any similarity between them. But others might have noticed – Mr Ash for instance.

Moray had drawn proceedings to a rapid close. "Mr Rufford has to leave, Thomas. A long journey home."

John had shaken the young man's hand, reluctant to release his hold, but Moray had pulled him away and led him out of the house into the cold November twilight and sent him on his way.

Later, in the darkness, the rain still hammering against the windscreen of his car, John had woken with a jolt. Intermittent blue lights in the rear view mirror had dazzled his eyes, and someone with a flashlight was banging on the driver's door. Half-asleep, he had wound down the window.

A young man in a fluorescent jacket had asked, "Everything all right, sir?" and rain had run off his peaked cap into the car.

"Yes, thank you, officer."

"A bit tired, are we, sir?" the young man enquired casually, hinting perhaps at another reason.

"Is there anywhere round here I could stay the night?"

"The Drovers' Rest's about a mile further on. Take the next left. You can't miss it."

"Thank you."

"Drive safely, sir."

And the patrol car had waited until he drove away.

At the left turn, the lights of a country pub had come into view, cheerfully defying the weather with a brightly lit sign offering B & B accommodation. He had pulled into a car park of puddles between areas of flattened hardcore, his BMW incongruous in the company of Land Rovers with sheep dogs barking from behind their grilles at the back. He had pulled his coat closer, turned up the collar and made a dash for the door.

The regulars, weather-beaten men with lean faces, sitting by the log fire in their tweed caps and jackets, had looked up briefly from their pints and noted his sombre garb. "Evenin'. Bad night to be out." He had agreed with them, stamping his feet on the 'welcome' mat by the door. The landlord, a broad fellow, evidently fond of home cooking, had provided the double whisky as requested, and yes, he had said, recognising his customer's distressed state, there was a room free at the back – "on the quiet side".

John had downed his drink in one, and two more in quick succession, seeking sweet oblivion. He had slumped onto the bed fully clothed, pulling the duvet around himself like a cocoon and sunk into unconsciousness. At some point in the night, he had woken to the sound of rain on the roof and fallen asleep again until the landlord had knocked on his door at nine-thirty, asking if he were all right and did he want some breakfast.

The journey home that day had been filled with recriminations and regret. He had gone to the funeral wanting Moray to know just how much he had always loved Laura; had wanted to see him bereft, as he himself had been, for so many years. Yes, he had wanted that satisfaction. It had been unworthy of him. She had chosen Robert Moray – and it had been her choice to make. Except ...

He opened his eyes. Above his fireplace was the pastel sketch of Rothwell Mere she had been working on the last time that they met. She had sent it to him later: a study of golden sunlight slanting across the mirrored surface of the lake; its dark backdrop of trees just coming into leaf; the reeds bedecked in their new bronze plumes; and ripples fanning outward behind a duck and her offspring, caught in the dying light. The piece was unsigned, but on the back she had written:

'To John. A memento of an enchanted place. May 1963. From Laura with love.'

He had framed it, and treasured it throughout the years between.

Had she known she was carrying his child? He did not think so. She had made light of their last loving, although it had been sudden and unplanned, and he had broken all his cherished rules to prove he loved her.

They had made a son that evening – his only son.

From the hi-fi, Pachabel's stately *Canon* rose to its crescendo and died away to silence.

There was a moment's pause before the achingly beautiful opening to another aria engulfed him.

John could feel his heart breaking, tearing itself apart. To the strains of *Dido's Lament* he wept, while in the hall, his phone rang on and on, incessantly.

CHAPTER THREE

The mud-spattered green Land Rover rumbled into the yard and parked up next to Robert's by the barn. The two dogs ran out of the sheds to greet it, barking and jumping up at the driver's door.

"Meg! Tod! Hey! Away with you! Leave him be!" Tom yelled at them. Brack, as usual, was still glued to his side, not caring to show such unbridled enthusiasm for someone else, even someone as close as Ian Robson.

Ian swung out of the cab onto the cobbles, encouraging his admirers with vigorous rubbing behind the ears. They yelped in delight. His own dogs in the back of the vehicle howled with indignation. "Your Dad about?" he asked.

Tom stroked Brack's head resting against his thigh. "He's inside," he said. He did not need to add that he had been there most of the morning.

Ian straightened from fussing the dogs and nodded. A year younger than his cousin, some said if it were not for Ian's beard, you would never tell them apart – except Robert suddenly looked much older. "I thought he might've gone down to Wallbridge mart on Wednesday," Ian was saying.

"He wasn't interested."

"Pity," Ian said. "There were some grand Swaledale hoggs for sale from off Black Hag Farm. Not a bad price either," he added. "Would've filled in for those gelds he got rid of this summer." Ian was a dairy man himself, but he had a good eye for sheep. "Gone quiet, has he?"

"Pretty much."

"What's he doing with his time, Tom? He's got to keep himself busy. No good moping around the house all day."

"He's up before me most mornings," Tom said. At least that was true. "Mucks out and takes hay up to the top field for the feeders. And there's the cooking and cleaning and things," he added trying to find something more positive to say.

Ian blew out his cheeks and stuffed his hands into his jacket pockets. "You don't have to pretend, Tom. You know it's not enough. Not for him. Not for you."

"He does his share."

"Does he? Not from where I'm standing, he doesn't. I bet if I went into the kitchen right now, he'd be just sitting there – doing nothing."

Tom could not deny it.

"Look," Ian said, putting his arm around Tom's shoulder, his tone softening, "I've seen all this before – after Ruth died. He went down like a stone. We couldn't shake him out of it. None of us could – Dad – me – no one. And God knows, we all tried."

Tom held his tongue. He could not explain that this time it was different – that this time Robert was mourning more than just the loss of his wife.

"Our Duncan's over at Sykeside this morning," Ian was saying, ignoring Tom's silence. "Ross says he doesn't want his old man under his feet, so I said I'd give Duncan a hand. There's a load of scrub to clear out. Do you think I could get your Dad to come down with me?"

The back door of the porch had opened. Robert was standing on the threshold in his stockinged feet. He was smoking his old pipe, a habit he had given up years ago. "Thought it was you, Ian," he said, squinting through the smoke. "You always drive the dogs crazy."

Ian ambled over, his wellingtons scuffing the cobbles. Meg and Tod danced around him ecstatically. "Wondered if you were doing anything this afternoon, Rob," Ian said a little too cheerily. "Just saying to Tom like, I'm off down to Sykeside. Duncan needs some help clearing out the scrub. Do you fancy coming? Just for a couple of hours like?"

Robert chewed on the stem of his pipe.

Ian was determined not to be beaten. "Come on, Rob," he said. "Get yourself out the house. Do you good to get away for a while."

Robert seemed in no hurry to agree. He folded his arms and blew out a slow, steady stream of smoke, watching it disperse in the wind. "Fretting over me, Ian?" he asked casually.

"Bloody right I am. Get your boots on will you, and do something useful."

Robert eyed them both, probably suspecting a conspiracy, before knocking out his pipe against the wall. "I'll get my boots then," he said with evident reluctance and retreated into the kitchen.

Ian beamed, thoroughly satisfied with a job well done. "Looks like we'll have to keep chivvying him for a while," he said, keeping his voice down so as not to be overheard.

Tom nodded. "I'll get the chainsaw. It's in the shed."

Ian called after him. "Duncan says you've got your name down for the Young Farmers' Quiz next week. Still going?"

"Not sure. Don't fancy leaving him on his own."

"Take him with you, Tom. Don't want you both going soft in the head, do we?" Ian was smiling, but there was no humour in his voice.

They had not been gone long before the familiar rattle of Wallace Armstrong's battered old red-and-white utility set the dogs barking once again. Tom shooed them away from getting under its wheels and stood back waiting for Wallace to clamber out of his seat. Brack stayed close, ears back, eyes watchful.

Wallace Armstrong was a big man not given to speedy thought or speech. Florid and round of face with greying, untidy hair thinning on top, he was bull-necked and barrel-chested with a voice to match; and had hands twice the size of anyone Tom knew. "Afternoon, Tom," Wallace said, hitching up his trousers as he lumbered across the cobbles ignoring the dogs. "Your Dad in?"

"He's just gone down to Sykeside with Ian, Mr Armstrong. He won't be back 'til dark."

"Ah well, not to worry, lad. It's you I really wanted a word with anyway, if truth be told."

Tom had been expecting this. "You'll come in for some tea then?" he offered.

"Don't mind if I do."

Brack followed them over to the house and lay down on the threshold of the porch, keeping guard when they went in.

Wallace heaved off his muddy wellingtons and made himself at home in the kitchen, his bulky stockinged feet up against the range for warmth. "Mary was just sayin' to me this morning like, we've seen nothin' of you since the funeral. Everythin' all right then?"

Tom poured them both a mug of hot strong tea and sat opposite his large visitor pondering how to answer him. "Dad's taken it hard," he said, dodging the real matter in hand as far as Wallace Armstrong was concerned.

The big man nodded, slurping the hot tea. "Grand cup," he said appreciatively, adding after a suitable pause. "How about you, lad? How's things wi' you?"

Tom opted for keeping his response simple. "I'm pretty busy," he said.

"Aye. You've got your hands full then?"

Tom agreed he'd got his hands full, and left it at that.

The conversation died, Wallace concentrating on his mug for a while. "Everythin' all right between you and wor Sal?" he asked suddenly.

"Everything's fine, Mr Armstrong," Tom said, trying to sound convincing.

Wallace pondered this for a moment. "Mary and me," he said, still concentrating hard on the contents of his mug, "Well – we just wondered like. You not bein' around much these last few weeks. Understandable, of course – I mean, your mam bein' so unwell an' all before. But – since the funeral an' everythin' …" He looked up anxiously, running out of things to say.

Tom's mind went a blank: he could hardly tell Wallace that Sarah had barely figured in his thoughts for some time now. "I'm sorry," he said, keeping the truth well-smothered. "I've had a lot on my mind." That at least was true. "I'll phone her tonight, Mr Armstrong. I promise."

This seemed to have the right effect. A broad smile slowly established itself on the big man's face. "I'll tell her that then, Tom. Wouldn't want anythin' to come between you two," he added solemnly. "You and her have known each other since Stanegate Infants. That's a long while."

Tom agreed it was.

Wallace nodded, as if confirming this to himself. "And you've been seein' her regular for a good year now," he added, pausing to let the gravity of this observation sink in.

Tom could not argue with this either.

Wallace was beginning to get into his stride. "Aye," he said. "You make a fine pair, you two. Everyone says so." He may as well have added that it was generally agreed an engagement was expected, followed fairly swiftly by marriage and the inevitable children.

Tom caught the drift. His mother's death had left a gap in the smooth running of Rigg End, even though she always put her art before baking or knitting, unlike Mary Armstrong, who was never happier than when she was turning out fruit cakes, or large woolly jumpers. To Wallace Armstrong the marriage between his daughter and Tom Moray would solve everything: Sarah would move into Rigg End providing housewifely duties that were now sadly missing. And even more important, as far as Wallace Armstrong was concerned, it would give him the reassurance of knowing Rattling Gate Farm would eventually pass to his hoped-for grandchildren, along with Rigg End, ensuring it would be a resilient and large enough holding to remain a viable economic entity in the future.

It was common knowledge Wallace had never entirely forgiven his elder daughter, Becky, for being so set against farming. Rebecca Armstrong had made this dislike quite explicit by marrying Jimmy Elliott – one of the two Elliott brothers running the car repair business in Wallbridge – instead of Eric Bell of Long Moss Farm up Ayburn way, who had always fancied her. Since then, all Wallace's hopes had been pinned on his younger daughter, Sarah – or 'wor Sal', as he called her. Unlike Becky, she had always wanted to be a farmer's wife – just like her mother. Uncomplicated and earnest, with blue eyes, hair the colour of dark honey, and an open, honest face sprinkled with freckles, Sarah was pretty rather than beautiful, and never happier than when she was busy. She loved everything about the farming life and adored children, helping out twice a week at the little nursery run by Wendy Haddon over at Whinrigg. Tom could not wish for a better wife. Everyone said so.

"You'll be comin' up to the quiz next week then?" Wallace was asking.

"I'm hoping to get Dad to come," Tom said, picking up on Ian's suggestion as a further reason for keeping Sarah at arm's length for a little longer. "Get him out of the house," he added for good measure.

Wallace finished his tea and heaved himself onto his feet. "Aye, lad. Good idea. We'll see you both there then." He paused as he pulled on his wellingtons. "I'll tell wor Sal you'll phone then?"

"Yes. Tonight. After supper."

The big man nodded. "After supper then," he said, wanting to be certain of his facts.

Tom waved him off and went back to stacking hay bales into the trailer to take up to the sheep. Brack watched him intently, ears pricked, waiting to help. Meg and Tod had curled up together, sound asleep by the barn wall.

Later, after Tom had shut the dogs into the sheds for the night, Ian's Land Rover rumbled back into the yard and came to a shuddering halt. Robert climbed down and collected the chainsaw from the back while Ian kept the engine running and his dogs howled to the tune of it.

"Need a hand tomorrow?" Tom asked above the din.

Ian wound down his window, grinning broadly. "Rob's already offered," he said.

Robert strode off to stow the chainsaw in the shed and said nothing.

Ian waited until he was out of earshot. "Doesn't like being organised," he said. "Bit of a bear with a sore head this afternoon. Thinks we're fussing over nothing like. When are Jamie and Flora back?"

"Next week."

"It'll do him good to see them. Won't do you any harm

either, I'd say. Take some of the strain off your back for a while, eh? Hey up," he added, noticing Robert was watching them from across the yard, "I'd better be off." He slammed the gears into reverse, completed a neat three-point turn, and with a cheery wave to Robert drove off, the vehicle bucking and bouncing down the ruts in the track.

Robert led the way into the house, clearly not in the mood to talk, and the silence continued through the nightly ritual of preparing supper.

Tom had come to dread this part of the day: his mother's absence from the supper table was painfully obvious, and he never knew how to deal with it. Sometimes he talked too much, an unstoppable stream of pointless remarks; at others, too little, because his head was empty of anything to say. Tonight was such a night.

"I don't need wet-nursing," Robert was saying testily, finally breaking the silence over their meal, his concentration firmly fixed on the lamb chops, mashed potato and swede on the plate before him. "I just need time."

"Ian's worried about you, Dad, that's all."

"I know he means well, but you can't bully someone into a better frame of mind, Tom. God knows," he added, looking up suddenly, "I am trying – it's just – difficult." He put down his knife and fork, fighting back emotion, the muscles in his jaw knotting and unknotting with the effort.

And once again, Tom could think of nothing very useful to say.

CHAPTER FOUR

That morning, John parked his car in its usual place, aware his state of mind had not improved much over the weekend.

Over the short distance between Lingford's High Street and his studio in Chester Place, he braced himself for what was to come: Gemma would want to know why he had not returned her calls. How could he explain? She had never understood the depth of his attachment to an unattainable woman. For three years she had been his 'nursemaid' as he called her – office manager, secretary, receptionist – always ensuring his diary was up-to-date and his deadlines met. Efficient, sophisticated and attractive, with short ash-blonde hair and a lovely figure, she had gladdened his eyes often enough. But she could not touch his soul, which was unfortunate.

Earlier in his Lothario-style career, she would have been a perfect pastime for a while, but that was far behind him now. Besides, he relied on her business-like ability to run things in his absence. Sex would have complicated things, and he had never – ever – mixed sex with his office life, although he had been tempted once or twice. He was also aware his fifty-six years to her thirty-one meant he was old enough to be her father, a sobering thought that reinforced the focus of his romantic inclinations on the woman who had turned him down twenty-five years ago.

He had not always been so abstemious. In fact, he had pretty much gone off the rails after Laura left him. Not at first. At first, he had remained convinced she would never go through with her hasty marriage, except the announcement in the *Lingford Herald* had shattered that particularly illusion. Afterwards, he had progressed into believing that given six months or so in the wilds of Northumberland, she would find herself isolated; that her marriage, rushed into as he saw it, would not stand the strain of wrenching her from all she knew; that she would grow tired of Robert Moray's taciturn tendencies and return to him – and to the more flamboyant lifestyle he could offer. No, he'd not gone off the rails in a moment of instantaneous combustion. He had held steadfast for that first year, determined to show her that regardless of his past predilections for short-term sexual liaisons, he had honestly meant his emotional attachment to her was total, and for ever.

His fall from grace had been spectacular and nothing to be proud of. It had in fact, he realised when he finally came to his senses, merely confirmed everything Laura had probably suspected of him – that he would, when things got tough, just slip back into former habits. And he had done precisely that.

It was the first anniversary of their last meeting that triggered his undoing. Unwisely, he had returned to Rothwell Mere, to the spot where they had parted, and there, surrounded by such intense memories, he had fallen into a melancholic and deeply maudlin state of mind. He had driven home determined to get drunk, a condition which he succeeded in achieving in a relatively short space of time, contrary to his usual practice of careful consumption. He had then embarked on a course of action which was truly despicable: he had re-ignited the interest of two of his former conquests simultaneously, and given them both cause to believe he regretted his decision to ditch them in the past. He had bedded Elizabeth Page three times before transferring his skills to Yvonne Naylor on alternate weekends, and continued in this unedifying manner for almost four months before he woke up one morning and looked in the mirror only to see himself in a new and very unpleasant light. In all the years he had indulged in casual liaisons with the opposite sex, he had never run two women at the same time. He had always operated his 'code of conduct' – if it could be described as such – according to very strict rules: no double-dealing; no lies; no intimation a relationship was anything other than a casual one; no promises of undying love. This last stricture of course had damned his chances of ever persuading Laura Driscoll that he was a changed man, or that she was the only sun in his heaven.

He consoled himself occasionally with the fact that he had finally been honest with them both, although he could never describe the outcome of his honesty as something he remembered with any sense of honour. He had, after all, broken Elizabeth's heart a second time, an unforgivable offence because she was naive and vulnerable, and was so elated when he took up with her again, in the same way he would have been if Laura had come back to him. Her tears and emotional collapse had frightened him. He had tried to make amends, writing a fulsome apology, accepting that his conduct had been unforgivable. But he neither expected, nor received a reply. Afterwards, he learned she had moved away, and several attempts to enquire after her well-being revealed nothing except his standing and reputation had taken a severe battering with their mutual acquaintances. Only his self-imposed celibacy over the years that followed had finally repaired some of the damage. As for Yvonne, made of sterner stuff, the memory of her rich vocabulary describing his shortcomings, and the welt she raised on his face, left a longer-lasting impression. He had finally learnt to his cost that taking out his frustration and anger on others had consequences. All of which turned him back in on himself and his obsession with Laura, an obsession Gemma found both irrational and irritating in equal parts.

Her own love life had not exactly run as smoothly as she might have hoped, but she had learned to move on. Five years before, she had married Ben Grosvenor, a well-heeled, good-looking man worthy of a second glance – someone she had known since their school-days in Chester. Which was why, when it all ended in an acrimonious divorce only a couple of years later, she had once remarked to John with brutal honesty, "God knows why I ever thought it would work. He was always 'Mummy's Darling' even then. Always at her beck and call," adding with some considerable feeling,

"She made my life hell." But with her self-confidence still intact, she had walked out of her marriage and into John's studio and applied for the job of 'office manager'. He was always grateful that she had.

Today was a particularly gloomy morning requiring some of Gemma's sparkle; one of those wintry days when daylight was permanently in short supply. The sky was a depressingly grey-brown, and the pavements puddled from earlier showers. Pausing to cross the road, John could see her behind the reception desk, immaculate as ever, engaged in a conversation on the phone. She did not look up when he came through the door, apparently having already seen his approach. The chill emanating from her was very evident.

She replaced the receiver. "Nice of you to come in this morning, Mr Rufford," she said, the formality of her greeting reinforcing precisely what she felt. She consulted her watch. "It's only ten-thirty. We can still expect miracles apparently." She looked up at him with her grey-blue eyes, challenging him to respond.

Sadly, he was not in the mood to rise to the bait.

"I suppose it's too much to ask why you've not bothered to answer my calls?" she went on, going back to jotting down notes on a pad in front of her.

"I'm sorry – I didn't get home until late Tuesday…"

"And today's Monday," she reminded him, giving him the benefit of a tight smile which was at odds with the generous line of her lips. "What happened to Wednesday, Thursday and Friday dare I ask? No – don't tell me. You went into a mental decline from which you haven't yet recovered."

He sighed. What was the point of agreeing with her? She would think him soft in the head. He took off his coat and hung it on the coat-stand by the door.

"Well, in view of your lack of communication," she went on. "I've rescheduled your meeting with the Cosgroves for Wednesday. They weren't exactly delighted when you didn't turn up on Friday. I said you'd been called away suddenly to a funeral – not exactly a lie, I suppose – but they were clearly put out you hadn't phoned – and Archie Baines was keen to remind you the 'County' deadline for the article on The Bell House is the seventh. He may call in later."

"Anything else?"

Another tight smile. "Oh, not much really. Mrs Shaw has telephoned three times wanting to make an appointment for her daughter Adeline's engagement portrait. Mr Mercer would like to discuss his new hotel brochure." She paused to flick through the notepad. "Mr Stevenson from the Tourism Department wants shots of the various canals in the area to include in the next edition of the Weaverdale newssheet – please telephone a.s.a.p. Oh – and your old Department rang to ask if they could book in a session for Councillor Mulvaney who's the new Chairman of Planning and Development. They want to include his photo in the next edition of the Year Book. You need to confirm dates and times with Rupert Reid – he apparently thinks I'm not capable of doing this." She closed the notebook and got up from behind the desk to face him. "Well?" she wanted to know, arching one very elegant eyebrow. "Are you going to tell me why you didn't phone, or have I to rely on a crystal ball?"

He shrugged. What could he genuinely say that would not become a protracted conversation he did not wish to have? Besides, what could he honestly confess? That he had suffered not just a monumental loss in his life, but had made a discovery that had knocked him sideways? That he had met the twenty-four year old son he never knew he had? He had absolutely no idea how he was going to handle this new intelligence, and until he had, it was better to keep quiet on the whole subject.

She was studying him now, a small frown on her otherwise smooth forehead. "I'm sorry," she said. "I didn't realise…" Her tone had softened. Perhaps his expression had betrayed the extent of his mental dislocation.

He censored what he could say. "It was much harder to deal with than I expected," he said, reducing everything to a simple, uncomplicated statement. "Much harder."

"Yes, I can see that. Go on, make your calls. I'll get you a coffee."

Her sudden kindness nearly undid him. He closed the door into his office and gathered his composure, and by the time she came through with his coffee and chocolate biscuit, he had managed to pacify not only his own agitation, but everyone else's as well. He was almost calm.

After that, she left him alone, and he was grateful because he needed time to think.

For seven days he had existed in a fog – and things were not getting any clearer. His thought processes had a habit of wandering off in all directions, wilfully refusing to help him sort out the mess he was in – and it was a big mess.

Nothing – absolutely nothing – was going to dislodge the need he now felt to keep in touch with Thomas Moray – except he had no idea how he could possibly do this. Robert Moray had been quite explicit. No further contact – and he had given him his word. Besides, there was the boy himself to think of: he was clearly ignorant of the truth, and John knew it was not his place to enlighten him. However selfish he may have been in the past, in his more reflective state, he appreciated only too well actions had consequences. The potential damage could be immeasurable. Sometimes, as it had been with Elizabeth, it could be irreparable as well. There must be no contact then. But just when he began to think rationally, he remembered how it felt to look into that young man's face and see himself so clearly reflected in that image; remembered taking his hand and feeling its warmth – warmth from the blood flowing in his veins that was both Laura's and his own. And his resolve would crumble and he was back to square one.

Other, wider concerns pressed in on him. His nearest and dearest: his father, Charles, forever angry with him for not settling down and getting married "like any sensible man"; his mother, Geraldine, caught in the buffer zone between them, trying with less and less success to deal with her husband's increasingly fragile state of mind and tetchiness; and his much younger brother, Michael, happily married to the beautiful Caroline for sixteen years, with three lovely daughters – Megan, Josie and Daisy – but no son.

No son – that single most cherished thing the old man wanted most of all in life – a grandson: it had become a fixation as the years passed that no amount of patient intervention by Geraldine could mollify.

For John, visits to his old family home at Sylvans in Little Retton had become increasingly depressing. Torn between the pleasure these brief encounters gave his mother, and the prickly conversations with his father, he often felt inadequate. But at least he could withstand the verbal lashings: he was well-practised in the art. Michael, on the other hand was ill-equipped, and had others to consider.

Michael had been his father's favourite from the moment he was born. He had followed in the altruistic footsteps of his grandfather and great-grandfather before him. He had made his father proud: delayed his university studies in 'sixty-three to join Red Cross volunteers in the devastated town of Skopje; obtained an honours degree in Nutrition and Dietetics on his return; and immediately volunteered again to go out to help alleviate the effects of the terrible famine in Biafra. He had met Caroline there and they had married on their return home.

Michael had always worked for the benefit of others: he knew no other way. Now in his mid-forties, selfless and devoted, he held the position of senior dietitian in a multidisciplinary team at the Kinnerswood and District General Hospital. His work on the integration of dietary needs into the care plans for post-operative and elderly patients had earned him a well-deserved reputation. But despite all this, Michael had begun to find himself the target of his father's pent up fury – and not just himself – Caroline and the girls were suddenly in the firing line as well.

"I can't talk to him any more," he had told John privately one bright spring afternoon earlier in the year over a glass of beer. "He's become irrational. First he blamed me – I could handle that. But now he's blaming Caroline – it's all her fault we haven't had a son. I'll not put her through that again."

The damage was done, and there was no going back. Michael had made his weekly pilgrimages to Sylvans on his own, and then, after a particularly distressing incident that summer, had resolved never to visit again. Geraldine had understood why, but it left her increasingly isolated, reliant on furtive phone calls and longed-for letters.

Michael's understandable defection however had thrown the spotlight back on John, and Charles' expectation over the years that his eldest son would finally pull himself together, get married and produce a Rufford heir remained unfulfilled. If John closed his eyes, he could hear his father's voice booming in his head as clearly as if he were in the room beside him; see the old man's agitation in the staring veins throbbing at his temples; and feel his own pulse quicken under the unstoppable onslaught. "God knows, John!" he could hear the old man bellow, "It's not as if you've never had the chance. You've had more women than I've had hot dinners! For God's sake – settle down. Get yourself married. Don't you want to have a son?"

And now he had that son, the living link to the woman he had loved beyond all reason – irrational behaviour as far as his father was concerned. "What's wrong with you?" Charles had demanded on more than one occasion in the past. "One minute you're in and out of bed with every woman who takes your fancy – the next you're mooning around like a love-sick calf for months on end over some woman who's given you the push. Sort yourself out, man! I want to see a grandson before I die." Now he had a grandson – but he would never see him.

A tentative knock on the door jolted John out of his reverie. His coffee had gone cold and the chocolate biscuit remained untouched on the plate. Gemma popped her head round the door. "John – Archie's here," she said, glancing over her shoulder at the visitor waiting in the reception area. She paused, evidently taking stock of the situation. "Have you time?" she asked, apparently prepared to give him the opportunity to say he hadn't, if he wanted to. "You look dreadful," she added lowering her voice so that Archie could not hear her. "I could say you've got another appointment, if you like."

John shook his head. "No, show him in. Life goes on, doesn't it?"

She gave him a weak smile. "All the time," she said, somewhat opaquely.

CHAPTER FIVE

On that drizzly Saturday evening in early December, the car park at Stanegate village hall was full to overflowing. Young Farmers and their supporters from hamlets beyond Ayburn to the west, Whiteburnmoss to the north and Whinrigg to the east, lured by the prospect of good food and even better crack, had turned out in force.

Inside, the atmosphere was hot and stuffy, a heady mix of lamb stew, strong local ale and raw tobacco smoke. The quiz had reached a satisfactory climax. Tension was running high.

"Right then," said Dougie Watson, delegated the responsibility of being the quiz-master for the evening, and enjoying his moment of power. "Last round. Current affairs." Groans from all sides. "Tom Moray ahead of the game like – but only just. Let's see if Duncan Robson can knock him off his bawk!"

Tom fluffed out imaginary feathers and clucked like a hen to general amusement and good-humoured banter.

Duncan was leaning forward, hands clasped tightly on the table in front of him, his brow deeply furrowed in concentration. Eighteen months older than Tom, this was his last chance to compete – and he visibly wanted to win.

A burst of applause. Duncan had answered correctly. Relief flooded his face. They were neck-and-neck now. Success hung on the final question. There was a buzz of excitement. Speculation. Would Tom snatch victory from under his rival's nose?

"All right then, everyone. Settle down. Settle down."

The hubbub died away. A tense silence filled the room.

Tom felt strangely calm: prepared to be the victor. And why not? Facts stuck to him like flies to flypaper. The quiz was a doddle, always was, when he took the trouble to enter it. School exams had never been a problem for him either, something that had irked Jamie in the past because he had always had to work hard to achieve. But then Jamie had always wanted to be an academic, like his Moray grandfather – another Robert – whereas Tom only wanted to run the farm. "You've got the brains to go to university, Tom Moray," Mr Gregson, his form teacher had said during a sixth form parents' evening, exasperated by this stubborn youth who had set his sights instead on Hawkrigg Agricultural College. "Don't sell yourself short," he had urged. "You could turn your hand to anything." To which Robert, ignoring this exhortation, had commented, "Do what you feel is best for you, Tom." And his mother, Tom remembered, had just smiled and said nothing. Perhaps she was thinking of John Rufford at the time.

The thought cut across his concentration.

"Which prime minister's statue was recently unveiled in London by ex-PM Harold Wilson?" Dougie was asking him.

Tom knew the answer. He looked across at Duncan, feeling the surge of triumph of someone on the brink of winning – and saw the desperation etched deep into his rival's honest face. Duncan knew the answer too.

"I'll have to hurry you like," Dougie was saying.

There were shouts of encouragement from all sides of the hall and then a breathless hush.

Tom hesitated – then made his choice. It seemed the right thing to do. He shook his head and threw up his hands. "Sorry," he said, feigning ignorance, " – it's gone."

Oohs and aahs to right and left. From the corner of his eye, Tom saw Robert raise an eyebrow.

Dougie paused, cranking up the tension and wanting to make the most of if. The room fell silent. "Duncan?" he asked.

Duncan, his face the picture of triumph, blurted out, "Clement Attlee!" to whoops and wild applause from his supporters round the room.

Tom felt a profound sense of relief. He offered his hand to the victor and stepped away from the table, happy to melt into the crowd of disappointed supporters back-slapping him while Dougie made a little speech and presented Duncan with the silver cup to much cheering and applause.

Supper was called, and to the inviting aroma of lamb stew everyone trooped into the adjoining room. Tom held back.

Sarah pushed her way through the press to reach him. She linked her arm through his, patting his hand reassuringly. "Never mind," she said looking up at him with an encouraging smile. But that was Sarah – always prepared to make the best of things. "Can't win every time," she said.

Tom nodded. Duncan deserved to win, he thought. He belonged to this place with his Douglas features, characteristics that had effortlessly come down through the generations of the Robsons and Morays: the red hair of varying hues; the fair skin; the similarity of facial structure, and with very few exceptions – the intensely green eyes. Duncan was part of the clan, whereas Tom now knew that he was not – and never could be. He felt apart: separate, and there was nothing he could do about it.

Somehow he got through the remainder of the evening, making mock of his forgetfulness. With Sarah amiably chatting to those around them at the table, he could make noncommittal comments here and there while his attention wandered off on its own.

Two tables further down, he noticed Wallace with Robert in earnest conversation. He was in no doubt what the topic was: every now and then, Wallace would cast a quick glance in Tom's direction. Robert, Tom noted, was just listening, nodding every once in a while, his concentration fixed on the bowl of jam roly-poly and custard in front of him. What he was thinking was a closed book. Sarah meanwhile was oblivious, too busy chatting with Alison and Beth Liddel from Hopeslaw Farm over Ayburn way.

"Close thing this time," Duncan said, bursting in on Tom's thoughts and grabbing a spare chair to sit down next to him. He planted the quiz trophy squarely on the table between them, a bald reminder he had won, in case Tom had forgotten.

Tom could see his own name inscribed on the winners' plaque for the previous year. "The best man should always win," he said, giving Duncan the benefit of his smile.

Duncan laughed and dug him in the ribs. "Is that so? Hey, Sarah, which one of us do you really fancy, lass?"

She turned, plainly irritated at having her conversation interrupted. "Honestly, Duncan!" she said, tutting at him. "What a question." She put her arm through Tom's, and gave an exasperated little sigh.

"I just thought – to the victor the spoils like."

"Well I'm sorry to disappoint you, Duncan Robson, but I'm not the Quiz Cup to be handed back and forward between the two of you!"

Duncan laughed. "Just checking," he said, dragging himself to his feet before slapping Tom on the back and returning to his table of triumphant supporters, trophy in hand.

Duncan's interest in Sarah was visible for anyone to see. He was a robust young man, hale and hearty like his elder brother, Ross, but as a second son with only thirty acres of woodland to his name, he stood little chance as far as Sarah Armstrong was concerned. When Ian finally retired, High Oakbank and its two-hundred-and-seventy-six acres would go to Ross and Liz, with their two young sons, Scott and Adam. Which was why Wallace was determined Sarah should remain firmly attached to Tom: he would take over Rigg End after Robert, and together, the Armstrong-Moray holding would stretch from the rough hill country north of the Wall down to the gentle south-facing slopes of The Rigg and the fertile pasture by the river.

But Sarah's attachment, Tom thought, had always been more about friendship than love, even during the past year, when they had been regularly going out together. She readily gave the impression they were very close, but that was all. Maybe it was just her way. Her parents were very protective after all – Mary Wallace in particular, with her staunch Methodism exerting a strong but loving influence over 'Wor Sal'. Sarah, he reflected, never allowed herself to become involved in too much intimacy – even when the opportunity arose. Nights out never ended with a snogging session in the car, for example; dances were always enjoyed for the sheer pleasure of taking part – there was never any smooching when the lights went down; and the back row of the cinema in Wallbridge was for watching the film, nothing more – no groping or fumbling. Sarah would always be loving, but never passionate. That was the deal, and he had never really questioned this in depth before. Perhaps he should have done. What did he really want from a woman? Donna would have known.

Donna. Donna Burdon. Even now, four years later, thinking about her could still rouse him.

They had met at Hawkrigg, she already in her final year – twenty-two to his twenty. She was something of an oddity – stocky, robust, prone to dressing like a man in her over-sized checked shirts and heavy cords, her hair pulled back into a single dark plait that hung down between her shoulder blades. She had a plain, round face, wore no make-up, and drank and swore like a trooper. From a farming family up in the far north of the county, she was tackling courses girls usually ran a mile from: Forestry and Land Management. She wielded a chainsaw as if it weighed nothing, set fences and handled a tractor with deceptive ease. The lads on her course enjoyed her rumbustious company, cheerfully accepting the possibility she was a lesbian with an eye on the girls taking the Small Animal Veterinary Diploma.

Hawkrigg College was a good forty miles south of Stanegate, just too far for daily travelling. Tom had taken up residence in one of the student halls, confident he could pull his weight back at Rigg End over the weekends and during the holidays. Robert had agreed and encouraged him. "You need to broaden your horizons, Tom." So he had broadened his horizons.

He had seen Donna often enough on campus during his first year, but they had never spoken. When they finally met, it was late one evening in the students' bar at the beginning of the summer term. Tom had become engrossed in the library, reading up on liver fluke and fly-strike prevention and cure. By the time he had turned up at the bar, his usual crowd had left. Donna was there with the lads from her own year, drinking most of them under the table, laughing uproariously at coarse jokes and providing some of her own. She seemed to have an unlimited supply.

Tom, sitting apart from this noisy crowd pondering the contents of his pint, was very much aware of her – and not just because of her raucous laughter. That night there was something about her: the way she moved if no one was looking; the way she leaned against the bar; the slight tilt of her head when she was listening; her evident ability to weigh up a situation and use it to her own advantage. She was not, he decided after some deliberation, what she seemed, or pretended to be.

Gradually the press in the bar had thinned. Eventually, the members of her group began to drift away, and she dismissed the last two with a hearty thump on the back and the tart retort, "Yeah – and you!"

With only her and himself left at the bar, it was as if she had switched on a magnetic beam and pointed it in his direction. He could physically feel it. With a determined toss of her head, she had flicked the thick plait out of the way and come over to join him, parking herself on the stool next to his.

He had finished his pint, very slowly, and turned to look at her.

"Penny for your thoughts," she had said in a low husky voice, looking him straight in the eyes, and presenting him with an entirely different persona.

Tom was cautious. Robert had given him sound advice at the beginning of the year. "Tom," he had said gravely, "You're going to be with a new crowd at college. There's going to be the temptation to sleep around. Try to keep your self-respect." It had proved a timely warning. Away from familiar faces, and by then, Sarah's willingness to be loosely associated with him, he quickly discovered girls liked to be around him, and he liked to be around them.

Flattered by their interest, he had also recognised that while he may give the impression of being the Last of the Red Hot Lovers, he was nonetheless unpractised in the arts of sexual niceties. Advice in leaflets and hectic couplings depicted on-screen were poor substitutes for actual hands-on experience, so to speak. Copying the astonishingly brief coitus practised by tups seemed unlikely to be appreciated. His recognition that he would be gauche, and possibly open to ridicule, had held him back. In the hot-house atmosphere of student gossip, it had been caution that had kept him chaste, not control of his desires. All of which had left him wondering how he could answer Donna's question, because under that over-sized lumberjack shirt was undoubtedly a pair of large, intriguing breasts, and she was deliberately leaning against the bar in such a way it was impossible to ignore them.

He remembered taking his time to answer, quietly contemplating his empty glass while she waited, unusually silent, her gaze never wavering. "I was wondering," he began, carefully picking his words, "why you pretend to be something you're not." It had been a bold statement, considering he had no idea if his assumption were correct.

She had raised an eyebrow. "And what about you, Lover Boy?"

He had not answered her, so she had provided him with an astonishing suggestion. "Perhaps we could work something out between us then?" And they had, on that first occasion finding the deserted boiler room quite adequate for their purpose. Her adeptness at bringing him to a speedy conclusion had left him breathless and exhilarated. And that was only the beginning.

Once, or sometimes twice, during the weekday evenings of that summer term, they would secretly rendezvous at the top of the long-abandoned miners' road, his Ford Escort bouncing and juddering over the bouldered surface like an untamed horse, until he reached the derelict miners' hut in the worked-out limestone quarry. She always arrived first, her battered 'Farmers' Blue' utility Land Rover parked up behind a massive slab of rock that had never been moved from the spot where it had landed years ago, blasted from its home high up on the quarry face. She had supplied the sleeping bag. He had been expected to supply the condoms. It was a remote and unromantic spot, often draughty and occasionally cold, but Donna had taught him in down-to-earth language and business-like efficiency everything he needed to know to satisfy a woman – and she was, he discovered, very much a woman. He had also learned a great deal about himself. Her 'anatomy lessons' as she liked to call them, had been thorough. But she had made one thing very clear – their encounters were entirely about 'having sex' and nothing whatever to do with 'making love'. "You're bloody good at it," she had informed him, much to his satisfaction at the time, but there was no emotional attachment whatsoever.

Once, after a particularly vigorous session, when she was lying on her back smoking a cigarette, one knee raised so he could still touch her if he wished, he had finally asked her outright, "Why do you pretend to be a lesby?"

She had tucked one arm behind her head and turned slightly to look at him, her eyes half closed against the curl of smoke from the cigarette. "To survive," she had said, enigmatically.

Her reply had puzzled him.

She had laughed out loud. "Don't be so bloody thick," she had said, without a trace of malice. "I'm a woman in a man's world, doing a 'man-thing'. Besides," she had added, propping herself up on one arm so he could admire the volume of her breasts and their large dark nipples all the better, "– it's safer. The blokes don't see me as someone they want to shag all the time. I'm just one of them."

It was the only time he had ever asked her anything about herself, and she never asked him anything at all. The end of term came, they had met for the last time at the hut, enjoyed a long and exhausting evening together – and parted. They had agreed not to exchange addresses or phone numbers, and that was that. Lessons over. He had returned to Rigg End for the holidays aware of being different; of being able to suss out what made one woman more attractive than another – and it was not always down to looks alone: some women just gave off certain vibrations, some without even knowing that they did. Sarah, he had suddenly realised, was not one of them. She was lovely and good-hearted, but had not a single ounce of sex-appeal as far as he was concerned. Maybe that was for the best, he convinced himself, as the months passed and Sarah and he had drifted into a more permanent relationship. Sarah would be a devoted wife and mother, and he would be able to make her feel good about herself, because he would know how.

Meanwhile, the demands of the farm sapped the greater part of his energy. But that did not stop Donna invading his dreams with a regularity he had come to accept. And with these exquisite erotic fantasies came the small, but increasingly insistent voice in his head that what he needed was a woman who really wanted him – body and soul. Sarah's cheerful disposition, he was beginning to suspect, might not be enough.

After the quiz, as Robert drove them back to Rigg End through the persistent drizzle, it was this uneasy thought that lodged in his brain.

Silence was increasingly becoming their companion when they were together, and Tom did not always have the mental energy to break it. Tonight was such a night, because Donna was in his thoughts. He was wondering if his desire to have full-blooded uninhibited sex, and not a pale imitation, had anything to do with his inheritance from John Rufford. Was it in his blood? He suspected that it was.

"You knew the answer, didn't you?" Robert was saying, breaking the silence between them, his concentration on the road ahead apparently undiminished.

"What?"

"To the last question. You knew the answer." Robert turned briefly to glance in his direction, his expression masked by the dark.

There was no point in lying.

"Why did you let Duncan win?"

"Because he wanted to. I can always win next year."

There was a longer silence before Robert observed quietly, "You don't always get a second chance, Tom. Remember that."

CHAPTER SIX

Jamie was gone only a little over half-an-hour before his ancient VW Beetle, headlights blazing, bumped its way back up the track announcing his return with an unnecessary toot of the horn that set Meg and Tod yelping and pawing at the closed door of their shed. He had barely cut the engine before Flora, decked out in a plum-coloured Puffa jacket and gaudy thick purple scarf, was out of the car and racing across the cobbles. "The train was on time," she said breathlessly, throwing her arms around her father, "so I didn't keep him long, did I? Oh, it's so good to see you, Dad! How are you? You're eating properly, aren't you?"

Her father could only nod, his pleasure at seeing her again mingled with a stronger emotion.

"Tom," she said, transferring her attention to him. "You are looking after him, aren't you?"

"We're looking after each other," he assured her, suddenly aware of just how much she looked like their mother – except for the reddish tinge to her hair. Is that what Robert saw?

Jamie unwound himself from behind the driver's seat and ambled after her with one of her college bags over his shoulder. He was his old self again: a student in worn-out looking jeans and leather jacket; his hair – tidied up for the funeral a month ago – running wild, a thick mass of ill-disciplined chestnut. "Hi, Tom," he said cheerfully, slapping him on the back. "Missed you this afternoon."

"I'd not got back from the mart," Tom said, trying to stifle the wider sense of distance he felt existed between them now. Jamie did not seem to notice anything amiss.

Robert was keen to get them both out of the wind. "Come on in, the pair of you. Tom's put the kettle's on."

Flora dragged Tom to one side. "I've got some things in the car," she said, evidently wanting a private word before they went in.

He followed her back to the car, ostensibly to help her with her bags.

She looked up at him anxiously. "He looks dreadful, Tom."

"He doesn't sleep well."

"But he's changed so much in a month! Even his voice sounds – I don't know – different." She shrugged, unable to express precisely what she meant.

"He says he needs time."

Their conversation was cut short. "Are you two coming in?" Jamie was demanding from the porch door. "Tea's brewed."

Tom lugged the rest of her bags into the kitchen. Jamie began pouring out the mugs of tea and passing them around.

"I brought some decorations I made at college," Flora said brightly, perhaps too brightly, unpacking the contents of a carrier bag onto the kitchen table. "I thought they might cheer the place up a bit." She pulled out a long garland of silver and gold foil in a snow-flake pattern, and another in shimmering bright green with holly and ivy leaves interspersed with bright red berries. "Do you like them? There's three of each, so there should be enough for the sitting room and kitchen, don't you think? I'll put them up after supper."

Her father was sitting by the range hugging his mug, his eyes brimming. He nodded, attempting a smile.

Flora beamed at him. "Oh – and I've made a –" She stopped herself in time. "A thingy for the front door," she finished lamely, unwrapping a circlet of pine interlaced with variegated ivy and scarlet silk poinsettia flowers – a wreath by any other name.

Jamie was more interested in practicalities, and the awkwardness of the moment was quickly dispelled by his wanting to know what arrangements were being made for Christmas.

"Tom and I haven't made any decisions yet," Robert said, looking embarrassed by having to admit this. "Ian and Bridie have invited us over for Christmas Day," he explained, sounding weary at the prospect. "They're having a big 'do'. Janet's back home, and Craig and Dana are flying over from Alberta. It'll be a full house," he added meaningfully, "with Ross, Liz and the boys as well."

There was an uncomfortable silence.

Jamie was frowning. Flora was biting her lip, evidently uncertain. Tom had no opinion to offer.

"Would you mind if we spent Christmas here, Dad?" Jamie suggested.

"What about you, Flora?" Robert asked.

She glanced nervously at Tom. "I know it's no change for you two, but – but," she went on, trying to sound positive, "it would be nice to stay here this year – just the three of us."

"Remembering happier times?" her father asked.

She nodded. "Jamie and I can rustle up the dinner, can't we?" she added, eager to press the case.

Jamie agreed. "We'll muddle through," he said, "as long as you don't mind if it's a bit rough round the edges. Hewitson's will still have a turkey left, won't they? I can buy one tomorrow if you like. Tom? What do you say?"

"I'll do whatever Dad wants," he said, aware he sounded unenthusiastic. Robert needed to get himself out more. Ian and Bridie had thought so too. Their invitation had offered the chance to break the cycle of depression that was steadily engulfing him. Christmas at Rigg End would be all about remembering the past, not about looking to the future.

"We'll stay here then," Robert said, visibly satisfied with this outcome.

Later, while Robert and Jamie washed and stacked the supper dishes, Tom offered to help Flora put up the decorations in the sitting room. Her enthusiasm for this task was infectious, and he needed her vitality more than she knew: it masked his tendency to wrap himself up in his own private anxieties.

He was at the top of the step-ladders pinning the last

streamer to a corner of the sitting room when she asked, "Where's the Christmas tree?"

"We haven't bought one," he said.

She was incredulous. "You haven't bought a Christmas tree? Why not?"

Regaining terra firma and folding up the ladders, Tom shrugged apologetically.

"Oh honestly, Tom!" she scolded him. "You're hopeless! Christmas without a Christmas tree! I'll get Jamie to buy one tomorrow on the way into Wallbridge. I saw a sign outside Skirs when we drove past. Let's buy a really big one to put up in the hall and then –" her eyes lit up with sudden inspiration, "– then we can invite everyone over here for Boxing Day. What do you think?"

Trust Flora to come up with the perfect answer: to fill the house with people for a festive, not sad, occasion; to lighten the darkened corners with a little joy and laughter.

She was already planning ahead. "Are the tree decorations still in the storeroom?"

"I think so."

"Let's go and see if they're okay. We don't want anything shabby, do we? Come on!"

Tom followed in her wake and reluctantly unlocked the door into the studio.

She put on the lights and shivered, hugging her Arran cardigan closer to herself for warmth. "Tom!" she said, turning to look at him, horrified by what she saw. "How could you leave it like this?"

He surveyed the place with fresh eyes. The day after the

funeral he had walked out of the studio and locked the door behind him, taking with him a new and unwelcome knowledge. He had never gone back. If he had, he would have been tempted to open the bottom drawer of the desk. Better to leave its contents out of sight and out of mind. To the best of his knowledge, Robert had never darkened the door either. It was as if the studio had ceased to exist for both of them.

The chill added to the doom-laden atmosphere of an abandoned place: the student clutter undisturbed; the unfinished study of Brack sitting on the cobbles in the yard, ears pricked, waiting to be called for a day's work, still on its easel, a lasting reminder of the day the artist Laura Douglas could no longer find the energy to paint; and by the window, the solid mahogany desk, stood like a challenge, the contents of the bottom right-hand drawer leaping to the forefront of his mind with a dreadful clarity.

Flora was tugging at his arm. "Tom?"

He recovered himself. "We – we haven't been able to touch anything," he explained.

"God – I can see that!" she said, screwing up her face in disgust. "It's like an old horror movie set – only worse!"

"Flora – it's not been easy here," he objected.

She relented, putting her arms around him. "Sorry," she said, burying her face in his jacket, the scent of her hair reminding him of honeysuckle. "I'm really sorry. I shouldn't have said that."

He surveyed the chaos over her head. She was right.

It was ghoulish to leave the place looking like Miss Haversham's wedding breakfast.

She was suddenly galvanised into action again. She picked up the painting of Brack and studied it for a moment. "How about getting this framed?" she suggested. "It doesn't matter if it isn't finished, does it? It's lovely. I'll ask Dad, if you like. And before I go back to college, I'll clear all this lot out." She encompassed the contents of the room with an expansive sweep of her hand.

The contents of the desk drawer loomed even larger in Tom's mind. "There's papers in Mam's desk I've got to sort out," he said, anxious to keep her from extending her enthusiasm into his territory.

"Oh, for heaven's sake, Tom, I'm not interested in the desk – it's all this student stuff – everything."

"Everything?"

"Everything."

"You don't want to use any of it?"

She was adamant. "No, Tom, I don't. This was Mam's place – not mine. Anyway –" She bit her lip and looked up at him, forcing an embarrassed smile. "Oh God, Tom," she said, adding a sigh for good measure, "there's something I've got to tell Dad, and I don't know how."

"What about?"

"About what I want to do when I leave college."

He waited while she wrestled with the problem of finding the right words.

She was becoming agitated.

"What is it?"

She picked at the cuff of her cardigan abstractedly. "Well – the thing is – I might not be coming back – to Rigg End," she said with a hopeless little shrug. "I couldn't tell him last time, Tom – not with Mam – you know ... I just couldn't."

"No – I can see that," he said, wondering how he could be so calm under the circumstances, his mind racing ahead to a time when the house would lose her too.

"You see," she was saying, "I know Jamie wants to go back to Edinburgh after he qualifies –"

"Edinburgh?"

"Oh, I knew he hadn't told you!" she said crossly. "There's a vacancy at Gowrie Academy – his old school. Uncle Sandy mentioned it. They're looking for a Classics graduate. He couldn't pass up a chance like that, now could he, Tom? Not with it being Dad's old school as well."

Tom heard himself say quite rationally, "No, of course not."

Flora was unstoppable. "So with Jamie going up to Edinburgh and me off to London –"

"London?" he repeated, wishing he could stop sounding like a stuck record. He was floundering under too much information.

She looked wretched. "Oh, Tom, how can I tell him? I've got an offer with a graphic design studio – in Hammersmith. We had an exhibition – at college – before half term. There were talent scouts. They saw the work I brought home to show Mam." She was beginning to gabble. "Obviously, the offer's conditional on my finishing the course – but it's a brilliant opportunity."

"Did Mam know – about the offer?"

She nodded. "She was really pleased for me, Tom. She promised she wouldn't say anything – in case it didn't work out. She didn't, did she?"

"No," he said simply, aware of the enormity of what he was about to say. "Mam was good at keeping secrets."

Jamie burst in on them, unaware of the drama he was interrupting. "On the news," he said, his voice catching in his throat. "A passenger plane. It's come down over Lockerbie. They think it's a bomb. There's hundreds dead."

They gathered solemnly in the sitting room in front of the television as the pictures flashed up on the screen: a scene of devastation; of Dante's *Inferno* in a small town just north of the Border. The world had gone mad.

Later, Tom went out into the yard for a while and looked up into the overcast night sky with Brack at his side. The clouds suddenly dispersed for a moment, and an almost full moon looked down on them, cold, unforgiving and lifeless, stretching out their shadows behind them on the damp cobbles bathed in its harsh blue light. Then it was gone, the next bank of cloud sweeping across its face obscuring it from view. Brack whined softly.

Small things mattered, Tom decided: Brack's wet nose nuzzling against him; the smell of the fresh straw in the hemmel that morning; the wet cobbles; the wood smoke from the sitting room fire. Larger things too: the security of his home, and the people who loved him. Life then, even with all its complexities and heartache, was too fragile a thing to take for granted.

CHAPTER SEVEN

The image of the severed flight-deck lying on its side in a Scottish field cast a pall over the Christmas festivities. The Carol Service at St Oswald's, usually such a joyful occasion, seemed inappropriate, God's message of Peace and Goodwill a form of words without meaning. Tom had left the service before it ended and walked the two miles home, glad to escape into the open air. No one mentioned his sudden departure over what proved to be a somewhat sombre Christmas lunch.

It was mid-afternoon by the time he loaded the hay bales onto the trailer and set off up the track with Brack beside him in the cab. The low winter sun broke through the clouds, and a blustery, but mild south-westerly greeted them when they reached the brow of the fell.

Sheltering against the stone dyke along the northern boundary, the ewes were waiting, heads already turned at the sound of the tractor's lumbering progress up the stony track. They looked in fine fettle, Tom thought, as they moved silently across the sloping ground towards them, a flowing wave of cream rough-fleeced Swaledales with charcoal faces and neat curved horns. They stayed back from the feeders, wary of the dog until Tom had spread the hay into the covered troughs.

He called Brack away, finding satisfaction in watching the flock push forward to feed. Most were in lamb, and his thoughts wandered into calculating whether it was worth keeping more Swaledales the following year – the upper fields could stand another fifty or so – or whether they should keep numbers down and breed more Mules instead. The Blue-Faced Leicester tup had been worth his price the previous year, his 'ladies' producing sturdy twins fetching a good price at the mart in October. But more Mules would put pressure on the grazing land over the summer. Robert would be reluctant to reduce the number of Limousins in favour of upland Galloways. But, there again, Limousins needed winter housing and extra feed. Wallace Armstrong swore by the Galloways. They could survive outdoors in almost any weather – so maybe …

His thoughts drifted off in another direction.

Sarah had been upset when he phoned rather belatedly after lunch to thank her for her present – a splendid knitted sweater for the cold winter days. "Aren't you coming over for tea?" she had asked, justifiably surprised by his unexpected defection so late in the day.

"I can't make it this year, Sarah," he had tried to explain. "I'm needed here."

She had accepted this with some reluctance.

"We're having a party tomorrow evening," he had told her, as if this might compensate for her injured feelings. "You could come over – if you like."

It was duplicitous of him to ask: the Armstrongs invariably had their Charlton in-laws over on Boxing Day, and Sarah would be expected to help out with the catering and hospitality, as she always did.

"You know I can't, Tom," she had said, sounding put out at his suggestion.

"Okay then," he had answered, a little sharper than he intended. "I'll see you sometime during the week." And he had hung up, irritated.

His annoyance had been slow to evaporate and it was good to get out of the house and feel the wind in his hair; to take in great gulps of it and fill his lungs almost to bursting; to listen to the sound of the rustling dried grasses, and let everything else go hang.

Suddenly, the dark shape of a hen harrier, with her blunt many-fingered wings outstretched, and short barred tail splayed, came soaring overhead. He watched her as she flapped and soared and flapped again, hunting for her prey along the boundary dyke. For several minutes she scoured the line of stones, then, finding nothing, she swooped away again to the north and out of sight over the crest of the fell, ignoring the presence of both man and dog.

Tom looked down. Brack was leaning against him, his warmth coming through the thick fabric of his cords. He rubbed the dog behind the ears to appreciative wheezing. "Time to go home," he said.

The light was fading. Tom climbed back up into the cab, Brack scrambling after him as he started the engine and they set off down the track towards the lower fields. Below them, across the lane on the opposite fell, the lights of High Oakbank could be seen above Rigg End's small plantation of larch and oak. Further off, in the distance, the yellow-orange glow of Wallbridge lit up the under-belly of the clouds. Dotted here and there in the darkness in between, twinkling lights marked out farmsteads scattered along the valley floor and the rising land to the south.

He brought the tractor to a stop, listening to the thrumming of its engine beating time with his heart. He was a fool, he thought. He might not be a Moray, or a Robson, but this place was his home. This was where he belonged – out on the fell with Brack and the sheep, or in the hemmel with the good-natured Limousins nudging him; with farming friends and neighbours exchanging crack down at the mart, or leaning over a pen sizing up the merits of this beast or that.

He wondered what Rufford had made of the place, perched in its isolation on the side of a hill. Probably not much. He would have noticed only the mud; the smell of beasts and the stench of muck piled high in the midden; the rutted track and rough cobbled yard; the basic facilities in the house; the lack of sophistication. If questioned, he would be polite, no doubt, but he would see things differently, and it hurt Tom to know the truth of it.

It was dark when they arrived back in the yard. He parked up the tractor in front of the hay barn and refilled the tank with diesel. Brack waited patiently to be let into the shed to curl up with Meg and Tod in the warmth of the straw.

With the stock settled, Tom kicked off his wellingtons

in the back porch and opened the door into the kitchen, bright with Flora's festive streamers and filled with the warm smell of fresh mince pies.

Flora welcomed him back with a large glass of sherry and a hug. "Jamie's challenged us to a game of ludo," she said with mischief in her eyes. "Come on – we've been waiting for you."

The following afternoon, when he returned from feeding the sheep, he found the house filled with noise and bustle. The Robsons had turned out in force to help with preparations for the party. Someone had brought a ghetto-blaster. It was in the hall blaring out well-known theme tunes from blockbuster films, *Dr Zhivago* in this case. Bridie and Liz were in the kitchen setting out the food with Flora; Duncan and Ross were lugging crates of local beer into the porch from the back of Duncan's pick-up; Janet, he was told, had gone down to Aitket Bank to fetch up old Harry and Maggie Fenwick when they were ready; while Craig and Dana, still jet-lagged, were sitting by the range drinking hot strong coffee and trying to keep out of everybody's way.

Oblivious of the music, Scott Robson, a harum-scarum boy of six, and his younger brother Adam, who was barely four, were tearing through the downstairs rooms conducting aerial warfare between the Jedi and the dark forces of Darth Vader. Careering into the hall, they collided with Ian helping to carry chairs into the sitting room. With a roar of bogus rage, he abandoned his load, scooping them both up, one under each arm, and carted them off, giggling and squirming, into the sitting room where they were instructed "to do something useful" by helping Great-uncle Robert stack logs in the wicker baskets by the fire.

Sitting at the bottom of the stairs, hidden by the vast Christmas tree Flora had laboriously decorated with tinsel and every bauble she could find, was Jamie, surrounded by a selection of multicoloured balloons. He looked exasperated.

"What's wrong, Little Brother," Tom asked above the expansive music of *Lawrence of Arabia*.

"These damned things get harder to blow up every year."

"You're out of practice, that's all. Too many hours with your head in a book. Here – pass some over."

Jamie obliged, continuing to struggle. "Damn!" he said, losing his grip on a curly yellow monster that shot across the hall into the sitting room causing shrieks of delight from the two youngsters who lurched after it trying in vain to catch it before it landed in a deflated heap on the sofa.

Tom squatted next to Jamie on the stairs and blew up a large blue sausage with ease.

"You make it look so bloody simple," Jamie complained.

Tom blew up another, just to prove the point, casually putting a knot in the end and tossing it up into the air. He watched it float down to join the others littering the hall. "Flora told me about Edinburgh," he said casually.

Jamie looked embarrassed. "Sorry. I should've told you. It's not definite, of course."

"Have you mentioned it to Dad?"

Jamie nodded.

"What did he say?"

"He said he was pleased." He did not sound entirely convinced.

Tom said nothing.

Jamie looked round at him, frowning slightly. "Anything wrong, Tom?"

"No. Should there be?"

Jamie tucked a long strand of errant red hair behind his ear and studied him more closely. "Are you worried about Dad?"

"He has a lot on his mind."

"And you haven't?"

Tom shook his head and stood up. "I need a bath," he said casually. "I stink of sheep. I'll catch up with you later."

Jamie nodded and went back to the laborious task of blowing up the balloons to *The Sound of Music*.

Tom soaked for some time, listening to cars arriving, doors banging, voices of cheery welcome and greeting. The house would be full again. It needed to be filled. Perhaps he and Sarah should get married after all – sooner rather than later. Start a family. Get on with life. He needed to look to the future himself. Jamie had – and so had Flora – even Flora. She had surprised him. She had always been ferociously single-minded, like her mother, but he had never thought of her as anything more than a home-bird. But she had gone off to college and found her wings. Now she was ready to fly. He should have known she would.

He closed his eyes. He wished Sarah had said she would come to the party. He wanted her to show commitment. Somewhere in the back of his mind it occurred to him that perhaps it was no longer a matter of whether he loved her enough, but whether she loved him at all.

The water had gone cold. He heaved himself out of it, towelling himself down vigorously, irritable again and out of sorts. For a brief moment, Donna came into his mind, with the inevitable result. He could have done with a good shagging.

When he finally came downstairs, spruced up and changed into a fresh shirt and jeans, the party was in full swing: the balloons were strung up in odd corners and down the bannister rail; the rooms were filling up with friends and neighbours gossiping over punch and sausage rolls; someone was laughing uproariously in the kitchen; Scott and Adam were being fussed over by all and sundry – not always to their liking; and from the ghetto-blaster, someone was crooning 'Winter Wonderland'.

Jamie was pushing through the crush to bring him a pint of beer. "I was going to check if you'd drowned," he shouted over the din, shoving the glass in his direction. "Here, I've managed to get it this far, drink up before it gets spilt." He paused, wrinkling his nose slightly. "Phew – Tom! Is that aftershave?"

"Thought I'd give it a try. Can't remember who bought it for me."

Jamie laughed. "Mam, most likely."

Robert never wore it, but of course, Tom remembered only too well, thinking of the last gathering of so many people in the house – John Rufford did. "Should I wash it off?" he asked, feeling it somehow betrayed the evident truth, even to those who did not know it. All that was needed was to look around the assembled throng and pick out every Robson and Moray in the room. Except him. Had no one *really* noticed how different he was from all the rest? It seemed to shout itself from the roof tops.

"Don't be daft," Jamie was saying. "Just knock 'em dead." And he was off again, pushing his way back through the crowd. Tom downed the drink in one long draught, enjoying the bitter tang of it.

It was then that he saw her, through a chink in the press of bodies filling the hall. She was standing by the fire in the sitting room, her concentration visibly not engaged in a conversation with Dana and Craig.

Janet. Five years older than himself. Ian and Bridie's only daughter. He had not seen her for more than three years. Now she was back.

He abandoned his empty glass on the hall table and manoeuvred his way towards the sitting room door, politely excusing himself as he went. There, he had an uninterrupted view of her, and he liked what he saw. She was as eye-catching as he remembered her, and not just because she was taller than most women – she was different. Contrary to the current fashion for lashings of lacquer cementing every strand of hair in place, her bright chestnut mane cascaded in almost wilful disorder onto her shoulders, free from any restraint. There was the added attraction of a pale-green loose-fitting mohair jumper with a scoop neck, and lying seductively against the soft swell of her lovely mature breasts, was a loop of amber beads.

She looked round, sipping her punch, and caught him watching her. She smiled faintly in his direction, turning away almost at once. It was the briefest of glances, but in that split second, Tom sensed a very definite Donna Burdon moment.

Very purposefully, he made his way over to her. Dana and Craig made room for him. "Hello, Janet," he said with a ready smile. "Long time no see."

She level-gazed him with those clear green eyes. "Tom. How are you?"

"Fine – and you?"

She cocked her head to one side. "Okay," she said, deflecting his attention by turning to her sister-in-law. "You know Dana, of course?"

Tom nodded, being polite. "We met when you came over after your engagement, didn't we?"

Dana was a solid Canadian girl, probably of Swedish extraction: flaxen haired; blue eyed. She was studying him very intently. "Sure, we did," she said, leaning forward and offering her cheek for him to kiss.

"Dana was telling me about job opportunities in Alberta," Janet informed him.

"There's *so* much going on around us right now," Dana said with great emphasis.

The twang in her voice was suddenly echoed by Craig's as he put his arm protectively around her. "Great place for kids too," he said, all trace of his Northumbrian lilt long gone.

Janet smiled, rather wanly. "I'm going to be an auntie again," she explained, and went back to sipping her punch.

Tom shook Craig's hand. "Congratulations. When's it due?"

Dana was keen to tell him. "May – they say – but who knows?" she added, smiling at him. "They change their minds every time I go for a check-up."

Craig was starting to steer her away. "Excuse us, will you? Dana's not met the Taits yet, and she's dying to be introduced."

Left on their own together, Janet seemed uncomfortable in his presence. Was he standing too close? She was scanning the room over the rim of her glass, feigning interest in finding other faces she might know.

"How are you – really?" Tom asked, sensing things were not quite as 'okay' as she made out.

She looked back at him briefly before studying the contents of her glass. "So-so," she said. "Got a temporary job as veterinary nurse at Sam Munro's – covering for maternity leave. God!" she added with some vehemence, "I seem to be surrounded by people having babies." She finished her drink in something of a rush, frowning into the empty glass.

"Shall I get you another?" he asked.

She shook her head. "Actually, I shouldn't have drunk that so quickly. I'm getting a headache."

"You need some fresh air."

He took the glass from her, leaving it on the kitchen table as he led the way through to the back porch. He closed the door behind them. It was suddenly peaceful, the hubbub of conversation and the insistent beat of Sonny and Cher's 'I've Got You Babe' muffled by the solidity of the door.

The space was more cramped than usual, filled with empty beer crates along with its day-to-day array of jackets, wellingtons and waterproofs. There was the strong aroma of sheep and cow muck. Outside, beyond the small-paned window, a fine rain had begun to fall. It glistened on the cobbles in the glow of the yard light. Tom opened the outer door to let in the air. It was a strangely balmy evening for December.

Janet leaned heavily against the door frame, arms folded, her face turned from him as she watched the rain. She was breathing deeply, her breasts rising and falling slowly beneath the soft fabric of her jumper. He could not take his eyes off them. Despite having downed only one pint, he felt intoxicated, and their proximity was tempting. He wanted to kiss them.

"What have you been doing with yourself since we last met?" he asked, trying to control the rapidly rising urge to reach out and touch her.

She was in no hurry to answer him, her concentration still on the rain. "Having an affair," she said almost casually, as if she were talking to herself. "A married man. Usual thing. Lots of empty promises." She shrugged it off as if it were nothing.

He was not sure what she expected him to say. It was a monumental admission.

She turned to face him. "Are you shocked?" she asked bluntly.

He shook his head, not knowing what else to do – or say.

She raised an enquiring eyebrow, evidently unconvinced.

"Why tell me?" he asked.

"You asked me what I'd been doing," she said, tilting her head slightly to one side.

He moved closer. There was the hint of a delicate perfume on her skin.

She was suddenly looking at him very intently. "Christ!" she whispered. "You're bloody dangerous, Tom Moray. I bet you eat girls for breakfast these days."

"No," he said, finding this vaguely amusing but imagining he could start by sampling her.

"Not even Sarah Armstrong?" she challenged him.

He shook his head, implying incredulity. "Sarah? Sarah's only a friend."

"That's not what I hear."

"Then you've heard wrong. We're not engaged." He finally gave in to temptation and ran the back of his hand lightly down the long sweep of her neck, contemplating the possibility he might go further.

She checked the progress of his hand. "Don't play with me, Tom," she warned.

"I'm not playing," he said, realising with a startling clarity that he meant it. She had just lit the spark he needed to set him on fire. Sarah had never even made the effort to fan the dying embers.

"You should stick to someone your own age," she said quietly, moving away from him towards the kitchen door.

He backed off and opened it for her, stepping aside so that nothing would appear amiss to curious eyes. She went through without looking back, and he watched her go, sensing that given the right time and place, she might be willing enough. Whether they would 'have sex' or 'make love' was something he could mull over at his leisure. But he wanted her.

CHAPTER EIGHT

John reached Little Retton on the outskirts of Shrewsbury by early afternoon and drove up the gravel drive to Sylvans knowing his mother would be waiting for him, eagerly scanning the road from her vantage point on the sitting room window seat. From there, he saw her wave to him.

"John!" she said, coming out onto the steps to greet him. "Oh, John, it's so lovely to see you." She embraced him, her face wreathed in smiles.

"It's good to see you too," he said, planting a kiss on her forehead, amazed as always at her cheerful resilience to withstand the provocation that had become so much a part of her life. At seventy-eight, apart from her silver hair, she looked so much younger. Her resolute determination not to be bowed down by circumstances seemed to be the power-house that kept her blooming in both body and spirit. "How was Christmas?" he asked as they linked arms and she ushered him up the steps and into the house.

"Oh – the usual. Up and down. It was nice of you to phone. He's probably forgotten, of course, so don't be cross."

"I won't be."

She beamed up at him again. "Here, let me take your coat. He's in the sitting room watching television." She led him in.

The room was warm, a fire blazing cheerfully in the grate augmenting the more than efficient heating system. An array of Christmas cards was ranged across the mantelpiece and in one of the inglenooks, a beautiful Norwegian spruce was festooned with its usual selection of Christmas decorations topped off with a star. In the other, the television was tuned into a light-hearted festive film suitable for the whole family – not a breast or buttock in sight. Sitting in the well-upholstered armchair in front of it, with his back to the door, was his father.

Squadron Leader Charles Frederick Rufford DFC and Bar, eighty-one years old with his trade-mark RAF moustache, was much less robust than he used to be, but still a commanding figure with a voice to match. His thick steel-grey hair showed no signs of thinning, even if his dark brown eyes were no longer quite as sharp as they once had been. Regardless of fashion, he could be found wearing beige twill trousers, a white shirt with a cravat, and a v-necked jumper. Today was no exception: he was decked out in his favourite primrose-yellow lambswool, fraying slightly at the cuffs.

"Charles," Geraldine was saying above the merry nonsense on the television. "Charles! John's here."

His father did not look round. "What's he doing here today?"

"He always comes on Boxing Day, dear, you know that."

The old man turned to face her, his face taut with vexation. "This is rubbish, Geraldine," he said, gesticulating at the television. "What have you put it on for? Complete rubbish!"

She shrugged slightly, smiling. "You thought you might like watch it, dear. Never mind. I'll turn it off if you like."

"No. I'll watch it anyway."

She ignored his irritation. "I'll leave you two boys to have a chat for a while, shall I? – bring in some tea later?"

Charles glowered at her over his shoulder. "I don't want tea! A large whisky – that's what I need – watching this rubbish!"

John walked round the chair and reached down to touch his father's shoulder. "Hello, Charles."

The old man looked up and studied him for a moment, sudden recognition registering on his face, but no hint of pleasure. "Oh – it's you. Had a good drive down?"

"Not bad. Not much traffic." It was difficult to think with the television so loud. "Shall I turn this rubbish off?" he offered, having learned it was wise to pick up on what was uppermost in his father's disordered thoughts.

Charles agreed with him. "Total rubbish. Always is these days. Don't know why I waste my time with it."

John clicked off the set using the remote that was on the table beside the old man.

"Damned clever that," Charles said, looking at the control as if for the first time. "Had a good drive down?"

"Yes – not bad," John repeated, making himself comfortable in the other armchair.

"I could drive from Chester to Shrewsbury in under an hour during the War," Charles said with satisfaction.

Highly unlikely, but never mind. John could already see the way the conversation was slipping back in time. It was best to let it flow and hope the topic of grandsons could be kept at bay.

"I flew Blenheims in 'thirty-nine. Did I ever tell you?"

"Once or twice."

"Ah, but did I tell you about the bombing raids in 'forty? – up in north-east Denmark?"

It would make little difference whether John had heard the story or not – and he had, on innumerable occasions in the past – Charles was already recounting his tale. "In August," the old man said, leaning forward confidentially. "Haamstede, I think it was – or maybe Evere. I forget which. Anyway – we caught them on the hop! Got a Staffelkapitan that trip. Bloody good show!" He thumped the arm of the chair, a broad smile suddenly lighting up his face. "Bloody good show, eh?"

John agreed.

The smile vanished into a thoughtful frown and sudden seriousness. "Couldn't catch 'em out twice though. No – they were ready for us the second time. Got shot to ribbons. Bloody 109s running rings round us – and flak coming up like it was bonfire night across the coast. Two of us made it back. Two – out of twelve." He shook his head, upset at the memory. "Bloody shambles. Lost Tubby Parker that trip," he added, staring into the fire. "Good chap, Tubby Parker. Always there for you."

"You got Shanklemann home."

A pause to remember. "Danny Shanklemann? Course I did! Damned fine fellow, Danny Shanklemann. Lost all his crew, you know. And his legs. Talked him back ..."

"They gave you the DFC for that, didn't they?"

The old man nodded, his concentration fixed on the flames in the hearth. "Got promoted. Did I tell you that? Moved on to Wellingtons." He perked up. "Good crates Wellingtons." He grew expansive. "You could make it home in a Wellington with half its side-beams blown to smithereens," he said, enthusiasm lighting up his face. "They'd patch it up and you'd be back in the cockpit in twenty-four hours – good as new. Damned good crates. Knocked the Blenheims into a cocked hat."

John nodded in agreement: it was all that was required.

His father had worked up a good head of steam now. "Did I ever tell you about the night missions over the Channel?" he asked, determined to continue anyway. "Bloody awful they were. Night after night. Pounding hell out of Jerry barges in the Channel ports. Invasion fleet, you see. All lined up ready to go. Had to stop 'em." He paused to reflect. "Battle of Britain, Churchill called it. Don't hear much about Bomber Command doing their bit, do you? All Fighter Command – Spitfires and Hurricanes – The Glory Boys. Pity about that. We lost nearly fifteen hundred men. Killed – missing – captured. God knows how many planes. Bloody shooting gallery. Did our bit all right." He lapsed into silence, sinking into his memories. But there was no mention of his final mission, or his second Award, or the shrapnel that had torn through the cockpit. No mention of the months spent in hospital afterwards: the string of operations; the long haul back to recovery each time; the physiotherapy and learning to walk again; the fragment still lodged in his head.

John could remember tedious train journeys with his mother in the summer holidays as a nine-year old, travelling to some god-forsaken RAF hospital who-knew-where: the forbidding Gothic building; the wards smelling of strong disinfectant that made him feel sick; the shattered men with shattered lives; and women weeping silently in corridors. He had been glad to start his new life as a boarder at De Montfort after Christmas. There he could forget the real world and bury himself in books and rugby.

Three years later, Charles had been invalided out, pensioned off and returned to Sylvans a changed man, bitter and angry in equal measure, incapable of holding down a job for long. He sensed failure. He had let down his Rufford forebears: his grandfather, George Edward Rufford, a wool merchant in Ludlow, steeped in Benthamite philanthropy; and his father, Frederick George Rufford, who had seen poverty and squalor on an appalling scale among the families of the coal mining and brickwork heartland of Shropshire, and devoted his life as Medical Officer of Sheckley Borough to the amelioration of these conditions. Charles had been imbued with the need for social reform since he was in his cradle. He had read Law at Oxford intending to stand for Parliament to achieve that goal; had married Geraldine, daughter of a Unitarian minister who had trained as a nurse and held similar views. He had high hopes of achieving great things himself, but defeating Fascism had taken precedence. In 'thirty-six, he had resigned his position with Sheckley Public Health Department and joined the RAF. John had been four, and he had grown up believing his father was an heroic figure: principled and brave. But the man who returned in 'forty-three, was someone else.

As the years passed, John remembered the shouting over trivial grievances, and Geraldine's determination not to be cowed by bouts of anger that could slip so easily, and without warning, into sudden violence. When Charles had threatened John, she had stood between them, explaining afterwards, nursing whatever injury Charles had inflicted on her, "I can remember your father as he was, John. A loving man. Don't be angry with him. He can't help himself, you know – and I still care for him."

Michael was born not long afterwards, his father's proof that he was, despite everything, still a man.

John had never resented Michael's late appearance on the scene: his sunny disposition blunted his father's tendency to rant and rave; the violence decreased; and eventually, the bark became worse than the bite.

But as time passed there were other, much less welcome changes. Charles became dissatisfied with everything John did, and though he bore these criticisms stoically at first, always striving to improve, he was baffled when his achievements were belittled. Eventually a sense of grievance made him stand his ground, and defiance, he discovered, was to prove his most effective weapon. Rebellion gave him power, and as a young man, he had used it. With hindsight, he regretted this: he had made things worse, not better; a battle waged against a damaged mind. But in these foundations lay the building blocks which stood solidly between them now, like the Berlin Wall. It was too late to tear them down.

Geraldine had come in with a tea tray already laid. "There we are," she said, smiling with satisfaction at her choice of Christmas cake and shortbread biscuits on a side plate with a paper doily.

John stood up and took the tray from her while she cleared a space on the coffee table. Charles was still lost in thought. He remained silent while his wife busied herself serving up tea and handing round the plates. It was as if she weren't there, John thought. How did she stand it? It had been this way for fifteen years.

"Charles?" she repeated. "Cake or biscuits?" offering him the choice.

He looked up, frowning in annoyance. "Why would I want cake or biscuits?" he asked sharply, glaring in her direction.

"It's three o'clock, dear," she said, the epitome of sweet reason. "You always have cake or biscuits with your tea at three."

"I'll have cake then," he said brusquely, evidently waiting for her to serve him with a slice, which she did. "Don't know why you make such a fuss about everything. Damned annoying – like your son here!" He glowered in John's direction, noticeably more agitated. "Why can't he get himself married, eh? All those bloody women he's had and he can't get himself married! What the hell's he waiting for? – the Second Coming? How much longer do I have to wait for a grandson, eh? – that's what I want to know! When are you going to marry that girl you keep mooning over?"

Geraldine sat down on the sofa with her plate on her lap and composed herself in the short silence that followed.

John's heart sank.

Charles was leaning over the side of his chair pointing a long finger in his direction. "Bloody selfish –"

Geraldine intervened. "Charles," she said in a finely balanced tone between firmness and politeness. "Not now, dear. We're having tea."

The old man harumphed and sat back again, pacified for the moment until he had eaten his cake. But his mind was set on its familiar path. More would follow. And, inevitably, it did. The finger was pointing again in John's direction. "You've spent your life defying me," Charles said, his eyes narrowing perceptibly as his anger built on itself.

Geraldine attempted conciliation. "Now you know that's not true, Charles."

Charles harumphed again.

"I preferred the Army, that's all," John said quietly, trying to deflect his father's anger. How many times had he said that?

Charles was unimpressed. He made a small explosive noise of contempt. "Rubbish!" he said. "Could have joined the University Air Squadron – got yourself commissioned." The old man was jabbing him in the shoulder now.

"You know I didn't want a commission," John said, trying to ignore the rhythmical prodding that was becoming more vigorous. "I wanted to be in the ranks."

"Bloody squaddies! Riff-raff – all of them!"

John continued with his well-practised rote of attempting a rational discussion. "They weren't all riff-raff. National Service was a catch-all."

The prodding continued. "Anyone with anything about them get's commissioned. What does that say about you, my lad? Bloody useless!"

No mention then of John's first-class law degree, nor the steady progress through the legal departments of several local authorities, nor even the culmination of a career as one of the youngest Chief Executives in nineteen-seventy-four. Of his son choosing to give up everything for photography, Charles had long since ceased to either comprehend or remember this event, and it had never been touched upon in recent times because of its potential to have explosive consequences.

"Charles! That's enough, now," Geraldine chided him gently. "You're getting yourself all upset. Have another slice of cake."

The old man frowned at the plate she was pushing in his direction, and was tempted.

John did not stay long afterwards: he felt too fragile.

With the television on at full blast again in the sitting room, Geraldine followed him out into the hall.

"I have to go," John said, feeling as guilty as hell at leaving her so soon.

"I know, dear," Geraldine was saying trying to put a brave face on things. "Not one of his better days, I'm afraid."

"You know he's getting worse," John said. "You can't go on like this. Next weekend – can you get someone to sit with him – for a couple of hours maybe? I'd like to drive you over to Michael's place for the afternoon. I know you miss seeing the girls – and they miss you."

Geraldine's face lit up at the prospect. "Oh, that would be lovely, John," she said, clutching his arm excitedly.

He hovered by the front door, suddenly compelled to tell her. "You know the girl I kept 'mooning over', as Charles puts it?" he said, listening to the roaring in his head. "She died a few weeks ago."

"Oh John! I'm so sorry."

"I went to her funeral – in Northumberland. She was only fifty. Much too young to die," he added, wondering how to tell his mother what he most wanted her to know. "I met someone," he said at last, hesitating over his words. "While I was there."

She was looking up at him, a small frown settling on her brow.

He stumbled on, wondering if he were doing the right thing in telling her. "It seems I have a son – his name's Thomas."

His news was greeted by a small silence. Geraldine gave it some thought before asking tentatively, "Hers?"

"Yes," he confessed, feeling the weight lift from his shoulders. "But it's complicated – he doesn't know I'm his father. It's been kept a secret."

"I see. So you can't tell him?"

"No, I can't. I have to consider his family."

"Yes – of course," she said, mulling this over.

He tried to smile. "I just wanted you to know – you have a grandson."

Tears were gathering in her eyes. She put her arms around him and held him close for a moment. "Thank you for telling me, John. I'm sorry Charles was so difficult today." She looked up at him, holding back her tears. "You can't tell him either, can you?" she said.

"I don't think he'd understand, do you?"

"No, probably not," she said with a little sigh. "Not now. He'd get very confused – and he's not easy to live with when he gets very confused." She squeezed his hand. "But perhaps you'll get the chance to see the boy again?" she said, trying to sound positive.

John shook his head. "No. I gave my word I'd never try to contact him. I can't go back on what I've promised."

Geraldine looked away quickly, searching for her handkerchief.

Behind them, his father's voice boomed out from the sitting room. "Geraldine! What are you doing? You've left me with this damned rubbish again!"

CHAPTER NINE

Flora in a pair of scruffy jeans, her hair dishevelled and impatiently pushed behind her ears, was standing hands on hips, surveying her handiwork. "What do you think, Tom?" Her voice echoed up into the empty recesses of the ceiling.

The studio was stripped bare. Except for the solid presence of the mahogany desk by the front window and the black leather chair behind it, all traces of its former self had been reduced to a whitewashed shell. The stools and easels had been moved into one of the sheds waiting to be collected – the art teacher from Wallbridge School had gratefully accepted these along with the stacks of paper, paints and pencils; the unfinished study of Brack was at Andy Dunne's Cardingwool Lane Gallery for framing; and their mother's remaining artwork had been taken down and carefully stored away in the box room upstairs. An agent from an auction house had asked if he could come to discuss possible options. Robert remained ambivalent and in no hurry to decide anything.

Tom looked around them. There was something unsettling about the dark solidity of the desk and its attendant chair surrounded by so much emptiness.

"Come on!" Flora was saying impatiently. "You're no help at all! What do you think?"

Perhaps to reduce the impact of the desk – not to mention its contents, Tom pushed aside the glass paperweight and balanced himself precariously on one corner, surveying the room from a different angle. "What else can it be used for, Flora? It's always been a studio – ever since I can remember."

"Well it can't just be left empty. It'll never be a dairy again, will it? And Dad seems determined not to use it."

Tom could have pointed out that with Jamie moving on, and Flora herself planning to do the same, the house was far too big as it was. It hardly helped that the studio had a Spartan feel to it that added nothing to its appeal, and it would cost a fortune to restore the half that had once been used as a snug. "Perhaps we should just accept we've no use for it and shut it up?" he suggested.

"We can't do that! You don't leave rooms 'shut up' these days, Tom. They go 'off' and smell all musty and horrible."

He shrugged, not wanting to be pressed on the subject. It was Wednesday. He would rather have been down at the mart discussing fatstock prices. Lambs were going for £40. It might be a good time to off-load the batch that were slightly under weight rather than hang on and see the prices fall. Ian had come round and persuaded Robert to go down to the mart with him to meet up with friends, but Flora had detained Tom because she said she needed "a bit of muscle" to help her clear out the studio.

"It's self-contained if we block up the door from the

hall," she was saying. "I suppose we could jolly it up a bit and let it out to someone."

"Who'd want to live here? It's not exactly 'homely', is it?"

She pirouetted, spreading her arms to encompass the whole space. "Artists, of course, stupid. Why not?" She was unstoppable now. "Look how many students said how much they loved the place."

"For a couple of weeks," he objected. "Not for a couple of months."

"Tom Moray, you've no soul," she said dismissively. "This is exactly what an artist wants. Why do you think Mam was so successful? – and just think about it – there'd be ..." She looked awkward for a moment and sighed regretfully. "Well – let's face it – there'd be more life around the place, wouldn't there?" She put her arms around him, resting her head on his shoulder. "Tom, I'm sorry, but what's it going to be like here when the Christmas decorations come down and everything goes back to being dark and gloomy? No students. Jamie and me gone. Just you and Dad. He's bad enough, but you're getting just the same – all broody and silent." She stood back from him, her lovely face suddenly serious. "You've changed, Tom. Really, you have. Some days you're somewhere else. What's wrong? Something's wrong." It could have been his mother asking him.

He shook his head. "It's nothing – just me being a pain."

"You've not fallen out with Sarah, have you? We haven't seen her since New Year's Eve."

"No – nothing like that," he said, wishing she would

drop the subject. "We're just busy, that's all. She's got the nursery job and I've got more to do here now that Mam's not around."

Flora was full of remorse. "Oh, Tom, I'm sorry – of course you have. I wasn't thinking."

"That's okay."

Her concern evaporated. She suddenly brightened. "I know – why not open up the old student block as a bunkhouse for walkers this year? Ask Chrissie Dixon to come back to do breakfasts and cleaning – like she used to do when the students were here?"

Once Flora got the bit between her teeth there was no stopping her: there was no problem that could not be solved; no difficulty that could not be overcome. All that was needed was a little imagination and a lot of energy, and she had both in abundance.

"Come on, Tom! Be positive!" she was saying. "What do you think?"

The sound of Ian's Land Rover coming to a stop in the yard relieved him of the need to drum up a suitable reply.

Robert invited Ian in, his presence only fuelling Flora's determination to expound her ideas to a wider audience.

"So I said," she explained. "Why not shut off the studio from the rest of the house – like it was when it was the dairy – and let it out to an artist – and – open up the old student dorm as a bunkhouse for walkers? Chrissie was only saying on New Year's Eve how much she missed her little job up at Rigg End."

Ian became her unexpected ally. "Makes sense, Rob," he

said. "You need to diversify these days. It wouldn't take a lot of organising either. It's what you need."

Robert looked up from the mug he was holding. "To bring some life back into the place?" he asked. "Is that what you mean?" It was a direct challenge.

Ian was not put off in the slightest. "No harm in that, is there? It's going to get pretty lonely up here with just the two of you."

To which Robert merely nodded.

"And come March you'll be busy lambing. You won't know whether you're coming or going. Why not ask Chrissie to help out in the house as well? As Flora says, she'd welcome the cash. Jackie's still off work with his back."

Robert frowned, studying the bottom of his empty mug. "I don't know, Ian. I'd like to think about it."

"Well, think on, Rob. It'd be no bad thing."

"Maybe." He glanced up at Tom. "Wallace had the idea Sarah could come down and cook for us now and then. Maybe do a bit of housekeeping as well," he added.

Tom wondered if everyone could see his ears burning. They were all looking at him. If ever a trap had been nicely sprung, this was surely it.

"You've embarrassed the lad," Ian said, finding this amusing. "What do you think, Tom?"

Flora added to the mix. "Oh Tom, why not?"

Somewhere in the maelstrom in his head, Tom heard himself say, "There'll be gossip if she comes here. It wouldn't be fair on her."

Ian was quick to stem any suggestion there might be

some impropriety in the arrangement. "She doesn't have to live-in," he stressed. "She could come down when she's needed like."

Tom wrestled with this notion, aping serious consideration that was so far wide of the mark he was certain everyone would see through his obvious deception. "As long as she's happy with that," he said. *He* was not. Far from it. He was being hedged in by other people's expectations, and the more those well-meaning souls interfered, the less inclined he felt to be pushed in the direction they wanted him to go.

"Well, that sounds like the best solution all round, Rob. Rent out the studio long-term, get the bunkhouse up and running for the summer and Chrissie to look after it, with Sarah to keep an eye on the house. They'd be a grand team, no doubt about it like."

The trouble was, the plan was perfect. And Tom knew it. Ian was right. Chrissie and Sarah had been friends since they were children. They would have the place running like clockwork in no time at all.

Robert was nodding. "I'll talk it over with Ralph Milburn," he said. "See what he thinks."

"You don't need an accountant to tell you it's a good idea, Rob."

"I'd like his opinion, all the same."

"Cautious as ever," Ian said, scraping back his chair as he stood up. "You can never hurry your father, Tom. Not if he doesn't want to be hurried."

Later that evening, when Robert and Tom were out in the hemmel checking the heifers in calf, Robert raised the subject again. He made it sound casual; something to talk about just to fill in the time as they moved down the line. "You didn't say much this afternoon," he said. "What do you really think – about the plan?"

"It makes sense, I suppose."

"You 'suppose'?"

"The rent would come in handy."

"You wouldn't mind someone else in the studio?"

"Would you?"

Robert straightened, giving his beast a friendly pat on its shaggy neck. He considered the question. "Maybe it's the best thing to do." He paused, mulling things over and moving on to the next beast, running his hand over her. "What about the idea for the bunkhouse?"

"It would be easy to run. Basic food. No laundry. Chrissie could handle it."

"I'm not sure I like the idea, Tom. We'd have strangers all over the place when we'll be too busy to keep an eye on them. Some folk are just plain stupid where beasts are concerned – letting dogs run amok – leaving gates open. There'll be new calves and lambs in every field come April."

"The footpaths are clear enough."

"Proper ramblers aren't the problem, are they, Tom? It's folk who think they can roam anywhere that cause the trouble."

"A few more locks – some warning notices. That should do it."

They moved on again to the next beast, Robert running his hand over her for a while. Eventually he turned to face him. "What have you really got against the idea of Sarah coming down?" he asked unexpectedly.

"What I said – there'll be gossip."

"So you say, but we're going to need help. With the best will in the world, we can't manage this level of stock and run a house as well. There aren't enough hours in the day."

"I'd rather we gave Chrissie the job if we give it to anyone."

"She's still got her own place to look after, Tom – and Jackie's not well. There'd be no harm in Sarah coming down – maybe a couple of days a week to keep an eye on the house."

Tom said nothing. What was the point of arguing? Robert had already made up his mind.

"Wallace keeps pushing," Robert said, letting the cow butt him gently with her head. "About you and Sarah," he added, making no great thing of it. "You don't like it, do you? – Wallace organising your life?"

It was best to be honest. "No," he said, relieved to get this out in the open at last. "I don't want to be pushed into marriage before I'm ready – and I don't think I'm ready – not yet."

"I can understand that. Wallace worries about the future, that's all."

"And that's what this is all about, isn't it? What Wallace Armstrong wants – me and Sarah – Rigg End and Rattling Gate." He realised he was beginning to sound like a petulant child throwing a tantrum.

Robert gave him a sideways glance.

"I'm sorry – but I'm not going to be pushed into marrying Sarah just because Wallace Armstrong wants me to."

"Aren't you in love with her?"

Now that was a straight question. No way out of that one, unless he make an obvious fudge of it. "I don't know, Dad," he said, honestly unable to say one way or the other. "I like her – and I'd always know where I stood with her but ..." He ran out of words, feeling he had not given a very good account of himself.

"But you're having doubts?"

"We're great friends – but there's nothing else. There's no – " He shrugged.

"Great passion?"

Tom scuffed the straw under his feet, studying his boots.

"I'll grant you friendship alone wouldn't suit me either, Tom. I know what I need, but sometimes friendship outlives passion. Sometimes it holds a marriage together – like glue – when everything else fails. For lots of folk, that's all they have."

"Maybe, but I don't think that's what I want from *my* marriage."

"Don't you think you should tell her, Tom? She's a nice lass. I wouldn't want to see her hurt."

"I know. It's just – well – I'm not thinking straight half the time these days," he confessed. He could have said more about the confusion in his head; about his uncertainties; about his loss of identity that troubled him more than anything else. But this was better left unsaid. Besides, there was no need to say it. From the expression on Robert's face, it was clear he understood precisely what lay at the root of everything that troubled him.

Robert came round from the other side of the cow to face him. "Do you know how I spend my nights, Tom?" he said, evidently pained to confess it. "I lie awake fretting – about losing your mother – about what's happened since – about how you must feel." He paused, shaking his head over his shortcomings. "I should've been honest with you right from the start – that night – after you found the photograph. I just couldn't. I hadn't the strength." The cow nudged her head up against his shoulder, distracting him for a moment. "But the questions aren't going to go away just because I want them to, are they?" He ruffled the thick dark hair on the cow's forehead. "Can you wait a few days – 'til Flora goes back to college? Then we can talk? Just the two of us?"

Tom nodded, and Flora called them in for supper.

CHAPTER TEN

A raw easterly was whipping along the platform. Flora hopped from one foot to another to keep warm, wisps of hair escaping from the hood of her Puffa jacket and flicking across her face. "I told Dad about London before we left," she said. "He was fine about it. I felt really stupid making such a big thing of it."

Tom pulled up the collar of his coat, his mind back at the farm. There was a loose panel on the north side of the hemmel that needed fixing. The train was late.

"I am doing the right thing, aren't I, Tom?" she was asking him, suddenly beset by second thoughts.

He honestly did not know. London was another planet as far as he was concerned, but he agreed with her anyway.

"I'm going down at half-term – to meet everyone," she added enthusiastically. "I'll miss seeing you all of course, but Jamie'll be back, so you won't miss me at all, will you?" She threaded her arm through his to keep warm and smiled up at him.

The two-coach diesel trundled into view and shuddered to a halt. Tom helped her gather her bags together and bundled them through the open door, slamming it shut.

She hung out of the window as the train began to move. "Have a great birthday, Tom. See you at Easter. Take care." The sing-song boom of the horn and the pulsating beat of the engine drowned out the rest of her words.

He stood watching the carriages slide away into the distance until they disappeared round the bend in the track. When he turned to leave, he had a strange notion something momentous had just happened, but had no idea what.

At Rigg End, Robert was waiting for him in the yard chewing on the stem of his unlit pipe. "Flora got off all right?" he asked.

"The train was late."

"You've just missed Ralph Milburn. He's going to look over the figures for us – for the diversification plans."

"You're going ahead with them then?"

"Maybe," Robert said. "I'll see what he says." He paused, sucking hard on the pipe. "Doing anything this morning?"

"There's that panel on the hemmel to fix. Thought I might take a look at the fencing out the back while I'm at it."

"We'll talk later then."

Tom nodded, too busy going through an expanding list of jobs that needed to be done to engage in chit-chat. Besides, the strange mood that had settled on him at the station had persisted and made him disinclined to talk. He was aware Robert had noticed his reticence. But if he had been asked to explain himself, he knew he would find it impossible. Better then not to be around in the first place. He went inside to search out a warmer pair of socks.

Flora had been right: the house, bare of decorations, had

an oppressive feel. He tried to ignore it, but as he turned to mount the stairs, he caught sight of the mahogany desk through the open door into the sitting room. Jamie had helped him move it into the space by the window, and anyone else would have said it fitted in well with the rest of the heavy old-fashioned furniture in the room. But to Tom, its locked drawer – and what was hidden inside – marked it out as an unwelcome addition.

Staring balefully at it, he realised there was something he should have done weeks ago.

That evening, Robert was in his own reflective mood. "We've got the house to ourselves again," he said, hunkering down in front of the fire to pull the logs together. "I'd forgotten how quiet it could be." He looked up suddenly, as if expecting Tom to ask him something.

Perhaps this was as good a time as any. Tom pulled himself out of his chair and retrieved his mother's letter from the desk. "I should've shown you this weeks ago," he said.

Robert looked at the folded sheet of paper and stood up, in no hurry to take it from him. "It was written to you, Tom, not me."

"All the same, I think you should read it."

Robert took it reluctantly, sitting down in his chair by the fire. He took out his reading glasses from their case on the table beside him and unfolded the letter, reading it slowly before handing it back. He returned the spectacles to their case without comment.

"When did she write it?" Tom asked.

"After the muddle over the receipt. Your mother had an instinct for things, Tom. She was convinced he'd come to the funeral."

"I still don't understand why she wrote it."

"She was sure you'd see the similarity between you if he came."

"But I didn't."

"She wasn't to know that. She wanted to tell you we'd been happy together – regardless of everything."

Tom looked down at the offending piece of paper in his hand. "And if he hadn't come?"

"I was to destroy the letter."

"So I would've never known the truth?"

"That's what she wanted."

"The truth doesn't go away because we want it to," Tom objected.

Robert shrugged this off. "Do you think she didn't know that, Tom? That's why she left you her family history – to show you every family has its secrets – and its reasons for keeping them."

Tom returned the letter to the drawer, and took out the notelet box. He wondered if he should mention it. "This is what I found," he said, handing it over.

Robert took it from him, looking puzzled. He slipped off the elastic band and opened the box. Bewildered, he took out the slender volume and examined its cover, evidently seeing it for the first time.

"Have you never seen this before?" Tom asked.

"No – never."

"His photograph's inside."

Robert flicked through the pages and the photograph fell into his lap. He picked it up and studied it for a moment, his face registering no emotion.

"I look just like him, don't I?"

Robert nodded, a tight smile hemming in the corners of his mouth. He returned the photograph and the book to the little box and closed it, carefully replacing the elastic band, as if he felt it necessary to keep John Rufford safely stowed out of sight.

"When did you find out? – about me?"

Robert was in no hurry to answer. "Not for a while," he said, reflecting on the memory that must have caused him pain.

"Didn't you suspect anything?" It seemed hard to believe.

Robert shook his head. "Your mother and I didn't wait 'til we were married, Tom," he explained, glancing up at him. "We thought you'd come early, that's all."

There were times when Tom wished Robert would restrain his frankness. "So when did you know?"

"The year after Jamie was born. We went up to Edinburgh – you, me, your mother and Jamie – to visit your Grandma Grace. It was her eightieth birthday. Everyone was there. Sandy and Mary had come over with their tribe – and Thomas and Una had come down from Aberdeen with young Gordon and the twins." He smiled at the remembrance of it. "It was one of those lovely summer afternoons, Tom. You youngsters were running wild outside and my mother thought it would be a good idea to have the birthday tea in the garden." His smile faded into serious reflection. "We sat on a tartan travel rug and had egg and cress sandwiches. Do you remember?"

Tom shook his head: he had no memory of the day at all.

Robert slipped back into his private world, staring at the fire. "Jamie was sitting in your mother's lap and I'd been tickling his toes, making him laugh. You were busy playing with your wooden train, chugging it up and down the lines on the rug by her feet. She said something to you and you looked up." He paused, recalling the moment. "I remember seeing her expression change. She was just looking at you – staring – and I turned to see what was wrong. That's when I saw ..." He stopped, unable to go on.

"You saw I didn't look like Jamie?"

"No, Tom, it wasn't that."

"What was it then?"

"Your expression, Tom. It happens, you know. Sometimes you get a fleeting glimpse of the man in the child."

"And you saw John Rufford?"

"We both saw it."

"Did she say anything?"

"No – neither of us did. Not then. That came later after we'd got the two of you tucked up in bed. I couldn't stop her crying, Tom. She kept repeating, over and over again, she hadn't known – wanting me to believe her." He leaned forward and put another log on the fire.

"Did you? – believe her?"

Robert settled back in his chair again watching the flames take hold. "Yes, I believed her – but at the time nothing would convince her I did. For months I was afraid she'd leave me – take you with her. I couldn't have borne that, Tom. I loved her too much. Loved you too."

A flurry of sparks scurried up the chimney as the log succumbed, the flames licking round it, hungry and fierce, like Robert's love, Tom thought, consuming everything: jealousy; anger; even resentment. "How did you convince her in the end?" he asked, " – that you still felt the same about her – about me?"

Robert glanced up at him. "How do you convince a woman of anything, Tom?" he asked, perhaps not expecting an answer. "You have to show her – day in, day out – that she's everything in the world to you." His voice had softened, remembering another time. "We made love in the hay barn one afternoon," he said dreamily, ignoring Tom's discomfort. "It was a drear autumn. I'd brought in the cows early and was piling up bales to take over to the hemmel. She brought me out a mug of tea because I was too busy to come into the kitchen for it. I remember the sun suddenly bursting through the clouds, and she was standing there, in the door way, lit up in this brilliant golden haze. She looked so beautiful." He paused, overcome by the memory of that moment. "I can remember the smell of the hay, and strands of it caught in her hair," he said. "Remember her laughing for the first time in months – and both of us looking tumbled and dishevelled in the kitchen afterwards." There was an expansive smile on his face, and he suddenly looked a much younger man. "Flora was born nine months later," he added, well-pleased with the outcome. There was a note of triumph in his voice. "That's what love can do for you, Tom – if you love someone enough."

Tom wondered what it was like to feel something so all-consuming. He wished he could feel something so intense for Sarah. But there was nothing except the easy acceptance of her company. He looked down at the notelet box still in his hand. There was another man whose love had outstripped the years, he thought. What was his state of mind now that he knew he had a son by the woman he had loved so devotedly for so long?

Robert had got up from his chair and was leaning against the mantelpiece. "Tom," he said, looking troubled by what he was about to say. "That day when I brought Rufford over to introduce him, I knew I was taking a gamble. I did it out of guilt because I felt I owed it to him – but that was all. I made him promise to leave the house quickly, and quietly, and not trouble us again."

"Has he been in touch?"

"No. He gave his word and he's kept it – but I shouldn't have asked him to make that promise in the first place. I'd no right to do that. He's your father. It wasn't up to me to decide."

"You were doing what you thought best."

Robert shook his head. "No, Tom," he said grimly, "I was being selfish. I'd just lost the woman I loved and I was afraid of losing you too." He bent down and put another log on the fire.

"Dad, you can't 'lose' me," Tom objected, feeling he was saying the obvious. "I'll never leave here. Rigg End's my home." But if he were honest, he could hear faint contradictions whispering in his ear, eager to be heard.

"Don't be too quick to close off your options," Robert was saying as he settled in his chair again. "You know the farm will be yours when I'm gone, don't you? You've helped to make it what it is. But if you found you wanted something else – remember what Mr Gregson said that night at parents' evening? – that you could turn your hand to anything? – you don't have to be a farmer. That was *my* choice, but it doesn't have to be yours."

"I don't want anything else," Tom insisted, hoping he sounded convincing enough to quell any doubts.

Robert was not to be put off. "Well, now perhaps you should think about it," he said, frowning hard at the grate.

Tom felt an icy hand grip his heart. "Do you *want* me to leave?" he asked, fearing this was where the conversation was heading.

Robert looked round sharply. "Christ! – no, Tom – that's not what I meant at all. I just wanted you to know I've no right to dictate how you should feel or what you should do with your life. Do you understand?"

Tom said he did, wondering if he were being entirely honest when he said it.

There was a strained silence between them for a while. "Do you remember your mother's place?" Robert asked suddenly. "Meeston Lodge – down in Cheshire? You went there with her once."

"Yes – when Grandma Driscoll died. I was about twelve, I think." For a moment, Tom could remember them both standing in the spacious hallway, his mother with her hands on her hips – the image of Flora in the studio after Christmas – surveying the boxes and plastic bags piled up ready to be taken to the charity shops in Weaversham. She had wanted to rid the place of all traces of her mother; to wipe away her memory once and for all.

"I think you should know," Robert was saying, " – it'll come out anyway soon enough – she's left the place to you in her Will."

His words did not sink in for a moment. "Why did she do that, Dad?" he asked, bewildered by what her motives might have been to do such a thing.

Robert paused before replying. "She thought you might need somewhere to go – if things didn't work out here."

"I don't understand."

"She thought if you ever found out about Rufford, you might need time and space to think things through for a while – on your own. Perhaps even make a fresh start. I did once," he reminded him.

"I'd never do that!"

"She didn't want to take the chance, Tom, that's all. Anyway," he went on, shifting in his chair and dropping the subject, "I've come to a decision. Flora's right – we need someone to help in the house. I know you're dead set against it, but I'm going to ask Sarah if she'd mind coming down a couple of days a week."

Tom could feel his heart sink. "No, Dad. It's a bad idea," he insisted.

Robert remained unconvinced. "Not from where I'm

standing, Tom. It'll make things easier if you have to go down to Cheshire for a while to deal with your mother's business. Ian and Duncan will be happy enough to help out on the farm side. You'll be able to go with a clear conscience without fretting over anything here. Oh – and while I think about it," he went on before Tom could catch up with him, "you don't need to tell Jamie and Flora anything you don't want them to know. I'll respect any decision you make."

Tom stared at the fire wondering what he was supposed to do.

CHAPTER ELEVEN

Being twenty-five was not all it was cracked up to be, Tom decided, when he woke up the following morning with a thick head and the knowledge he had made a spectacular fool of himself the night before, getting blind drunk up at The Gate with half the Stanegate Young Farmers there to witness it. He had managed to spill a pint of good ale over the thick lovat-green jumper Sarah had knitted him for Christmas, and had been bundled into the back of Dougie Watson's pick-up with Duncan and one of the Liddel boys holding his head over the side while he spewed up all the way back to Rigg End.

He had overslept as a result, and by the time he got himself pulled round, Robert had already left to complete the hedge cutting down on the green lane. In the kitchen, draped over the airer above the range like silent accusers, were the ale-sodden jeans and jumper, freshly washed and left to dry.

Robert made no comment when he came home for lunch. Perhaps he felt no need: he understood the reasons behind Tom's strange behaviour.

Two days later, Sarah's red Fiat 127 negotiated the

potholes in the track to become a regular feature in their lives.

"She won't be here every day, Tom," Robert explained over their bacon and eggs that morning. "She's still got her job over at Whinrigg Nursery twice a week."

But in no time at all, she made her presence felt. Rooms that had languished since Flora had gone back to college were rapidly put into order; old newspapers discarded; the ash in the grate emptied; the hearth swept clean; everywhere downstairs hoovered and dusted. She was setting her sights on the upper floor when Tom put his foot down. "I'd rather look after my own things," he had said when she threatened to invade his room one morning.

Robert however was less inclined to put such limits on her enthusiasm. By the end of the first week, the house had been given an early spring-clean from top to bottom. The kitchen, almost inevitably, became her domain, and her cooking and baking skills were readily transferred from Rattling Gate to Rigg End, along with her determination to oversee a regular schedule of laundry. Life at Rigg End had not been so organised for months.

Robert seemed unperturbed by this sudden dislocation of their lives. Tom, on the other hand, disconcerted at first, began to actively resent the loss of homeliness and the casual clutter of day-to-day living. Sarah, he soon realised, could not abide anything out of place: half-read newspapers, put down in a hurry in the kitchen after lunch, were promptly folded and placed in the paper rack in the sitting room; breakfast plates left stacked in the drainer were dried and put away in the dresser; outer jackets left over the backs of the kitchen chairs were hung up in the back porch; and the haphazard notes of varying ages and sizes pinned to the notice board by the back door were systematically reviewed at regular intervals, with only the relevant few allowed to remain in place.

There was nothing malicious in her regime, Tom realised, but her persistence in maintaining an immaculate home seemed somehow to reflect badly on the more relaxed attitude his mother had adopted towards housekeeping. He found himself wondering whether Sarah, when she had visited Rigg End in the past, had thought the place needed more attention than it was getting. It irked him to think that she had. But it irked him even more when her enthusiasm spilled over into more personal matters.

"Tom!" she said, frowning at him disapprovingly that Thursday morning. "You were wearing that shirt when I came on Tuesday!" Considering he soaked himself in the bath every night, and the thick twill was perfect for the time of year, he took this criticism to heart.

Matters came to a head the same day over lunch. Tom arrived a few minutes late and found Robert, spectacles balanced on the end of his nose, engrossed in the weekly fatstock prices in the *Wallbridge Mart* which he had spread out on the kitchen table. He was smoking his old pipe, thick curls of smoke drifting upwards on the warmth from the range. The table was already set with a basket of crusty rolls and a slab of butter – a situation he seemed to have ignored, pushing aside cutlery to make a suitable space for his paper – and Sarah was preparing to serve up a hearty bowl of game soup.

Tom took him to task. "What's this then, Dad? Smoking over lunch?"

Robert looked up, taken by surprise. "Ah – forgot," he said, looking sheepish, and was about to knock out the pipe when Sarah made her views known. "Oh, Tom!" she said disapprovingly. "Let him alone. A man's got to have some pleasure in life."

Robert paused for a moment, evidently as startled by her intervention as Tom, but all the same, he knocked out the pipe into the ash tray, and the meal was passed in an atmosphere of strained politeness.

Tom spent the rest of the afternoon in a furious state of mind, and when at last they had the house to themselves over supper, he could no longer keep silent. "This isn't going to work, Dad," he said, raising the topic without warning.

Robert looked bemused. "What isn't?" he asked.

"Sarah – coming here."

"She's looking after the place well enough, isn't she?"

"It's not about the way she's looking after the place, Dad," Tom said, realising he was still angry, and it showed.

"What is it then?"

"It's – it's lots of things."

Robert briefly contemplated his half-eaten chop then put down his knife and fork, giving Tom his undivided attention.

"She's getting on my nerves, Dad. I'm sorry – but she is. I can't move for her tidying up behind me. It's not like it's our home any more."

"Maybe she thinks we want things that way."

"Maybe she does, but that doesn't give her the right to interfere." He would have liked to say more, but decided against it.

Robert gave the matter some thought, returning to cutting up his chop with careful deliberation. "I'll have a word with her," he said after a while. "Tell her we're not used to so much attention to detail."

Sarah was so contrite when they next met, Tom felt both uncharitable and guilt-ridden in equal parts. "I'm sorry, Tom," she said earnestly. "I thought you'd want the place the way your mam had it – before she took ill, I mean," a response which only made him feel worse.

Sarah was right of course: his mother had kept the place neat and tidy, if not exactly spotless, up until the previous spring. It had gradually gone downhill over the summer into the autumn, until Flora had pushed things into place before the funeral. After that, the general air of quiet neglect had crept in and become part of their everyday life. They had simply stopped noticing. Sarah had merely reinstated the place to its former self – or at least her version of it.

"And I'd never want to come between you and your dad, Tom," she insisted, holding onto his arm, concern written large on her honest, open face. "You know I'd never want that."

Suitably chastened, Tom quietly resolved not to be so judgemental in future. He would be grateful for all the devotion and care being showered on both of them. Sarah had, after all, offered her time unconditionally and for little recompense.

So the days passed, and it became easier to accept her presence as the workload of household chores was taken from his shoulders and he could devote more of his energy to the farm. Some of the ewes had been brought indoors needing to be kept an eye on, and the corrugated roof on one of the lambing sheds was working loose. There were ditches to be cleared and a couple of new gates to be installed.

Robert was equally as grateful. "The house doesn't seem so empty," he said one evening with an air of quiet satisfaction, and Tom knew what he meant.

Keeping busy outside, Tom discovered, was a useful distraction: it stopped him thinking too much – most of all about John Rufford. His shadowy presence could be locked away in the back of his mind, resurfacing only at odd moments before tiredness took over and sleep washed everything away. Occasionally, he was surprised to discover he could forget him for a whole day at a time.

February was almost upon them. Ralph Milburn had given the bunkhouse the thumbs up and renovating the building became a priority with the lengthening days. Tom had been energetically wielding a paint brush all morning when he emerged into the yard spattered with white-wash, ready for lunch. Sarah was standing on the cobbles staring up at the clear blue sky.

"Look at them, Tom!" she said excitedly pointing at a long skein of geese honking noisily overhead, their ragged

V shifting and changing with every beat of their wings. "Greylags going north again! There'll be no more snow this winter!" Her eyes were shining with delight, and she turned back to watch them flap their way over the tops of the oaks and larches and out of sight.

Tom was suddenly aware of how lovely she looked standing there, totally absorbed, unaware of him appraising her. For the first time he thought how natural it was to see her in the yard, a part of their lives. There was a sudden, very definite jolt under his ribs. Yes, he thought, I *could* marry Sarah. I *should* marry Sarah. Stop worrying about John Rufford. What was the point? Get on with life. Settle down. Raise a family.

The last of the geese disappeared behind the trees and she turned to look at him again. "It won't be long before it's Spring, Tom!" she was saying, oblivious of his interest. "Just think of it! There'll be snowdrops down the lane, and crocus in the tubs at the front door!" She was like a small child in her enthusiasm.

Her excitement was infectious. Regardless of his spattered state, he put his arms around her waist, eager to hold her. She looked up at him, astonished at this sudden show of affection.

He did not kiss her immediately, just made his intention clear by gently moving a stray strand of hair from her forehead, and looking fondly into her slightly startled eyes. When he did finally kiss her, it was neither casual, nor overtly demanding, but delicate, in the way he had learned from Donna, which wordlessly spoke of a very definite aim in mind: a shameless declaration that he wanted to take things much further than a kiss. Surely, he thought, she could feel just how hard he was against her.

At first, perhaps because she was taken by surprise, she did not resist, but then, quite definitely, she began to push him from her. She stood back, like a small bird watching a potential predator. "Tom!" she said hoarsely. "What do you think you're doing?"

He was used to a certain coyness from her, but this was more than he expected. Surely this was why she was at Rigg End, wasn't it? – to bring them closer? Why was she here, if not for this? "I thought that's what you wanted," he said.

She was frowning at him. "What do you mean?" she asked crossly, clearly not happy at this turn of events. "I was only looking at the geese."

"Don't you want a cuddle?"

"No," she said very definitely. "Not that way – not before we're married." She looked about her anxiously. "It's not right taking advantage of me when there's no one else around."

"You seemed to be enjoying it," he said, feeling he was justified in pointing this out.

She hesitated, uncertain how to respond to this. She looked down at the cobbles, unable to meet his eyes. "Mam said I should be careful, that's all," she said. "Being here – with you – on our own sometimes." She gave him a nervous smile.

His reaction must have registered clearly on his face.

"She didn't mean I wasn't safe with you, Tom," she struggled to explain.

"Well, that's nice to know."

"Don't say that."

"It doesn't bother your Dad – about your being here."

"That's not the point," she protested.

"Christ, Sarah, I don't know where I am with you!" he said, losing patience and forgetting she disliked blasphemy.

"Oh Tom, you know how I feel about you." There was a note of pleading in her voice.

"No, I don't. One minute you're hanging onto me like a limpet – the next you're pushing me off. Honestly, Sarah, if you want me to marry you, you could at least show me you wanted – you know." He stumbled around for less crude terminology than Donna would have used, and failed.

She looked uneasy. "Mam says that's what all men want," she said, still frowning. "Then once they've got it, they lose interest."

Considering all the years they had known each other and he had never once overstepped the mark, he was taken aback by her suggestion. "So I'm just some bloke who wants to try his hand, am I?" he stormed, really very angry now.

"You know I didn't mean that!"

"I don't know what you mean, Sarah. You go on and on about how much you want children – but from where I'm standing it looks like you don't want what it takes to get them in the first place."

"That's not true!" She was nearly in tears.

"Then for Christ's sake, at least show me you like the

idea of me touching you – or maybe that you quite fancy the idea of touching me. We don't have to go all the way, you know – but I don't want a wife who thinks shagging's only for making babies – and puts up with it the rest of the time. That'd make me feel like some kind of – I don't know – rotten pervert." Sarah's eyes had grown wider and wider as he spoke, whether from shock at his unexpected language, or because he had plainly told her what he wanted from her, he had no idea, but Robert's Land Rover coming into the yard provided a necessary end to this painful conversation.

Brack came out of the barn to bark a greeting.

"Tom!" Robert called over as he slammed the door shut and ambled across the yard. "Can you go down to Wallbridge for me this afternoon? There're some antibiotics waiting at the vets. I promised Ian I'd go back and do some hedge-laying or I'd have gone myself." He stopped, looking between them. "Anything the matter?" he asked.

Tom forced a smile. "Nothing at all," he said. "Some geese came over – flying north. We were watching them."

"That's a good sign then."

Tom agreed and went into the house to scrub up for lunch while Sarah tried her best to pretend nothing out of the ordinary had happened. Tom was certain neither of them had managed to hide the awkwardness between them. So be it. It couldn't be helped.

Wallbridge was bathed in unseasonal afternoon sunshine when he parked his car on High Side north of the river. He wanted to walk. It was a pleasant afternoon, and he stopped for a while to lean over the old seventeenth century double-arched bridge, watching the lazy flow of the clear water across the shallows by St Edward's Church on the southern bank. The worn sandstone under his hands had absorbed the sun and was warm to the touch.

He had been glad to quit the farm. His encounter with Sarah had left him angry. For the first time, he had genuinely believed he could make his life with her, and it had all blown up in his face. How could she expect him to propose marriage if she was so unresponsive? Would it always be like that? Or was she just hemmed in by her mother's warnings and it would all be resolved once they tied the knot? Did he want to take that chance? What if, deep down, she disliked physical contact beyond a simple embrace? He knew he could never live with that. Donna Burdon had demonstrated only too well he needed more. A lot more.

He turned down Reivers' Lane off the market square, through noisy groups of pupils walking up from Wallbridge School, their grey and red-trimmed blazers mingling with afternoon shoppers. It seemed a lifetime ago since he had been a part of their crowd, laughing and joking with his friends as far as the bus stops on High Side. How often had he travelled home with Sarah on the single-decker bound for Drumlinfield, helping with her Maths homework because she said he explained it much better than Mr Trotter? How often had he walked her down from the top lane to Rattling Gate and trudging the mile-and-a-half through all weather to Rigg End when he could have got the bus to Aitket Bank instead, and got home an hour sooner? Countless times. Well, now he knew what she really thought of him. He would leave her alone, he decided. See if she came to her senses. He would find some excuse not to take her to the Young Farmers' St Valentine's Dance. Let someone else have that pleasure.

The glass door into Gillow and Munro's Veterinary Practice buzzed when he opened it. There was a surgery in session, and beyond the reception area was an assortment of dogs, and cats in baskets, their anxious owners sitting around the waiting room walls on grey plastic chairs. The air was thick with the pungent smell of disinfectant and animal fear.

Janet Robson got up from behind the receptionist's desk automatically, only noticing who had come in at the last moment when she glanced up. "Tom," she said, with a cautious smile. They had not spoken or seen one another since their encounter on Boxing Day. Today, she looked stunning, he thought, her bright chestnut hair pulled back into a neat bunch at the nape of her neck; her immaculate short-sleeved uniform cinched in at the waist, accentuating her figure; the neck just open enough to draw his eyes to the potential view if he could undo another button.

As he smiled back, he could not get it out of his head that Janet simply out-shone Sarah in every way. Feeling both thwarted and rejected in equal parts, he badly needed someone to put that right. Donna would have known what to do. So too, he surmised, would Janet.

She was waiting for him to speak.

"Dad says there's some antibiotics for me to pick up," he said, never taking his eyes from hers.

A yellow light went on in the waiting room. Janet returned his gaze briefly. "Mrs Henderson," she said to a small, grey-haired woman clutching a large wicker cat basket on the seat next to her. "You can go in now."

The woman got up, struggling to lift her burden.

Tom was surprised no one offered to carry it for her. "Would you like some help?" he asked, tearing himself away from Janet.

The old lady looked up at him as if he had come down from heaven in a blaze of glory. Her anxious face lit up for a moment. "Oh, would you, pet? That's so kind of you." And she beamed at him.

He lifted the basket gingerly, the low sound of an animal in pain prompting extra care as he followed behind its fretful owner into the surgery.

When he returned, Janet was studying him thoughtfully. She passed over the box he had come to collect. "That's ten pounds fifty," she said casually, adding, "I hear Sarah's over at Rigg End these days," as he handed over his three five pound notes.

He agreed, making light of it. "Just helping out," he said.

She raised an eyebrow, pushing the change back across the desk towards him.

"Not in that way," he assured her quietly, trapping her hand under his, and looking directly into her green eyes.

She looked right back at him with a Mona Lisa smile.

CHAPTER TWELVE

A fitful sun filtered through gaps in the steel-grey clouds as John stepped down off the stile that led from the lay-by into the field. The footpath was unusually soft underfoot for the time of year, and he picked his way with care to avoid the mud, following the meandering progress of the track up the slight incline to the crest of hill. He paused, as he always did at the top, to take in the view of the gently rolling landscape spread out in front of him with the mere at its heart.

Rothwell Mere. It had changed little over the years, the mingling shadows and reflections of the trees, the reeds and sky, as strangely compelling as ever. Laura had described the place as magical – and it was. Today, its surface was calm, unruffled by the slightest breeze: perfect, except he lacked the motivation to seek out the interplay of light and shade, or the image of a bent reed caught in the water. The scene was set; his camera was ready; but he was not. He felt dead inside. He could not stir himself.

For the first few years after Laura left him, he had returned to this spot on late spring evenings. He half believed he might conjure her up, as it seemed he had done the last time that they met. He would tell himself she would be there, waiting for him; that everything would change, and his longed-for happy-ever-after ending would come to pass. Except, like most fairy tales, it was nothing more than a fanciful concoction lacking substance. She was never there.

Still clinging to hope, he had persuaded himself he had misjudged his choice of season: he should have made his pilgrimages in the depths of winter when he had first brought her to the mere. As the years passed and hope faded, he still came to wait in vain, like the love-sick calf his father had so dismissively called him.

Somehow the brooding silence of the place in its winter garb suited his state of mind better. Like a religious zealot mortifying his flesh, he needed the pain. He would stand on the small pebbles that lined the margins, the water lapping at his feet, reciting over and over again to himself the lines of Keats' poem, "The sedge is withered by the lake, and no birds sing", letting the despair of those lines etch ever deeper into his soul. It was he, not Robert Moray, who had become the Pale Knight, alone and palely loitering.

And when, like the heron that had taken flight all those years ago, Laura had never returned, its absence somehow became bound up with hers.

He stirred himself out of his reverie and picked his way down the muddy path to his usual spot where the tufted grass gave way to the strand of small, rounded pebbles, and stood, staring out across the silent stretch of water, feeling desolate. The heron was not there. Why should it be?

After a few moments, he turned to leave, resolving never to return again. Enough was enough.

And then, it came – noiselessly, on curved silver-grey wings, swooping down from somewhere high up in the oaks to land, with delicate precision, barely twenty yards away in the shallows by the reeds. It stood erect, long neck craned, its head turned in his direction, its bright eyes noting his presence with a penetrating gaze.

He dared not move. In the silence, his heart thumped against the prison bars of his ribs, bursting to be free.

Somewhere in the trees a soft breeze rustled dead leaves, and a lonely crow cawed forlornly.

Inside his head, he could hear himself repeating over and over again – Don't go. Please don't go.

The bird did not stir. The seconds passed. Suddenly, as if deciding the man was nothing of importance, it cocked its head, its attention shifting to the water at its feet, and the possibility of some tasty morsel in the mud.

John waited, spell-bound. He had been granted this precious moment; he must cherish it. If he were allowed to take but one photograph, it would be enough, he resolved. Let the heron be the last photograph he would ever take of Rothwell Mere.

Holding his breath, he slowly lifted the camera into position. The heron was perfectly framed in the viewfinder. It continued to disregard him, apparently unconcerned. He adjusted the focal length, his lungs close to bursting, and heard the shutter click.

The heron turned and blinked.

Surely it would fly! He exhaled slowly and painfully, his breathing dropping to a shallow, noiseless sound.

The bird remained perfectly still, head on one side, regarding him as a curiosity perhaps, nothing more.

Emboldened, he chanced another shot; and another; and another – on and on until he could take no more and the film whirred softly as it rewound itself into its cassette.

The heron turned to look at him again, dipping its head slightly, as if bowing in acknowledgement. Then, with an elegant slowness, it picked up its long brown legs and stepped delicately out of sight into the shelter of the reeds.

Exhilaration flooded through him. He turned and sprinted up the path towards the crest of the hill, breathless and filled with an overwhelming sense of happiness. Ridiculous. He paused and turned, taking in the scene for the last time. "Thank you!" he called out, hearing his voice swallowed up by the silence.

His head was buzzing, a weird excitement fizzing inside him. Like champagne. The urge to share this extraordinary sensation with someone – anyone – became irresistible.

Gemma was surprised to see him on her doorstep on a Sunday afternoon, and he was equally as surprised to find himself standing there.

He knew she lived in a small-scale development on the outskirts of Lingford. The little town houses had been crammed into an area once occupied by a grand Victorian dwelling belonging to a cotton merchant from Liverpool. He vaguely remembered her telling him she had mortgaged herself to the hilt to purchase it after her divorce, sacrificing her little car to secure the deposit. But the location was right, she had said: it was within easy walking distance of the studio and suited her well enough.

"John?" she said, her grey-blue eyes clearly registering astonishment when she opened the door. She was dressed casually – a sight unusual in itself – wearing a long checked shirt over faded blue jeans. Her hair was roughly brushed back from her face and tucked behind her ears, and her face was devoid of make-up. She looked natural and enchanting.

He suddenly felt embarrassed by his unannounced intrusion into her private world, realising his supposed reason for calling was patently ridiculous. What in heaven's name would she make of his rambling account of seeing the heron at Rothwell Mere at last? – or of using up a whole reel of film to photograph it?

He smiled optimistically, hoping at the very least to be blessed with some reasonable level of verbal coherence. "I – er – I've been out taking photographs," he managed at last.

If she appeared mystified by this intelligence, it was nothing to be wondered at – it was after all what he did for a living.

"At Rothwell Mere," he added.

She nodded, awaiting further elucidation.

"Of the heron!" he announced enthusiastically.

Gemma was well acquainted with the story of the heron – and Rothwell Mere. Too well acquainted perhaps to feel the need to comment beyond expressing her opinion that she was pleased his annual pilgrimage on this occasion had not been in vain.

"Can I come in?" he asked, not wanting to prolong his conversation on the doorstep.

She glanced anxiously at his BMW parked outside her gate, evidently disconcerted by his presence. From somewhere inside the house there was girlish laughter, and he heard a flirtatious female voice enquire, "Is this your new boyfriend, Gemma?"

She coloured visibly. "My younger sisters," she explained.

Behind her in the hall, a slightly younger version of herself appeared in the doorway and viewed him with evident curiosity, promptly disappearing again to relay the necessary information to a third party. There was more laughter.

He began to wish he had never come.

There was further commotion in the hall, and much suppressed giggling as two young women emerged pulling on their coats and giving him the eye as they passed him on their way out. "Don't worry about us. We only dropped in for a chat. Lovely to see you, Gem. Have fun!" And they were off down the road, laughing and waving goodbye as they went.

Gemma remained staunchly guarding her front door, watching them leave.

"I obviously picked a bad time," he said, regretting his impulsiveness: he had never given a moment's thought to the likelihood she might have visitors – and even less to the possibility she might be entertaining a man. "Thoughtless of me," he added.

She stood back reluctantly to let him in.

He discovered her small lounge was simply furnished: a two-seat sofa with a chair to match in grey, black and red stripes; a teak bookcase with a hi-fi on a low table next to it for magazines and papers; a coffee table with empty mugs on coasters and an opened biscuit barrel; and in front of the coal-effect gas fire, a sheepskin rug on an dark grey cord carpet. Full-length black and red striped curtains framed the small window, and a large shiny black and crimson vase stood in the corner displaying an array of artificial cornflowers and scarlet poppies with charcoal centres. It reminded John of the simplicity of his first home in Lower Chursley: basic and unpretentious. He had entertained Laura there.

"You'll have to forgive the place," Gemma was saying, busily picking up an assortment of magazines from the sofa where her sisters had abandoned them. "Karen and Tara always leave a mess. Do you want a coffee?" She was being polite, nothing more.

"Um – no – thank you. I won't stay long."

"Well – sit down then," she suggested, indicating the sofa and retreating to the single chair by the fire where she curled up against a cushion and waited for his explanation.

The room was warm. He sat down and unzipped his padded walking jacket, but she made no offer to relieve him of it.

"I had to share this with someone," he began, somewhat lamely he thought on reflection. "Seeing the heron today – at Rothwell Mere. It – it was – " He wrestled with the need to find the right word. "Astonishing," he managed at last, although this did not quite match up to how he felt. "A kind of – release – if you like," he went on, floundering more than a little. "A new beginning. I really can't express exactly how I felt – it was like being given a whole new life."

She said nothing.

Her silence was difficult to fathom. He looked down at his hands, clutching one another tightly as he leaned forward, braced against his knees. "I – er – I'm really sorry, Gemma. This must be of no interest to you whatsoever."

Her cool evaluative gaze swept over him briefly before she suddenly got up and cleared away the three mugs, disappearing through the door into the kitchen. He heard the sound of a kettle being filled and switched on. "I'm making another coffee," she said. "Are you sure you don't want one?"

It seemed he was being pressed to stay a little longer. He relented.

She brought in two fresh mugs and handed him one before retreating again to her seat by the fire, watching him with the intensity of a cat. "You know," she said, in what sounded like a school teacher talking to a wayward pupil. "Sometimes I think you're slightly unhinged."

He laughed off the idea, but not without recognising there was an element of truth in it.

"You go around in a world of your own most of the time. The rest of us could drop off the planet, and you wouldn't notice."

"That's not true in your case, Gemma, you know that. I rely on you too much."

"Oh yes, to keep your diary up-to-date, remind you of appointments and so on, but as a person, I'm invisible – always have been." Her tone was decidedly critical. "Let's be frank – you know absolutely nothing about me except I'm a divorced thirty-one year old who has occasional days off, goes on a fortnight's holiday every year to somewhere or other, and knows how you like your coffee. I often feel I'm nothing more than an extra piece of furniture in the office."

He was appalled that she should think so.

She went on without waiting for him to contradict her. "I know you never mix business with pleasure – you made that perfectly clear from the start – and I understood why – eventually, although I admit I didn't to begin with. In fact I quite fancied having a fling with you when you took me on. I thought that's what you wanted, you see, if I'm honest. You looked the sort who did. Good looking, mature man – unattached, or so I thought – money to spend – flashy car." She sighed. "There've been times in my life, John, when things were going horribly wrong, and you never even noticed. Not so much as a flicker of interest."

He had no answer for her: she had held up a mirror to him and shown him the extent of his self-absorption. It was all true. He had wallowed in his sense of loss and injustice: a solitary martyr.

"So," she was saying, in the absence of him finding anything to put forward in his defence, "You've had this revelation, and you decided to come round here and share it with me. Any particular reason?"

He had no idea.

"Well?"

He heard himself laugh. "I honestly don't know," he confessed, beginning to feel absurd.

"Really?" she asked caustically. "So you suddenly decided, hey – I'm free of all this baggage I've been carrying around for all these years – why don't I go round to Gemma's and tell her just how amazingly fantastic I feel? She'll be thrilled. Is that it?"

He had no answer.

"Who do you think I am, John?" she said, her anger visible in the heightened colour of her cheeks. "Just a dumping ground for your messy emotions?"

He put down his mug, its contents untouched. She was right. He had been prepared to indulge himself at her expense, and what was worse, he suddenly realised, was that his determination to tell her about the heron was nothing more than a flimsy excuse. What lay behind it was something else: he wanted to tell her about his son, and minutely examine all the complexities that surrounded this discovery, whether she wanted to know them or not. He got to his feet. "I'm sorry. I'd better go."

She made no attempt to stop him. "Yes," she said. "Perhaps you should. I honestly don't want to hear any more about your crazy life."

He suddenly felt very small indeed.

She unfolded herself from the chair and led the way to the door. "By the way," she added with heavy sarcasm. "Just in case you might be interested, I do actually have a boyfriend – after all this time. He's called Timothy, he's a land agent, and we've been seeing each other for about two months. He's tall, dark and handsome, and he's taking me out tonight to Sparston Hall – for a slap-up meal. You might like to ask me if I had a good time when you see me tomorrow."

He forced a smile – and let her show him out.

Fate it seemed could still draw blood. He drove home to Lower Chursley with memories crowding in again. Sparston Hall. He had taken Laura there on their first date: wined her, dined her, and afterwards – afterwards, he had bedded her and discovered she was something special. And that had been the start of everything that followed.

CHAPTER THIRTEEN

Still smarting over what he saw as Sarah's coldness, Tom decided to make himself scarce when she was due to come down the following Tuesday.

Jonty Tait from Black Hag provided him with the perfect excuse over a pint at The Gate on the Monday evening. "Old Jack got hi'sel wrapped up in wire yesterday," he said. "You couldn't bring up your dog tomorrow, could you, Tom? Help me out wi' tekkin' the hoggs in off the top like?"

Tom was only too happy to oblige.

On the Thursday, he spent the day down at Sykeside Plantation with Duncan, and just when he was wondering how to avoid committing himself to the usual Saturday night out with Sarah, it was one of her mother's many brothers who unwittingly came to his rescue.

He got back to Rigg End just as Sarah was getting into her car to leave.

She was subdued, evidently aware he was avoiding her. "I can't go out with you this weekend," she said with a nervous smile. "Uncle Billy and Auntie Josie are having their Twenty-Fifth over in Gateshead."

"Right," Tom said offhandedly. What did she expect him to say? Besides, his mind was mulling over other possibilities: Janet.

In the kitchen, he found Robert reading the paper. "She caught you then?" he said, looking up briefly.

Tom mumbled something to the effect she had.

"You'll have time to yourself on Saturday then," Robert said, folding up the paper and looking at him over the top of his spectacles.

"Do you need me around?"

Robert shook his head. "Give yourself the day off, Tom. We'll be busy enough in a week or two."

"I might go down to Wallbridge. See if Dougie Watson's around."

But Dougie Watson had his mind on other things that morning. "Aw Tom," he said with a shake of his head. "I'm right sorry, but I'm off over to Newcastle wi' Billy Henderson. The lads are playin' at home this weekend like." He paused, adding as an afterthought, "Do yuh wanna come wi' us?" He was being polite because he knew very well Tom had no interest in football.

Tom idled away the rest of the morning looking around Cunningham's latest range of tractors and planning how he could best spend his time that afternoon. One thought struck him as the most obvious.

Just before twelve, he sauntered down Reivers' Lane and happened to be passing Gillow and Munro's as Janet came out to lock up. Except chance had nothing to do with it: his timing had been perfect.

"Hello, Janet" he said, standing as close to her as he dared without seeming to be intrusive.

She turned. "Tom!" she said, surprised by his sudden appearance. She looked concerned. "Is it urgent?" she asked, entirely misunderstanding his mission. "Surgery's closed now for the weekend."

"Not exactly urgent. I just forgot to ask for something last time I came."

She waited for an explanation, suspecting nothing.

He stuck his hands nonchalantly in his pockets and smiled at her engagingly. "I forgot to ask you out for a date."

She frowned at him, taken aback for a moment. "Don't be silly," she said, clearly irritated by what she saw as adolescent behaviour. She turned away from him and checked the door was secure without further comment before setting off at a brisk pace up the lane.

He caught up with her.

"Look," she said curtly, not pausing in her progress. "I don't know what you're up to, Tom, but I'll not have you do to Sarah what Geoffrey Frayling did to me."

Geoffrey Frayling. He pondered the name. The man must have been blind as well as stupid. "I told you," he insisted, " – we're not engaged," adding for good measure, "Not likely to be either."

"Oh – and why's that?"

"We don't – 'click'," he said, surprised how good it felt to openly admit it.

"I see. And we do?" she asked tartly.

He felt bold enough to agree with her. "Boxing Day?" he reminded her.

She gave him a scathing sideways glance. "We'd both been drinking, Tom."

He was not going to let her off that lightly. "Not that much," he pointed out. She made no further comment, so he put the question. "It wasn't the drink, was it?"

This seemed to annoy her even more. She gave an audible irritated sigh. "I don't know why I told you about Geoffrey – all right? Forget it, will you? Don't think I'm around for the asking just because I've had an affair."

He was affronted to imagine this was what she thought. Many things about her had occupied his mind of late, but this was definitely not one of them.

She strode on, ignoring his protestations of innocence.

"I'm serious," he said, pressing his case. "I want to go out with you."

"Oh, for heaven's sake, Tom!" she snapped, deciding on what seemed to be the spur of the moment to tell him she was going to The Sycamore for lunch, and then shopping afterwards. "Will that do?" she challenged him.

It was not quite what he had in mind, but it was better than nothing.

The Sycamore Café, with its hanging sign depicting the well-known sycamore tree on the Roman Wall, was a small family-run business on Sheep Street just off the market square. It was popular because it had a reputation for good food and good service. It was not an obvious choice for anyone interested in a discreet venue. Perhaps that was why she chose it – to deflect any possible interest in the pair of them.

There was only one table free in the corner by the window. Tom sat with his back facing the rest of the lunchtime clientele while she took off her coat and put it over the back of her chair.

He studied the menu, trying to disregard the open neck of her blouse. She chose a beef sandwich with a side salad and he ordered the same for himself, except he chose chips instead. She refused to let him pay for her meal. Whether this was to satisfy the curiosity of those at the neighbouring tables, or because she did not want to be in the position of owing him anything, he could not decide.

Surrounded as they were by the lunchtime gossip and chatter of others, it was difficult to advance his cause without being overheard, but, he reflected as they ate their meal largely in silence, this might be for the best: he would not appear too pushy. So he continued to restrict himself to polite pleasantries and the occasional furtive appreciation of her breasts.

The conversation drifted along in this way for some time until he happened to mention he had not seen her over at High Oakbank Farm for some time.

"That's because I live in Wallbridge now," she informed him casually over her cup of tea.

He was genuinely surprised. No one had mentioned it.

"No, they wouldn't," she explained. "They're all embarrassed."

"Why?"

"Because it didn't work out – me moving back."

"What happened?"

"Nothing *happened*. It was just the atmosphere. No one said anything – but I knew what they were thinking –" She dropped her voice to a low whisper. " 'What did you expect getting involved with a married man?' – 'We told you it would all end in tears.' " She paused, thinking this over. "They were right though, weren't they?" she added philosophically. "Maybe that's what I couldn't stand – that – and the silent condemnation." She gave the word extra emphasis.

Tom had no intention of being judgemental. Ian and Bridie had fixed views: she must have known they would see her transgression as something deeply shameful. He kept his thoughts to himself: he had a mother who had been less than blameless.

It was almost one o'clock. The quartet of women gossiping at the next table collected their belongings and left for the bus back to Ayburn. Several others did the same. The sense of being overheard diminished.

"You haven't asked me where I'm living," she observed, evidently surprised by this.

"You'll tell me if you want me to know," he said, shamelessly hoping she would.

She ignored this obvious opening, asking instead, "Have you told Sarah you don't want to marry her?"

"I've told her what I want from a marriage," he hedged.

"What *do* you want?"

"More than she can give me," he said, increasingly aware

he was finding it difficult to concentrate on the conversation without letting his mind wander into the realms of the desire he felt for her. Just by sitting there, looking at him the way she did, she could rouse him to a considerable state of neediness.

"How did she it take it?" she was asking, those magnificent green eyes never wavering from his.

"Not very well."

She poured herself a second cup of tea and continued to study him closely. "So what happens now?"

"I don't know. Dad wants her to help out at Rigg End. I'd prefer it if she wasn't there. I don't want her hanging around thinking I'll change my mind."

"Will you?"

"No." He could be definite about that. "Anyway," he said, aware he was blundering into a topic he never intended to raise. "It's not just about me and Sarah – there're other things."

"Really?" There was a half-smile on her lips, expecting a revelation.

He felt cross with himself for stirring her curiosity. Thoughts about his own passion had brought his mother and John Rufford into his mind. "We all have secrets," he said, trying to defuse her interest. "Some we can share – some we can't."

"I see," she said. "Then I won't ask."

He was grateful for her discretion.

The one-o'clock-lunchers were drifting in, and the tables were beginning to fill again.

"Well," she said, finishing her tea and adopting an air of brisk efficiency, "as I told you – I've got some weekend shopping to do."

"I'll come with you, if you like?" he offered.

She was amused by this. "To the supermarket?"

He feigned bewilderment that she should find this idea extraordinary. "Why not?" he said, trying to sound mildly offended. "I can get a couple of things – and – " he paused for effect, " – and I can walk you home with your bags." From her expression, he could see exactly what she thought of this: that he was being artful – which he was.

They went shopping, and dutifully, as he had promised, he relieved her of her two heavy plastic carrier bags, like an attentive slave.

Her studio flat, he discovered, was above the travel agent's office on High Side. It had an anonymous door next to a large window displaying enticing posters advertising holidays in the sun.

She opened the door and took the bags from him, showing no inclination to invite him inside.

"Can I come in?" he asked. He very much wanted to.

She gave his proposition some thought. "No," she said, smiling at him and glancing briefly in the direction of the group of people waiting at the bus stop who had taken notice of them. "That wouldn't be a good idea."

"Can I see you again?" he asked, lowering his voice.

"I'm off on Monday," she said.

"Would you like me to come round?"

"If you like," she said, with an air of casual indifference.

"After lunch?"

She nodded, smiled, and closed the door.

He strode back across the bridge to where he had parked his car, feeling as light as air. Deferring pleasure, he decided, added to the contemplation of it.

On Monday, he arranged to meet Willie Robertson for a pie and a pint at The Ploughman down by the Mart. He wanted a valid excuse to be in Wallbridge and left a note for Robert saying he would be back around five. He purposely parked on High Side and ambled down to Low End across the bridge as anyone might if they were enjoying an afternoon stroll. It was a pleasant enough day, after all. After lunch, and a detour via the barber's, he strolled back again.

When he rang the bell, she opened the door almost immediately. She was dressed in her soft mohair sweater and a pair of black denims. Her hair was loose around her shoulders. She looked amazing.

"Come in," she said, ushering him in and closing the door quickly behind him. There was the warm aroma of fresh coffee. He let her lead the way up the stairs, admiring the view of her from behind.

The flat was small, but from the rear window it looked out across the river and St Edward's, a fine sunny aspect, even on an early February day. She had furnished it simply and kept it uncluttered. He took off his jacket and she poured out the coffee.

They never drank the coffee.

They dispensed with preliminaries and spent the afternoon on her bed. She never questioned why he came 'prepared', and he never asked her why she changed her mind and decided to have sex with him: he did not care.

Afterwards, he remembered that sunny afternoon as one of the most intoxicating of his life.

She was exquisite, her skin almost translucent in the pale afternoon light. Her breasts, capped with neat pink nipples, were mature and beautifully rounded. He loved them. After Janet, Sarah's remained a mystery he no longer had any interest in. Janet's accentuated the slimness of her waist and the swell of her hips which drew his eyes downward over her smooth, softly rounded belly to the soft bush of chestnut hair between her thighs, an altar he had worshipped at for some considerable time that afternoon. The scent of her still filled his head.

Lying next to her, his arm under her waist as she curled up against him, he would have been content to die. It was an astonishing sensation.

The afternoon had slipped by.

She stirred and eased herself away from him.

"You're lovely," he said.

She leaned over and kissed him lightly. It had the inevitable effect. "So are you," she said with a knowing smile, turning away from him and sitting up. "What time did you say you'd be back?"

"Around five," he said, running his fingers down the length of her spine, in no hurry to disturb his comfortable languor.

"It's half-four. You'd better be going."

"Do you want to get rid of me?" he asked.

Ignoring him, she reached for her jumper, abandoned on the floor, and pulled it over her head, flicking her hair free of it. "No," she said, getting up and sitting herself at the dressing table from where she could study him in the mirror. He liked her doing that. "Just being practical," she said and began to brush her hair with quick, decisive strokes.

Reluctantly, he got up and began dressing, aware she was still watching him.

She piled her hair up into an unruly bunch on the top of her head, hastily fixing it in place so that loose strands broke free, framing her face. It made her look more desirable than ever. "What excuse did you make for coming here?" she was asking him.

He turned his mind from the possibility of upending her again and concentrated on the question. "Said I was meeting up with Willie Robertson for a beer and a bite at The Ploughman."

"And did you?"

"Yes. Don't you believe me?"

She laughed, mocking him.

He leaned over to kiss the nape of her neck. "Do you want to do this again sometime?" he asked, breathing in the warm scent of her. He wanted her again. She did not reply and he looked up.

She was studying their combined reflection in the mirror, her expression betraying caution. "You're serious, aren't you –" she said, looking troubled. "You really don't mean to marry Sarah, do you?"

"No, I don't. I don't love her" He ran a hand lightly over

her cheek, down the sweep of her neck to the warm curve of her breast and let it rest there for a while, comfortably at home.

Her face was serious. "Because of what we've done?"

"No." He wanted to reassure her on that point. "I'm not the right man for her, that's all." Of course, it wasn't quite all. There was the small matter of John Rufford...

"Don't keep her hanging on if there's no hope, Tom. It's unkind. Just tell her."

She was right – he should make a clean break of it – he just didn't know how.

The sun was sinking, catching the west-end gable of St Edward's and casting a long shadow into the room. Janet looked at her watch. "It's almost five."

He began putting on his jacket. "Do you want to see me again?" he asked.

She paused for a moment. "I don't know. I'm not sure where this is leading."

"Does it matter?"

She gave him a sad smile. "Probably not."

"Tomorrow night then?" he suggested hopefully.

She shook her head. "No – leave it for a day or two. I want some time to myself."

He had no wish to rush her: it would be better that way. "Thursday?" he offered.

"Maybe," she said, leading him to the door.

They reached the bottom of the stairs and he stopped for a moment to kiss her, his hand moving up under the welt of the jumper, seeking out the warm soft place between her thighs. In the days and nights until they met again, he wanted to remember how she felt.

Chapter Fourteen

When Tom arrived home, Robert was peeling potatoes for the evening meal. "Anything I can do?"

Robert looked up. "No. There's some hot pot in the oven. Bridie brought it over this afternoon. Had some to spare, she said."

Tom rolled up his shirt sleeves and ran the hot water in the sink to scrub up.

Robert moved over to give him room.

There was a definite moment when Tom felt Robert's eyes on him. "Had a good afternoon then? – with Willie?" he was asking him.

He sensed Robert suspected something. He was not sure what. "Had a good crack over lunch," he answered casually. "He's thinking of renting a few acres over at Fossetdale down by Jimmy Turnbull's place. Maybe get in some draft ewes over the summer."

Robert nodded and finished cutting up the potatoes, piling them into a pan of boiling water on the range. He dried his hands with a deliberate slowness it was impossible to ignore and carefully folded the towel to hang up on the rail.

Tom could almost touch the silence that had sprung up between them: it had a very definite presence.

"Wallace came over this morning after you'd gone," Robert said, pouring out two large mugs of tea and pushing one in Tom's direction. "Said you and Sarah had fallen out. Asked if I knew why." He paused briefly. "I said maybe you were the best person to ask, not me." He looked up, waiting for an answer.

"We had an argument."

"What about?"

"I wanted to give her a cuddle that's all. She didn't want me to."

"Did you lose your temper?"

"Maybe – yes – she gave me the brush off. Why? What's she been saying?"

The pan on the range was bubbling vigorous, the lid rumbling on the rim as the steam pushed its way out and billowed up to the ceiling. Robert reached over and set it at an angle to quieten it. "Nothing," he said. "That's the trouble. He can't work out what's going on between you."

Tom could feel himself becoming increasingly irritable. He wanted to think about Janet, not talk about Sarah. "I told you, Dad – nothing's been going on between us."

Robert drained his mug and considered the dregs. "So she's not pregnant then?"

"Chance would be a fine thing!"

"That's all right then."

There was something about this observation that warned

Tom not to say anything further. Robert poured himself more tea before asking, "Seeing someone else?"

It was difficult not to betray himself when faced with such a direct question. In any case, he disliked lying. "I've seen Janet a couple of times, that's all."

Robert nodded, quietly concentrating on his tea. "Today?" he asked.

"Yes – after Willie went home. We had a chat."

There was a noticeable pause. Robert was frowning. "I think you had more than a chat, Tom. I can smell her scent all over you. She wore it at our Boxing Day party."

It was a long time since Tom had felt himself blush, but the heat of it rose like a tidal wave up his neck and across his cheeks to the tips of his ears in an unstoppable rush.

The timer on the window sill rang shrilly and Robert got up and lifted the potatoes off the range, draining them into the sink in a cloud of steam. "Is it serious?" he asked.

Tom shook his head.

Robert's silence spoke volumes. Tom could almost read his thoughts – like father, like son. It was an uncomfortable sensation.

"Janet's got history," Robert was saying.

"I know."

"You won't be doing her any favours if you're only having a fling. You won't be doing yourself any either," he added. "Gossip's like mud – it sticks."

"We're not children, Dad."

"No, you're not – either of you. But you're playing with

fire. And I'm not just talking about how the Armstrongs will take it – I'm talking about Ian and Bridie as well."

Tom felt he was being cornered. "What Janet and me get up to is our business – no one else's."

Robert said nothing. He served up the meal and they ate in silence, Tom wishing he could simply ignore what had been said – except there was truth in it. In Stanegate's closely-knit farming community, family feuds could last for generations.

The silence continued through the rice pudding and washing up.

Robert sat down at the table again looking weary. "None of this would've happened if your mother hadn't died," he said bitterly. "You'd never have known about Rufford. You'd have gone on seeing Sarah without giving it a second thought. Next year – maybe the year after – you'd have got married, had a family. I'm not saying this was right, but ..." His sense of hopelessness was written on his face. "But now you've lost your footing and you've nothing left to cling to."

"I can't help feeling different, Dad."

Robert sighed and stood up, putting an understanding arm around his shoulders. "I'm not blaming you, Tom. I'm just sorry Sarah's been caught up in this wretched mess. She's a good-hearted, uncomplicated girl. She doesn't deserve to have her life turned upside down like this."

"I didn't set out to hurt her."

"I know that."

"I just can't marry her – not now."

"Then make a clean break of it, Tom. Tell her tomorrow.

I'll leave it up to her if she wants to carry on looking after the house. I doubt she will, but I won't stop her if she does. She does a good job and I'll offer to pay a proper wage for her time. I'll not have Wallace thinking we've taken advantage of her – although I've no doubt he'll think we have."

Tom felt wretched. "I'm sorry, Dad."

"It's not your fault. Maybe we both misunderstood your mother. Maybe she saw Sarah wasn't the right girl for you after all. Maybe she was afraid you were letting time slip by and not seeing you were making a mistake. I don't know."

"Will you be around tomorrow – after I've told her?"

"I'll make sure I am. Are you going up now?"

"I think I will."

"Goodnight then."

"Goodnight, Dad."

"Oh – by the way, Tom. There's a letter for you from Crozier's. I left it on the hall table. Probably about your mother's Will."

Tom turned at the door. "Dad – what do you think Mam would have thought about me and Janet?"

Robert paused before he answered. "You and Janet?" he said. "I think she'd have seen something she recognised."

Tom knew exactly what he meant.

The following morning, as soon as Sarah arrived, Tom asked her to join him in the kitchen. It had not been an easy night, and he still had no idea how he could make what he had to say any less upsetting.

She was sitting opposite him, already anxious, perhaps

suspecting what was coming, her hands clasped in front of her on the table, fiddling with her handkerchief. Her brow was furrowed, her concentration fixed on her fingers twisting the cloth round and round on itself.

Tom cleared his throat. "This isn't easy for me, Sarah," he began, struggling to remember the well-turned phrases he had practised so meticulously the night before. "I've been thinking a lot recently ... since – well since that business in the yard and – " His tongue seemed to be sticking to the roof of his mouth. "And – "

She was biting her lip, not looking at him.

"And – I don't think things'll work out for us."

She looked up at him, astonished, as if he had pronounced the earth was flat, or the moon was made of green cheese. "You don't mean that, Tom," she said indignantly. "It's just because I said 'no' to you, isn't it?"

"No – it's not, Sarah –"

"Yes it is," she said, cutting him off mid-flow, colour rising in her cheeks.

"It isn't – honestly," he insisted, trying to keep calm as her agitation visibly increased. "It's my fault – I know. I should've said something sooner."

"So all that lovey-dovey stuff was just a pack of lies, was it?"

He had expected tears, pleading, even expressions of undying love. He had not bargained on her being so angry. She had wrong-footed him completely. "No – it wasn't," he insisted, trying to rescue the situation as quickly as possible. "I was trying to make things work, that's all. When they didn't, I should've said something straightaway." Christ! Nothing was coming out the way he intended.

"What are you saying, Tom?" she demanded.

He plunged on, just wanting to get it over with as soon as possible. "I really can't marry you, Sarah. I'm sorry."

She sat back in the chair, her eyes wide with disbelief. "You don't mean that!" she insisted.

"I know you don't want to believe it, but we wouldn't be happy together." Keep going, said the voice in his head. "You need someone who won't ask so much of you – you know what I mean."

"It would be different if we were married," she persisted.

"No, it wouldn't. You're not keen on the sex thing, are you? I mean, you wouldn't want it as much as I'd want it, would you?" Not like Janet, he thought. Not like Donna. With Sarah it was even impossible to talk about sex without feeling hideously uncomfortable. Telling her she could never satisfy him would be unforgivably cruel.

Her anger was beginning to dissolve into uncertainty. He could almost read her thoughts. "I know this'll upset your dad, Sarah," he said, sensing this was now uppermost in her mind, "but he wouldn't want you to be unhappy, would he?"

Tears suddenly welled up and spilled down her cheeks. She wiped them away hastily, trying to maintain a sense of dignity under duress while Tom sat watching, feeling miserable. That it should come to this, he thought. After all the years growing up together. It was a tragedy of sorts.

He stood up, not wanting to prolong the discussion.

"I've told Dad," he said, "and he'll talk to you – about things – here." He pushed his chair under the table trying to remember what else he had intended to say.

She just looked up at him, red-eyed and perplexed by the speed in which her world had crumbled around her.

"Anyway," he said, clutching at straws now, "I might be away for a while. There's some business of Mam's I might have to see to – down in Cheshire."

She just nodded.

He ventured an apologetic smile and left her in the kitchen, feeling he had handled things very badly. Not something to be proud of. He pulled on his wellingtons and went out into the yard and the unexpected pleasure of a bright frosty morning. Calling Brack from the barn, he headed off up the well-worn track onto The Rigg: he wanted the wind on his face; his blood pumping through his veins, and time to think of Janet. She took his mind off Sarah, the rest of life's larger problems, and the outcome of the invitation by Messrs Crozier & Co, Solicitors of Proctor's Lane, Wallbridge to call into their office that Friday to discuss the terms of his mother's Will.

On the Thursday morning, as Robert had expected, Sarah was absent from the farm. She phoned to say she wanted time to think things through. Beyond giving Tom the news, Robert made no comment, but the potential lack of help around the house was clearly on his mind. Feeling responsible, Tom spent his spare time that afternoon tidying up the sitting room. That evening, he went down to Wallbridge and met Janet.

She was quiet as he walked her home through the darkened streets.

"I've told Sarah," he said, thinking perhaps this was on her mind.

She did not ask what the outcome had been, merely nodded her acceptance that he had done the right thing.

In her flat, there was little time for talking until later. Exhausted but exhilarated, Tom felt supremely happy. He had no sense of guilt, or any remorse, just the intoxicating pleasure of indulging himself unshackled by expectations, duty or responsibility. It was a heady brew. Donna would have understood.

Afterwards, wrapped up in her duvet, they drank coffee in the semi-darkened room lit only by her bedside lamp.

He put his arm around her and brought her closer. She was dishevelled and smoothed out by his loving and he thought she looked incredibly beautiful. "I'm not going to the dance on Saturday," he said knowing what he really wanted. "Can I come here instead?"

She studied his face for a moment before she answered him. "If you like," she said with a slight smile.

"Would you let me stay – the night?" he asked.

She did not say 'no'. Instead, she asked, "What about Robert?"

"He knows I'm seeing you."

"Did you tell him?"

"No – he guessed. Your perfume. He remembered it from Boxing Day."

She looked thoughtful. "I should have been more careful. Did he warn you off?"

"He thinks we're playing with fire."

"He's right – we are."

"Then you'd prefer me not to stay?"

"I didn't say that," she said. "But it makes sense to be careful."

He took this as a 'yes'. "What time shall I come then?" he asked.

"After nine. There aren't so many people around then."

"After nine, then," he said, turning his attention to his rising desire for her again.

He left before closing time at The Dog and Stick to avoid being seen by anyone who knew him, and all Robert said on his return was, "Don't forget you're going to Crozier's tomorrow."

Crozier's occupied the end property in a row of Georgian houses off the market square. Sometime during the 1890s, it had become the offices of Eustace and Oswald Crozier, two local brothers who had qualified to practise law. Their descendants continued to run the firm.

Tom had rarely crossed the threshold, having little reason to spend time there. One of the current partners, Mr Brian Taylor, had come up to the farm a couple of times during the autumn, so Tom knew him by sight.

Mr Taylor shook his hand and sank back into his chair on the far side of his enormous desk piled high with buff-coloured folders tied up with pink tape. He was a round, jovial man in his mid-fifties, a popular raconteur and after-dinner speaker with a wealth of anecdotes to fit any occasion. Blessed with a fine head of swept-back flaxen hair and a fresh, smooth complexion, he looked younger than his years, although his choice of clothes – heavy double-breasted tweed suits – gave him the appearance of belonging to an earlier age.

Mr Taylor's office was small and smelt of dust and cigarette smoke, its dark oak furniture much too large for the dimensions it occupied. In navigating his way around the desk to welcome visitors, his ample girth was always in danger of dislodging a bundle of files. Behind him, the glazing in the sash window filtered the afternoon sunlight through a haze of accumulated tobacco smoke and prolonged neglect.

Tom tried to concentrate, a large part of his mind still in bed with Janet. "But in your case," Mr Taylor was saying, reading from a document in front of him, "there's the additional bequest of Meeston Lodge and the associated funds to meet the cost of running it. I suppose you know this was her family home before she married? It's been rented out for several years now."

Tom agreed he knew its history.

"The management of the property is in the hands of Barker Fawcett in Lingford. They took over your grandfather's business, Driscoll & Jackson after Mr Jackson died. The previous tenant gave notice last October, and your mother decided, in view of her declining health, it would be better to leave the property unoccupied for the time being. She's made no stipulations as to what you should do with it when it's transferred into your name, but if you decided to sell rather than rent, the deeds are held by the solicitors

Gorst & Parr." He looked up from the document and smiled broadly. "I understand there's a family connection there?"

"My Great-aunt Cynthia was married to Mr Gorst Senior," Tom said, thinking he could also have added that his mother had once been engaged to their eldest son, Oliver.

Mr Taylor's voice had an underlying drone, like the Northumbrian pipes, and Tom found his attention wandering again, this time mulling over the reasons for his mother's gift. All those intimate talks between mother and son when she had questioned his determination to stay on the farm made sense now. He had taken these to be intellectual exercises, debating over the pros and cons of a thing; the sort of stimulating conversation Jamie delighted in – encouraged by Robert – which had eventually drawn in Flora as she grew older and more self-confident.

Jamie and Flora – the true heirs of Robert and Laura Moray – had set their horizons further than the boundaries of Rigg End. Perhaps this had troubled his mother most: they were the true inheritors, yet the farm meant nothing to them, while John Rufford's boy had put his roots firmly into the soil without the ties of blood.

Perhaps he had convinced her he was right until the threat of Rufford's reappearance had thrust her latent doubts and fears into the forefront of her mind. Had she imagined her son's reactions? – his sense of grievance at years of deceit? – his simultaneous loss of face and place? Had she asked herself – "What will he do?" – and known in her heart he would not simply shrug his shoulders with casual indifference.

Mr Taylor was standing up, offering to shake his hand. Tom automatically shook it, said what he hoped was suitable under the circumstances, and made his way down the stairs and out of the building.

CHAPTER FIFTEEN

Robert was setting down fresh straw in the hemmel. Tom came straight out with it. "I'm staying at Janet's tomorrow night," he said. "I'll be back early Sunday for the sheep."

Robert continued spreading the straw. "Better stay on 'til lunch time," he said, without looking up. "Won't draw so much attention if you do. Folk'll think you've just called round that morning."

Tom felt defensive. "We know what we're doing."

Robert was not going to be drawn on the subject. "That's all right then, isn't it." A statement, not a question. "Did Barry Taylor give you all the details?" he asked, moving on to other matters.

"About the Lodge?"

"Yes. You should get off down there to see the place, Tom. Decide what you want to do with it. You've got a week or so before lambing starts. Good time to go."

"Would you mind?"

Robert straightened. "Mind?" he said, frowning. "Why should I mind, Tom? The place is your responsibility." He heaved another bale down from the pile and cut it free of the twine. "Get yourself off," he insisted. "Talk things over with the letting agents – maybe see someone at Gorst and Parr while you're about it. Your mother never liked the idea of leaving the place empty – just felt it was the right thing to do at the time."

"Any idea where I could stay?"

"You could try the George Hotel at Weaversham. Good spot to be – midway between Meeston and Lingford. Give them a call." He leaned on his fork for a moment. "You should get yourself a new car, as well," he said. "You want something reliable if you're travelling all that way. Hetherington's have got a sale on. You could see what they've got tomorrow afternoon. Get yourself some supper at The Black Grouse afterwards – if you're staying on in Wallbridge." Beyond this, he had nothing further to say about Tom's decision to spend the night at Janet's.

The following afternoon, Ken Hetherington was only too pleased to show Tom around his showroom. Moving on one of his shiny new models was clearly uppermost in his mind, even if it meant taking Tom's old banger in part exchange, and Tom had no difficulty in pondering long enough to land himself a good deal. He left an hour later feeling well-pleased with himself: his metallic silver Golf would be ready to collect the following Saturday.

The combination of self-satisfaction at his purchase, and the potential pleasures of the night ahead left him feeling mellow. He wandered through the town in the light rain going nowhere in particular until opening time, making his way through the narrow streets of Low End to Cardingwool Lane and the unremarkable exterior of The Black Grouse, sandwiched between a turf accountant's and a charity shop. It was an old inn, dating back to sometime in the 1700s, frequented mostly by men of Robert's age rather than his own: men who disliked the fruit machines and loud music of places like The Hen and Harrier in Goodacre Street, or The Dog and Stick up on High Side, with their noise and bustle, raucously laughing girls, darts matches and pool tables. It served up home cooking on a modest scale for those who came for a pie and a pint, and the chance to catch up on local crack. The men who sat around the low tables in front of the fire were generally from farms to the south of the town; dairy farmers who bred Friesians and whose lives revolved around the current state of milk prices. They were ruddy-faced men, stout and thick-necked for the most part, welcoming enough to those who farmed 'up on the Wall', but equally ready to regard them as a different tribe. Robert occasionally frequented the place on market days, but his suggestion that Tom should choose to go there smacked of something else: the need for Tom to be discreet if he intended seeing Janet. None of Tom's contemporaries, or their kin, would be in The Black Grouse that Saturday: the St Valentine's Dance up at Stanegate would be the main attraction.

When Tom lifted the latch into the narrow entrance, there were few regulars at the bar, two or three heads turning briefly to see who had come in. He was early and the atmosphere, usually thick with smoke and the smell of stale ale, was less in evidence.

Bobby Dobson, Landlord, was a cheery fellow in his early forties, pleased to see anyone come through his door.

"Evenin', lad," he said with a broad smile. "What can I get you?"

Tom ordered his food, and nursing his pint, settled himself in one of the pews by the door still within sight of the hearty fire blazing in the hearth. From this strategic spot, he could slip out later without anyone seeing him leave.

As time passed, the bar became more crowded and the general hubbub of conversation and good-humoured banter increased. Tom, engrossed in reading his glossy car brochure between mouthsful of steak pie, chips and peas felt comfortably invisible, and even a little smug.

The last person he expected, or wanted to see at that moment was Wallace Armstrong. But there he was, at the bar when Tom happened to look up. He had no idea how long he had been there. Their eyes met. Wallace nodded, and came lumbering over with a pint of bitter clutched in his paw-like hand.

"Evenin' Tom."

"Mr Armstrong."

"Expectin' someone?"

"No."

"Right then." He sat himself down opposite placing his pint carefully on the table between them.

Tom waited for whatever might follow.

Wallace cast a passing glance at the brochure. "Buyin' a new car, then?" he asked.

Tom needed no divination to guess a prospective car purchase was unlikely to be uppermost in Wallace Armstrong's mind.

"Saw you comin' out of Hetherington's place," the big man went on.

Tom had the uncomfortable feeling he might have been followed. There was no way this unwelcome meeting had happened by chance. Wallace's preferred watering hole was The Gate. If he had chosen to come to The Black Grouse, he was a man on a mission.

"Not goin' to the dance tonight then?" Wallace asked bluntly, concentrating on his beer.

"No," Tom said, keeping things simple.

Wallace began turning the pint mug on its beer mat, his huge hand rotating the glass with care. "Wor Sal's not either," he said, looking up suddenly and fixing Tom with a perplexed frown.

Tom had expected belligerence, not bewilderment, but Wallace seemed genuinely unable to grasp the sudden shift in circumstances. There was no bluster, no raising of his voice, just a quiet incomprehension.

"What's happened between you two then? I can't get any sense out of her. She says you don't want to marry her. Is that true, lad?"

Tom nodded. He did not want to elaborate further, but Wallace would want some kind of explanation. It was best to be honest. "I'd never make her happy, Mr Armstrong, that's the truth of it."

"And it's just come to you like – after all these years?"

Tom nodded again.

Wallace shook his great head, still wrestling with how this could have happened.

Tom tried explaining. "We've been friends, Mr Armstrong. Nothing more – and –" He stumbled, wondering if it were wise to raise the subject, "and I think I want more from a marriage than Sarah wants."

Wallace rotated his pint once more before leaning forward confidentially and looking Tom straight in the eye. "Sometimes it teks a lass a while to get used to things," he said, understanding precisely what Tom was hinting at. "I knows that. They don't all want it at first like. But they gets used to it." Perhaps he was speaking from experience. Mary's strict upbringing must have been quite an obstacle in its time.

Tom stood his ground. "I'd rather she wanted it in the first place," he said.

"Give her time, lad. She'll come round to your way of thinkin'. Just give her time." Wallace was pleading, not just for his daughter, but for himself.

There was no easy way to lessen the impact of dashing the man's hopes. But anything less than complete demolition would only give him cause to cling on to cherished notions that were dead in the water. And that would be worse. Best to say precisely how things stood. "I don't want to marry her, Mr Armstrong," he said. "I'm sorry, but that's the end of it."

The frown on Wallace's brow deepened. His pint of beer remained undrunk as he stared into its depths. "I hear you've tekkin' up with the Robson girl," he said after a moment's pause for thought.

Tom steadied himself. "Janet?" he said, feigning incredulity.

"Aye – Janet. The red-haired lass."

Tom kept his mask firmly in place, retreating behind his raised glass and taking two large gulps which threatened to choke him.

"You've been seen together," Wallace informed him with a slight nod as if to confirm the truth of this.

"Aye – she's family," Tom said, adopting an air of being affronted by the suggestion, and stating the obvious as far as Wallace was concerned, even though Tom knew this was no longer the case. "Had a bite together at The Sycamore. Helped carry her shopping home. What's wrong with that?"

Wallace nodded and took his first sip of beer, relishing its taste. "Must have been hard for the Robsons – her comin' back like that," he observed, implying much more than he said. "Mind she's a grand looking lass like," he added sagely after some thought. "A grand looking lass." He stared straight into Tom's eyes as he said it.

"Aye, she is," Tom agreed, finishing his drink and getting up to go.

Wallace held onto his arm. "Goin' home then?"

"Want to show Dad what I've bought," Tom said, flourishing the brochure in front of Wallace's face. "See if he approves."

Wallace sank back, crestfallen. "Aye lad – you do that."

Outside, the rain had stopped, blown away on a stiff wind. The sky was clearing. Tom sauntered back to the station car park, stopping every now and then to check if he were being followed. He sat in the car for a while and waited, glancing up at the rear view mirror every now and then. After half an hour, there was still no sign of Wallace.

He timed his walk back through the town and over the bridge very precisely. At nine o'clock there were few people about with the exception of two groups of well-oiled town-boys on a pub crawl, too much in their cups to notice him.

Janet opened the door to him with a smile. Her hair was loose around her shoulders and she was dressed simply, but stunningly in a plain cream open-necked blouse with full sleeves over a full-length skirt with broad diagonal stripes in three shades of green. When she led the way upstairs, he noticed her feet were bare, and the soft fabric of the skirt swished around her ankles.

She had lit the room with thick, scented candles in tumblers on the window sills, the warmth of the flames reflecting in the glass, and from the hi-fi drifted James Taylor's melancholy rendition of 'Fire and Rain'. It brought back memories.

Curious, Tom picked up the cassette and read through the list of recordings hand-written on the back in thick black biro. It was a personal selection of American country ballads: James Taylor; Judy Collins; Bob Dylan; Johnny Cash. "One of Ross's?" he asked.

She leaned over his shoulder, arms around his waist. "Mm," she said, kissing him lightly on the neck. "I found it this morning in with a box of stuff I'd not opened. Must have had it for years. I should give it back to him." She laid her head on his shoulder. "Do you remember this song?"

How could he forget? He was in his early teens and finding life confusing. "I remember Ross singing it," he said.

"At the barn dance we had at High Oakbank," she reminded him, although he needed no reminding.

"He was all dressed up in his cowboy gear, sitting on the hay bales strumming his guitar," Tom said, laughing at the memory. "Filling in for the band when they went off to the bar. He was pretty good too."

"Mm, he was, wasn't he?" she said. "And I caught you eyeing me up while Ross was playing it, if I remember rightly." she added, releasing him from her grasp. "You must have been all of fifteen." There was a hint of a smile on her face. "My God – how time flies."

He put down the cassette and reached out for her. "I liked what I saw," he said softly, pulling her close to him, remembering how he had looked at her for the first time through a man's eyes, wondering what it would be like to touch her – and wanting to do more. Now he knew – and it was better than he had ever imagined.

She ran her fingers through his hair. "I think I must have known – even then – that we'd do this someday," she said, pressing herself against him, her eyes searching his face as if she were trying to remember the smallest detail.

There was something in her urgency that should have warned him. For some time afterwards, they lay listening to the music in the tumbled chaos of her bed. At some point, she got up and rewound the tape, setting it to play again before returning to curl up against him.

Two of the candles guttered, letting the room sink into semi-darkness. James Taylor sang on.

'...*I've seen lonely days that I thought would never end ...*'

Tom could feel himself drifting off into a light doze as he listened to the words, sensing their melancholy, but ignoring it. He was blissfully content.

'...*but I always thought I'd see you again ...*

Eventually, she stirred and unwound herself from him. Sleepily, he reached out to bring her back, but she was already beyond his grasp.

The pale light from the crescent moon shone in through the window, catching her briefly in a ghostly hue as she moved about the room. He loved the sight of her. "Come back to bed," he said, listening to the huskiness in his voice that betrayed his rising desire for her again.

She shook her head. "Not yet."

He heard the sound of glasses being set on the table, the pop of a cork, and the gurgle of liquid as she filled them. "What are you doing?" he asked, propping himself up to watch her.

"Marking the occasion," she said, coming back to the bed and handing him one of the glasses. "I bought some sparkling wine – another bad habit I've picked up since I've been away." She sat next to him, looking magnificent in the half-light, her long hair in happy disorder on her breasts. She brought her glass to his. "To the future," she said. "To whatever it holds – for both of us."

A small chill ran through him as he drank the toast. From out of nowhere came the image of John Rufford hidden in

The Rubaiyat, and the words of the poem marked by his photograph.

Ah, fill the cup – what boots it to repeat how time is slipping underneath our feet...

"I overheard something today," she was saying, turning away from him, her voice strangely distant. "I was at the check-out – and this old biddy standing in the next aisle said to her wide-eyed little friend – 'There's that Robson woman I was telling you about. She's after Robert Moray's lad now.' " She glanced round at him. "She wanted me to hear her say it, Tom. I could tell – by the way she smiled at me." She was visibly upset. "I made a terrible mistake coming back. There's always someone ready to spread gossip."

Tom could only think how quickly word had reached Wallace.

Janet had reached out to touch his face. "I don't belong here any more, Tom."

"Don't be daft!"

"No, it's true. I don't even talk the same language. Haven't you noticed?" She leaned forward pulling the duvet from him and kissed him lightly, stirring him again. She looked up at him with sad, defiant eyes. "You shag me – I fuck you."

He sensed a deep unease begin to gnaw at the pit of his stomach. "Are you going to leave?" he asked, already suspecting that she was.

She nodded.

"When?" He heard his voice shaking as he said it.

She looked away for a moment and drained her glass.

"As soon as I can. I've still got friends down in Hampshire. I can bunk up with them until I get a job – find a place of my own." She tried to smile. "Tom – don't look like that."

"Like what?"

"Like – oh, I don't know – "

He reached out for her. "I'll miss you," he said, unable to stop himself admitting it.

She escaped his hold and got up suddenly to stand by the window, the pale moonlight leaving her partially silhouetted against the pane. She looked so lovely, it made him ache. "I'll miss you too," she said, glancing back at him for a moment. "I know I shouldn't. This wasn't meant to be anything permanent, was it?"

He shook his head, and put down his glass on the floor, the wine suddenly bitter to the taste. "Come back to bed," he said. "I want to hold you."

When she curled up next to him, he held her close, burying his face in the warmth of her hair as she laid her head on his shoulder. Her perfume filled his head, and the thought of losing her made him feel weak. "You might be gone when I get back," he heard himself whisper, giving voice to his fears.

She looked up. "Where are you going?"

"Mam's left me her family place in Cheshire. Dad said I should go down and look it over."

"When will you go?"

"Maybe next weekend."

"For how long?"

"A few days – maybe a week – maybe more. I don't know.

Nothing's settled." He could hear his voice catching in his throat.

The final notes of James Taylor's 'You've Got a Friend' faded away and the cassette switched itself off.

She eased herself from him and sat up. "There's something else, isn't there, Tom? What's wrong?"

He ignored the warning voices in his head, tired of pretending silence was an option. "I've discovered something I can't handle," he said, knowing there were a thousand-and-one reasons why he should not tell her. But the urge to unburden himself to someone had suddenly become overwhelming.

"Is that the secret you told me you couldn't share?" she asked quietly.

"Yes."

"Then you must keep it to yourself," she said, laying a finger on his lips to silence him.

"Jan, if I don't tell someone, I think my head'll burst."

"Why do you want to tell me?"

"Because I know I can trust you. Because you're going away."

She smiled sadly.

He heard himself take in a long, uneven breath. "Robert's not my father," he said, the words sounding strangely alien to his ears. "I'm a cuckoo in the nest."

There was a long pause while she considered this. "When did you find out?"

"The day after Mam's funeral. I found a photograph of this man she knew before she was married. John Rufford. I look just like him."

"Does Robert know about him?"

"Yes – he's known for years."

She ran her fingers through his hair. "What are you going to do?"

"I don't know. I'm not sure who I am any more."

A cloud covered the moon and the sound of rain began to patter against the window. With infinite gentleness, she wrapped him in her arms, cradling his head against her breasts. "We're both adrift, aren't we, Tom?" she whispered, stroking his hair.

"Yes – I suppose we are." He breathed in the scent of her; felt her warmth; heard her heart beating. "Do you really have to leave, Jan?"

"Yes," she said, rocking him as she might a hurt child. "I can't stay."

He felt the emptiness conjured up by her words begin to eat into his soul. "Then make love to me. If tonight's all we have, I want to remember you making love to me."

The last of the candles flickered and went out.

CHAPTER SIXTEEN

Bernard Makepeace, noted eccentric, local historian of the arcane and obscure, and regular contributor to the county magazine, was standing on his doorstep dressed in an old donkey jacket. "Mr Rufford?" He pumped John's hand energetically after introducing himself, his mop of disorganised white hair bobbing enthusiastically as he did so. "Good of you to see me," he said with a broad smile. Between his deep-set, piercingly pale blue eyes, an alarmingly large aquiline nose jutted out over a short straggly white beard. "Parked the car in front of your garage. Hope you don't mind."

A cursory glance in that direction revealed the old shooting-brake had been drawn up somewhat haphazardly on the gravel, and appeared to have been abandoned without much thought to its position . "No – that's fine," John assured him.

"Splendid. Splendid. Came as soon as I could. Know your work, of course – from the mag. Can't think why I've never been in touch before." He paused, stepping over the threshold with exaggerated care. "This way, is it?" he asked, with all the visible excitement of a child about to meet Father Christmas.

John followed his eager diminutive visitor through the hall and into the sitting room.

Makepeace stopped for a moment in the doorway. "Ah!" he said, enraptured, suddenly advancing at speed, skirting the intervening furniture in a series of little side-steps reminiscent of Fred Astaire. "Ah!" he repeated, standing in front of the fireplace, his head tilted back to study the pastel sketch. "Rothwell Mere! Incredible piece of work!" He peered closer. "Unsigned. Yours?"

John shook his head. "A friend gave it to me."

"Astonishing! Primitive and primal! Captured it exactly! Such power!" He turned suddenly to face him. "I never thought, you know. Silly of me. There you were, right in front of my nose, so to speak. Would never have dawned on me if Davey hadn't mentioned it." Davey was one of the sub-editors on the county magazine. "Said, 'Why not try John Rufford?' He gave me your number at the studio. Very helpful girl you've got there. Gemma something-or-other. Sorry – hopeless at names unless they've got a date attached to them. It's the way my mind works, you know."

"Gemma Mortimer," John said.

"Yes – that's the one." Makepeace took off his old donkey jacket, dumping it on the floor before making himself at home in the chair next to the coffee table. He was a bizarre sight: threadbare brown cords, a cerise shirt, tartan tie and pea-green velvet jacket, his feet encased in thick blue walking socks stuffed into scuffed tan sandals. No one who knew him was sure whether this outlandish mode of dress was contrived, or the result of a simple lack of interest in the niceties of fashion. John tended to think it was the latter. Bernard Makepeace was on another planet.

"Coffee or tea?" John asked, beginning to regard his guest as a hyperactive garden gnome minus the floppy hat.

"Oh no – nothing for me, thank you – unless you've got any elderflower cordial?"

John apologised for his lack of elderflower cordial.

"No matter. No matter. By all means, of course, have something yourself." There was the briefest of pauses before the next onslaught of words caught up with John in the kitchen. "I have to say I was bowled over by the news. Couldn't believe my luck when your lady assistant – Gemma what's-her-name told me. Who would have thought it? A whole collection of photographs! Couldn't wait to see them. You didn't mind me coming round like this? Wasn't sure I'd find you back from your latest assignment. Harkley Manor, wasn't it? Fascinating place. They say there's a ghost in the east wing. Not sure about that, of course, but it makes a good story. Did an article on it a couple of years ago."

John returned with his coffee and made himself comfortable in his recliner wondering when Makepeace would finally get round to the reason for his visit. Gemma had been somewhat opaque when she rang. "Something about Rothwell Mere," she said icily. "Are you free today? He'd like to come over and see you."

The topic of Rothwell Mere was never likely to bring out the best in Gemma, John realised. Their relationship had become noticeably more prickly since his unannounced visit the previous weekend. His efforts to be less self-absorbed appeared to have fallen on stony ground.

"Well I suppose you're wondering what this is all about?" Makepeace was saying, leaning forward in his chair, his bony fingers grasping his knees in a vice-like grip.

"Something to do with Rothwell Mere, I understand."

Makepeace nodded vigorously. "Indeed it is. Not what I intended in the first place, of course – researching something else entirely. But there you are – that's what happens. You start out on one project and end up with another." He laughed uproariously at this, his meagre frame shaken to its core in an alarming fashion. "Anyway," he continued, "I was reading up on witches in the seventeenth century for an article about six months ago – there's an amazing archive on them, you know – in Bebbington Hall. Don't think the Weaverdale District Historical Society know just how much stuff they've got tucked away on some of their shelves. A gold mine – absolute gold mine. Anyway – as I was saying, I was pursuing this line of enquiry – particularly about the appalling habit of throwing witches into water to see if they would sink or swim – and there it was! In Hepplethwaite's *Journey Through the North – 1784*. A passing reference to the trial of Betsey Burrows! March 1649. Named as a witch by her employer for consorting with demons and casting spells on her pigs so that they died 'most horribly'. Foot and mouth most likely," he added with a grim smile. "So the poor woman was thrown into Rothwell Mere."

"Where she drowned?"

"No – no. She floated – which of course proved she was

a witch. She was dragged out to be hanged on the orders of Adam Bradley – ghastly man. One of those self-appointed witch-finders of the time. Misogynist of course. Anyway, Betsey seems to have escaped – and vanished completely. Hepplethwaite says her persecutors swore the devil had turned her into a crow and she flew away, but years later – when Bradley was exposed as a fraud – another story went the rounds that Betsey had been innocent after all – and had been transformed into a swan – or some-such. Lots of stuff like that, I'm afraid. All nonsense of course, but *fascinating*." Makepeace beamed, evidently thrilled by this discovery. "Well this set me off. Had there ever been a Rothwell village close to the mere? Absolutely no trace – even before the Black Death. Nearest habitation in the sixteen-hundreds was Monksfield – six miles away at least – with a perfectly adequate duck pond for the purposes of drowning a witch. So why, I asked myself, had Betsey been hauled off to Rothwell Mere? And this is the interesting bit," he added, emphasising the point with a bony finger. "Found an old notebook belonging to a Josiah Watt of Holdingstone – another hamlet about ten miles further south. Not very legible in places. Bits missing here and there, but enough left to get the gist of it. Written between 1661 and 1664. Amazing fellow – journeyman carpenter. Kept quite remarkably detailed accounts of his travels. Anyway – yes – he wrote down what he'd been told about a witch trial in Monksfield. Seems Betsey was employed by a widow, Elizabeth Bolton who complained Betsey regularly fell into a trance and went wandering off. Had to be brought back any number of times apparently. And where do you think they used to find her?"

"Rothwell Mere?"

Makepeace nodded. "Every time. The poor girl was probably afflicted with something or other. Who knows? But," he added, his pale blue eyes riveting John in his seat, "and this is the *really* interesting bit – Josiah says, 'those who lived at Monksfield feared for their lives. For the mere was said to be the haunt of sprites, and demons who inhabited the wood close by. And it is still held today that no man or woman is safe from the devil's hand who goes there without they wear a cross.' All superstitious nonsense, of course, but *very* powerful at the time."

"So Betsey was doubly damned when she floated?"

"Yes, indeed. Proof positive it was a place of demonic influence. Alas, Josiah doesn't throw any more light on how she escaped hanging. Maybe her executioners just took fright and fled – got spooked perhaps? – made up the story she was rescued by the devil? But this got me thinking. There's always something behind these stories – myths – legends – whatever you call them. How did Rothwell Mere get its reputation for magic?" He sat back in the chair, evidently waiting for a hypothesis from his listener.

John declared himself unable to supply it.

"Don't you feel it – when you're there?" Makepeace pointed dramatically at Laura's sketch. "There's something about the place?"

"Yes – there is something."

"Exactly!" Makepeace leaned forward in his chair again.

"So I thought, why not look further back? So I did." At this point, he looked inordinately pleased with himself. "Earliest reference? – *Celtic!*" he said emphatically. "One of their water shrines! There's a collection of finds in Lingford Museum. Bracelets – knives – brooches – that sort of thing. Amazing! Possible druidical connections too. An ancient oak grove. All the evidence is much later, of course. Fascinating reference by Aethelric in County Archives – seventh-century monk living in a religious community – possibly near Monksfield, who knows? – all in very shaky Latin, I'm afraid. Complains people are drifting back to pagan ways – offering gifts at 'Roffa's Well by a grove of oaks'. He's not at all pleased! Threatens everyone with hell and damnation!" He laughed uproariously at this, slapping his thighs. "Later references to 'Rolf's Well' after the Norman invasion and a heretical sect in the mid-1100s. And there you have it! The early Church decided this was definitely not a place for good Christian souls to visit – and it stuck! – suitably elaborated by the presence of demons et cetera in the Middle Ages, of course –" He stopped suddenly, perhaps aware his host was being very forbearing. "Ah – forgive me – I rattle on once I get going. There's so much more – about how the well was transformed into a mere – but mustn't bore you with it. No – no. Must keep to the point."

John smiled encouragingly.

"To cut a long story short – I've so much material, it would make a splendid book. Absolutely splendid. But I need photographs, you see. Atmospheric photographs. And I wondered – if I found what I wanted in your collection

– would you agree to me using them? – under terms that suit, of course."

John got up from the recliner and retrieved four of his photographic albums from his bookcase. "You're welcome to see if there's anything you want," he said, handing them over. They were not his complete collection, of course. There were some that were for his eyes only – of Laura down by the margins of the mere, muffled up against the cold, picking her way along the shoreline studying the ice; turning in answer to him calling out her name; laughing at him for taking pictures of her. These had no place under the gaze of Bernard Makepeace.

His visitor had whipped out a pair of dusty reading spectacles from his jacket pocket and was carefully turning the pages of the albums, his eyes consuming the contents like a hungry man devours a meal. "Oh yes – yes," he kept saying. "Perfectly splendid. Perfectly splendid." Followed by a sudden exclamation. "Ah! Look! This is wonderful," pointing to a particular print. "The oak grove! Magnificent! Stark and menacing with the sun behind it! Perfect. Perfect. And this too!" he said, indicating the photograph mounted below: an evocative study of the harsh winter sunlight slanting through broken reeds, casting a lattice of tangled shadows across the muted brilliance of the frozen surface of the mere.

It was the photograph Laura had selected as her favourite from all those he had taken on that special day. "It captures the magic," he remembered her saying. Makepeace had seen it too.

Like so much in life that can make you stop and wonder at coincidence, John thought, this sudden convergence of two entirely separate lives and times seemed predestined. He felt a generosity of spirit he had lacked for so many years, and the unlikely benefactor of his sense of well-being was this strange, eccentric fellow who had never crossed his path before. "Take them with you, if you like," he offered. "Let me know which ones you want and I'll dig out the negatives for you."

"That's extraordinarily kind of you."

"Not at all. You're very welcome. It's good to know they can be of some use."

"It's an absolute treasure trove, Mr Rufford. An absolute treasure trove. How many years have you been photographing the mere?"

"About thirty."

"Astonishing! Any particular reason?" Makepeace was studying him with intense interest over the top of his spectacles.

John chose to be airily dismissive. "Just a whim."

Makepeace shook his head vigorously. "No – no," he said firmly. "This is an obsession – a *grand* obsession." He made it sound impressive.

John simply smiled: his reasons were his own.

Makepeace was looking through the albums again. "You don't have any with birds on, do you? Crows perhaps? Swans?"

"Not in there – but I've just developed some. If you'll give a me a moment?"

"Of course – of course."

John retrieved the treasured prints from his study upstairs, handing them over with the strangest sensation that perhaps everything in life was preordained.

Makepeace carefully examined each of them in turn, his eyes growing wider with every image. "Oh my!" he said very softly, suddenly looking up. "A heron!"

"I've been waiting more than twenty-five years for those particular shots," John explained. "Saw a heron take off from the mere in 1963, but hadn't got the camera ready. I've gone back every year hoping to see one."

"And you never did? – until this year?"

"Not until this year."

"Fascinating," Makepeace said, spreading the photographs out in front of him on the coffee table, his eyes darting from one to another. "Really fascinating," he repeated. "You see one of the stories – about Betsey – was she was actually changed into a heron. I think Godwin mentioned it – in 1674. 'And her soul flew up and she escaped her persecutors.' Something like that. Put an entirely new complexion on things, as you can imagine." He laughed again. "Of course, nothing particularly unusual about a heron in a mere, is there? And some fine mature oak trees close by for its nest?" He cut himself short, clearing his throat. "Ah – you must forgive me digressing for a moment – but it really is astonishing. Herons have all sorts of symbolic meanings, you see – find them in twelfth century bestiaries all over the place. Herons taking flight are supposed to herald a storm brewing, apparently."

John confessed his ignorance of such things.

"Yes, indeed. The heron symbolised the soul of someone fleeing from the storm of persecution whipped up by the Devil. Poor Betsey, eh? Turned into a crow, she was certain to be damned. Turned into a heron, and suddenly," he snapped his fingers, "suddenly, she's entirely blameless. Heigh-ho. Such is life."

Makepeace's unstoppable prattling receded into the distance. John had stopped listening, his thoughts drifting elsewhere. He was thinking of the heron taking flight on that long-ago day in January which had presaged a storm indeed – his own turbulent state of mind for more than twenty-five wretched years, and he remembered how it felt to see the bird return: the elation; the sheer joy of it. Foolishness, of course, but he smiled, recalling it.

CHAPTER SEVENTEEN

Brack wanted to go with him. He whined pathetically when told to stay, and lifted a paw, urging forgiveness for some unknown misdemeanour when Tom rubbed him fondly behind the ears. They had been inseparable ever since Robert had taken Tom up to Liddel's place to choose any dog he wanted from Tammy's litter for his Twenty-first. It was a wrench to leave him behind, looking forlorn and leaning protectively against Robert in the yard.

And despite the pleasure in his new car, Tom found the journey tedious. It was a typical day in early March, bright and blustery with occasional fierce showers. Spring seemed to be holding its breath in the North, not yet ready to burst into life; everywhere was still dressed in sullen khaki with gaunt trees etched against the sky.

He turned onto the motorway after an hour of driving against a strong westerly, and headed south over the wilderness places of Cumbria, where hardy sheep grazed the sparse moorland turf, and into a gentler landscape of farms and fields that was northern Lancashire.

He stopped at one of the service stations for a meal: a soulless place of concrete and glass. It was relatively quiet, being that dead time before Easter, and there were few customers in the café waiting to be served. With his tea in a fragile plastic cup, and his apology for a ham and tomato sandwich, he sat by a window overlooking the traffic speeding past, and felt unaccountably dispirited. Surely he should feel something? He was going to claim his inheritance – to meet people he had never met before – by any standards, an adventure. But his acquisition of the Lodge seemed a remote concept – unreal – and he felt strangely uninvolved.

His mother had rarely spoken of her family home, her life there too painful to recall. And his single visit had left him with few memories beyond her determination to remove any trace of his grandmother's occupation of the place: the black plastic sacks piled in the hall; removal men coming and going; and his boredom with the process – a twelve-year-old wanting to be busy doing something else.

By mid-afternoon, the scenery had changed as the motorway cut through the Cheshire landscape: there were hedges, not walls; the grass was greener, and lambs were already out with their mothers in the fields. There were more trees and the steadings stood in open ground, unafraid of the elements. The horizon too was further off. There were no broad-breasted fells to block out the low ambit of a winter sun. And the clouds were small and fluffy, with flat bottoms as they scudded over the plain.

He came off the motorway, a by-pass taking him round Lingford with its new general hospital and leisure centre, and housing estates springing up everywhere. Then he was heading south again through a narrow strip of green belt before a signpost welcomed safe drivers into Weaversham. Before long, he found himself driving down a busy thoroughfare with small shops on either side, the only concession to the modern world, a mini-market with its garish window posters on a corner site. Ahead, he could make out the hanging sign of a plump, red-faced fellow in an oversized powdered wig. Above, mounted on the bracket, was a gilded wooden crown. He turned left, and followed the signs into The George Hotel car park at the rear.

His room, he discovered, looked out across the ranks of cars, not a particularly inspiring view. But the room itself was pleasant enough, if a little faded.

Necessity had given him no option but a double bed. "We don't have single rooms, sir," the receptionist had said. Tom stared at it and wished he could have brought Janet with him, away from prying eyes and gossip, to where he could revel in her company. But Janet was already moving on, leaving him behind. He might never see her again.

At a loose end and in low spirits, he wandered out into the town. In a small pedestrianised square, he found a pleasant sitting area between raised flower beds filled with brightly coloured primula. It was sheltered there in the late afternoon sun, and finding an empty bench, he passed the time listening to those who came and went around him: giggling schoolgirls with their friends; casual shoppers with heavy bags, eager to ease their feet; and lovers, snatching precious moments in each other's company. How he envied them.

He saw himself the stranger in their midst: his clothes practical rather than fashionable; his speech, with its mix of Scots-Northumbrian parlance and slight lilt, at odds with those around him. He could hear his mother's voice and intonation, which he had learnt to copy when he chose, and wondered if he were wise to choose it now, rather than be taken for a rough country yokel of no breeding and possibly less education. Robert had been taken for such. Prejudice and ignorance, combined with overt snobbery, had reduced him in the eyes of others, people who had never troubled to learn there was more to this quiet man than met the eye.

At the bar after supper – or dinner – as it was described on the menu posted at the entrance to the hotel restaurant, he noted the same differences that marked him out among the small groups of reps and salesmen who were patrons of the place. He kept himself apart, phoning Robert later to report his safe arrival, finding comfort in the familiarity of tone and speech.

The following morning he drove south out of Weaversham towards Redbridge, and took the junction heading east to Meeston along a winding B-road with mature oaks and well-trimmed hedges on either side. Neat farm complexes in red brick were set back from the road, their smart aluminium agricultural buildings surrounded by lush green fields for dairy cows to graze in over summer. Along the sky-line ran the dark shape of the Pennine hills, their low profile a distant prospect across the plain.

He passed through the hamlet of Dobbs Green, over a packhorse bridge and not long after, drove past the sign for

Meeston. A crossroads lay ahead. He slowed down, passing the war memorial in its cobbled area outside the village store, and then beyond the weavers' cottages, the Meeston Arms with its cheerful wooden planters filled with early tulips. Set back on higher ground stood the old church of St Wilfrid, surrounded by sycamores, ash and wild cherry trees, its venerable yews sheltering the graves in the churchyard. His grandfather, James Driscoll, was buried there. His grandmother, Daphne, was entombed elsewhere, with her Harriman relations in their vault at Broxley, a decision taken by his mother, much to the distress of the vicar of St Wilfrid's at the time. But then he knew nothing of the realities of their loveless marriage or its consequences.

Opposite the church were the two stone pillars set in the high red-brick wall marking the entrance into Meeston Lodge.

Tom drove onto the freshly laid gravel on the driveway and turned off the engine. He was early. Mr Warburton, acting on behalf of Messrs Barker Fawcett, had arranged to meet him with the keys to the property at ten. It was only quarter-to.

It was a fine sunny morning and bright yellow and purple crocus were open in the beds on either side of the door, with daffodil spears bursting into flower beside them. Early bees were prospecting among the purple and pink heads of pulmonaria between the well-pruned dormant shrubs, and flocks of chattering blue tits were darting from branch to branch seeking out insects.

He got out of the car and surveyed the house with its

fine double fronted bay windows and steps leading up to the porch, its Georgian proportions elegant and pleasing to the eye.

Not long afterwards, a metallic blue Sierra pulled into the drive behind him, and a tall man in his late-thirties wearing aviator-style spectacles emerged from behind the wheel. He was every inch a professional man in his dark suit, striped shirt with a white collar and maroon tie. He extended a hand as he approached. "Mr Moray?" he asked with a smile, his voice a rice baritone. "Mark Warburton – Barker Fawcett. I see you're admiring the house."

Tom shook his hand and mentally adjusted his speech. "It looks very fine," he said.

"Your mother was very particular about maintenance, Mr Moray. Would you like to see inside first?"

Tom followed him up the steps and into the half-panelled hall. The atmosphere was unexpectedly warm and welcoming.

"Your mother suggested we leave the heating on over the winter," Mr Warburton explained. "To prevent problems. Never does to leave a house at the mercy of the weather. She ensured, of course, that adequate funds were available for this. I'm sure you agree, it's money well spent?"

Tom agreed, trying to reconcile his memories of the place with his surroundings: it seemed much less gloomy than he remembered.

"Have you been here before?" Mr Warburton was asking him.

"Yes – about thirteen years ago."

"Ah, then you know the parquet flooring extends throughout the downstairs rooms – with the exception of the back porch and kitchen of course – there's still terracotta tiling in those areas." Mr Warburton led the way into the sitting room. "The decorations have no doubt changed since you were here last. There were major alterations to the house in 1977 – before my time – new fireplaces and a completely new central heating system. A more modern bathroom suite and kitchen were installed in 1983, and the interior of the house was completely redecorated again two years ago." He paused in his account to allow Tom sufficient time to evaluate the decor. "It's quite a tasteful wallpaper, I think you'll agree," he continued with some satisfaction. "A Regency style seems to suit the dimensions of the house."

Tom made some comment along the lines that he agreed with Mr Warburton's assessment, and wandered over to the window to admire the view of the drive and shrubbery bathed in soft spring sunshine.

"West facing," Mr Warburton explained. "Particularly lovely on summer evenings. The dining room has the advantage of a similar orientation," he added, leading the way across the hall. And following a brief inspection, conducted Tom down the hallway again into what had once been his grandfather's study, and later his mother's studio. "A very pleasant room indeed," Mr Warburton said, noticing Tom's particular interest in it before leading him towards the back of the house. "And here we have what is a very attractive dining kitchen with all the latest appliances. The dishwasher is next to the sink unit." He pulled down the oak-fronted door for Tom's inspection but did not linger. "The utility room and laundry are through here," he said, opening a side door to reveal where the boiler was housed together with a large washing machine and tumble dryer. To Tom's eyes, everything about the place made Rigg End seem very lowly and unexceptional. Had his mother ever thought so? "Shall we go upstairs?" Mr Warburton was asking.

Tom could remember little, except the turn in the stairs with the half-landing, its window looking out across the walled garden and beyond, to where Meeston Woods met the eastern boundary. At the top of the stairs, across the spacious landing, he had a vague recollection of the three generously-sized bedrooms all with fire places, long since removed; the little dressing room over the front door; and an antiquated bathroom now completely refurbished with a pale cream suite and an electric shower over the bath.

Mr Warburton continued his tour at a brisk pace, taking him downstairs once more and out onto the drive, securing the front door behind him as they left. He led the way past the orchard and round to the pathway through the rhododendrons into the vegetable garden. "The old greenhouses were replaced about ten years ago, I believe, along with the garden shed. I should explain this area is still let separately to Nether Meeston Farm. Mr Benyon Junior continues to cultivate it as an allotment as part of his contract to maintain the gardens. But of course, you may wish to terminate this arrangement if you decide to sell." It was a considerable area, roughly dug over and cleared ready for spring planting. The earth was a rich dark brown, drying out in the sun, and a robin was busily hunting for worms between the clods. It watched them warily for a few moments, then continued its search, ignoring their presence.

Tom let Mr Warburton walk back through the rhododendrons. Alone for a moment, he could envisage Robert as a younger man, working here in solitude – the quiet, introspective man his mother had turned to in her time of need. He could almost see him there, bent over his spade, turning to see her coming through the rhododendrons to meet him. It was a strange, unsettling sensation.

Mr Warburton was calling him. "Mr Moray? Ah – I thought I'd lost you for a moment. Everything all right?"

Tom assured him that it was and followed him back onto the drive.

"Now this is the old stable block," Mr Warburton was saying with an expansive sweep of his hand taking in the single storey building abutting the garden wall. "It was renovated around 1980, I believe and – as you can see – it's now a very fine double garage." He unlocked one of the doors, sliding it upwards to reveal the spacious interior with shelving and cupboards, closing it after their cursory inspection and heading down the drive again towards a wooden door set into a recess of the western wall. "And here, of course," he explained, pausing to wait for Tom to catch up with him, "is the side door through into the walled garden." He lifted the latch and they walked into the seclusion offered by the high walls with the espaliers spread-eagled against them. The flower beds between the gravel paths were tidy and planted out with well-pruned roses. "Up the steps, of course," Mr Warburton was saying, pointing in the direction of the house, "is the rear door into the utility and laundry, and access to the back porch and terrace." He paused, waiting perhaps for a question, or comment. "Is there anything you'd like to ask?"

"No – thank you. Everything is very satisfactory."

Mr Warburton looked suitably pleased. "Mrs Moray had every confidence in Barker Fawcett," he said, " – particularly in view of her late father's connections with the firm. And of course," he added, leading the way back out onto the drive and closing the side gate behind them, "if you decide to continue renting out the property, we would be happy to act on your behalf on similar terms."

"Thank you. I'd like to think about it."

"Of course. There's no point in rushing things. Are you staying long in the area?"

"A few days."

Mr Warburton handed him the keys. "Can I suggest you call into our office before you return to Northumberland? – talk over your preliminary thoughts with us? There are one or two administrative details to sort out now you own the property."

Tom agreed he would.

"I'll leave you then to look round at your leisure. If there's anything else you wish to discuss – any questions – you have our number?"

"Yes. Thank you for your time."

They shook hands and Mr Warburton got into his car and drove away.

Tom stood in the driveway for a while listening to the birdsong filling the air. His mother's presence seemed strangely close. He turned, leaving the Lodge behind him and crossed the road, stepping through the gate into the tranquil precincts of St Wilfrid's Church. There was a pilgrimage to make. A gravestone to acknowledge.

CHAPTER EIGHTEEN

At the door to his bright and airy office, Oliver Gorst, senior partner of Gorst & Parr, shook Tom's hand briefly.

"Mr Gorst," Tom said.

"Do please call me Oliver, Thomas." A thin smile passed fleetingly across his gaunt features. He was tall man, untouched by middle-aged spread. His slim figure was dressed in a well-tailored charcoal suit, a crisp white shirt and dark blue tie with a yellow and white motif, his immaculately trimmed greying hair and moustache adding to the overall impression of someone well-used to commanding both attention and respect. "Won't you sit down?" he suggested, indicating with an elegant sweep of his hand one of the four well-upholstered black leather chairs ranged around a glass-topped coffee table. All very modern. All very different from Crozier & Co in Wallbridge.

When Tom had visited Gorst & Parr thirteen years ago, the office was situated in a dark and brooding Victorian building, filled with mahogany and cigar smoke. The firm had evidently prospered in the intervening years: the brushed aluminium plaque at the entrance to the new offices at 18 Tilverton Square announced the presence of six other highly qualified practitioners of the law, as well as two conveyancers, and an estate agency by the same name.

Tom made himself comfortable while Oliver ordered coffee over the intercom on his well-organised, uncluttered desk. "I'm sorry Julius Parr isn't here at the moment," he said, coming over to join him, and crossing his long legs as he leaned back in his chair. "He's out visiting one of his elderly clients this morning."

Tom noted the clearly enunciated speech and adjusted his own accordingly. "I called on impulse," he explained. "I should have telephoned first." The pitch and tone sounded about right, he thought.

A small nod of acknowledgement. "I'm afraid I know very little of your mother's affairs, Thomas. Wills and Trusts – not my forté. I spend most of my time in court," he added. "Your mother's contact with us was originally in the hands of Mr Parr Senior. Perhaps you know. Julius took over his father's clients when Horace retired."

"I understand."

There was a knock at the door and an attractive young woman in her late teens or early twenties entered carrying a small tray with two coffee cups, a sugar bowl and a plate of assorted biscuits. She was tall and willowy in a navy-blue close-fitting suit with an open-necked stripy blouse which revealed a gold chain nestling at the base of her throat. Her wavy shoulder-length auburn hair framed a heart-shaped face, with high cheek bones and large wide-set hazel eyes. She cast a quick glance in Tom's direction.

"Thank you, Sophie," Oliver said as she placed the tray on the coffee table in front of them.

She acknowledged his thanks with a nod, turning as she left the room to glance briefly once again in Tom's direction. It was difficult to ignore her interest.

"My daughter," Oliver was saying as he offered Tom a biscuit. "Gap year. Has no idea what she wants to do. I suggested a stint here to fill in her time."

Tom nodded, selecting a chocolate digestive, trying to identify some similarity between the bright young thing he had just seen and the stiff personage sitting opposite. They were chalk and cheese.

"So – you've seen Meeston Lodge?"

"Yes. It's not the way I remember it."

The thin smile resurrected itself. "I've not been there for several years. Nice enough at the time. A little old-fashioned perhaps even then. The early sixties," he added, glancing up from stirring his coffee.

"It's been renovated since."

"Ah. Do you think you'll sell?"

"I haven't decided yet."

"Barker Fawcett have been very diligent, I believe. You've met Mr Warburton, I presume?"

"Yes – he showed me round yesterday."

"Excellent man, Mr Warburton. Should you decide to sell, of course, we can provide you with all estate agency requirements here. Useful having everything under one roof."

Tom agreed.

"I did wonder if that was your reason for calling on us today."

Tom paused, aware of the delicacy of what he was about to say. Opposite him, he kept reminding himself – because frankly it seemed so unlikely – was his mother's ex-fiancé – her cousin. "I'm here for another reason," he said, picking through the phrases he had mulled over soaking in the bath the previous evening at The George. "My father suggested I should try to contact my mother's relations while I was in the area."

A small frown settled on Oliver's brow. He put down his spoon and sipped delicately at his coffee. "Not many of us left in these parts these days, I'm afraid," he said after a moment's reflection. "My mother lives in Spain now. Perhaps you hadn't heard. Moved there after my father died in seventy-seven. Has a rather splendid villa near Alicante. Usually spend Christmas there. Take Gregory – my eldest – and Sophie when I can. Gregory's in his last year at Cambridge. I've every hope he'll be joining the firm." He was evidently pleased at this prospect.

Tom noted there was no mention of the beautiful Claudia: Claudia, the wilful daughter of Horace and Phyllis Parr who had ensnared Oliver for his money, and caused ructions between the Gorsts and Parrs. Sophie, Tom deduced, without any evidence to the contrary, had inherited her mother's looks.

"There's my sister Rosemary, of course," Oliver was saying. "Your mother and she were very close at one time when they were younger."

"Yes."

"She and Julius have two children – Damien and Marcia – but they're both at university at the moment – and my brother, Stephen, emigrated to the States – last year," he added. "So – as I said – not many of us left in these parts now." The thin smile etched itself once more into his face. "Did you ever visit your Great-aunts Millicent and Sylvia?"

"I stayed with them at Hazeldene Court when I came down with my mother."

"Ah – yes, of course, when Daphne died. I'd forgotten. Not an easy woman, your grandmother," he added as an afterthought.

"No. I never met her." He could have elaborated further that she had never expressed any wish to meet him either – nor Jamie nor Flora – never having forgiven her daughter for marrying someone she regarded as beneath her social status.

"So different from her sisters," Oliver was saying, musing on this fact for a moment. "Did you know Millicent and Sylvia went into a home in Redbridge about eight years ago?"

"Yes – they kept in touch with us."

"Ah – did they?" He considered this information while chewing carefully on a Rich Tea biscuit. "They never said. Miss visiting them, you know. They were very frail by then, of course. Well into their eighties. Strange how people die within a few weeks of each other when they've been very close all their lives, isn't it?" He frowned. "Did your mother come down for their funerals? I don't remember seeing her."

"My mother was never fond of funerals."

"No – her father's was particularly fraught, if I remember." There was a long pause followed by a slight clearing of the throat. "I'm sorry about your mother, Thomas. Not something you expect to happen at such an early age."

"No."

"Came as quite a shock when your father wrote to us."

Tom noted Oliver did not mention Robert's letter had been sent after the funeral – something his mother had particularly requested. "He appreciated your condolences," he said, keeping things brief.

"The least we could do – apart, of course, from offering you our services – if they were ever required."

"Thank you."

In the small silence that followed, Tom became aware that Oliver was studying him. "You know," Oliver said awkwardly, "In all those years your father was at the Lodge our paths never crossed. Not once. Another world in those days, of course," he added with a slight hint of embarrassment that Robert's station in life had been regarded as somewhat lowly – and possibly beneath notice. "I do remember Millicent saying – many years ago, of course – there was more to your father than met the eye. He's keeping well, is he?"

"He's managing reasonably well."

"Yes – of course. A great loss for him – and many in the art world too, I understand."

"Yes – she was highly thought of in certain quarters."

"I went to an exhibition of hers a few years ago – in York, if I remember. Very impressive." He did not say whether he had bought any of her work. Looking at the standard Van Gogh prints adorning the walls, Tom thought it unlikely. "Do have another biscuit, won't you?" Oliver suggested.

Tom declined the offer and finished his coffee, wondering if Oliver might summon Sophie to refill his cup. But his hospitality fell short in that department.

Oliver was studying him again. "You must forgive me," he said, the frown on his forehead deepening perceptibly, "But you do remind me of someone. Perhaps I did meet your father after all – who knows? I just can't remember when."

Tom felt the heat rising in his face and looked down at the empty cup until the moment passed.

He had never for a moment suspected Oliver might know – or have known John Rufford. Why should he? But the thought alarmed him. Was this the reason his mother had wanted to keep Oliver from her funeral? To prevent them meeting? Would she be equally appalled at the thought Robert had unintentionally brought about the very situation she had sought to avoid? He checked his watch, feigning concern at the time. "I'm sorry, I'm probably keeping you from another client. I'll make an appointment to see Mr Parr – Julius – tomorrow perhaps – if I can." He stood up, eager to change the subject. "Thank you for the coffee."

Oliver unwound himself from his seat and offered his hand. "Not at all. By the way," he added, a little cautiously. "Are you free for lunch? I usually take Sophie to The Bebbington on Station Road on Wednesdays, and I would, under normal circumstances have invited you to join us, but I need to be in Flockton for two." He hesitated, the frown on his forehead re-establishing itself. "Would it be an imposition if I asked you to stand in for me?"

Tom had no hesitation in offering to take on this onerous task.

Oliver seemed relieved. "I'm sure she'll find your company more to her liking than mine, Thomas. I realise I can be very dull at times," he added with an embarrassed smile. "I'll introduce you properly on the way out, then you can make whatever arrangements suit best. Just ask for the bill to be added to my account, will you?"

The Bebbington belonged to the era of grand railway hotels, all polished stone and grandeur, high ornate plaster ceilings and wood panelling. The restaurant had a certain old-world charm about it with its thick-piled carpet of an elaborate floral design, elegant chairs with padded backs and arms, and every table set just so, with white damask table cloths and the condiments neatly clustered at the centre.

Tom would have preferred somewhere less formal or stuffy, but Sophie seemed happy enough with the arrangement. They were shown to Mr Gorst's regular table by a deferential head waiter, and she made her choice without any reference to the menu. The fare was nothing elaborate, to Tom's relief, and he had no difficulty in selecting what he felt would be appropriate in view of the dinner he was anticipating later at The George. He suggested wine, which she declined on the grounds her father would disapprove.

"Daddy says we're related," she said, propping her chin on her hands as she studied him across the table.

Her curiosity in him was gratifying and he was flattered by her attention. "Second cousins, I think," he offered, not entirely sure if this were correct. His mind was becoming more focused on the way she kept playing with the gold chain around her neck, aware this was becoming dangerously distracting.

She leaned forward slightly. "Did you know about me?" she asked. "I mean, did you even know I existed?" This seemed to trouble her.

He shook his head.

"What about Greg? He's three years older than me."

"No, I didn't know about Gregory either."

"And I didn't know about you – not 'til today. Don't you think that's strange?"

From what Tom knew of the family history, it was not at all strange, but what he should and should not mention, was a potential minefield he had no wish to enter. "Too many hurt feelings in the past, I suppose," he suggested.

The waiter brought his soup and she sat watching him eat it. "Is it true Daddy was once engaged to your mother?"

"A long time ago."

"Daddy never wants to talk about the past. He clams up and goes all prickly. I can't get anyone else to tell me either. There's this 'great conspiracy'," she added, emphasising the words dramatically. "It really annoys me. Anyone would think I'm a child."

"You're no child," he said, thinking aloud and immediately regretting it. He was surprised to see her blush and look away, watching passing traffic outside the window while he finished his soup.

The waiter took his empty bowl and brought the main course.

She contemplated her breaded plaice before carefully separating the white flesh from the skin. "Do *you* know what happened?" she asked suddenly, apparently hoping that he did.

He censored his answer, determined not to be the cause of further misunderstandings or animosity. Sometimes, he had learned, silence is the best option. With this in mind, he gave a somewhat truncated version of events. "I know that after your father and my mother decided not to get married – they both found someone else. Caused a bit of a rumpus at the time."

"Yes – but why did it cause a rumpus?"

"Something to do with the terms of an inheritance, I think," Tom said, cutting out any details of both romances which had caused far greater ripples in various family circles.

"Oh – that stupid Harriman fortune business!" she said, attacking her fish with some vigour. "Did you know Daddy inherited everything – even though he didn't marry your mother?" The unfairness of this arcane provision of Edward Harriman's Will clearly irritated her.

"Yes."

"I heard people say Mummy only married Daddy for his money."

"I don't know anything about that."

"I think she did. Did you know they'd split up?" she persisted.

He chewed thoughtfully on a particularly tough slice of lamb, wondering why he had ever imagined a town hotel would be capable of serving up anything remotely similar to the quality he was used to. "I'd heard. None of the details though."

She put down her knife and fork in a very determined manner. "Well I don't mind telling you what happened. Mummy dumped us," she said brutally. "When I was three. Daddy never got over it." Anger had brought colour into her cheeks. "We were packed off to boarding schools a-s-a-p. Poor Daddy – I know he can be a bit of a bore at times, but what else could he do left with two young children?" She stopped suddenly. "Sorry, I need to explode sometimes, and there's no one else I can talk to. What about you? Tell me about yourself."

Keep it simple, Tom thought. Don't on any account say something you might regret.

Noticing his hesitation, she gave a small embarrassed laugh. "Oh trust me – now I've put you off completely! Daddy says I'm always doing that – putting my foot in it. Ignore me, Tom – I can call you Tom, can I? Thomas sounds a bit too formal, don't you think?"

He agreed with her and the conversation died for a while until they had finished their meal.

But her curiosity could not be stifled long. When the waiter had taken their plates, she leaned forward again across the table and asked him in a stage whisper, "Did your mother really run off with the gardener?" She evidently thought this was very romantic and seemed oblivious to the possibility she was being horribly patronising.

Tom was taken aback for a moment. "No," he said, gathering his wits and feeling the need to set the record straight without compromising himself in the process. "She married Robert Moray, a farmer from Northumberland, who happened to help out in the garden at Meeston Lodge."

Her eyes widened. "Oh – there I go again! That was really thoughtless of me!"

"You can't help it if that's what you've been told."

"No, but I can be more careful what I say." She reached out and touched his hand. "I really am sorry." Her eyes betrayed more than she knew. "You must think I'm very stupid."

"You're forgiven," he said, making light of her offence, but warning bells were ringing in his ears. There was a fragile naivety about her: a vulnerability. She was no Donna, or Jan. She was a porcelain doll, precious and very easy to break in the wrong hands.

"Are we still friends?" she was asking him earnestly, still holding his hand.

The waiter interrupted, bringing their puddings and placing them on the table with exaggerated care, expressing the hope they would enjoy them.

"Say we are," she insisted, looking earnestly into his eyes.

He nodded, picking up his spoon and concentrating hard on his larger than expected portion of rhubarb crumble, its custard collapsing into the bowl around it. He wanted

Jan, and this fawn-like creature was stirring more than his interest. He began to panic.

Tomorrow, he decided, resolving to resist all temptation, he would go home. He would not stay a moment longer. He would certainly not make any attempt to discover the whereabouts of his father and add this to the heady mix of emotions engulfing him. No – he would call in at Barker Fawcett in the morning and deal with whatever was necessary; telephone Gorst & Parr, thank Oliver for his hospitality, and apologise to Julius Parr for not making his acquaintance on this occasion; but most of all, he would keep Sophie Gorst at arm's length.

CHAPTER NINETEEN

Tom got out of the car to be greeted by a short, ecstatic bark as Brack bounded towards him across the cobbles. He bent down to fuss the dog, breathing in familiar smells and feeling the sharp edge of the wind in his face. It was good to be home. Meeston Lodge, Weaversham and Lingford felt a million miles away.

Robert came out from the lambing shed and stood in the yard, his cords and jacket threaded with straw spills from the bales. From inside the shed came the urgent bleating of a new-born lamb. The bleating became more insistent.

"Good job I came back early then," Tom said glancing across at the shed.

Robert nodded. "Started last night. Didn't want to take the chance you'd get held up somewhere so I've asked Duncan if he'd come over later to help out. Hope you don't mind him treading on your patch."

Tom heaved his bag out of the back of the car. "No – that's fine by me," he said. "I'll be in better fettle tomorrow night if I get some sleep."

"You didn't fancy staying on then? – in Weaversham?"

"No. Too much to do here," Tom said, keeping the real reasons to himself.

Robert stuffed his hands in his pockets and studied the cobbles at his feet. "Might have been better if you had," he said, glancing up briefly.

Tom put down his bag. "Why? What's happened?"

Robert looked embarrassed by his news. "Sarah's back. Came up on Tuesday."

Sarah was the last person Tom wanted to see at that moment. He had hoped her pride would keep her away from Rigg End – at least for a while. Why had she come back? He suspected her motives. "If she thinks I'll change my mind, Dad – she's wrong," he said, hearing the truculent tone in his voice.

"She says she knows that."

"Well, I hope she does – because we're going nowhere, and the sooner she accepts that the better."

Robert glanced over in the direction of the kitchen. "Don't make a big thing of it, Tom," he said, lowering his voice and trying to mollify him. "She's glad of the extra money, that's all. Says it makes her feel more independent."

Tom gritted his teeth and tried to be charitable. "That's all right then," he said, knowing full well he did not mean a word of it.

"Well, even if it doesn't suit you, Tom, I'm not sorry to see her back. We'll need all the help we can get now lambing's started."

There was no arguing to be done on that point.

"And she's making us a fine stew for supper tonight,"

Robert was saying, possibly hoping to assuage Tom's ill-humour.

Tom picked up his bag and headed for the house with Brack in tow, in no mood to be bought off by the promise of a stew.

In the kitchen, Sarah was dicing vegetables. She must have seen them in the yard – maybe overheard them too. "Hello, Tom," she said with a nervous smile.

Tom nodded, intent on taking his bag up to his room, not engaging in a conversation he had no wish to have.

"It's a good thing you're back," she said quietly.

Her tone begged the question – why?

She piled the vegetables into a pot and filled it with water. "He's in a bad way," she said, drying her hands with deliberate slowness.

"What do you mean?"

She frowned slightly, concentrating on what she had to say. "When I came up on Tuesday – to talk things over – about coming back and that." She paused, struggling to get her story right. "Well – it was gone ten – and I'd not phoned or anything to say I was coming 'cos I thought he'd be out in the sheds. But he wasn't. He was just sitting there," she said, pointing at the table. "No breakfast. Not even shaved." She bit her lip. "Should I have told you?"

Tom nodded. "Yes – I'm glad you have. Thanks."

"Don't tell him I told you, will you?"

"No, I won't."

She looked relieved.

He went upstairs and got changed feeling he had made

the right decision after all to come back when he did. Robert was still too fragile to be left alone for long.

When he went outside, Robert was in the lambing shed leaning on the barred gate scanning a practised eye over the ewes. "Looks like there'll be a couple more due before supper," he said.

"I'll take over, if you like," Tom offered.

Robert turned suddenly and embraced him in a grip of iron, emotion catching at his voice. "I'm glad you're back, Tom," he whispered fiercely.

Tom held him fast. "I'm not going anywhere," he said.

The moment passed. Robert pulled back, mastering his self-control, and turned away quickly, striding out of the shed. "I'll look over the cows then," he said. A low mooing greeted his arrival across the yard.

By dusk, Tom had seen several more lambs safely penned with their mothers in the comfortable warmth of the bales. There would be more overnight mostly likely, but none was imminent. With time on his hands, he strolled over to the hemmel.

The lights were on and Robert was in a back stall talking softly to one of the red heifers. It was her first calving and she was visibly distressed, restlessly shifting to and fro, kicking up the straw.

"Problems?" Tom asked.

Robert nodded, passing a halter over her neck. "Can you hold her steady, Tom? I need to find out what's going on."

Tom took the rope, preparing to brace himself against the side of the stall as Robert took off his jacket and gloved up.

The cow shifted, rolling her eyes, Robert straining to reach inside, his face pressed hard against her flanks. "Twins," he said, pulling his arm free. "Legs everywhere. I'd better get Munro to have a look at her."

"I'll give him a call."

But both Munro and Harry Gillow were out, and there was nothing to do but stay with the beast and hope for the best.

Robert continued soothing her. She leaned against him, lowing softly. He stroked her neck. "Flora was on the phone while you were away," he said, filling in time with casual conversation. "Wanted to know what we were doing about the plans we'd talked about at Christmas." He drew in a long breath, letting it out slowly. "Didn't know what to tell her, Tom. She keeps on about the studio – had I decided to rent it out – what had Ralph Milburn said –"

"What has he said?"

"That there's not a cat in hell's chance the Planners will agree to it being converted into a separate domestic unit."

"Are you sorry?"

Robert shook his head. "I never liked the idea – you know that."

The cow lifted her head suddenly and pulled away, shifting backwards and forwards, pulling at the rope.

"Easy girl," Robert said. "Not long now." She settled again, looking at him with large, anxious eyes. He continued stroking her, running his hand down her neck. She nudged him, resting her great head against his chest. "I've had an idea, Tom – but I wanted to talk it over with you first." He paused, looking mildly embarrassed by his suggestion. "I know you and Duncan don't always see eye to eye – "

"We don't mean anything by it."

"Maybe not, but would you want him around the place all the time?"

Under the circumstances, Tom was unsure he should have any say in the matter.

"There's going to be changes over at High Oakbank," Robert was saying. "Ian and Bridie are thinking of winding down – letting Ross and Liz take over the farm. Ross wants to shift over to beef and lamb production – move out of milk altogether. There's not enough profit in a small-scale unit now."

"Where does that leave Duncan?"

"Pretty much out of a job."

"Unless he helps out here – if I'm not around."

"I wasn't thinking of that, Tom. I know he's said a couple of times he'd like to try his hand at making furniture – nothing fancy. Farmhouse tables, chairs – that sort of thing. He understands wood. I think he could make a go of it. The trouble is Ross'll need every shed he's got for cattle housing and feed. There'll be no room for a workshop."

"But there would be here – in the studio – is that what you're thinking?"

Robert nodded. "What do you think?"

"I think it makes sense."

Robert looked pleased. "So do I," he said, as Sam Munro's utility drove up into the yard.

An hour later, two healthy bull calves were bedded down in the straw with their mother.

"Keep an eye on her for a while longer, Rob," Munro said, scrubbing up at the sink afterwards. "She's still not sure what to make of them. By the way," he added, "that drench you wanted on Monday – there's another batch due in the morning. Do you want me to put a couple of litres to one side for you tomorrow? I could put it on the bill."

"If you wouldn't mind, Sam," Robert said, turning to look pointedly in Tom's direction. "I'm sure Tom won't mind picking it up for me."

Tom could feel his ears burning, but he waited until Munro had gone before giving Robert a piece of his mind. "Why did you tell him that, Dad? – After what I told you?" he said, trying not let his anger get the better of him.

Robert's expression was infuriatingly blank.

"Don't play dumb, Dad! You know Jan and I agreed to make a clean break of it! We said – that's it – it's over." Christ! – had Robert any idea how hard it had been to say goodbye to her that Sunday morning and walk away? – possibly for ever? "She'll think I've gone soft in the head turning up again," he persisted. He could hear himself whingeing like a small child about to throw a tantrum.

Robert raised an eyebrow, visibly unimpressed by his performance. "Tom," he said with considerable emphasis, as if his patience were being strained to breaking point, "I saw Janet on Monday. She came right out with it – asked me if I knew when you were coming home. I said I didn't. Now if you don't think that's an invitation to go down to Munro's tomorrow and tell her that you're back, I don't know what is."

The sound of Duncan's Land Rover coming up the track cut short any further discussion, and Tom was left quietly seething, unable to press his case further.

"Hi, Tom!" Duncan said cheerily, unaware of the atmosphere he had blundered into. "Rob didn't think you'd be back yet."

"I didn't expect to be."

"You won't be needing me tonight then, Rob?"

"Oh I wouldn't say that, Duncan," Robert said, slapping Tom on the back with unnecessary bonhomie. "He's had a long drive, and he'll be fit for nothing if he's up all night," adding almost wilfully, to Tom's way of thinking, "I need him up early tomorrow morning. He's going down to Munro's for me."

Duncan paused from unloading his gear from the car and glanced at Tom, looking for a moment as if he were about to say something before thinking better of it.

"Come and join us for supper, Duncan," Robert was saying, maintaining an air of joviality. "Sarah's making us a grand stew."

Duncan brightened up. "Ah man, I wouldn't say no to some of Sarah's stew," he said enthusiastically.

Too rattled by Robert's conniving to be cooped up making polite conversation, Tom excused himself to check on progress in the lambing shed.

When he finally came into the kitchen, the others were already seated at the table. For a brief moment he had a strange sense of disorientation – or something akin to it he could not put a name to. It was a familiar, yet strangely alien scene: Robert at his usual place, a young man to his left – who wasn't Jamie; and serving up the meal, a young woman – who was neither Flora, nor his mother. He sat down feeling himself slipping inexorably out of sight, invisible to those around him. And the oddest notion came into his head – that if he were ever to leave Rigg End, Robert might not be on his own after all.

"So, after Tom and I talked it over," he heard Robert saying, "we agreed it made sense to offer you the place as a workshop – if you wanted it, that is."

Duncan looked like a small boy who had been given a much-wanted Christmas present. "Aye, I would!" he said, grinning like a Cheshire Cat. "And don't think I'll take it for free and gratis like," he added earnestly. "If I make a go of it, I'll pay rent. And if I don't, you'll have free labour out of me, I can promise you that."

Robert offered his hand across the table and Duncan shook it. The deal was struck.

After supper, Duncan helped Sarah clear away the dishes while Robert and Tom went out to check up on the cow.

She ignored them watching her, nuzzling each of her calves in turn, her long rasping tongue lovingly raking across their backs as they suckled.

"She's doing better than I expected," Robert said reflectively, turning from leaning on the gate to put his arm across Tom's shoulder. "You were very quiet over supper, Tom."

There was no point in raking over previous irritation, or giving voice to his strange sense of dislocation. "I'm tired, that's all," he said, prepared to think there might be some truth in this. "I'll be fine after a few hours' sleep."

"You're not still angry with me? – over Janet?"

"No," he said, although he was.

"You'll go down to Munro's then?"

Tom nodded.

"Make the most of it, Tom."

"I know, Dad – I may not get a second chance."

Robert patted him on the shoulder. "Right then, get yourself off. See you tomorrow."

Tom left him to his vigil watching over the cow and went up to bed, his head full of contradictions wondering what he could possibly say to Janet that had not already been said.

Chapter Twenty

Geraldine, wrapped up in her mohair scarf against a sudden change in the March weather, was engrossed in watching the world go by as John drove her from Little Retton to Michael's home in the fashionable part of Kinnerswood, its individually designed 1930s' properties a pleasing mix of wet-dash and reddish-brown brick. Her pleasure at these all too brief excursions was almost tangible. At regular intervals, she would turn and smile at him, her face filled with delight at the prospect of the afternoon ahead.

Barely twenty minutes later they had arrived at Upton Drive where Michael and Caroline were already waiting for them.

"Come on in, Geraldine. It's cold," urged Caroline as she rushed forward to help her out of the car. And linking arms, they hurried like a pair of giggling schoolgirls towards the porch and the waiting trio of excited granddaughters. "Lovely to see you again, John," Caroline called back to him over her shoulder. The girls waved to him briefly, their attention quickly diverted by their eagerness to tell Geraldine their news.

Michael sauntered down the path to meet him. "We're

in the minority," he said with a wry smile in the direction of the departing womenfolk. "Too many females of the species. Do you fancy lying low in my den for a while? There'll be no place for us mere men in the conservatory once the women get going. I'll get us some coffee."

The den summed up Michael's world: bookshelves crammed with reference works on nutrition, social histories and geopolitical topics; a small work desk with a word processor and a collection of open books haphazardly piled on top of one another vying for the limited space available.

"Another project?" John asked, settling into the armchair provided for visitors in the corner of the room.

Michael handed him a large mug of coffee and perched himself on his swivel chair, surveying the apparent chaos on his desk. "My team's setting up an educational programme for other healthcare professionals," he said casually. "The effects of poor nutrition – they often get overlooked in diagnosis and care of patients. Caroline did something similar last year for the immigrants referred to Langton Clinic."

John felt he should be impressed.

From beyond the door into the conservatory came the sound of women's talk and ready laughter.

Michael glanced over his shoulder in their direction. "I'm very grateful, John," he said, apparently embarrassed by having to mention this. "These visits mean a lot to everyone. Makes me feel as guilty as hell I can't do anything to organise them myself."

"Glad to help out," John said, conscious he could have

driven Geraldine over far more often if his self-absorption had been less, and his awareness of others' needs more finely tuned.

"How is the old man?" Michael was asking, perhaps more out of habit than affection.

"Much the same."

"Does he know you bring Geraldine here?"

"No – I just tell him I'm taking her out for a spin. He can understand that. Keeps him happy. Besides, now he's got Kenneth to help chew the fat over old times, he's in his element. I doubt he'll remember she's been out five minutes after we get back."

Kenneth had been a godsend to Geraldine: a willing listener provided by the local veterans' association; a man who had seen war service himself in the RAF and survived unscathed physically and mentally, but who understood the trauma of those less fortunate. His cheerful disposition, mischievous sense of humour, and calm unflappability in difficult situations, had helped Geraldine reconcile her notion of continuing to do the right thing by her husband with her increasing desire to see her younger son and his family.

"I'm worried about her, John. How much longer before he gets too much to handle?"

"Difficult to tell. He seems fairly stable at the moment. What he's like when I'm not there of course, I can't say. But you know our mother – determined – not given to histrionics, even under duress."

"She's a saint."

"She'd not thank you for saying so."

"Does she talk about the future?"

John shook his head. "She won't hear of him going into a home. I get short shrift if I suggest it. She says he has good days when he's fine. I don't see much evidence of it, but who knows? Maybe that's the man she wants to hang on to. The man she loved." He considered his half-drunk mug of coffee. It was easy enough to put himself in her place, knowing as he did how love can make someone seem irrational as far as the rest of the world was concerned.

Another peel of laughter from the conservatory made him turn to look through the door. Geraldine was telling a story. Her granddaughters were enthralled: Megan, almost a woman at fourteen, sitting on the edge of her seat; Josie, two years younger, less poised, all legs and arms like a young filly, sprawled on a bean bag; and Daisy, the baby of the three, not quite ten, eyes like saucers as she listened, curled up in the corner of the wicker sofa hugging a cushion.

Caroline, relaxed and smiling next to Geraldine, saw John watching them. She raised an eyebrow and he smiled back, acknowledging his eavesdropping. She was a lovely woman, he thought. Not just in the way she looked, although that afternoon she looked particularly fine, her dark hair piled up into a loose bun on the top of her head, accentuating the curve of her slender neck. She was intelligent and witty; generous and loving; a professional woman in her own right, and Michael had been cheerfully and lastingly besotted all their married life.

Perhaps being besotted was a trait that he and Michael

shared, inherited from Geraldine: in her case a crusty old man who had once been dashing, charming, and capable of great bravery; in her sons', their separate attachment to determined young women who decided their own future and were willing to share it with someone whom they loved. Caroline Saunders had seen her future with Michael Rufford. Laura Driscoll had chosen Robert Moray.

If things had been different, John could imagine a life where Geraldine – and Charles for that matter – had come to visit him in Lower Chursley, or wherever he had finally settled with Laura, Thomas – and who knew how many other children they might have had together? He could envisage a new home with expansive lawns, mature trees – a sturdy oak perhaps, or a horse chestnut for conkers – a swing, or even a tree-house with a rope ladder. There would be gatherings of family and friends on the patio on warm summer evenings; weekends with Michael, Caroline and the girls ...

"John?"

He looked up.

Michael was frowning at him. "You were miles away," he said.

"Sorry – just thinking."

"I could see that. Something you want to share?"

John shook his head and finished the coffee, dismissing his inattention as something of no importance.

"The old man been on at you again?"

"Oh – he's always on at me. Nothing new there. Wouldn't be a visit to Sylvans without him taking a swipe at me, would it?"

Michael found a space on his cluttered desk and put down his empty mug. "I'm sorry about Laura," he said quietly. "Geraldine told me when she rang last week. I know how much she meant to you."

"She still does."

Michael gave him a sad smile.

"I know you think I'm off my rocker – but that's how it is."

"I'd probably feel the same if I lost Caroline."

A burst of animated conversation from the conservatory interrupted them.

"Did Geraldine say anything else?" John asked. He wondered if she had.

Michael frowned, mulling over the question. "No," he said. "Was there something else?"

In the pause that followed, John listened to the regular bump of his heart quicken a little. "Yes, there was actually," he heard himself say in an almost nonchalant manner. "Something quite extraordinary."

Michael was patiently waiting to be enlightened.

Unexpectedly, John experienced a burst of joy bubble up inside him, like the surge of emotion triggered by an exquisite piece of music – or by the sight of a heron at the mere.

"Well? Don't keep me in suspense, John."

"I have a son," he said, hearing the unintentional triumph in his voice. "A grown-up son I never knew I had."

Michael just looked at him. "Are you joking?" he said.

"Would I joke about something as serious as that?"

"No – of course not – stupid of me."

"It's true, Michael – I have a son."

"When did you find out?"

"The day of Laura's funeral. I met him – briefly."

"Does *he* know who you are?"

"No, and his 'father' made it very clear that's the way it had to stay."

Michael frowned. "You're sure he's yours?"

The image of the boy sprang into John's mind, pin sharp. "Oh, he's mine all right – the spitting image of you and me at his age."

"So, what happens now?"

"Nothing."

"Nothing!" Michael glanced anxiously over his shoulder perhaps fearing his exclamation had been heard in the conservatory. "Are you out of your mind?" he went on, reduced to speaking in an exaggerated stage whisper. "It's what Charles always wanted – a grandson! He'll be over the moon –"

"Michael, how can I tell him? He's never going to see him."

"Can't you do *something*?"

"Don't you think I want to?"

The door from the conservatory opened, and Caroline came in still laughing. "Geraldine's been telling the girls all about her escapades at school," she said. "I thought I'd better leave her to it." Her merriment faded, sensing the tension in the room. "I'm sorry – have I interrupted something?"

Michael shrugged, and glanced in John's direction, not knowing what to say.

John felt strangely liberated. "I was telling Michael my news," he said, watching her reaction in a detached sort of way he found oddly agreeable. "I've a grown-up son I never knew I had."

She paused, perching herself on the arm of Michael's chair, all trace of laughter draining from her face. "I see," she said very quietly.

Michael looked up at her with a strained smile. "Geraldine knows," he told her. "We were just discussing the impossibility of telling Charles."

She nodded understandingly. "Is he Laura's?" she asked.

"He is."

She apparently expected this. "Where is he?"

"On the farm in Northumberland."

"With the man she married?"

"Yes."

"Does the boy know you're his father?"

"No. And I'm afraid that's the way it has to stay. He has a brother and sister – or rather a half-brother and sister."

"How sad," she said after a moment's reflection. "He has another family he doesn't know exists."

"It's not my place to tell him."

"No, perhaps not."

"It's what comes of sowing wild oats," he added, trying to sound philosophical. "There's a price to pay."

"Yes," she said softly. "There always is."

For a moment, no one spoke and a strange stillness settled on the room.

"Well," Caroline said at last, getting to her feet, "I

promised Geraldine some tea before you took her home. She'll be wondering what I've been up to all this time."

Michael waited until she had gone. "Is there really nothing you can do, John?" he asked.

"At two in the morning, I toy with the idea of jumping into the car and heading off up the motorway. I don't, of course. I can't just go blundering into someone else's life like that. If there was an easy way to do it, believe me, Michael, I would. He's my son." Even the word left an ache.

"You've already lost so much time together. It seems wrong somehow."

"Oh – it's about more than that, Michael. I want him to know how much I loved his mother. I think that's important – because I did, you know that – with all my heart and soul. I think that matters."

Michael nodded, agreeing with him.

On the journey home, Geraldine, observant as always, noticed his lack of conversation. "Did you tell them?" she asked. "About your boy?"

"Yes. Do you disapprove?"

"Goodness, John, why should I? He could turn up on our doorsteps next week, and then where would we all be?"

He laughed at such a notion.

"Oh, you can laugh, John. But what if he did? What if his 'father' decided to tell him the truth?"

The memory of Robert Moray standing guard in front of his house that cold November day was still painfully clear. "Unlikely, I'm afraid."

"Well – you never know," she said, turning her attention

to the view of familiar places on the outskirts of Little Retton as they passed. "Life's full of surprises – good and bad."

"And what would we tell Charles if he did?"

She frowned for a moment and shrugged off the problem. "We'd have to deal with it the best we could, wouldn't we? We'd think of something."

"I admire your confidence, Mother."

"I'm not in the least bit confident, John, but if I can learn to live with the Battle of Britain on a daily basis – and all the other muddles in your father's head – I'd like to think I had the strength to deal with something as important as a visit from our grandson."

"I've no doubt you'd deal with it admirably – but I can't imagine Charles understanding any of it. He'd just get angry and confused."

"Who knows, John. It would be just like Charles to be contrary – take it in his stride and confound us all." She smiled briefly and turned away.

When they arrived back at Sylvans, Kenneth opened the door to them, beaming broadly. "Had a nice afternoon?" he asked as John helped Geraldine out of the car.

"Lovely, thank you. And you?"

"Not bad at all," he said cheerfully. "We've just come back from a difficult mission over the Channel Ports, you know. Bombing barges again. We get better at it every time!"

From inside the house, the brusque tones of Squadron Leader Rufford demanded to know why the front door had been left open yet again.

CHAPTER TWENTY-ONE

Tom walked the twenty new Blackface hoggs up the track to the clean pasture of the six-acre field high up on The Rigg and closed the gate behind them. With Brack at his feet, he leaned against the metal bars, watching them fan out across the breast of the hill exploring their new home stopping now and then to nibble the fresh grass. They were a fine flock.

The hazy September sun was warm on his back. It felt good and he slipped effortlessly into a reflective mood.

The spring and summer had slid past, days blending into weeks, then months of hard, unremitting work. There had been successes and failures, triumphs and tragedies – two sides of the same coin in any stockman's life.

Lambing had gone better than usual despite the cold snap at the end of March. None of the lambs had needed bottle feeding – a round-the-clock ritual that could leave a man asleep on his feet. No, he could not complain. Most of the ewes had dropped sturdy twins, and the few with singletons or stillborns had successfully fostered orphans or the occasional unwanted triplet.

Robert had seen a couple of the early calves fail to thrive, but that was all, and only that week, he had sold off half-a-dozen stirks over at Drumlinfield, and got a good price for them. Things could have been worse, and Ralph Milburn was pleased enough to say the balance sheet wasn't looking too bad at all for the time of year.

April had been unseasonably cool and wet, and one of the owlets in the barn had died. But May had seen a sudden burst of warm, sunny days. Tom had moved the sheep up onto The Rigg to give the home fields a rest, and the cows had been moved out of the hemmel onto one of the lower pastures by the river. Almost overnight, the larch trees behind the farm had been stippled in brilliant green and the verges in the lane filled with bluebells, lady's smock and crane's bill. A year ago, Tom thought, his mother would have painted them.

The house martins and swallows returned, setting up home in the sheds as usual, swooping and twittering between the buildings with giddying speed, filling the lengthening twilight with aerial displays. Down in the valley there was silaging and haymaking, the lanes filled with tractors and trailers from morning to night, and now the barn was full, ready for winter.

June saw the start of the annual round of shearing sheep, with its back-breaking days and the camaraderie of neighbour helping neighbour with the compensation of strong liquor of an evening to help dull aches and pains, and the prospect of bagging £2 a fleece. Good days, followed by sheep dipping and selecting lambs for fatstock marts, and heifers and bullocks to sell on, and the start of the regular round of agricultural shows in August with the chance to bring home a rosette or two. Over at Ayburn, Tom and Brack had pipped Eric Bell and Minty at the sheepdog trials, and Robert had come away from Drumlinfield with the Limousin Champion's Cup for Rigg End Rosie, snatching victory from Jarred Liddel's Hopeslaw Honeysuckle. All in all, not a bad year for Robert and himself.

Elsewhere, Tom reflected, it had been a summer of change. Some good – some bad.

In far-off Poland, Solidarity had triumphed. In China, a solitary student had outfaced an army tank in Tiananmen Square.

Closer to home, equally momentous events had taken place. In June, Becky Elliott had moved back to Rattling Gate with little Kylie, barely three years old. It was common knowledge her Jimmy had taken up with a young lass barely out of school that spring and put her in the family way. Becky took out her bitterness on everyone. Most evenings, Wallace was up at The Gate staring into his beer, wondering why life was so complicated while Mary tried to keep the peace back home. But Sarah, compliant and placid, had become an easy target for her sister's pent up rage.

At High Oakbank, Ian and Bridie had moved out to Oakbank Cottage leaving Ross and Liz to run the farm, and Liz was expecting another baby some time in the New Year. Without making much of it, Duncan had moved out into a one-bedroomed cottage down at Birks Farm and seemed content enough. Most days, he was up at Rigg End in the old studio, wood turning, drilling and sanding to the accompaniment of Tina Turner or Whitney Houston – not always welcome to Tom's ears – but it would have been churlish to complain: Duncan was always ready to lend a hand whenever he was needed.

By mid-summer, the bunkhouse had been given the green light from the Tourist Board and opened its doors to ramblers walking the Tourist Trail along the Wall. The slow trickle had become a steady stream, needing someone on hand to welcome visitors. At first, Chrissie Dixon had come up to run the place. But then Jackie took a nasty fall, and Chrissie had to leave to nurse him. Sarah had taken the bull by the horns. "I could run the bunkhouse over summer, if you like," she had offered.

"Life's not much fun at home for her these days," Robert had said when they had talked it over. "We could make one of the storerooms a bed-sit for her." So they had, although Tom had reservations. So here, away from the main house – and free from any perceived impropriety on Mary's part that her daughter was 'living-in' – Sarah had installed herself with a few possessions brought from home and some of Duncan's handmade furniture. Tom could not complain: Sarah ran both the bunkhouse and Rigg End with exemplary efficiency. She took bookings; welcomed guests; ensured everywhere was spick-and-span; kept careful accounts; cooked meals; dealt with all the laundry, and made herself indispensable.

That summer, Rigg End had come to life again. When the evenings were fine, Tom would find Robert in the yard, sitting on the wooden seat Duncan had made for him, smoking his pipe, watching the swallows and house martins swooping overhead, silently contemplating the changes going on around him. Some were nearer to his heart than others.

Like the young swallows and house martins, Jamie and Flora had flown the nest.

Jamie's visits were rare, and phone calls only brief affairs. Edinburgh and the prospect of his new career filled his life. He had found a flat in Leith and could talk of little else. Other things were on his mind as well – his youngest cousin, Lesley, twenty-two and working in an old bookshop not far from the Academy, had caught his eye and captured his heart.

Flora too was rarely seen, promising to come, then crying off without much warning. Something unexpected had turned up. No doubt it had, but Tom could see her willingness to disappoint her father often left him deeply hurt. She had gone from college to London barely pausing for breath, sharing a basement flat with two other girls, caught up in the dizzying, crowded world of the metropolis far removed from the wild and lonely places of the North. There was a boyfriend – and then another – as she flitted recklessly between the two.

At the end of July, she had come home briefly to celebrate her twenty-first. Jamie had come home too but not for long, off touring Greece before the start of term.

They were different people now: Jamie no longer the bedraggled student, but a smart young man, transformed into what he would become – the Classics master with a position to uphold; Flora, quite the opposite, the style and colour of her hair bizarre; her choice of clothes bewildering and often garish.

They had become strangers: independent; the focus of their lives elsewhere; their mother's death receding in their thoughts and growing fainter all the time. As autumn loomed, Robert's brooding silences were something they ignored and never mentioned. Better not to ask what troubled him. They were flying now, and wanted nothing that might bring them down to earth.

Even Sarah noticed. "Don't they see how sad he is when they're in such a rush to go?" she had asked Tom, and he had excused their lack of interest because he understood: time and distance had opened up a gulf that none knew how to bridge. Perhaps it was unbridgable. Robert's intensity was often hard to bear and after they had left, he would retreat into a world of silence for days on end, leaving Sarah even more perplexed. "I don't understand, Tom," she would say, with that little troubled frown of hers. "He still has you."

And Tom remembered saying nothing, racked by such an innocent remark, knowing he was part of Robert's sense of loneliness and loss.

Now summer was almost gone, rowan berries a gaudy red and the barley in the lower fields a rippling golden sea. In the lanes between the purpling brambles, stinging nettles thrived, catching the fingers of unwary foragers. And in the woods, fungi sprouted from fallen timber and sprang up in exotic shapes and colours. Late afternoons were filled with house martins and swallows circling above the yard in twittering family groups, preparing to travel south to warmer climes. And in the twilight, bats came out to hunt, flitting erratically across the darkening sky as the evenings drew in. Autumn, with all its sombre memories, was hovering in early morning mists.

A light breeze rustled the drying grasses by the gate. Brack whined softly and stood up, eager for home. "Not yet," Tom said, enjoying the solid weight of the dog against his leg, and the heat of the sun still warm across his back.

For him, the passing year had brought little time to stop and think. Extra chores had come his way with walkers on the farm. He and Brack had walked many miles that summer, monitoring gates that should be closed; checking stiles for wear and tear; putting signs in place advising dogs must be on kept on leads. And most nights after supper, weariness had summoned him to bed before the light had left the sky. There had been little time or energy to ponder how things might have turned out if he had stayed away for longer back in March. But he had come home, heartsick and homesick – and was glad he had. There was no urgent need to travel south again. Mr Warburton had found new tenants for the Lodge who seemed very keen to stay. And the lovely Sophie Gorst had written saying she was off to Italy for the summer, but hoped their paths would cross again. He had not written back but she sent him several glossy postcards promising to write with all her news when she returned. She never did and he put her from his mind.

But other matters were less easy to resolve: John Rufford was one; Janet Robson the other.

Rufford had become the unwelcome ghost that came to haunt him every morning when he shaved; and Janet's absence was an abiding ache that refused to be dislodged, his memory of her still as sharp as on that wild, wet day in March when last they met.

He had driven down to Wallbridge torn between the desire to see her and the strong conviction he should not. They had said their last goodbyes. He should have left it at that.

Instead, he had walked across the town heedless of the pelting rain and arrived outside Munro's with his hair plastered to his face. For a moment he had contemplated turning round and going home. Nothing would be lost if he did, he had convinced himself, except the moment passed. He had opened the door; she had risen to meet him; and he had looked into her eyes – clear, green eyes that spoke of just how much he meant to her – and he had felt the jolt in his chest echo in his head. "I've come for the drench," he had said, feeling daft because he had intended saying something else much closer to his heart. But the waiting room was full and everyone was watching them.

She had smiled faintly, saying for anyone to hear, "Sam said you'd be coming down for it," adding quietly, "I'm glad you came. I hoped you would." And she had looked so beautiful it had caught him unawares.

He had reached out for the container, putting his hand on hers, and she had smiled. A dog had started howling miserably so that no one overheard him when he asked, "Promise you'll write – when you're settled."

She had nodded, implying that she would.

Releasing her hand quickly, he had picked up the container and gone out into the slanting rain, the blood roaring in his head.

No letter ever came, and Duncan had been strangely vague whenever he was asked about her. She was never anywhere for long, he said.

Perhaps that was why she never wrote. But Tom wished with all his heart and soul she had.

CHAPTER TWENTY-TWO

Duncan was leaning over the gate watching Tom checking the straps on the harness for the Blue-faced Leicester tup standing defiantly on the far side of the pen. "I could help with him, if you like," he offered.

"You're not busy then?"

Duncan shrugged. "Not in the mood," he said.

"You can swing him over for me," Tom suggested.

"Playing up, is he?"

"Can't wait to get at 'em," Tom said with a nod in the direction of the first batch of Swaledale ewes grazing on the lush grass of the home field. He had brought them down from The Rigg a couple of weeks before and now they were in prime condition for mating.

Duncan climbed over the gate and cornered the tup while its attention was fixed on Tom. He hauled it over onto its back and held it steady with his legs while Tom fixed the harness in place. The beast looked indignant.

"So what's wrong?" Tom asked as he fixed the green raddle to the harness on the tup's chest. There had to be something wrong to bring Duncan out from his workshop so early.

Duncan shrugged again. His head was bent over the tup and the morning sunlight on his red hair made it several shades lighter – more like his sister's, Tom thought, letting his mind wander for a moment.

With the job done, Tom opened the gate into the home field and Duncan swung the beast back onto its feet. "Hey-up!" he said, giving the tup a hearty thwack on the rear to send it on its way.

Several ewes lifted their heads at the commotion and turned their smudged charcoal faces in the direction of the tup, registering his presence. They inspected their prospective mate and his considerable possibilities with unblinking interest. He was a fine fellow. By the next day, most, if not all of them, would have the tell-tale green markings on their rumps showing just how much he had impressed them.

Tom closed the gate, watching the tup take stock of his harem while he waited for Duncan to join him. He had a good idea what was troubling him.

Over the summer, Tom had watched Duncan's attempts to attach himself to Sarah with the mild curiosity of a casual bystander watching a boisterous young puppy continually getting slapped down for disobedience.

From the moment Duncan set up his workshop at Rigg End, he had made himself available whenever Sarah needed help, no matter how busy he was himself. His endeavours to make her little room in the bunkhouse as comfortable as possible were clearly labours of love, not easily overlooked. Except Sarah seemed to overlook them as signs of his devotion. It was not that she was unappreciative, but she never said or did anything to encourage him in any way. Attraction was fickle, Tom reflected, letting his mind drift back to Donna Burdon for a moment and her extraordinary sensuality despite her plain, peasant face.

Duncan began idly scuffing the bottom bar of the gate with his foot. "I thought like," he began hesitantly, screwing up his face in puzzlement, "that when you and Sarah – you know – didn't make a go of things, maybe she'd take up with me. But she doesn't seem interested."

"Maybe you're trying too hard," was all Tom could think of as a possible suggestion. "Come on up to The Gate tonight after supper. I'll buy you a pint."

"Aye, all right then."

There was a women's darts match in full swing when they arrived – Whinrigg versus Ayburn Ladies – and most of the regulars were crowded into the games area, barracking or supporting the contestants, according to fancy. The air was thick with smoke and raucous commentary.

Archie Ramsey, landlord of The Gate, was busy keeping his customers well supplied. "Here for the darts?" he asked Tom as he paid for the drinks.

"No – just brought Duncan up for a pint."

"You may as well join Willie, then. He's over in his usual corner."

In the far pew tucked away from the noisy distractions, Willie Robertson was watching proceedings over the top of his glass. "Expecting anyone?" Tom asked: it was always better to check whether Willie had some business in hand.

"No, man – you can join me if yuh like."

They settled in the pew opposite him, no one in a hurry to start a conversation. Willie was never one for talking unless there was some point to it. He was a well-built, swarthy man, with piercingly dark eyes under a mop of thick black dishevelled hair. He lived somewhere up beyond Ayburn, but no one seemed to know precisely where, and he had connections with wheeler-dealers all along the Border. He was fiercely loyal to his friends, but not a man to cross. Some said he had Traveller blood. He certainly had a way with horses, knew how to trade in sheep, made some of his living from gambling, and knew how to fight. But after drinking copious amounts of ale, he was known to play the Northumbrian pipes with such a melancholy air, he could reduce even an audience of the roughest men to tears.

Someone threw a triple and loud cheering drowned out the groans of the opposing side.

Willie leaned across the table and touched Duncan's arm. "Ah hear yer doin' a bit o' furniture mekkin' down at Rigg End," he said in a low voice, implying this was something not to be discussed too loudly. "Ah've tekkin' on one o' Tommy Ridley's sheds o'er Ayburn way fer a spell like – doin' up furniture an' things mysel'. Yuh might o' heard."

Duncan nodded. Willie probably had other irons in the fire, but it was better not to ask.

Willie took a long draught of his beer, making sure he had Duncan's full attention. "If yuh let me have some o' yor frames like," he suggested, his gaze never wavering for an instant, "ah could put some grand rush seats in fer yuh. What d'yuh say?"

Duncan thought for a moment and they shook hands on it.

"Come o'er on Saturday then," Willie said, downing the rest of his beer.

Duncan said he would.

Noiselessly, Willie rose from his seat. "Ah'll be goin' then," he said, and with the elusiveness of a shadow, he left.

"He'll do a good job for you," Tom said. "Did Harry and Maggie Fenwick's kitchen chairs for them a couple of weeks back. They're good as new now."

Duncan continued drinking his beer with slow deliberation. "Aye – well," he said, "Going over to Willie's place'll keep me out of Sarah's way for a while. Maybe she'll start missing having me around."

Tom thought it was wise to say nothing.

Duncan's absence that Saturday morning coincided with Tom's decision to strip down the engine in the old tractor, and Sarah's determination to enter her six jars of bramble jelly in the Stanegate Autumn Fayre. She had never entered anything before, but perhaps because she felt more independent and self-confident at Rigg End, she had decided she would make her mark.

The Fayre was the one annual event guaranteed to bring out the competitive spirit in everyone for miles around, from the usually mild-mannered Reverend Hespin of St Oswald's, known for his bee-keeping and heather honey, to the stalwart members of the Ayburn, Stanegate and Whinrigg Gardening

Club, with their giant onions and marrows, and the W.I., famed for their decorative flower arrangements, jams and cakes. Winning mattered, and Sarah suddenly wanted to be one of the winners – except her trusty old car chose that Saturday of all days to let her down.

In his oil-stained overalls, his head under the tractor bonnet and grease half way up to his elbows, Tom could hear the dry, uncommunicative cough-cough-coughing of a car engine refusing to burst into life.

"Tom!" he heard her call out plaintively. "Tom! It won't start." He looked across the yard. Her face was the picture of agonised frustration.

A brief glance at the indicator panel revealed the problem. "Your battery's flat," he said, aware as soon as he pronounced this verdict, he should offer to give her a lift up to the village hall. Except that by the time he had scrubbed up and changed, she would probably miss the deadline for competition entries – or at least that was what he told himself at the time. The true reason was less gallant: he wanted to spend the afternoon at High Oakbank with Ross, and the sooner he finished the work on the tractor the better.

Robert appeared at the back porch wearing his reading spectacles, apparently awaiting an explanation for the disturbance of his peace. He had been in one of his silent moods all morning, retreating into fatstock prices from which he refused to be drawn, despite Sarah's best endeavours.

"Battery's dead," Tom called across to him. "Can you run Sarah up to Stanegate, Dad? I've not got time to change."

For months afterwards, Tom wondered if his unwillingness to help lay at the heart of everything that followed. Perhaps not. Consequences stem from the conjunction of several purely random events. But the thought dogged him all the same.

It was much later, as dusk was falling, he got back from High Oakbank after a pleasant afternoon's crack and a glass of beer. He felt generally benevolent towards his fellow creatures, and had worked up an appetite doing nothing in particular.

As he closed the kitchen door, he could sense the tension in the room. "Sorry I'm late," he said, although he knew he wasn't.

Sarah, swathed in her apron, was silently stirring the gravy on top of the range. She did not look round.

Robert was sitting, his forearms on the table, his concentration fixed on the empty space between his knife and fork. His mouth was set hard and he was visibly seething.

No one spoke.

Not sure what to make of things, Tom scrubbed up and sat down at his usual place. "How did it go?" he asked, trying hard to sound cheerful. "With the bramble jelly?"

Sarah turned briefly, smiling nervously. "Oh," she said. "I got First Prize."

"Hey – well done!"

She acknowledged this with a slight bob of the head.

Robert remained glaring at the table, his rage undiminished.

"Much competition?" Tom persisted.

Sarah nodded. "A few," she said, glancing quickly in Robert's direction.

It was impossible to ignore Robert's silence any longer. "You all right, Dad?"

Robert looked up fiercely. "Why shouldn't I be?" he demanded in a tone that clearly indicated he did not require an answer.

Silence descended again.

Tom sensed Robert was censuring him for putting his own interests before everyone else's. He felt uncomfortable. Yes, he should have made the effort and taken Sarah to the Fayre; he should not have off-loaded the responsibility onto Robert and obliged him to spend his whole afternoon making polite conversation, rather than sitting in his comfortable kitchen chair reading the *Farmers' Gazette*. Sarah's success with her bramble jelly had evidently been of little consolation for all those wasted hours as far as Robert was concerned.

The meal began and continued in an uneasy silence.

Tom could stand it no longer. "Ross was saying he's thinking of buying a bull," he said, surprised to find his voice louder than he intended it. "From the Sinclair place in Scotland," he added, dropping the volume a couple of notches. "Has he mentioned it?"

Robert made no effort to look up from his roast beef. "Yes, he mentioned it."

"Said you were thinking of going halves with him if he goes ahead."

A long pause. "I might."

Tom tried to catch Sarah's eye, but failed. She cleared away the plates, served up the steamed pudding, ate her portion very quickly and set about tidying everything away.

Robert finished eating and stood up, scraping his chair against the floor. "I'm off to bed," he announced, although it was barely eight-thirty. "Goodnight," he said, nodding briefly to Sarah. The door closed behind him and Tom heard his footsteps heavy on the stairs.

He turned to Sarah. "What's wrong?" he asked. "Something's wrong."

She shook her head. "Oh, don't ask, Tom, please."

He persisted. "If he blames me for not taking you to the Fayre, he should say so," he said, feeling he should make amends any way he could. "I don't want him taking his bad moods out on you."

She bit her lip and turned away, hastily stacking the last few plates in the drainer.

"I'm sorry," he said, determined to set things right with her. "I should have made the effort." He put a hand on her shoulder to prove he meant what he said.

She pulled away from him quickly, looking anxious. "If you don't mind, Tom, I think I'll turn in now too. Lots to do tomorrow."

"Right – yes, of course," he said, and he was left standing alone in the kitchen feeling he had managed to wreck a perfectly good day for everyone.

Over Sunday there was little improvement in the atmosphere, Sarah keeping to herself in the bunkhouse after meals; Robert remaining tight-lipped and uncommunicative. Tired of trying to make amends without getting anywhere, Tom took himself off the farm and went down to Aitket Bank to spend some time with Harry and Maggie Fenwick, who were always pleased to see him.

On Monday morning, Duncan arrived early. He beckoned Tom into the workshop. "Aw man," he said, visibly agitated. "Have you heard what happened up at the Fayre on Saturday?"

Tom could honestly say he had not.

"Aw – there was a load of trouble. I couldn't believe what I heard like. I was up at The Gate with Willie last night – and everyone was talking about it."

Tom waited to be enlightened.

Duncan's agitation extended to include several chair legs he had left to one side ready for sanding that morning: he seemed unable to decide which one to start on first.

"Come on, Duncan – out with it. What happened?"

Duncan finally selected one of the legs and began sanding it vigorously. He shook his head over what he was about to say. "Becky Elliott, Tom," he said, blowing out his cheeks in disbelief. "They said she'd turned up at the Fayre – right out of it. Been drinking cider all afternoon. Started shouting her mouth off – saying things."

"What things?"

"About what goes on up here like – between you, me and Sarah." His sanding had suddenly become even more vigorous.

Tom heard himself give a strangled laugh.

"Aye, well you can laugh Tom Moray, but it's not funny. She said Sarah Armstrong could get a first prize for a lot more than her bramble jelly up at Rigg End."

"What!"

"Aw, I won't say what else she said, but it'll be all round the neighbourhood by now, I can tell you that."

Tom was too busy coming to terms with Becky's nonsense to take on board the likely consequences. "Oh, come on, Duncan – who's going to believe her?"

Duncan turned his attention to a second leg. "Some folk'll believe anything," he said, turning red under his freckles, his moral outrage spreading down across his neck. "Not much you and me can do about that is there? We're all tarred with the same brush now."

Tom sensed something dreadful had happened but could not quite put his finger on what it was: it was more than just the accusation, or the possible consequences; it was what might lie beyond.

"Well, I suppose we should be thankful for small mercies like," Duncan was saying, upending a chair frame and beginning to knock a leg into place. "Looks like Wallace got her away before your dad got wind of it."

Tom said nothing. He was in no doubt Robert knew precisely every last detail of what had been said: it explained the dreadful silences; Sarah keeping a low profile; Robert seething.

"Families, eh?" Duncan was saying between blows of the mallet. "Who'd have 'em?" And the mallet came down hard again.

Tom heard himself mumble something in agreement, while his thoughts wheeled off on their own. Had Becky given voice to Mary Armstrong's private fears? – that Sarah had left herself wide open to tittle-tattle when she'd come to stay at Rigg End? – that some folk, and not just Becky, would enjoy spicing up their gossip with that extra ounce of malice? One thing was certain, however false the allegations, Sarah would have to leave Rigg End – and sooner rather than later. Maybe Robert knew that too.

CHAPTER TWENTY-THREE

Tom could hear the blood swooshing in his ears. Given half the chance, he would have murdered Becky Elliott.

From the doorway of the back porch, he heard Robert calling. "Tom! Can you spare a minute?" His tone was brusque.

Reluctantly, Tom joined him in the kitchen, his thoughts still boiling in his brain.

"Sit down, Tom. We need to talk."

No need to ask what about, Tom thought.

Robert was sitting opposite him deep in thought, contemplating his hands clenched tightly together on the table in front of him. "You've heard what happened? – up at the Fayre?" he asked curtly.

"Just now – from Duncan."

"And where did he hear about it?"

"Up at The Gate – yesterday evening."

The muscles in Robert's jaw tightened into a visible knot. "I hope you don't think I believe any of Becky Elliott's nonsense?"

"No, of course not. But you've not exactly been easy to live with the last couple of days. I thought you were mad at me for not taking Sarah up to the Fayre."

"I'd have come straight out with it if I'd thought that. Has Duncan said anything to Sarah – about what he's heard?"

"I don't think so."

"Best if he didn't then. She's been upset enough already. It'll only set her off again. No point in doing that."

"I don't think he'd want to tell her – he's too keen on her."

"Then I'm sorry she doesn't feel the same."

It struck Tom as an odd comment, but he let it pass.

Whatever was on Robert's mind, he was in no hurry to share it for the moment. He went back to concentrating on his hands and very slowly prised them apart, placing them palms down on the table in front of him, the fingers splayed wide as if to keep something firmly in its place. "I've had to make a decision," he said, "About Sarah." His attention remained fixed on his hands.

Tom expected what he saw as inevitable. "She can't stay here, can she? Not now."

Robert looked up sharply. "What option has she got, Tom?" he asked, giving him a glacial stare. "She can't afford a place of her own. She can't go back to Rattling Gate – not with Becky there. What's she supposed to do?"

Tom could feel the hairs on the back of his neck prickling against his collar. He had no answer.

"No – there's only one honourable thing to do, Tom, and I've done it," Robert said, pausing briefly before making his announcement. "I've asked Sarah to marry me."

Tom was stunned into silence for a moment. "*Marry* you!" he heard himself say, unable to mask the incredulity in his voice: shock, disbelief, mockery even – all rolled into one. "And she said 'yes'?" He pushed back his chair and got up. Had Robert taken leave of his senses? Had Sarah?

Robert's expression was as cold as carved stone. "Why not?" he said defiantly. "It solves everything."

"Don't be daft, Dad. You can't *marry* her! She's too young – and she's – she's –" He bit his tongue. He had already said too much. "She's not right for you," he finished lamely.

Robert appeared unfazed by this observation. If anything, it seemed to strengthen his determination. "In what way, Tom?" he challenged him.

Tom hesitated, not knowing if he would regret what he was about to say – but he said it anyway. "She's not interested in what you need – what Mam gave you."

"A warm bed?" Robert asked bluntly. "Is that what you mean?"

"Well – yes." Christ! Surely he didn't want him to spell it out!

Robert leaned back in his chair and looked up at him. For the briefest of moments, Tom thought he saw something in Robert's eyes that registered not anger, or resentment, but pity. It was a profoundly uncomfortable sensation.

"I'm not too demanding these days, Tom. I'll suit her well enough. That's all I ask."

Tom heard himself give a derisive snort. He turned to leave. He did not want to hear the details. He just wanted to get out of the kitchen – out of the house.

From behind him, he heard Robert say in tones that demanded compliance. "Sit down, Tom. We need to discuss this."

"I don't want to discuss it, Dad."

"Then at least have the courtesy to hear me out."

They faced one another across the kitchen, an unexpected antagonism springing up between them.

Tom's mind was reeling: this was not supposed to happen.

"I'm under no illusions," Robert was saying, his words washing over Tom like a tidal wave. "I know everyone will say the same – that I'm too old for her. And I know this year's taken its toll – I'm not the man I used to be – the mirror tells me that. But –" He paused, seeking understanding, a softness beginning to smooth away the hard lines etched into his face, "this past summer, Tom – since she's been here, I've grown comfortable having her around. I'd miss her if she had to go, that's the truth of it. Do you understand?"

Tom had no idea if he did.

"Besides," Robert went on, ignoring Tom's silence, "I feel responsible for what's happened – asking her to come here in the first place."

"That's no reason to marry her!"

"It is in my book if I want her to stay – and I want her to stay." The old steely determination was firmly back in its place.

An impasse. Tom could feel his energy to continue the argument draining away. "Do you love her?" he asked, because he could barely believe it was possible.

Robert looked down for a moment, perhaps embarrassed to admit what his true feelings really were. "Not in the same way I loved your mother," he said. "I could never feel that way again about a woman. But I've grown fond of her, Tom – and she says she's fond of me."

"Is that enough? – to marry her?"

Robert reflected on this for a moment. "Yes – I believe it is," he said. "And she's a cheerful soul to have around the place," he added. "I'll need that in the months to come. She'll be the only one I can rely on to rescue me from these black moods that take me."

"Oh – I see," Tom said, aware he was raising his voice. "You don't think I can help you? Well, thanks a lot."

"Tom – Tom – don't be angry. I'm not saying that at all. I just can't go on pretending, even if you can."

"What do you mean, Dad?"

"I mean – when I look at you, I can't help seeing what I see. And the older you get – much as it hurts me to say it – the more you look like him. Sometimes I can't bear it, Tom. I'm back at Meeston Lodge – on the drive, seeing him standing there waiting for your mother, leaning against his car, confident, good looking, the world at his feet – a young buck turning to look at an older stag. It hurts – because I loved her and I love you like my own. But you're not mine, and sometimes that makes me feel worse. It's not your fault. I don't hold it against you. I love you too much."

There was a terrible silence.

Tom let that lie. How could he argue against the truth? "What about Jamie and Flora?" he asked. "You've still got them."

Robert shook his head. "When did we last see either of them?" he asked sadly.

Tom had to think hard to remember. "July – Flora's birthday."

Robert nodded: point made. "And when was the last time either of them phoned?"

Tom had no need to answer: there had been a deafening silence for weeks now.

"You've stuck it out here, Tom – over this summer. But I can't fool myself much longer. Sooner or later, you'll need to leave – even if it's only for a short time. I'm reconciled to that." He paused for a moment to master himself. "I know I'll find it hard without you. I found it hard in March. I didn't think I would. But I don't want you staying just on my account, do you understand? I'm starting again. I don't want to hold you back. Your father's out there, Tom, keeping his distance because I asked him to. You can't turn your back on him for ever."

Tom felt numb. Nothing had prepared him for this conversation and he stood mutely staring at the table trying to think rationally while Robert's words flowed round him and over him, and he felt he was drowning with nothing left to cling to.

"Penny for your thoughts," Robert was asking.

"Have you set a date?" It was all Tom could think of on the spur of the moment: a useful question without any sense of reality behind the words.

"Before the end of October. Nothing grand. The Registry Office in Wallbridge. Will you come? I won't press you, if you don't want to. I'd understand."

Tom nodded, wondering why he was prepared to acquiesce to something he so bitterly resented. "What about Jamie and Flora?" he asked.

"I'll tell them – after we're married – not before."

Tom had no energy left to argue. "They'll be upset," he warned. On reflection, he thought later, this might have been an understatement.

Robert appeared undeterred. "Oh, I'm sure they will," he said with a grim smile. "Maybe – for a day or two," he added. "But I daresay, given time, they'll be glad enough I've got Sarah to look after me. It'll take the trouble off their shoulders, and they can get on with their lives. That's what they want now." There was no bitterness in his tone, only a quiet resignation that his children had flown the nest and that he and Rigg End no longer figured very largely in their lives.

Tom felt profoundly sad. "Will Sarah really make you happy, Dad?" he asked, barely able to believe this was remotely possible.

"Maybe you should ask her yourself," Robert said with a faint smile.

Tom strode out into the yard wondering if he had lost his grip on reality. Anger had given way for the moment to confusion and muddled thinking. Robert and Sarah? Nothing made sense.

Brack came bounding out from the shed to greet him, tail up, ready for anything. Tom, his senses still reeling, sent him back with a curt, "No!"

The dog sank to the ground by the barn door, ears back, his head on his paws, looking the picture of misery. Tom turned away, in no mood to relent.

Outside the bunkhouse door, he paused before knocking. Behind him, from the direction of the workshop, he could hear the tap-tap-tapping of Duncan assembling another chair. His heart sank. Duncan would be deeply hurt when he heard the news.

Sarah did not answer immediately. When she finally opened the door, she stepped back defensively as if she were afraid he might barge past her in a rage.

"Can I come in?" he asked.

She looked nervous. "Yes – of course," she said, showing him in and offering him the wicker chair in the far corner. She hesitated before asking, "Would you like some tea?"

He said 'yes' out of politeness and found himself fidgeting waiting for the kettle to boil. The atmosphere seemed overcharged and liable to crackle and burst into flames at any moment.

The tea was made, but still nothing was said.

She handed him one of her floral china mugs, brimming almost to over-flowing, and retreated to the ladder-back chair behind the table, clutching her own mug in both hands like a shield. She was silent, waiting for him to speak.

He resolved he would not. Let her speak for herself, if she dared.

She was biting her lip. "You must be very angry," she said at last, her voice scarcely above a whisper.

He sipped at the tea. It was too hot to drink.

Her anxious eyes studied him over the rim of her mug. "I don't know what you must think."

"Does it matter what I think?" he asked, wrestling with a heady mix of emotions that was doing nothing to help the situation.

"Of course it matters. He's your dad."

Her innocence nearly undid him. It was all he could do just to ask her, "Do you care for him?"

She nodded.

"I shan't say the obvious then," although he did. "He's too old for you. Perhaps you think that let's you off the hook," he added, wishing afterwards he had not said it.

She frowned, evidently not sure what he was driving at.

He blundered on. "He's a passionate man, Sarah, whatever he might tell you. Will you be able to love him enough?" It was a brutal question, badly put. "You never gave me the impression you liked the idea of sex," he went on, aware he was treading on thin ice and yet quite unable to stop himself. Christ! – he thought, did he have to put it so bluntly?

She did not blink. In fact, there was a sudden fierceness about her he had never seen before. "I feel comfortable with him, Tom. I wasn't always comfortable with you." She was bold enough to look him straight in the eyes. "Sometimes – sometimes you were too much for me."

"Too much?" He had no idea what she was talking about.

"When you looked at me," she said, putting down her mug and struggling to find the right words. "You would get this 'look' on your face," she said. "I can't describe it – not exactly – but it would put me in a panic. I couldn't help it." She shrugged, evidently troubled by her inability to explain herself.

Tom drank his tea slowly. How was she to know? Janet had joked about it. *I bet you eat girls for breakfast these days.*

"Robert's different," she was saying. "Maybe I need an older man."

"And what about Duncan? How's he going to take it?"

She frowned.

"You know he's in love with you."

"Maybe he is," she said, " – but he doesn't *need* me. Your dad needs me."

"And that's enough, is it?"

She nodded.

"You know this is going to set tongues wagging more than they are already, don't you?"

There was a sudden fire in her eyes. "I'd rather they wagged over a marriage than no marriage, Tom – and I do care for him. Honestly."

Downing the remainder of his tea in one long draught, Tom got to his feet and made for the door. "Christ, Sarah!" he said, throwing caution and good manners to the wind. "I hope you bloody do!"

"Don't be angry, Tom," she pleaded. "He's a lonely, tenderhearted man who needs someone to love. He says he needs me. I think he does."

Tom was too angry to contradict her.

She had got up and was standing holding on to the

handle of the door, preventing him from leaving. "Say you understand," she said earnestly. "Say you're glad for both of us."

He said something. Later, he could not remember what. But it must have been enough, because she had briefly touched him on the arm before he left, and kissed him lightly on the cheek.

Suddenly, standing outside the bunkhouse door, feeling oddly detached from everything around him, Tom remembered his mother's letter written all those months ago. *Sarah is a lovely girl. Don't take too long to decide if you love her enough.* Had she suspected Robert might seek solace with this girl? Surely not! Yet, perhaps she had. Was it possible? Maybe it had been her way of warning him – that if he felt anything at all for Sarah he must act, not let things drift on from month to month, heedless of the consequences. He had not understood. Now it mattered little: his affection for Sarah had never been that strong. He should stand back and let things take their course.

Brack was still waiting by the barn, looking forlorn. Tom called out to him and the dog came bounding over, yelping his delight at being forgiven for whatever misdemeanour had banished him from Tom's good books. Together they went out through the gate leading up the track and onto the broad open land beyond The Rigg.

Tom wanted the isolation of space around him, the broad sweep of an empty landscape and the warm sweet scent of dry grasses filling his head, because everything else had a tinge of madness. He needed some perspective;

some proper sense of what was happening. He would go back when everything was clear, and not before.

He headed north, away from the farm, following sheep tracks beyond the boundary fields into the empty tracts of crag and mire with Brack keeping close at his heels.

The miles slipped by. Later, up by the Wall, in a landscape of desolation, with the lapwings and curlews for company, Tom sat on an ancient lichen-covered stone half buried in the bog, Brack at his feet, and watched the sky turn pale and milky from the west, and columns of rain march closer, falling from a dark line of leaden cloud. The wind sprang up running before it, chilling the air.

As the light faded, he headed home.

It was dark when he reached the shelter of the farm, the rain running down his face and neck, soaking into his shirt. Meg and Tod barked their greeting from the shed and he left Brack with them, snug and warm at last in the comfort of the straw.

Across the yard, the porch light lit up the slanting rain, and cast a yellow glow onto the curved wet cobbles. He lifted the latch and took off his sodden jacket hanging it up to dry. He could hear voices talking softly beyond the kitchen door.

In the kitchen's welcoming warmth, Sarah and Robert were waiting, standing by the range, holding hands. They turned as he came in, anxious smiles on their faces.

Until that moment, Tom had wondered what he truly felt about this match. Now he was reconciled. He stepped forward and embraced them both in turn. "I wish you every happiness," he said – and knew at last that despite all his reservations, he meant it.

CHAPTER TWENTY-FOUR

The Grange, just outside the hamlet of Flockton and a ten minute drive south from Weaversham, was an attractive two-storey Tudor red brick, tall-chimneyed country house with mullioned windows and diamond leaded lights. Bernard Makepeace could be relied upon to give anyone interested in its history a detailed and minute account of its chequered, and sometimes gory, past. After several reincarnations over the centuries, its present owners had transformed it into a conference centre and it was now widely regarded as *the* venue for prestigious events.

That Saturday lunch time in mid-October, the main dining room was filled with around a-hundred-and-fifty guests who had been invited to join the literary nobility of the area for the 1989 Rural Cheshire Book of the Year Awards. A splendid three-course luncheon had been served with two fine wines (a Sauvignon Blanc from the Loire with a Merlot for those who preferred red), and the proceedings had reached the point where coffee and mints were being distributed, and speculation was rife as to who would, or would not, receive an Award this time around.

At the top table, the five judges and two organisers of

the event were enjoying the frisson of expectation in the atmosphere. Before them, scattered amongst the twenty or so tables, were the anxious authors of the twelve short-listed books. As the warming effect of the wines took hold, the general hubbub of conversation grew louder. John, trying hard to appear attentive to the intensely detailed literary argument of the elderly lady next to him who was bedecked in an abundance of gold jewellery and heavy make-up, was more interested in watching Bernard Makepeace sitting opposite.

Bernard was a constant source of fascination: his wardrobe a kaleidoscope of possibilities. Despite the preponderance of smart suits, Bernard was wearing an assortment of oddly mismatched items with little regard for the importance of the occasion. This cheerful garden gnome, his head bobbing up and down as he spoke enthusiastically to his neighbour on this subject, or that, was a truly astonishing sight. To mark the event, his one concession was the clear evidence he had trimmed his beard, if not perhaps very successfully. Beneath his velvet jacket with elbow patches was a green shirt of startling brilliance, and around his neck he had somewhat hastily arranged a cravat of a colourful paisley design. Below the level of the table cloth were other eye-catching elements: the baggy blue trousers of an uncertain age, thick pink socks and the inevitable open-toed sandals.

In other surroundings, Bernard would have been a figure of derision, but amongst these, his soul-mates with their common interest in the literature, landscape and heritage

of the area, he was happily accepted for what he was –
thoroughly eccentric, perhaps more than a little mad, but
a brilliant writer, historian and raconteur.

Over the summer, Bernard had rapidly become part of
John's life. From their first meeting, an unlikely friendship
had developed. John welcomed it. In Bernard's company,
he could forget his father's declining health, Gemma's
burgeoning love-affair that he still could not bring himself
to mention, and the dull abiding ache for the son he would
never know.

Bernard's researches into Rothwell Mere had, as Bernard
himself had predicted, produced enough material for a
good-sized book. Ten chapters to be precise, ranging from
the mysterious prehistory of the Celts up until the late
Victorian age. His visits to Lower Chursley to pour over
John's photographic albums and discuss his choice of prints
had become increasingly frequent, and there was always one
print that was precisely what Bernard wanted to illustrate
the subject matter in hand. "Splendid! Splendid!" he would
say on every new discovery, his pale-blue eyes filled with
evident delight. And so their collaboration had flourished,
beginning with Bernard's hardback masterpiece, *A Forbidden
Place: The Dark History of Rothwell Mere*. It had been
published by County Publications in early June with both
their names emblazoned on the cover, a collaboration to be
seen as the centrepiece of every local bookshop window.
John found this oddly satisfying, moreso because Bernard,
without understanding its significance, had picked the single
most poignant photograph of John's entire collection to

grace the cover – the atmospheric scene Laura had chosen all those years ago.

That summer, the arcane topic of the mere and its mysterious history seemed to catch the public mood. Demand for the book outstripped supply quite early on and a second run was hastily arranged. Its popularity spread. There had been a couple of articles in the literary section of the larger local newspapers, a news report on local radio and TV, and the BBC had been in touch over the possibility of a documentary sometime in the future. Nomination for the Rural Cheshire Book of the Year Award became a foregone conclusion. Winning it, in Bernard's view, would be the crowning achievement. But he took nothing for granted. "Strong competition this year," he had said to John, nodding sagely. "Marjorie Tailforth's *Ley Lines in the Plain*. Excellent. Read it?"

To which John had been forced to confess he had not, the subject never having fired his interest.

But Bernard was always interested – in anything and everything – and his enthusiasm to continue their collaboration soon became evident. "I've had this project on the back burner for a while," he had announced over his elderflower cordial on John's terrace one sunny afternoon in July. "Done the research of course. Need illustrations. Or photographs. Interested?"

After which John, without being entirely sure he had ever actually agreed, found himself ferrying Bernard to the Welsh Border on joint expeditions to explore Wardsley Castle and its extensive grounds. It was a magnificent, ramshackle pile, its history stretching back a thousand years hacked out in solid stone and layered in the architecture of each succeeding age. There were meetings with its current owner, the Fourteenth Earl; agreements reached over access to the habitable areas; negotiations successfully concluded, and another book was in the making.

The Chairman of the judging panel, Dexter Hughes, a dignified and well respected author, was standing, calling the room to order, tapping his water glass delicately with the back of his coffee spoon. The general hubbub died away. "Ladies and gentlemen," he began, his voice booming across the room. "Can I begin the more formal part of these proceedings with a vote of thanks to Heather and Keith Hill for organising this splendid event yet again." General applause. "Can I also extend my appreciation to the other members of the panel – Charlotte Parker, David Pritchard, Marion Thomas and David Sutton –" to which each nodded and smiled in turn, "– for their unstinting commitment to reading all the books submitted and for taking so much time out of their busy schedules to give careful consideration to each and every one of them." More applause. "And now to the moment you've all been waiting for – the final decision of the panel." A slight pause, designed to heighten the tension. "I have to say this has been an exceptional year for entries, not only because of the quality of scholarly research so ably demonstrated by authors in the non-fiction category, but also by the powerful prose written so brilliantly in the works of fiction we had before us." He cleared his throat, donned his reading glasses and consulted the notes on the table in front of him. "In the fiction category, after a great deal of discussion, it was decided the prize this year should be awarded to – Kerry Shaddon – for her evocative novel based on the life of Emily Baines – *The Single Rose.*"

To appreciative applause and cheering, a blushing young woman in an elegantly tailored cream suit got to her feet and made her way between the tables to receive her framed certificate and handsome cheque. She made a short, pretty speech which John found captivating while Bernard fidgeted with his napkin in nervous anticipation.

"And now to the non-fiction category," the Chairman said as a hush settled once again. "Here again, the standard was extremely high. But it was the unanimous decision of the panel that there was one entry which deserved to be recognised as having outstanding merit." His gaze swept over the assembled company searching out the author in question. The hush deepened. "The prize for non-fiction this year," he said, pausing again for effect, "is awarded jointly to – Bernard Makepeace and John Leighton Rufford for their excellent collaborative work, *A Forbidden Place: The Dark History of Rothwell Mere.*"

Bernard was already standing, a broad smile spreading across his face, bobbing his gratitude to all those around him slapping him on the back and congratulating him. John heard his own, "Bravo! Well done!" as he applauded the little man, his own contribution of little account, he felt: the text was all Bernard's; the photographs incidental. But Bernard had turned, beaming at him, urging him to follow, and John was suddenly aware of the lady next to him taking hold of his arm and physically pushing him up onto his feet. "Go on! Go on!" she was saying in rich commanding tones that brooked no contradiction.

John disliked forced public visibility: he preferred meeting people on his own terms and in his own way. He was selective and cautious, because success in personal encounters mattered to him, and he had honed this strategy to a fine art over the years. So, like a peacock, he knew when to make a show, and when to quietly go about his business.

He stood up, mentally unprepared, automatically buttoned up the jacket of his lounge suit and reluctantly followed the bizarre figure of Bernard Makepeace shambling his way between the tables. The sheer incongruity of their pairing was both disconcerting and vaguely amusing at the same time. If others thought the same, they were too polite, even after several glasses of exceptionally good wine, to give any hint of what they might be thinking.

Later, his memory of this moment of triumph was blurred. He could remember the applause; the Chairman shaking Bernard's hand vigorously as he handed him his prize; of Bernard moving graciously to one side; of having his own hand shaken equally as vigorously; of a certificate and cheque being handed over; the demand for press photographs that followed; and of trying to adopt an air of suitable humility and gratitude – and most of all, trying to hide the sense of feeling vaguely foolish.

But the moment was soon passed. Bernard relieved him of the necessity of delivering an ill-thought-through speech. The little man had taken centre stage and was beaming round at everyone. There was an air of expectation and complete silence.

In the blink of an eye, the audience was in the palm of Bernard's hand. His speech was lively, witty and short. He was gracious in his thanks, generous to his competitors, encompassed everyone present, and gave John the perfect excuse to restrict himself in total to a simple nod, a deprecating smile of acknowledgement, and an even simpler, "Thank you."

"Realised," Bernard whispered to him on their way back to their seats to general applause. "Not your sort of thing – this," he added, taking in the entirety of the room with a little gesture of his hand.

"No."

"Thought not."

There were a few closing remarks on the part of the Chairman and the organisers, and the assembled company were invited to linger for the remainder of the afternoon in the lounge bar if they wished so that staff could clear the dining room for a later function.

The hubbub resumed and the tables began to empty as people drifted through to the comfortable seating in the adjoining room.

John, hoping to disengage himself from the attentions of the lady with the abundance of gold jewellery, excused himself on the grounds he wanted to leave the framed certificate in the care of Reception. This duly done, he found there was already a sizable crowd in the lounge when he arrived. Most of the easy chairs ranged around coffee tables were occupied. At the bar, Bernard had attracted a coterie of admirers. John felt no compulsion to join him.

Standing further down the bar was Kerry Shaddon with her own group of admirers clustered around her. There was a great deal of light-hearted laughter and she was slightly flushed. She briefly caught sight of him over the rim of her glass as she finished her drink and smiled.

Her disciples peeled back in deference to the presence of another winner as he joined their circle. "Congratulations," he said.

She blushed visibly. "Thank you. I never expected to win." She put down her empty glass on the bar and gathered her composure. Her disciples began to drift away. They had become superfluous, and knew it.

John watched her discomfort, finding it mildly amusing. "Would you like another drink?" he offered.

She smiled prettily. "Oh – yes. Thank you."

"More ... Sauvignon?"

She nodded.

The barman, hovering at her elbow responded to John's casual indication that her glass was empty and filled it immediately.

"You're not having one yourself?" she asked.

"No. I'm driving."

"Ah." She looked him straight in the eye and openly evaluated him. "If I didn't know better, Mr Rufford," she said, tilting her head slightly, "I'd say you were trying to pick me up."

The directness of this comment, and the intonation of

her voice, had unsettling echoes of the past. John suddenly found himself thrust back in time, engaged in delightful verbal sparring with a young woman he had just met and intended to get to know a great deal better: Laura. The recollection knocked the breath from him for a moment. He shook his head, trying to brush aside Kerry Shaddon's comment with a dismissive wave of the hand. "Wouldn't dream of it," he said as nonchalantly as he could manage. But the thought left a very definite ache that was much less easy to dismiss.

A smartly dressed young man in his late twenties with light brown wavy hair and strong features appeared out of nowhere and put his arm protectively around Kerry's waist, kissing her cheek. "Read my Kerry's novel, have you, Mr Rufford?" the young man asked with evident animosity.

John noted the possessive adjective. She's mine – hands off. He made no attempt to lie. "No," he said casually, keeping his tone light. "I'm sorry to say I haven't. Bernard keeps me too busy with his projects, I'm afraid," he added, remembering to smile. A smart answer, but it did not fool either of his listeners.

The young man managed a tight-lipped smile in return. "Sorry to drag you away, love," he said to Kerry, evidently far from sorry, "but Colin and Helen want a chat before they leave. Excuse us, won't you, Mr Rufford."

John acknowledged their departure, noting her parting glance in his direction. At another time, now long in the past, he thought, he would have bedded her with ease and thought little of it.

A hand tapped him on the shoulder, and a man's voice said, "Hello, John."

He turned, frowning, recognising the voice rather than the features. "Julius?" If he sounded incredulous, he was sorry, but it was hard to equate this plump, middle-aged man with thinning hair, to the energetic, sleek, slightly mad-cap Julius Parr he had known and worked with as a younger man.

His companion nodded, patting his expanding waistline. "I know – too many Law Society dinners. Lethal things. I'm morphing into my old man these days," he added, which was true: his plump features and receding hairline reminiscent of the quietly spoken Horace Parr, younger partner of Gorst & Parr, a man permanently confused by the waywardness of his children, not least by the beautiful but volatile Claudia.

Julius was looking him up and down. "You look just the same, damn you, John Rufford," he said, frowning in mock irritation.

John ignored the jibe. "What are you doing here?" he asked. After his recent brush with Kerry Shaddon, it almost seemed like Fate: he had not seen Julius since the early 1960s, when the Parr siblings held boisterous parties in the cellar of their parents' home, Highfield House, and where John had met Laura, his life changed for ever by that first astonishing encounter.

"Sitting in for Rosemary," Julius was explaining *sotto voce*. "Not my usual scene."

"How is she?"

"Oh, fine. Fine. Spends a lot of time in Italy these days – now the twins are up at uni. We have a villa there, you know – in Tuscany," he explained, adding hastily, "Join her as often as I can," clearly wanting to explain her absence did not in any way raise questions as to the state of their marriage. "Italian cooking," he went on, patting his stomach again. "Doesn't help." He laughed, and for a moment there was a brief glimpse of the young man who used to call himself 'Jules', who drove like a maniac and became besotted with his clever and elegant cousin, Rosemary Gorst. "You married yet?" John heard him ask.

"No." A simple, painful word.

"Probably for the best," Julius observed. "Noticed you were still up to your old tricks," he added, with a nod in the direction of the departed Kerry.

"Not really."

"No?" Julius had raised a sceptical eyebrow. "Could have fooled me, John Rufford. Once a Lothario, always a Lothario."

John shrugged off the comment.

"Anyway, I should be congratulating you," Julius was saying. "Terrific photographs. Do you remember the rotten snaps I used to take?" he asked, dismissing his woeful attempts with an embarrassed smile. "Bloody awful things. Can I get you a drink?"

John declined the offer and waited for Julius to be served his whisky and soda.

"How did you get mixed up with Makepeace?" Julius asked.

"Through the County magazine."

"Ah, yes – of course. Seen your name on lots of things. Done well for yourself."

"Couldn't stand local government in the end. Too much petty Party politics. You?"

"Felt the same. Went into the family firm when the old man retired. Right thing to do at the time. Joined Oliver. You remember Oliver?"

John remembered Oliver.

"His marriage fell apart you know. Not surprising. Claudia and Oliver! My God! Chalk and cheese! She left him in seventy-three, you know. Rocked him something rotten. Everyone said he should have stuck it out with his other cousin – Laura. Did you ever meet Laura Driscoll?"

John felt a knife twist in his heart. He leaned heavily against the bar for support. "Yes," he managed with difficulty. "At one of your parties."

"Those were the days, eh? Did you know she ended up marrying the gardener at Meeston Lodge? Never met the man myself. Swanned off up to his farm in the wilds of Northumberland. Caused quite a stir."

"So I heard."

Julius rambled on between sips of whisky, blissfully unaware of the distress he was causing. "Made a name for herself in the art world apparently. Died last year. Only fifty. Terrible."

John nodded, incapable of any rational reply.

"Do you remember her old family home? – Meeston Lodge?"

"Yes – I drove you there once."

"Of course you did! Remember now – the night of my leaving do from the old Town Clerk's Department." Julius was well away now, lost in reminiscing. "I took some of my photos round of her twenty-first, didn't I? Apparently her mother threw the first lot out. Can't think why," he added with a laugh. "Shouldn't speak ill of the dead, I suppose, but my God – Daphne Driscoll was the original Gorgon. One glance from her and you were stone dead."

John could clearly recall the icy reception that had greeted him on the first occasion he had visited the Lodge.

"Anyway, for some reason Laura left the family pile to her eldest boy. He came down for a couple of days back in March to give it the once-over."

John felt the thud in his chest and took a moment to recover himself.

"I'm sorry I missed him," Julius was saying, frowning into his tumbler. "Oliver said he was quite a personable young man. Not the country yokel we'd expected after all. Reminded him of someone, he said – but couldn't quite remember who. Sophie – that's Oliver's daughter by the way – was quite taken with him apparently. Smitten, in fact."

John found himself concentrating very hard on the shiny surface of the bar. The reflection of the late afternoon sunlight through the window was beginning to slip into a soft purple autumn twilight. His heart was racing. He wanted to go home.

CHAPTER TWENTY-FIVE

No one could accuse Robert Moray of being coy about his proposed marriage to Sarah Armstrong: he told everyone he met. He seemed to relish the notoriety, meeting gossip head on with a steely determination and grim humour.

"Let them rattle on, Tom," he would say, dismissing the tittle-tattle out of hand. "They'll soon tire of it when something else comes along. I can bear it."

And they did rattle on, not least because no one had supposed, or even briefly entertained the thought, that Robert Moray would remarry. Or if they had, their imaginations had certainly not lighted upon Sarah Armstrong as his intended, a twenty-four year old to his sixty-one. Some were outraged and called it 'indecent'; others shook their heads and tutted disapprovingly; while those closer to the couple saw things differently.

Ian and Bridie were relieved. "He'll have someone to help him through November," they said. "It's for the best."

Duncan, perhaps because he already knew his cause was lost, accepted Sarah's choice, wishing them well. But for several days he stayed away from the farm, going down to his plantation at Sykeside, chainsaw in hand, determined to cut back dead wood. And when he did return, he announced he would be working up at Willie Robertson's place for a few weeks. He kept his disappointment to himself.

Wallace, bewildered by this latest turn of events, said he was pleased his daughter had finally found someone who really cared for her, a thinly veiled criticism of Tom's indifference. Mary's initial reaction remained a closed book. She would have liked a church wedding, was all she said to Robert, but when Sarah said she was perfectly happy with the Registry Office, that was the end of the matter. Becky, of course, would not be invited.

Within a week, the tongues fell silent.

They married on the Monday morning, 23rd October. It was Robert's birthday. He was sixty-two going on twenty-five, a rejuvenated man. And Sarah looked up into his eyes with such tenderness, it touched the heart. Tom saw the change in both of them. Love, even when not understood by others, was a force not to be underestimated.

After the ceremony, there was a small celebration at the Stewart Arms Hotel in Wallbridge: Robert and Sarah, Wallace and Mary, Ian and Bridie – and Tom. Like the wedding, a quiet affair.

Later, back at the farm, Tom put his bag into the back of the car and gave Brack stern instructions to behave himself while he was gone. Robert and Sarah stood in the yard, arms around one another, and waved him off. "I'll be back by the end of the week to help bring up the cows," Tom called back through the open window. And when he drove away, he could see Brack in the rear view mirror, sitting forlornly where he had left him, watching him go.

It was dark when he reached Weaversham.

He persuaded himself he had a perfectly valid reason for returning: Mr Warburton had telephoned. The Ingrams had extended their tenancy of Meeston Lodge for a further six months, but they would like him to consider the possibility of their purchasing the property at some time in the future. It would have been simpler to have discussed the pros and cons of this over the phone, but Tom wanted an excuse to get away, and this seemed as good a reason as any.

But the true reason was the marriage. On a wedding night, three was definitely one too many. He was uncomfortable with the thought of Sarah in his mother's bed; of Robert making love to her; of perhaps hearing sounds he did not want to hear; and of coming down to breakfast the following day pretending he had not. Robert had understood.

So he returned to Weaversham, and thought himself stupid to have gone to such lengths to make himself scarce. He could just as well have travelled up to Fife with Ross to look at Sinclair's bull, and spent a few days up there. Instead, he had arranged to meet Mark Warburton on the Wednesday afternoon. The rest of the time he would idle away, playing at being a tourist. He would make no attempt to find his father, or meet up with Julius Parr – or Oliver Gorst for that matter. Nor would he seek any contact with Sophie: this would simply lead to complications wiser to avoid. He wanted peace and quiet, and time to adjust. Then he would go home and life would go on.

At The George, they had given him the same room as before, its dull familiarity a welcome sight. He closed the door behind him dropping his bag on the floor, and stretched himself out on the double bed, tucking his hands behind his head and staring up at the ceiling. He was thinking about Robert and Sarah. Thinking about Janet. He was lonely. Why had she never written? Even just a few lines? Just to tell him where she was. He frowned at the crack running along the ceiling overhead. It seemed larger than he remembered. He wanted her. Now. In this bed. Wanted her touch. Wanted her in his arms. He ached for her. Why had she not written?

At odds with the world, he fell asleep.

After breakfast the following morning, he wandered out into Weaversham's High Street. It was a bright, crisp day after a light frost, and the town was busy, the half-term holiday bringing families out to make the most of a pleasant autumn day. With no destination in mind, he strolled along the main street window shopping. But by mid-morning, he had explored everything there was to see, and beyond some interesting architecture in the little side streets, there was nothing much to occupy his time. Briefly, he toyed with the idea of going down to Meeston to visit the Lodge, just to keep in touch with the place, but the mood passed.

For a while, he sat drinking coffee and eating toasted teacake in a small café, watching the comings and goings of people around him, casually eavesdropping on their conversations and hearing once again the sound of his mother's voice. It brought home to him his solitary state. He finished the teacake, drained his coffee and left.

Despite his determination to avoid Lingford, he decided he would drive there after all, have lunch and head out into the surrounding countryside for the afternoon. He remembered places his mother had spoken of: Pickerton; Hunters Green where she had gone to school, and Smallcross with a roadside shrine that dated back to the Early Middle Ages. He would begin his explorations there, visit a new location every day, and the week would soon pass.

He parked well away from Tiverton Square, avoiding Gorst & Parr, and walked through the less busy side streets towards the town centre. At the end of a narrow pedestrianised lane filled with bijou shops selling perfumes, jewellery and ornaments, he came out unexpectedly into an open grassy area surrounded by fine black-painted iron railings, topped by fleur-de-lys picked out in gold. Within this imposing precinct stood the early Victorian sandstone edifice of the parish church of St Barnabas, built by subscription in 1842, according to the brass plaque at the gate, after a devastating fire had reduced the ancient medieval church to a smouldering ruin. He stood for a while, admiring this sturdy no-nonsense structure raised by the public-spirited enthusiasm of Victorian Lingfordians, who seemed to know precisely what they wanted. Turning to leave, he walked straight into Oliver Gorst, complete with black Crombie, umbrella and brief case. He had appeared from nowhere.

"Thomas! Thomas Moray!" Oliver said, already shaking his hand vigorously. "Good heavens! What are you doing here? Are you down for long?"

"A few days," Tom said, adjusting his speech to match that of his interrogator.

"Why didn't you say you were coming?"

Tom's head was empty of any logical reply.

"Decided to sell?" Oliver was asking, not waiting for an answer.

"I'm not sure."

The clock on the church tower struck twelve.

Oliver checked his watch. "Meeting anyone?"

"No – just looking for somewhere to eat."

"I'm having lunch with Gregory over at The Greyfriars. Come and join us." And without allowing Tom any say in the matter, he propelled him by the arm across the road towards the pub in question, ushering him through the old oak doors into the warm, fuggy interior.

Inside, many of the plush red seats around the walls were already taken, and several men were standing at the bar waiting to be served, a comfortable mix of professional suits and casual jeans and jackets. Unidentifiable anodyne music was playing from the speakers on the wall. Of the men at the bar, Tom had no difficulty in picking out Gregory Gorst. He was a younger version of his father with the same distinctive profile: tall, slim, smartly dressed in a steel-grey trench-coat over a dark suit and white shirt. But there the similarity ceased: his face was less gaunt; he was clean-shaven, and his thick wavy hair was the attractive auburn of his sister's. He was clearly as much a Parr as a Gorst.

"Gregory," Oliver said, tapping the younger man on the shoulder. "I'd like to introduce you to someone."

Gregory turned, evaluating his father's companion. He had his sister's hazel eyes and engaging smile.

"Thomas Moray," Oliver was saying, " – down from Northumberland for a few days. Bumped into him outside St Barnabas'."

They shook hands firmly.

Gregory's smile had become expansive. "Pleased to meet you," he said, his rich baritone revealing an expensive private education that would stand him in good stead in any profession. "Can you join us for lunch?" he was asking.

Compared to his father, Gregory was easy company. He had none of Oliver's stiffness. He was affable, and determined not to let his father's business dominate the conversation. He was curious, without being intrusive when Tom chose to be non-committal or purposely vague. Gregory, he sensed, had recognised his reluctance to discuss family matters. He was grateful: Robert Moray's decision to remarry was a topic Tom had no intention of divulging. But there was one topic Gregory was decidedly interested in: whether there was a woman in Tom's life. He was tactful, but persistent, and seemed pleased to discover the fact that there was not.

After lunch, when Oliver left to meet a client, Gregory ordered another round, showing no inclination to follow his father back to the office. Tom wondered if he were just being polite. "Am I keeping you?" he asked.

Gregory shook his head and smiled. "Not at all," he said. "I'm not part of the firm just yet. Not sure I want to be, to be honest. Wouldn't tell the Old Man that, of course. Not 'til I've made up my mind." He opened a gold cigarette case and offered Tom an expensive looking cigarette, lighting up one for himself with an equally expensive looking lighter when Tom refused.

"What would you do instead?"

"Oh – I'm not sure," Gregory said, inhaling deeply and squinting through the ensuing cloud of smoke. "Don't want to close off my options too soon, do I? A law degree opens lots of doors. I'd like to take time out for a while. A bit like Sophie, I suppose."

Tom concentrated on his beer.

"You met Sophie, didn't you? – in March?" His tone was mildly inquisitive.

"Yes – briefly."

"She's been in Italy most of the summer – in Callistini with Aunt Rosemary – near Florence," Gregory explained, becoming expansive. "Pretty place. Up in the hills."

Tom said nothing.

There was a noticeable pause while Gregory pondered his half-drained tumbler of whisky. "She wrote to you, didn't she?" he asked, frowning slightly, giving the impression he was thinking aloud.

"A couple of postcards."

Gregory nodded. "She's taking French and Italian now,"

he said casually. "At the European Language School in Oxford. Home for half-term at the moment. Staying at my place. I've got a flat not far from where you're staying in Weaversham." Another noticeable pause. "Why not come round tonight for supper – if you're not doing anything? Meet up with her again?"

The image of Sophie as Tom remembered her in March was as clear to him as if it had been yesterday: the well-tailored navy blue suit; the striped blouse open at the neck revealing the gold chain at her throat; the lovely heart-shaped face with high cheek bones; the wide-set hazel eyes, and the obvious vulnerability she displayed without being remotely aware of it.

Gregory was smiling a little too knowingly. Did he suspect there had been anything between them? Tom had no idea how he could disabuse him of this without his fervent denial being misinterpreted as an attempt to cover up a relationship.

"She could do with some company," Gregory was saying looking him straight in the eyes over the rim of his whisky glass. "Got herself into a bit of tangle with someone – in Italy. Not quite over him," he added.

Tom just nodded understandingly, glad he had not been responsible for breaking her heart.

"Needs cheering up," Gregory insisted. "How about it? I'm sure she'd love to see you."

"I'd be very dull company," Tom found himself saying, grasping at straws. "I don't think fatstock prices and grass yields would interest her that much."

Gregory's gaze did not waver. "I'm her brother, Tom. I'm looking at you and I can tell you – you're just what she needs. Break the spell for her, will you?"

"I don't want to make matters worse," Tom heard himself saying.

Gregory laughed softly and finished his drink. "You won't," he said with the kind of conviction it was hard to argue with. "She's not as fragile as you remember," he added, showing an insight into her previous vulnerability Tom did not expect. "Will you come?"

So he had said he would.

Idly driving round the countryside later that afternoon, his thoughts ran wild. Why – he asked himself repeatedly – had he agreed to such a proposal? – to provide Sophie with some unspecified form of diversion – possibly of a sexual nature? Because, by accepting Gregory's invitation, it appeared on the surface at least, he had done precisely that. It was both demeaning and indefensible. He should be ashamed of himself.

Other thoughts were even less attractive. Was he simply intent on indulging himself and using her as an excuse because Janet had gone out of his life? Was the idea of tupping her simply to satisfy his curiosity? Or perhaps what was worse – because it was so mean-spirited – was he, deep down, resentful of Robert's wedded bliss? Did he just want a woman – any woman – no matter who? And did he lack the basic honesty to admit it? He hoped not.

He should cry off. Phone Gregory at his office and decline the offer – keep his conscience clear. But he did nothing. Instead, he persuaded himself he was over-reacting to a simple invitation. Perhaps Gregory had not equated 'cheering up' with anything more than a convivial evening of good food, good wine and good company. It was perfectly possible.

But whatever motivation spurred him on that evening, he called in at the barber's shop on High Street on his way to Grenville Terrace. "Better safe than sorry," as Donna would have said.

CHAPTER TWENTY-SIX

The flat was on the first floor of a substantial sandstone property in Grenville Terrace, little more than a ten minute stroll from The George. The high-ceilinged white communal hallway, with its frosted glass lights, smelt of fresh paint and looked pristine. The stairs were covered in a dense midnight blue carpet, and the bannisters were stripped back to the original wood. There was an air of casual affluence about the place, and an indifference to cost.

Tom rang the expensive brass doorbell outside the flat.

Sophie opened the door almost immediately. He took a moment to readjust his memory of her. Her hair was longer with a parting at the side, and she looked very chic in beige slacks with a dark mushroom slim-fitting sweater that emphasised her breasts, a gold chain with a lovers'-knot pendant nestling between them.

"Tom!" she said with a welcoming smile. "It's so lovely to see you again!" And she leaned forward to kiss him lightly on the cheek. There was a brief encounter with her perfume, delicate and tantalising.

Gregory emerged into the hall holding a glass of red wine. "Come on in, Tom. You're in good time." He looked sleek and polished dressed in casual light-grey slacks and cream silk shirt. They could both have stepped out of the pages of a glossy magazine.

Tom was instantly conscious he was wearing more robust clothing than either of his hosts – his twill trousers and the thick moleskin shirt under his tweed jacket perfectly adequate for evenings at The George, but not quite right for an evening 'at home' with the well-heeled Gorsts.

"Can I take your jacket?" Sophie was asking.

He surrendered it, trying to ignore the fact he felt distinctly over-dressed.

They led him into the elegant lounge, furnished with deep-cushioned chairs and a sofa covered in a soft grey-green fabric on a thick-piled carpet of a darker hue, with heavy brocade curtains to match. There were side lights on glass-topped tables, and fitted light-oak shelves from floor to ceiling on one wall, filled with books. The remaining walls were a pale cream, bare below the ornate plaster coving where cherubs held garlands of flowers picked out in gold. From the hi-fi speakers came the lulling notes of lush orchestral music designed not to intrude, and an enticing aroma drifted out from the kitchen.

"Lasagne's in the oven," Gregory said. "The real McCoy. Sophie's a fantastic cook. Didn't you know? Have a glass of wine. Best Rosso di Toscana." And before Tom could decline, Gregory had furnished him with a generously filled glass and topped up his own.

Through the archway leading into the dining area, Tom noticed, the highly-polished oval table was already set for three, and another bottle of the same vintage was open and ready to drink. He would be well provided for, Gregory had seen to that.

Gregory was indeed the perfect host, offering the armchair next to the Adams-style fireplace, its artificial fire pumping out heat. "Glad you decided to come," he said, stationing himself in the remaining armchair and leaving Sophie the only option of sitting on the sofa opposite, giving Tom an uninterrupted view of her.

There were the usual pleasantries, Gregory ensuring Tom's glass remained permanently full, while Sophie persuaded him to try the selection of stuffed black and green olives from a small white ramekin on the table beside him. Tom ate them more out of curiosity than pleasure.

During the progress of the meal, through the antipasto of roasted red and green peppers with almonds doused in olive oil, and the main course of lasagne with a salad on the side, conversation revolved mainly around Italian cuisine and Sophie's expertise in that direction. Tom was happy to provide his own congratulations on the excellence of her culinary skills, which seemed to satisfy both his hosts. Once this topic had been exhausted, the conversation shifted to Gregory. He appeared eager to give an account of how he came by the flat; its many advantages, both in size and location; how useful it was to have an extra room with an en suite for guests for instance, even down to the more prosaic benefits, such as the electric showers in the bathrooms and integrated appliances in the kitchen.

"I love staying here," Sophie enthused over another glass of wine. "It's so much nicer than Daddy's gloomy old place over in Lingford. Oh God – it's like a mausoleum." She rolled her eyes at the thought of it.

"What she really wants," Gregory confided to Tom, "is her own place, isn't it, Sis?"

She sighed prettily. "Don't I just. I'm off tomorrow to spend a few days with my friend Maddie before I go back to Oxford. She's found this sweet little flat in Harrogate – and I am *so* envious."

And so the meal progressed. Interestingly, Tom noticed, through the fog of intoxication that was beginning to insinuate itself into his brain, neither of them made any attempt to interrogate him on anything: there were no enquiries about family, friends or life on the farm, and Tom began to suspect Gregory had noted his reluctance to discuss certain topics when they last met, and had warned Sophie off making any mention of these.

The main course cleared away, the conversation turned back to Italian cuisine. Sophie made a great play about the dessert – "lamponi e more al limone" – as she was eager to describe it, throwing herself into the Italian pronunciation with evident enthusiasm. In this case, Tom was as complimentary as he could be over what he saw as a dish of raspberries and brambles with a dash of lemon and a sprig of mint leaves, something Sarah would have put together in a trice, although possibly with less flamboyance – and without the mint. This somehow led on to discussing Sophie's decision to take languages rather than read law;

the part their Aunt Rosemary had played in this; the advice she had given on the subsequent choice of college, and so on, and so on. And the wine continued to flow. A third bottle was opened. The topic of Sophie's summer sojourn in Italy was alluded to only in passing, and only in relation to her determination to learn how to cook Italian food to Italian standards.

The meal finally drawing to a close, Gregory suggested they retired to the lounge where Tom was served strong coffee and a large brandy. He began to feel distinctly disorientated: a silent observer of a performance that had been meticulously planned in which he would ultimately be required to play the starring rôle.

Shortly before nine, Gregory suddenly and unexpectedly excused himself. "Sorry – I've got a taxi coming to pick me up," he said nonchalantly. "Arranged to meet a friend down at The White Peacock this evening. Didn't want to cancel the arrangement." He gave them both a somewhat contrived smile.

With Gregory gone, there was a curiously embarrassing hiatus. Sophie got up suddenly and put on another tape of orchestral music. "Would you like some more coffee?" she asked brightly.

Tom declined: it was not to his taste, but he had no wish to offend.

She settled back on the sofa, leaning against the arm, her shoes discarded and legs stretched out along the cushions. Very Roman, Tom thought.

He waited to see what was planned next.

"I'm sorry I didn't write," she said apologetically, "after I'd promised."

"It doesn't matter."

"Oh, but it does matter," she said with great seriousness. "I said I'd write – and I didn't." Her fingers played with the fringe along the edge of the cushion. She kept looking over at him, apparently expecting him to say something. Finally, she asked, "Did Greg tell you?"

"About what?"

"What happened in Italy?" She was looking at him very directly.

He feigned ignorance.

"He didn't tell you about Matteo? Matteo Bacchelli?"

"No." A truthful answer: Gregory had never mentioned Matteo by name. "He just said you needed cheering up." On reflection, Tom thought this might be regarded this as something of a bold statement, but she let it pass.

"I fell madly in love," she said casually, as if it were an everyday occurrence. "Oh I know it sounds silly – everyone has a fling when they go on holidays abroad, don't they?"

Tom had never been on a holiday abroad, except for a school trip to France – which hardly counted – and a holiday romance was never part of the itinerary. Medieval castles, churches, and museums, yes – very definitely on the 'things-to-do' list, but a romantic attachment? – never. Besides, at thirteen, girls had held no interest for him whatsoever: they were alien beings who giggled a great deal, going into secretive huddles, or being malicious and spiteful to one another.

"But I fell for Matteo one-hundred-per-cent," she was saying.

"Did he feel the same – about you?" Tom asked, although he was more interested in the very definite effect the brandy was having on his senses.

"I thought he did. But – who knows? He's Italian after all," she added, as if this explained everything. Perhaps it did.

It was clear from the pause that followed, he was expected to continue with the theme. Through the increasing haze of brandy and wine, he asked the first thing that came into his head. "How did you meet him?"

"His parents were staying with the Antoninis for the summer," she explained. "The Antoninis are neighbours of Aunt Rosemary. They have a villa just down the road – nearer the town."

"Callistini?" he offered, pleased he could remember the name from lunch time after so much alcohol. He was beginning to suspect he would have a thick head in the morning.

"Yes. It's a pretty little place. All tiny streets and picturesque piazzas," she was saying, absent-mindedly stroking the fringe again, her eyes concentrating on what she was doing. "It's up in the hills just outside Florence. Anyway," she went on, remembering his original question, "Matteo's a friend of Dario's – that's how we met."

Now she had lost him entirely. "Dario?" he asked.

"The son of the Antoninis," she explained. "He asked Matteo to come down to spend the summer with him –

from Milan," she added, as if this were important. "But then Dario got himself a girlfriend, and Matteo was a spare part."

"And you fell for him."

"Big time," she confessed.

"Tall, dark and handsome, I suppose?" Tom said, wondering why he thought this was appropriate: he would not normally make such a trite remark.

She cocked her head to one side and thought about this. "Mm," she said, after due consideration. "A bit like you."

For a nasty moment, the photograph of John Rufford came to mind. Tom struggled to concentrate, deflecting her observation with a dismissive laugh. Christ! How did he get into this state? He was beginning to take a serious interest in how she might look if he removed her sweater.

"So what happened?" he asked, aware he was now definitely making conversation for conversation's sake while most of his mind was concentrating on the possibility Sophie really fancied him. But did she want him enough to go to bed with him? Or was the brandy just fuddling his brain into thinking that she did? He was now most definitely in the mood to do something about it.

Sophie shrugged. "What happened?" she said, repeating his question. "He left. Just went." She frowned, thinking this over. "I think his father had him lined up to marry someone in Milan. Some girl with pots of money probably. The Bacchellis are filthy rich, you see. Maybe I wasn't rich enough." She looked quite cross about this.

Tom continued drinking the brandy, wishing he could stop fantasising about undressing her.

She looked up at him suddenly. "Honestly," she said, still frowning. "You really do look like him. It's weird." It clearly unsettled her.

Tom carefully swallowed the last of the brandy and put down the glass on the table beside him. This was it then, he decided. This was why he was here. "Do you mind?" he heard himself ask in an off-hand, careless sort of way, making sure she was looking at him as he spoke.

She shook her head, smiling nervously, and began twisting the lovers'-knot pendant round and round with her fingers.

Tom eased himself forward and reached out, placing his hand over hers. "You'll break the chain," he said softly, feeling the rise and fall of her breasts under his touch.

She just looked at him, her mouth parting slightly.

Certain now, he stood up and uncurled her from the comfortable nest she had made for herself on the sofa. With great care, he brought her closer and began to unfasten the chain. "You don't want to break it, do you?" he said, smiling at her and placing it carefully on the table.

She shook her head.

He did not rush things. Almost casually, he let his hands rest on her hips as he leaned forward to kiss her neck. Her scent was intoxicating. He could hear her breathing coming in little gasps. "Do you want to go to bed with me?" he asked. "Say no now if you don't." He looked her straight in the eyes. She did not answer him, and when he began to lift her sweater, she raised her arms so it would slip easily over her head. He paused before unhooking the clasp on her bra. The view was as lovely as his anticipation of it.

In the end he stayed the night, and awoke with a thick head to a strange room with daylight slanting through the crack in the heavy brocade curtains. At first, he had no clear idea where he was, until the elaborate coving on the ceiling reminded him. Under the tumbled duvet, he was naked, and Sophie Gorst's warm, smooth body was curled up next to him, still sleeping, her hair in delightful disorder. He closed his eyes against the light and drifted back into a doze.

Eventually, the sounds of the day began to intrude: the traffic on the road outside; distant music coming from the downstairs flat; a jackdaw 'chuck-chucking' from the gable end above the window.

Sophie stirred and stretched luxuriously with a deep, satisfied sigh.

"What time is it?" he asked.

"Nearly half-nine," she said, consulting the bedside clock before turning to smile at him and heaving an audible sigh of regret. "I've got to get up," she apologised. "I've not packed yet and my train's at one."

"Pity," he said, ignoring the fact for the moment that he had an appointment with Mark Warburton at two.

She extricated herself from the mess of bedding and he watched her pad around the room naked, picking up discarded clothing from the night before. He liked the look of her: her slim, lithe, almost boyish figure with its neat buttocks and flat belly; her petit breasts he could cup in his hands with ease; and the pretty light brown bush between her thighs that was like thistledown to touch. If the muzziness in his head had been less, he would have been tempted to summon her back and give her another good tupping, but she had found her wrap, and was swathing herself in it, removing temptation from his sight. She caught him watching her.

"You look fantastic," he said.

She sat down next to him, ignoring the compliment and ran a finger over his jaw. "And you look like a hedgehog," she said, not remotely likely to respond to any further advances, even if he felt able to provide them. "Greg's got a spare shaver. Shall I get it for you before you go?"

"If you like. Where is he by the way?"

"Probably meeting a client," she said, offhandedly. "I heard him go out about eight o'clock." She was suddenly thoughtful. "When Greg invited you over," she asked hesitantly, "did he suggest ... ?" She looked embarrassed.

"What?" Tom asked, acting dumb.

She paused, biting her lip and looking awkward, trying to shrug off her suspicions. "Taking me to bed?"

"No," he said, laughing this off and hoping he sounded convincing.

She did not look impressed. "Are you sure? He didn't ... hint at anything? He doesn't usually go to The White Peacock during the week, that's all."

Tom stuck to his guns. "He just said he thought you needed cheering up."

"So you always carry skinnies with you, do you?" she asked accusingly. "In case a girl needs 'cheering up'?"

"Skinnies?"

"Don't pretend you don't know what I mean," she said, becoming cross with him. "Condoms – rubbers – French letters – whatever you call them."

He tried turning on the charm. "Life can be full of surprises," he said, wondering if this would satisfy her curiosity.

Except her curiosity was far from satisfied. She studied him for a moment before asking, "Have you had sex with lots of girls, Tom?"

He took his time to answer. "A few," he said cautiously, hoping she would not press him for exact numbers or engage him in a discussion on the pros and cons of quality versus quantity.

"Was I any good? – compared with the others?" she was asking earnestly.

Christ! What was he supposed to say? She was eager but unimaginative compared with Donna or Janet. He had kept things simple.

"What I mean is – am I boring? – in bed?" The thought clearly troubled her.

He ran his fingers through her hair. "I've no complaints," he said, making sure he looked her straight in the eyes as he said it.

"But there are other things, aren't there? I mean – " She looked uncomfortable. "Maybe that's why Matteo lost interest."

"You don't have to do things you're not ready for," Tom said, hoping he sounded convincing enough. "They happen when they happen – with the right person." Janet, he thought. With Janet.

"Maybe you could teach me sometime," she suggested, apparently seriously mulling over this possibility. And when he did not reply, she shrugged, dismissing his reluctance and got to her feet. "I'll make us some breakfast, shall I?" she suggested. And he agreed.

When she had gone, Tom threw aside the duvet and dressed quickly. He had indulged himself long enough. It was time to go.

CHAPTER TWENTY-SEVEN

"The Ingrams are prepared to offer you a sum well above what we would regard as the market value for the Lodge, Mr Moray," Mr Warburton was saying. "In the current financial climate this is an attractive proposition, but –" and here he paused to indicate his slight reservation, "there's no doubt it's a fine property, and you may well feel it would be prudent to hold on to it."

Tom's ability to think was suffering from the surfeit of alcohol the previous evening and from what had followed. His night with Sophie had left him unsettled. He had thoroughly, if somewhat drunkenly, enjoyed her, as any man might indulging in a one-night stand. But this put him on a par with the young men in Wallbridge whom he had always openly despised because they would pick up girls at the Rainbow Disco on a Saturday night for the sole purpose of having them up against the wall behind the auction mart afterwards. He was equally uncomfortable with the knowledge he had used Sophie as a convenient surrogate, except, he kept telling himself, that was precisely the rôle she had allocated to him. Nonetheless, he felt tainted by the casualness of their encounter and the knowledge he had been gullible enough to be encouraged in the enterprise by her brother.

"What would you like to do?" Mr Warburton was asking, evidently for the second time from the expression on his face – strained patience.

Christ! – Tom had absolutely no idea, except for the nagging doubt at the back of his mind that at some stage in his life he might indeed need the bolt-hole his mother had provided. "I'd rather not sell," he said, managing to rid his mind of other thoughts, and adding in case he seemed too intractable, "For the moment."

So it was agreed to leave matters as they were for the time being, and Tom came away clear on this point at least, if nothing else.

Feeling decidedly at odds with himself, he drove straight back to Weaversham, relieved that he could console himself with the knowledge Sophie would now be safely out of his way in Harrogate.

He arrived at The George to find a message from Oliver suggesting a luncheon engagement at one o'clock at The Bebbington in Lingford on the Friday to meet with Julius Parr.

Tom spent most of Thursday driving around the countryside in a prolonged state of self-recrimination and introspection, contemplating the uncomfortable prospect of sitting opposite Oliver at lunch the following day trying to forget he had spent a large slice of Tuesday evening tupping his daughter.

The Friday morning dragged. After breakfast, he idled

away his time in the Residents' Lounge trying to read his daily paper. Instead, he found himself listening to those around him: the tone of their voices; their manner of speaking; and the topics that filled their conversations. Almost without knowing it, he realised, he was already slipping into adopting their nuances and phraseology, their mannerisms and vocabulary, sloughing off his hard northern vowels and sing-song intonation, only occasionally lapsing into the soft burr he had absorbed from his years with Robert – a tendency Sophie had regarded as 'charming'.

Robert. Sarah. Rigg End. Even Brack. The miles of wilderness beyond the Wall. For two days, he had barely given them a thought. But when it came to meeting Julius Parr, who was no doubt as urbane as Oliver, he felt the need to demonstrate his northern roots. Rather than dress casually, he chose to wear the suit he had worn for Robert and Sarah's wedding. Not the height of fashion perhaps, but made from traditional, finely woven cloth well-tailored, courtesy of Bell & Lomax of Wallbridge (by Royal Appointment), and therefore appropriate for his introduction as the inheritor of Meeston Lodge.

What he had expected of Julius Parr however, was not the rotund individual who waved cheerily to them from the entrance of the dining room at The Bebbington, and who proceeded to weave his way awkwardly between the intervening diners to join them. He was immaculate – that much Tom had anticipated – with his dark pin-striped suit with waistcoat to match, white shirt and navy tie with alternating diagonal silver bands. But although supposedly younger than Oliver, Julius' receding hairline, slightly florid complexion and expanding waistline made him look much older.

"Sorry I'm a little late," Julius said breathlessly, addressing himself to Oliver.

"No – no," Oliver assured him graciously, standing up to greet him. "We were a little early." Tom rose from his seat too, preparing for the introduction. With an elegant sweep of his hand, Oliver said, "Julius, I'd like you to meet Thomas Moray. Thomas – Julius Parr."

Julius extended his hand, turning from Oliver as he did so. He looked directly at Tom for the first time, the shock registering on his face almost at once. There was a terrible momentary silence. Julius opened his mouth, but said nothing.

"Pleased to meet you," Tom said, filling the void and shaking the proffered hand which turned limp in his grasp.

Julius blinked. "Oh – yes – yes – of course. Lovely to meet you at last," he managed, licking his lips nervously.

Oliver frowned. "Are you all right, Julius?" he asked.

Julius recovered himself sufficiently to release Tom's hand and sit down hurriedly in his chair. "Perfectly, Oliver. Perfectly. Just a little rushed to get here, that's all." And he smiled broadly to confirm everything was entirely as it should be – except it clearly was not.

Tom and Oliver sat down while Julius fiddled with his napkin.

"We haven't ordered yet," Oliver assured him.

"Good. Good," came the overly bright reply. "Lovely weather for the time of year," he added inconsequentially. Evidently realising this comment was entirely superfluous and therefore embarrassing, he turned his attention to the menu, studying it for a moment with intense concentration before hastily fumbling in his top pocket for a pair of half-moon reading spectacles.

Oliver, watching this performance, wore an expression of deepening concern. Something had happened that was beyond his comprehension.

Tom knew exactly what had happened. Somewhere in the pit of his stomach was a dreadful gnawing sensation that knocked all thoughts of food from his mind. It was pure panic, and the terrible urge to make any excuse he could think of, no matter how flimsy, to remove himself from this untenable situation, no matter how flimsy. His heart-rate was rocketing.

Except it was already too late. The damage was done. Somehow, Julius knew the truth.

A series of further alarmingly inconsequential and fractured observations followed concerning the options available on the menu. The tension mounted and became almost tangible. Julius was overly jovial, Oliver increasingly perplexed, and Tom could feel sweat breaking out on his upper lip. The situation was only defused by the timely arrival of the waiter, poised with his polite smile, pencil and little note pad ready to take their orders.

Tom's interest in the sea-food salad, steak diane with all the trimmings, and a blackcurrant cheesecake to round things off, evaporated. Instead, he chose mushroom soup, Sophie's lightly breaded plaice, and decided on cheese and biscuits instead of a dessert. Anything more elaborate, he felt, was unlikely to remain in his stomach for very long. For the same reason, he politely declined Oliver's offer of wine and asked for a glass of iced water instead. Oliver mistakenly seemed to take this as an excellent indicator of his sobriety, of which he evidently approved. Julius meanwhile, opted for the pâte, beef wellington and chocolate torte to follow, ordering a glass of house red, and promptly drinking most of it as soon as it arrived – something that did not go unnoticed by Oliver.

"Thomas thinks it would be wiser not to sell Meeston Lodge, Julius," Oliver said, as he picked his way through his side salad.

Julius looked up from spreading a liberal amount of pâte onto an oatcake. "Ah," he said, flourishing his knife. "Yes – always difficult to know what to do for the best, isn't it? To sell or not to sell, that is the question – so to speak. Pros and cons."

Oliver frowned, evidently feeling this approach was less than helpful.

"No harm in taking time to make a decision, is there?" Tom added, although he had already come to the conclusion he was incapable of finishing his soup.

Oliver was indulgent. "Quite right. Quite right," he said, his faint smile indicating his approval. "An asset sold is an asset lost. Your mother must have had a very good reason to leave you such an excellent legacy."

Julius choked, and the proceedings came to an enforced halt while he recovered himself.

And so the meal limped on from one topic to the next, Oliver gradually preferring to engage Tom rather than Julius, the latter evidently becoming an embarrassment to him by making incoherent responses to questions whenever he was invited to give an opinion. And when Julius excused himself between the main course and dessert, Oliver was eager to apologise for some of the more bizarre statements his partner had expressed. "You really must forgive him, Thomas," he said, evidently far from pleased with the performance he had witnessed so far. "He's really not himself today."

Tom was at pains to reassure him. "Perhaps there's something on his mind he doesn't want to mention," he said, surprised by his own temerity in providing this explanation.

"Well, it's not like Julius at all. Not at all," Oliver said, adding after a moment's serious reflection, "Of course he might be going down with 'flu. Perfectly possible at this time of year, I suppose – and he does look quite flushed, don't you think?"

Tom agreed Julius did look quite flushed, but he thought the wine might be the more probable cause.

With the arrival of coffee and mints, and the seclusion offered by a group of easy chairs in an alcove away from the bright autumn sunlight slanting through the windows, Oliver directed the conversation towards his sister Rosemary's next trip to Italy at Christmas, and Julius was able to wax eloquent on the latest improvements to the villa which he thought Oliver would approve of. The topic of Sophie's last trip to Tuscany during the summer was mercifully not raised.

At two-thirty, Oliver consulted his watch and said he was meeting a client at three and would they excuse him.

Julius announced as it was Friday he was free for the remainder of the afternoon. "I'll see you in the office on Monday, Oliver," he said, almost dismissively, an observation which seemed to add to Oliver's concern over his partner's welfare.

"Yes – of course," Oliver said with a slight frown as he stood up. Tom got to his feet, offering Oliver his hand. He shook it abstractedly. "When are you travelling home?" he asked, possibly more out of politeness than interest.

"Sunday," Tom said.

"Well – do keep in touch this time, won't you?"

Tom nodded, but did not promise, and with a polite smile, Oliver departed.

Tom settled back in his seat and waited for Julius to explain himself. He did not have long to wait.

Julius coughed politely. "I'm sorry," he said with a nervous little laugh, "You must have thought me a complete fool earlier. I was just – I wasn't – quite myself."

Tom acknowledged his apology with an understanding nod while his mind wheeled off into the realms of all the possibilities that lay ahead.

"Silly of me," Julius was saying. "But I was rather taken aback when we met, you see. You reminded me of someone." He was smiling broadly now, shaking his head at his apparent foolishness.

Silence, Tom decided, no longer seemed a sensible option. "Anyone in particular?" he asked casually.

Julius tutted. "Goodness – no! Complete nonsense on my part. You couldn't possibly be related."

Tom smiled the particular smile he knew from the photograph in his mother's notelet box, and waited for the reaction.

Julius gulped: it was perfectly clear he knew that smile. He stirred his coffee a little too vigorously and looked increasingly discomfited.

"Do you know John Rufford?" Tom asked him bluntly.

Julius' head came up with a jerk. "Um – yes, I do, as a matter of fact," he said with a nervous smile. "Used to work together back in the 'sixties."

"Have you seen him lately?"

"Last week, strangely enough. First time in ages."

Tom took the bull by the horns. "I think he might be my father," he said, aware he was giving this statement a casualness that might seem somewhat misplaced under the circumstances.

Interestingly, Julius showed no inclination to contradict him. He simply stopped stirring his coffee and carefully replaced the spoon in its saucer, pondering for a moment before asking, "Do you have any particular reason for believing this?" There was an enquiring smile on his face that did not fool Tom for a minute: Julius clearly believed he was, but had no intention of committing himself too soon.

"I found his photograph – in one of my mother's books. Do you know how they met?"

Julius began fiddling with his collar where it bit into his neck. "Probably my fault, I'm afraid," he said, evidently embarrassed by this. "We younger Parrs used to have regular parties at home in the cellar, you see," he explained. "I think it must have been just before Christmas in 'sixty-two – not long before your mother and Oliver broke off their engagement anyway. Yes – that was it. We went out round the pubs in Weaversham raising money carol singing, if I remember. My sister Antonia was very keen on good causes at the time. Anyway, we all trooped back to the parents' place for a party and I remember seeing John chatting up your mother, and warning her to give him a wide berth, so to speak." He paused, obviously uncomfortable with what he was about to say. "Oh dear, this is very difficult," he confessed, fiddling with his collar again. "You see, Thomas, John had a bit of a reputation in those days."

"For the ladies?"

Julius gave him an apologetic smile. "Nothing obvious," he assured him. "No office romances or anything like that. No – he was always very discreet. Never revealed who they were. But he made no secret he had a way with women. Sorry – that was insensitive."

Tom let the comment pass. "Did you never suspect? – about him and my mother?"

"No – I don't think anyone did. Although," he added confidentially, "I'm not sure Rosemary's dear old Aunts Millie and Sylvie didn't know a thing or two. I remember her saying – oh, quite a number of years ago now – she'd overheard them discussing your visit – after your grandmother's death – something about how taken aback they'd been when they met you. But as soon as they realised Rosemary could overhear them, they clammed up."

"They must have known him."

"Well if they did, Thomas, they never mentioned it to anyone."

"I think he must have been very much in love with my mother. I can't think why he would come to the funeral otherwise."

Julius looked astonished. "He went to her funeral? Good grief! And you didn't know who he was?"

"No – not until later – when I found the photograph."

"I see."

"What can you tell me about him?"

Julius looked apologetic. "Not much, I'm afraid. We went our separate ways, you see, in 'sixty-three. I went off to Chester when Rosemary and I got married. He stayed on at the Town Hall. Did very well for himself. Became Chief Executive of Weaverdale eventually. Gave it all up suddenly about ten years ago. Took up photography. He's been working with a local historian recently providing photographs for a book on some obscure beauty spot – not sure what all the fuss was about actually – but anyway, between them they walked off with one of the Rural Cheshire Book of the Year Awards – that's where I met him last week –" He stopped short, a look of horror on his face. "Oh – good God!" he said, pummelling his forehead furiously. "And there was me rabbiting on to him about Laura's death – you inheriting Meeston Lodge – and coming down to see Oliver in March."

"And he said nothing?"

"Not a thing! But I remember him going very quiet afterwards. Yes – very quiet indeed."

"Do you think I should try to get in touch with him?"

"That's for you to decide, Thomas. But if you do, then I suggest you do it sooner rather than later. The *Lingford Herald* comes out later this afternoon, and there'll almost certainly be photographs of the Awards winners in the book review section. I think – if you don't mind me saying, this may draw attention not just to him – but to you. People around here – and in Weaversham too, I shouldn't wonder – will almost certainly notice the similarity between you. You're like two peas in a pod."

"Do you mean Oliver?"

Julius nodded. "And word will get around."

So, Oliver would finally make the connection he had almost made in March; Sophie no doubt would regard the news as adding spice to their brief liaison, and being Sophie, would be incapable of keeping this particular piece of news to herself; and Rufford, somewhere down the line, would ultimately hear that Tom had been in the area, asking questions.

Julius drew their meeting to a close. Somewhat awkwardly, they shook hands on the steps of The Bebbington as the clock at St Barnabas struck four, and went their separate ways.

In something of a daze, Tom headed down the high street towards the car park, stopping every now and then to gaze into this shop window or that without much idea why, or to what end. His mind was disconnected, free-wheeling through the afternoon with Julius, not knowing what to do for the best.

He read the large poster in the book shop window several times. 'Rural Cheshire Book of the Year Award – Non-fiction Prize – Book signing here Saturday, 28 October 10.00 a.m. – noon.' Behind this, an assistant was busily arranging books. In the centre of the display she had placed the winning entry, the names of the co-authors emblazoned on the glossy front cover. Bernard Makepeace. John Leighton Rufford.

Tom stood for a while, his concentration fixed on the name. John Leighton Rufford. Almost without thinking, he turned up the collar of his coat and went through the door, wondering what possessed him to take such a risk. There were several other people in the shop, and he feigned interest in a couple of gardening titles before moving over to inspect the stack of books on the table nearest the window. *A Forbidden Place: The Dark History of Rothwell Mere.* He picked up a copy and turned it over. On the back were two photographs of the collaborators: Bernard Makepeace, an odd-looking man with wild hair and a straggly beard; and John Leighton Rufford, immaculate and well-groomed, the image of the man he remembered so well, with his sad smile, and dark, penetrating gaze.

He took the book to the counter, trying not to engage too readily with the cheerful young sales assistant who was keen to advertise the book signing event the following day.

"It's going to be very popular," she said enthusiastically as she wrapped his purchase. "Why not come back tomorrow and get it signed?"

He thanked her briefly for the suggestion, and left, pretending to be in no particular rush. For some time afterwards, he sat in the car listening to his heart thumping against his ribs.

CHAPTER TWENTY-EIGHT

As Julius had predicted, the *Lingford Herald* gave wide coverage to the literary event at The Grange. There were photographs of the judges and a prominent feature on the nominated titles and winners. The photographs were good, clear and well-printed, and Tom had no difficulty in finding the likeness of the man he was looking for. Rufford was standing to one side behind Bernard Makepeace, his expression betraying a mixture of puzzlement and pleasure – a raised eyebrow and slight smile. What was he to make of this man? Too many contradictions. Not enough to go on.

Tom put aside the paper and turned his attention to the book, peeling back the cellotape keeping it safely wrapped inside its coloured paper bag. It felt like an act of great moment. Jamie would have likened it to being initiated into the Eleusian Mysteries – but then Jamie always enjoyed being overly dramatic. Nevertheless, it definitely felt extraordinarily significant: it opened a small window into the world of a man about whom he knew so little, and needed to know much more.

He decided to forego an unnecessary dinner and keep to his room. He would read the book, study the photographs –

of which there were many – and try to understand the man who lay behind them. He sat on the bed, his back propped up against the headboard and switched on the bedside light.

The biography appearing with the photograph on the back of the cover was brief. It gave him little more to go on beyond what he had already gleaned from Julius Parr, apart from the additional information that John Rufford had been born in Shropshire and attended the De Montfort School where he had become Head Boy. This last nugget of information mattered: here was a man who had succeeded from a relatively early age and gone on to achieve more. Robert's successor must, at the very least, be his equal: he had overcome personal tragedy; built up a thriving farming business; supported and encouraged his wife's artistic talents; raised three children and given them the opportunities they craved. Robert Moray would be a hard act to follow.

Flicking through the pages, Tom discovered the text was surprisingly engaging. He had expected it to be dry and achingly dull – like the volume on the bookshelves at Rigg End devoted to Roman settlements along the Wall written sometime back in the 'thirties by Robert's academic father – but it was nothing of the sort. Nowhere in the text or introduction however, was there any explanation as to why John Rufford had spent years of his life returning to photograph the mere at various times of the year, mostly in winter: it was simply mentioned in passing as something he had done, and was left unaccounted for.

The photographs themselves were atmospheric: sometimes reminiscent of Gothic horror in black and white; others mystical, veiled in filtered light; and sometimes deeply melancholic. The few coloured prints of winter scenes in sunlight were oddly threatening: stark outlines of trees or reeds set against piercingly blue or silver-frosted skies, or deep, hard-edged shadows thrown onto the ground like a challenge. All were devoid of any living creature with the exception of one, a beautiful study of a grey heron standing sentinel-like in the shallows. It was easy to understand how the myths and legends springing up over the centuries had been conjured into being. Here was a place not to be visited without a sacred talisman to protect you against evil. So what had brought John Rufford back, year after year? A ghost? A private demon?

Wrapped up in this strangely compelling world, Tom lost track of time. He finished the last chapter, closed the book, and discovered almost four hours had slipped by unnoticed. It had gone ten o'clock.

He pulled himself off the bed, finding his legs stiff from being stretched out straight for so long. He was little nearer understanding John Rufford now, he realised, than he had been earlier that afternoon.

He put on the television and made himself a mug of tea, sitting back on the bed with a stack of pillows behind his head, flicking from one channel to the next. Nothing appealed. Without much enthusiasm, he watched a protracted discussion on the ramifications of the disintegration of the Soviet Union, and the possible reunification of Germany. An empire was crumbling. The

Cold War was slipping into history. But their significance, and likely impact on his life, seemed distant and uninvolving. He switched off the TV.

Subconsciously, he realised, he had decided what to do. Prevarication was no longer an option. He would seek out John Rufford: circumstances had made it possible.

He would need to be cautious. He was about to impose himself on someone else's life without warning. He must make allowances, and be prepared to walk away. It was an uncomfortable thought.

He lay awake for some time rehearsing what to say, rephrasing this or that, and too often getting tied up in verbal knots. Mentally exhausted, he fell asleep sometime in the early hours, waking with a start at the sound of other hotel guests walking past his door deep in conversation, and daylight creeping through the crack in the curtains. The clock said eight-thirty. He got up, muddle-headed, and doused his face in cold water. The shock cleared his brain but he felt shaky, the way he used to feel before school examinations: taut; a tightly coiled spring lodged in the pit of his stomach.

When he threw back the curtains, a light frost was melting on the roofs of the cars in the hazy autumn sun. It was a good sign, he decided, seeking reassurance in small things.

He had no appetite for breakfast. Instead, he made a coffee and ate the two digestive biscuits left over in the china dish on the hospitality tray. He planned to drive over from Weaversham around eleven-fifteen, park and reconnoitre

Lingford Books with enough time to spare before noon. He was prepared for the possibility Bernard Makepeace might be on his own, but if Rufford were there too, it would be better not to blunder in and introduce himself in front of strangers.

When he arrived in Lingford, the streets were crowded with Saturday morning shoppers. Many were admiring inventive shop window displays with Halloween themes: witches on broom sticks; black bats and grinning pumpkins. At Lingford Books, someone had gone to great trouble since the previous day to cut out silhouettes of leafless trees, their trunks framing the sides of the window, the branches overlapping at the top. The window itself was brightly lit, with a spotlight directed on the central display. Behind the visible stack of books, a cluster of people were waiting patiently. Who they were waiting for, it was impossible to tell, the press of bodies blocking out the view beyond. Tom strolled past, then crossed the street and doubled back taking his time. He felt remarkably calm, his heart beat a slow and steady rhythm in his chest.

The clock at St Barnabas' church struck twelve. He recrossed the street opposite the book shop, giving him an uninterrupted view of the activity within. There was a knot of people just inside the door; the sound of laughter, and movement at the back; the brief image of two men getting up from behind a table. He walked on, stopping in front of the window of the adjacent shop. He feigned interest in the mortgage deals and savings rates on offer and waited. Three people came out clutching their purchases and went their separate ways after a moment or two of lively conversation and accompanying laughter. The door closed behind them.

Tom could feel his heartbeat quicken as the minutes passed.

Then suddenly, the door opened, and Bernard Makepeace shambled out, talking to someone over his shoulder. There was a brief conversation before he turned, and with a cheery wave, walked off down the street. A moment later, John Rufford appeared on the doorstep, shaking hands with the proprietor before stepping out onto the pavement. He paused for a moment, taking stock of the day, buttoning his jacket against the chill in the air.

Tom felt the thud in his chest as he stepped forward. "Mr Rufford?"

★★★

John awoke to the now familiar pattern of events: the momentary shift from sleeping to waking when anything was possible; realisation dawning; the sensation of an iron grip fastening around his heart; the dropping away of hope, and the ache it left behind.

Autumn brought its leaden memories: almost a year since Laura's death; almost a year since he had stumbled on the truth, given his word to Robert Moray, and come away shaken to the core.

He lay on the makeshift bed upstairs in his study and stared at the ceiling. On a personal level, his life was going nowhere.

For almost a year, he had cherished the notion Robert

Moray would relent, divulge the truth, and the boy would get in touch. On this slim hope, he had built a fantasy determined to recognise Thomas Moray as his son, even though this would lay bare his past and expose it as less than honourable. He would do this because he felt he should: he could give Charles the grandson he longed for; Geraldine the pleasure of seeing the old man content at last; Michael and Caroline a nephew, and a dashing cousin for Megan, Josie and Daisy to idolise.

It was a dream built on insubstantial air. He had no idea why Moray should feel under any obligation to relent or revoke his decision: he had brought up the boy, nurtured him and made him heir to the farm they worked together. And the boy was not a boy, but a man – almost twenty-six by now – and well able to decide on matters for himself no doubt.

Beneath the hope lay fear – that Moray had relented after all, and it was Thomas who had chosen to keep his distance. As the months passed, and the hoped-for meeting never came, this fear intensified, plunging John into the depths of despair not even Bernard's persistence could hope to penetrate. His meeting with Julius Parr the previous week had only added to his feelings of hopelessness.

With the shortening days and the remorseless approach of November, these bouts of depression became less easy to dispel. Today was such a day. Not even the bright morning could lift his spirits. He had made a mess of things, and like the boxer in the Simon and Garfunkel song, he felt he had squandered his existence.

Meanwhile, life went on: his father's grip on reality was inexorably slipping away, telephone conversations with Geraldine too often punctuated by his incoherent ramblings in the background; Gemma had found consolation elsewhere; and that summer, realisation had dawned he was now fifty-seven, facing a desolate and lonely future.

The alarm bleeped, and he turned it off. Another day.

The book signings had been organised by Bernard and he had gone to great lengths to make them a success. "No point in hiding our lights under bushels," he had said. And he had a point. Naturally gregarious and garrulous, he thrived on these events. Anyone and everyone taking the time and trouble to come was treated like royalty. Each person was made to feel special: the shy, the verbose, the overly clever and the abysmally stupid. It mattered not one jot to him. They were buying his book – that's what mattered.

But for John, the prospect of spending a morning under these circumstances felt more like a penance. He could not rid himself of the guilty notion he was there on false pretences: his input had been minimal; every photograph already taken, just waiting for Bernard to decide which ones to choose. And of course, there was the book itself – Rothwell Mere – and all the memories that surrounded it, reinforcing his appalling sense of loss.

It took considerable will-power to pull himself out of bed and shave.

He chose to dress simply: Bernard would more than make up for any lack of flamboyance on his part. Besides, it was easier to merge into the background where he properly belonged.

When he arrived at Lingford Books, Bernard was already in full flow with the proprietor over the arrangements. "Ah – John," he said enthusiastically. "We're over here. Mr Percival's put out a couple of dozen copies on the side table. The rest are round the back. Easy to reach when they're needed." He evidently expected great demand.

Mr Percival introduced the three sales assistants who would provide back-up during the morning. There was an air of excitement; a buzz it was difficult to ignore.

John settled himself behind the table and accepted a coffee from one of the assistants. She was young, and very attractive. "Is there anything else I can get you, Mr Rufford?" she offered helpfully.

He closed his mind to the obvious. "No thank you," he said politely and looked away.

People began drifting in and soon Bernard had a knot of disciples waiting for his attention. No one seemed to mind if they were kept waiting while he exchanged witticisms and jovial banter with one of their number. Their turn would come.

John dutifully signed each copy, smiling briefly at the purchaser. Most were indifferent to his lack of conversation. One or two, who were interested in photography, enquired about his choice of shutter speed for this or that shot; whether he used a filter, and what type of film he would recommend. It was nice to be asked, but he felt the questions were raised out of something to say rather than a genuine desire to seek his advice. One man in particular was obviously no novice, but for some reason felt obliged to engage him in a protracted discussion on the pros and cons of processing one's own black and white prints. But when he finally left, he seemed to consider it had been time well spent.

Several coffees later, he heard the clock at St Barnabas' church strike twelve and the last three customers were eventually ushered out the door by Mr Percival.

Bernard was supremely happy. "Can't thank you enough, Mr Percival," he said, rising from his seat and pumping the proprietor's hand. "And you too, of course, ladies," he added, beaming in the direction of the three assistants at the counter who smiled back at him, pleased to be remembered.

John stood up from the table and returned his pen to an inside pocket, contemplating what to do with the afternoon. Perhaps he should telephone Geraldine.

"An excellent turn-out, don't you think, gentlemen?" Mr Percival was saying, evidently well-pleased with the number of books no longer taking up space in his store room. "Good to see so many people interested in local history."

Bernard's eyes twinkled. "Witches and demons, Mr Percival. All down to witches and demons, I'm afraid. We all love a bit of horror." He made the prospect sound deliciously wicked.

Mr Percival agreed.

"Still all right for Wednesday, John?" Bernard asked him as he headed through the door.

"Yes – about one o'clock?"

"Splendid. Splendid." And with a cheery wave to all and sundry, Bernard was gone, bobbing and weaving down the street between the Saturday shoppers.

John thanked Mr Percival and the three ladies, who evidently appreciated his smile, and stepped out into the autumn sunshine. There was a slight chill in the air. He breathed it in and buttoned up his jacket to keep the cold at bay.

Someone was calling his name. "Mr Rufford?"

He glanced up, expecting to see someone he might have met earlier. Instead, he found himself facing the image of his younger self.

There was a momentary sense of unreality followed almost at once by something akin to a physical blow to the chest. He could barely breathe, and a roar was filling his head with thunder. From a great distance, as if in a dream, he heard himself ask, "Thomas?" while everyone and everything around him slipped away into a silent, all-pervading fog.

The image smiled, acknowledging his question with a nod.

CHAPTER TWENTY-NINE

The strapping young man in the black leather jacket, chambray shirt and denims, was offering to shake his hand. John shook it, an automatic reaction, and remembered the warm, firm grip of almost a year ago: solid and reliable, like the young man himself with his tanned features, broad shoulders, and a face that mirrored his own.

The thumping in John's chest echoed the beat of a muffled drum inside his head, a distraction that bedevilled his clarity of thought. He was unprepared; floundering; his ability to think confounded. What should he say? It mattered. He could think of nothing rational that might pass for conversation, while beneath the thrumming in his brain, his joy was bubbling up, bursting through the tumbled thoughts and feelings, a rollercoaster of emotions. He heard himself ask, "Are you down visiting relatives?" A startlingly stupid question under the circumstances. A Freudian slip, surely?

The answer? – no – not specifically. Meeston Lodge was mentioned, a vague reference to Oliver Gorst – and a meeting with Julius Parr.

John was hearing the voice, a pleasant tenor with a slight

lilt hidden just below the surface and a hint of Scottish burr. He was hearing the words, but not attending to their meaning: they came to him from far away, on the other side of the dinning in his ears, through strange distorting filters. Unreal. Yet beautiful.

Odd recollections sprang into his mind. School assemblies. Standing in the silence on the stage. Aware of himself. As Head Boy, reading from St Matthew's gospel. The heavy bible on the lectern. His hands resting on the open page. The smell of polished wood, mingling with old leather and ancient printer's ink. The hushed hall filled with well-scrubbed faces, all turned upwards, listening to him say the words:

This is my beloved Son in whom I am well pleased.

He could hear his voice, clear and strong through the mists of time, caught in the rafters by a faint echo.

In whom I am well pleased.

He wrenched himself out of the past, the present demanding his more urgent attention, befuddled though he was. He found himself blundering on. "Are you staying in Lingford?" he was asking. Did it matter? No. Words. Just words. Anything to stop a vacuum springing up between them. Anything to give him time to find his footing on some firmer ground, and if not that, then at least to let the dreadful clamour in his ears die away.

No, John heard him say. He was staying in Weaversham – at The George.

And then the suddenness of what he dreaded most: an embarrassed empty silence; each facing the other across the barrier of time and space, coming to terms with a new and hard reality.

There was agony written in those deep brown eyes, a desolation Tom had seen before, almost a year ago, at his mother's funeral. He had not understood the reason then. He was wiser now. The months had passed but here he was again, seeing in the same face, the same expression: a mask of self-control; emotion held at bay – but only just.

"I wanted to meet you," he found himself saying. He had planned to say something else entirely, but could no longer remember precisely what. Surely it was more?

There was a raised eyebrow in response, but nothing else: surprise registering, feigned or otherwise.

"Robert said I should," Tom went on, sensing his listener's reluctance to admit to anything too soon.

"Did he tell you? – about me?"

"No, I found your photograph. The one you gave my mother."

"Ah." A long pause ensued. "Have you known for long?" A simple enquiry wrapped up in politeness and a wan smile that was quickly gone.

"Since the day after her funeral."

This knowledge seemed to hurt: there was a noticeable wince before Rufford said, "That long?" What had he expected?

"I couldn't come any sooner," Tom said, hearing his defensiveness reflected in his voice. "I wasn't ready."

Rufford acknowledged his explanation with a ghost of a smile. "No – of course not. Not easy for you."

An anguished silence sprang up again between them.

Rufford stuffed one hand in his trouser pocket, frowned and cleared his throat. "I didn't know – about you – last year," he said, evidently wanting to make this clear. "I would never have come – to the funeral – if I'd known it would cause ... unnecessary ..." He trailed off, struggling to find the right words and failing.

Tom could see the man's emotions held in check by sheer force of will and deep embedded stubbornness.

"I hope there were no – repercussions – afterwards?"

"No."

An audible sigh of relief.

Another silence wedged itself between them.

Rufford suddenly looked away, swallowing hard, his jaw clenched in defiance at the unwarranted betrayal of his self-control as a tear slid unbidden down his cheek.

All Tom's carefully rehearsed phrases evaporated into nothingness. Words suddenly seemed inadequate. Deprived of speech, he stepped forward and embraced the man, the strong familiar scent of aftershave filling his head.

Rufford was holding him fast.

A young couple walking past turned to stare, then walked on, glancing back, whispering to one another, and shaking their heads.

Recovering quickly, John pulled back, stifling this unseemly and unwarranted display, determined to rescue some shreds of his dignity if at all possible. Maudlin behaviour was not a pretty sight. He despised it in others. How much more indefensible then in himself? He found his handkerchief in his trouser pocket and wiped away the tears with a casual, dismissive gesture. A speck of dirt in his eyes, nothing more.

The young man was trying to put a brave face on things. "I bought your book," he was saying with a nervous smile, flourishing his copy in the general direction of the bookshop window. A long pause, followed by, "Congratulations – on winning the Award."

Relieved to be given time to compose himself, John gathered his wits and made an attempt at casual conversation. "Thank you," he said, wanting to acknowledge the compliment without over-egging his achievement. "I can't lay claim to any of the text of course – just the photographs," he added, feeling this was necessary.

The young man was standing, head cocked to one side. He reminded John of Michael: the same stance; the same inclination of the head. They were frighteningly alike.

"They're very powerful," the young man was saying, " – the photographs. Why did you go back? – to the mere? – all those times?"

Why? Good God! What a question! A thousand treasured memories stored away for years sprang into John's head. "A fixation," he managed, hoping this would serve the moment. "An obsession – some might say."

The young man nodded, studying the cover of the book, deep in thought.

Silence again.

John fought down rising panic, not knowing what to do. Was this brief moment all that they would have to share?

Would the boy look up, smile, shake his hand again and say 'goodbye'? Heaven forbid! He must not let him go so easily! "How long are you staying – in Weaversham?" he asked, desperate to detain him.

"I'm leaving tomorrow."

An iron band tightened round John's heart. So little time. So many questions to ask. So many things to tell: about Geraldine and Charles; Michael, Caroline and the girls; and most of all about the love he had harboured for so many years. He must tell him that, however short the time – that above anything else.

A tentative enquiry then? No unseemly begging or pleading.

The church clock struck the half-hour. Rufford made a play of unnecessarily checking his watch. "Have you time to spare?" he asked, his face betraying his anxiety. "A spot of lunch, perhaps?"

Tom nodded. He had come this far. There was nothing to lose in going further, and possibly everything to gain. Life at Rigg End was changing. He must not close his mind to this. Robert had offered him the opportunity to choose, and this man, it seemed, was eager to claim him – on the surface at least. Tom could read something of it in his eyes.

"There's an old inn out by the canal at Farley Heath," Rufford was saying, his nervousness dogging his enthusiasm. "We could have lunch there, if you like? A twenty-minute drive?"

And Tom agreed, wondering what was so special about the old inn that made Rufford suggest they should eat there.

The dark-blue BMW with its personalised number plate was parked not far from where Tom had left his car. The interior was immaculate and devoid of clutter. There were no dog hairs, and the passenger seat was noticeably firm and little used. Tucked neatly away on the driver's shelf was a pair of black leather driving gloves and nothing else. There was no hint of perfume, just the scent of aftershave. A solitary man then – living a solitary life.

They travelled out of Lingford, soon away from the new executive housing estates on the outskirts of the town into winding lanes fringed with trees in autumn colours, fields on either side, some ploughed, others with dairy cows still out, grazing contentedly in the unexpected warmth of the October sun. It had an alien feel, this landscape: too soft for Tom's liking, if he were honest; too well-manicured. It lacked that element of danger he was used to by the Wall, where mists and rain could whip out of nowhere and lead you into a bog if you lost your bearings. There was no challenge here. Nothing to stir the spirit or the blood; nothing to lift a man out of himself and make him more than he was.

After a few miles, they reached the canal and followed the gently meandering line of its towpath for a while. Further on, they passed a sign welcoming safe drivers to Farley Heath, and drove through a small village, little more than a cluster of rustic brick cottages with a tiny church set back from the road. Driving out once more into open country, a long, low double-fronted building of russet brick with a red-tiled roof came into view. There were three bull's-eye sash windows either side of the door, and smoke curling lazily from one of the tall chimneys.

Rufford slowed down and pulled off the road into a small, newly laid tarmacked area. Several sleek cars were already parked in front of the smart, freshly-painted white wooden fence.

Rufford cut the engine and stared out of the window for a moment. "I've not been here for years," he said with a sad smile.

CHAPTER THIRTY

Above the porch was a new sign depicting a black shire horse with a white flash and fetlocks, hauling a bottle-green narrowboat past the image of the inn in the background. The old sign, John remembered, had been more crudely painted.

"I came here with your mother a couple of times," he said as they got out of the car, feeling it was necessary to explain his choice of venue.

Inside, the place was not much changed, except the smoke-stained oak-beamed ceiling and the plastered walls were now a pristine white where the burnished horse brasses hung on leather straps between the windows. A log fire burned in the same iron cradle on the red-tiled hearth beneath the arched brick fireplace; the pewter mugs of every shape and size still stood on the high shelves above the bar; and the high-backed dark-oak pews ranged along the walls, with their tables set between them were as he remembered them, only the cushions, their plain deep crimson gone, were now covered in a busy floral fabric of beige, plum and green to match the curtains.

The pew nearest the fire was already taken, the four occupants – two middle-aged couples – deep in conversation. John paused for a moment remembering how Laura and he had sat there, eager to keep warm on that cold January day. They had left the car and walked down the towpath half-a-mile or so as far as the bridge and back again, in step all the way. They had been comfortable together, and he had known, even then, she was different from the other women in his life. All the old questions came back to haunt him. Why had he not been honest with himself? – with her? – put aside his idle foolery? The answer was simple – he had not known how. Instead, he had acted out a part, reinforcing his image in her eyes, and damning himself forever.

"Has it changed much?" Thomas was asking.

"Not much," he said.

Except the barman had. No longer the tubby, balding, middle-aged man who knew John; knew he came here with his many lady-friends for a quiet tête-à-tête and drinks before seducing them. Now there was a fresh-faced young fellow in white shirt and black waistcoat, greeting newcomers with a practised smile, serving their drinks with brisk efficiency and handing them the menu – a more sophisticated choice on offer than before. The clientele was different too: well-heeled married couples out with friends, prepared to pay for more exotic food and a wider choice of drink, spending their leisure time in the company of others of their kind. There were no seducers here; no couples leaning close across the tables, whispering to one another; no meaningful glances.

*

Tom took their drinks to an unoccupied pew, putting distance between themselves and other diners. He wanted privacy. Over the rim of his pint of best local ale, he studied the man whose looks he had inherited, and wondered if he had grown up under his tutelage, and not Robert Moray's, whether he would have followed in his path. It seemed possible. Donna and Janet had weighed up his potential. Maybe Sophie Gorst had done the same. They had all seen what he could have been, except he knew he lacked that certain style; that easy manner born of total self-assurance; of knowing that the world lay at your feet. He was no less self-assured among the men up by the Wall, but more rough-hewn; less refined; made different by days of hard work in the fields and heavy labour handling sheep; his hands large; his gait a rolling stride.

At the bar, Rufford was leaning nonchalantly on one elbow, menu in hand, engaging the barman in casual conversation with the occasional elegant gesture to emphasise something he was saying. Some of the women sitting at the tables in the centre of the room had noticed him. It was easy to see why, seeing what they saw – a man blessed with brooding good looks and charming smile, whose every movement seemed effortless and uncontrived. He drew them like moths to a flame. It would take little more than a glance, a smile, and they would be his. He was a man men envied, and maybe feared. Tom could see it in their faces: their eyes betrayed their thoughts.

Rufford had finished placing their order and was sauntering over to join him. He moved fluidly, like a cat,

Tom thought. Perfectly balanced. Ready to pounce. The women smiled at him as he passed, and he ignored them with the studied indifference of a monk. Was he always so abstemious? Or was this just a show, put on for Tom's benefit alone? It was hard to believe Rufford had shut himself away from the pleasures of the flesh, devoting his life to a woman who had put herself beyond his reach for ever. He was too potent. Too attractive. Was it all a lie? Maybe he would find out that it was, and he would be freed from any sense of obligation to this man beyond acknowledging him for what he was – his father; free to go home with a clear conscience, and get on with his life as best he could.

Rufford sat down in the pew opposite, his eyes filled with undisguised pleasure. The intensity of his gaze never wavered.

Tom found it disconcerting.

Rufford apologised. "I'm sorry," he said. "I can't get used to you being here. It's rather like a dream. There are so many questions I want to ask. So much I want to tell you. Where do I begin?"

"I don't know much about you."

"What do you know?"

"What I read on the book cover. What Julius told me – about when you worked together."

"Did Robert say anything?"

"He said you were rivals – that's all."

"Nothing else?"

"He was more worried about how I'd handle the truth – about him not being my father. It wasn't easy for him."

"No – I'm sure it wasn't – or for you," Rufford added, after a moment's reflection.

Tom let that lie. It was too big a subject.

Rufford did not press him.

Tom could hear the rich tones of a woman somewhere behind him recounting minute details of an exotic holiday cruise to a silent listener. Her voice intruded on his thoughts. He tried to concentrate, clearing his mind. "Robert feels guilty, you know," he said, feeling Rufford deserved to be told.

"Guilty? Why should he feel guilty?" Rufford appeared bemused by the idea.

"For telling you not to get in touch."

"I don't think I could hold that against him."

"Still – he feels bad about it."

"Then he shouldn't, Thomas. It's what I deserve," Rufford said stoically, downing half his drink of dry ginger with ice and swirling the remainder round the bottom of the tumbler, frowning at its progress. "Before I met your mother, I lived a very selfish life. I'm not proud of it," he added after some reflection. "Defied my father out of sheer bloody-mindedness. Joined the Army as a squaddie. Discovered women." There was a brief hint of bravado, soon dispelled. "Allowed an officer's wife to seduce me – just for the hell of it. After that, I found I could pretty much pick and choose any woman I wanted." He stopped himself and looked away, perhaps fearing he had overstepped the mark.

Their conversation was interrupted by the arrival of their meal, the barman swooping the large oval plates down onto the table with a flourish, presenting them with cutlery wrapped in white paper serviettes and dismissing himself with a polite nod.

"Julius said you had a reputation."

Rufford began picking at his side-salad without any apparent interest in it. "I'd no scruples, Thomas," he said, a ghost of a smile briefly flickering into life. "None whatever. It was a game I played. Even set the rules. Thought it was clever to say I was a 'pastime' – a convenient short-term arrangement for mutual gratification – nothing more." He paused, glancing up across the table. "I'm sorry, perhaps you don't want to hear this."

It made uncomfortable listening, but Donna would have understood – and by association, so did Tom. "You 'had sex' – you didn't 'make love'," he said casually, tucking into his steak and roast potatoes.

Rufford raised an eyebrow, apparently taking stock.

"I do know the difference," Tom said, stifling the impulse to add, 'Like father, like son'. Instead, he asked, because it puzzled him more than anything else, "So why did my mother go out with you?" Julius had warned her. What had made her change her mind? Just his charm? His good looks? It was possible. He was magnetic enough.

Rufford did not answer immediately. He ate a little of the salad, toyed with his steak, and sank into a reverie. After a while, he stirred himself. "We first met at the Parrs'," he said. "At one of their parties."

"Yes, Julius told me."

"Ah – did he? She was engaged to Oliver then. You know about that, I suppose?"

Tom nodded.

"She gave me the brush off," Rufford said, suddenly smiling at the memory: the same sensuous smile captured in the photograph.

"And the second time?"

"She was free to choose."

"After Oliver?"

"Yes. I traded on that. I guessed at what she wanted – the freedom she'd never had before – to be herself. I was right."

Tom shifted in his seat, keeping his head down.

Rufford sensed his discomfort. "She accepted my conditions," he insisted. "A short-term affair – a couple of months at the most – and ..." His expression changed. A frown settled on his brow. He shrugged slightly, as if dismissing some passing inconvenient thought. "And then I fell in love." The frown dissolved into a full-blooded smile.

"She broke it off, didn't she?"

Rufford nodded, the smile soon gone. "Yes. Did Robert tell you why?"

There was no easy way of telling him. "She thought you'd never change. You'd grow tired of her. Want someone else." It sounded brutal.

Rufford looked pained. "That's not what she said. It was something to do with her father – something she wouldn't tell me – about his past."

"There was that too."

Rufford pondered this for a moment. "I see. I made light of it at the time."

"Maybe that's why she never told you."

Rufford put down his knife and fork, his meal apparently no longer of any interest to him. Perhaps he understood for the first time why he had so signally failed to convince her he was serious – about anything. He looked up suddenly. "Do *you* know what it was? – about her father?"

Tom remembered the family history in its folder in the mahogany desk; his mother's careful notes setting it all out; shame and guilt in equal portions harboured for so many years by her father who had lived a lie and discovered worse. If she had felt unable to reveal his story, then neither could he, for her sake. "It was what he knew about his family," he said, keeping things simple. "He was ashamed," he added, hoping Rufford would not press him further.

Rufford took the hint. "Did Robert know?" he asked.

"He knew some of it. It was family history."

"Ah – of course. I could never compete with that, could I?"

"No, probably not."

Further down the room, someone laughed out loud, and others followed. A tale well-told perhaps. The laughter died away and the general hubbub of casual chatter resumed once more.

"What happened at Rothwell Mere?" Tom asked at last, certain whatever it was, two people had been bound together over the years by its invisible thread.

Rufford gave a low, hollow laugh. "What happened?" he said, shaking his head as he wrestled with the memories. "Nothing. Everything."

★

Where to begin? John censored the finer details – of the night they had spent together – of the intensity of their love-making. Children never want to hear such things. Instead he told the story of their walk to the mere on that bright, bitingly cold January morning; the heron taking flight from the reeds at their approach; the silver mist hovering between the trees; the photographs he had taken – the one Laura had chosen later as her favourite, now gracing the cover of Bernard's book; the strangeness of the place – its magic that had touched them both; and the realisation that something had happened he could not ignore. "That's where it began," he said, hearing his voice soften with the memory of how he felt that day. "That's when I began to believe I was unshakeably in love with her."

Thomas was looking straight at him. "What made her any different from the rest?" he was asking.

"Everything. Her spirit. Her defiance. Her determination to find her own way. She wasn't like other young women at the time, Thomas. She wanted something more – for herself. To make the most of her talent – her art. There was a fire in her that thrilled me to the core."

"Did you ever tell her?"

"Not until it was too late."

Don't take too long to decide if you love her enough.

"We met for the last time at the mere," Rufford was saying, "That May." The pain of that final meeting was written on his face. "By accident," he added, maybe wanting to emphasise there had been nothing improper between them – no secret assignation. "I didn't know she and Robert were engaged. I didn't know –" He stopped himself, but Tom had no doubt what he was going to say – that he had not known she was pregnant at the time – and not with Robert's child. "She was sketching," Rufford went on, pretending nothing untoward had been said. "I'd told her the mere looked its best on spring evenings. She must have remembered."

"Was that the sketch she sent you?"

"You know about it?"

"Yes. She told Robert."

"Really?" Rufford appeared strangely elated by this discovery.

"She said she didn't think you'd keep it."

"I've treasured it. Always will."

"Is that why you keep going back – to the mere?"

Rufford nodded, finishing his drink.

"What made you start collecting? Robert said you'd been buying her work for years."

Rufford laughed softly, studying his empty glass. "An indulgence," he said, looking mildly embarrassed. "I wanted to feel close to her – even if we never met again." He paused. "Do you believe that?" He looked up suddenly, seeking reassurance – no, demanding it.

Did Tom believe it? He was unsure, but there was something about Rufford's intensity that was more than bluff or bluster: it was a kind of desperation; a need beyond a simple statement or acknowledgment that he had been believed – he needed absolute certainty.

CHAPTER THIRTY-ONE

"Would you like to come over to Lower Chursley?" Rufford was asking him as they left the inn, clearly hoping he would agree to the suggestion. "I'd like to show you around my place if you can spare the time."

Tom agreed, wondering what else he would discover about this man that had not already been revealed over lunch.

They followed a minor road flanked by managed woodland for several miles. Every now and then, clearings in the trees revealed old estate cottages with black and white Tudor-style gables and diamond-paned casements. Their tall, exotically shaped chimneys rose dramatically from the flanks of their steeply sloping red-tiled roofs.

Just before the village, they turned off the road into a lane between cut hedges of hazel and alder, and after a few yards came to a side entrance off the lane. On the gate post, an expensive black metal sign, with letters picked out in gold, told Tom they had arrived at Rufford's home, Westercot.

Rufford cut the engine and got out of the car waiting for Tom to join him.

On the driveway, sheltered by laurels, there was the

distinctive tang of pungent black creosote emanating from a timber garage nearby, and the thick scent of a woodland in autumn: the sweetness of decay and fungi; and the damp mustiness of fallen leaves.

Tom followed Rufford along the curving gravel path that led to the front of the house. The garden was a picturesque mix of lawns and borders with perennials and shrubs in autumnal disarray: blue and cream hydrangeas; a deep crimson weigela induced to flower a second time by the unseasonal warmth; and skimmias, equally confused, attracting foraging bees late in the year.

The house was double-fronted, one of the estate properties from its style of architecture. Around its solid oak front door, a small-leaved cotoneaster, thick with bright red berries, clung lovingly to a trellis on the wall.

There was so much to remember, Tom thought. Everything, in fact: he might never visit here again.

Inside the house, the hallway was light and airy, the walls unadorned except for a bevelled oval mirror which captured the afternoon sun, casting bright rainbow colours down the hallway to the foot of the stairs. But for all the brilliance, the atmosphere seemed strangely cold: melancholic; waiting.

"I live mostly at the back if I'm working on a project," Rufford was saying, leading Tom to a door beyond the stairs and revealing a second, smaller hallway to the rear. "This used to be the adjoining cottage," he explained. "Knocked into one sometime in the 'fifties, I believe."

It must have been a very humble place, Tom thought, with its separate entrance hidden away at the back, out of sight. A simple affair, its tiny kitchen transformed into a dark-room, the window blanked out, the work surface housing an enlarger, a measuring jug and thermometer, with photographic trays laid out in tandem by the sink. There was a selection of brown glass bottles on the shelves above and stocks of paper tightly wrapped against the light. A clothes line, with red and blue plastic pegs here and there along its length, stretched from the side of the shelves to a batten on the wall opposite, and behind a partly-opened door, Tom could see a white-tiled washroom with a shower in the corner. Simplicity itself.

"My study's upstairs," Rufford said, showing him the way.

On a narrow landing at the top of the staircase were two doors. Behind the door on the right, Tom could make out storage boxes and a couple of tripods leaning against the wall. The door on the left was closed. "I work in here," Rufford said, opening the door into a small attic room. He stood back, letting Tom go through.

There was a grey filing cabinet facing the door and next to this a functional desk and typist's chair. On the wall above was a year chart with random multicoloured symbols and reminders written in black marker pen. On the desk itself was an open note pad with hand-written jottings in biro, a desk lamp, a magnifying glass mounted on a stand, and an open binder with strips of negatives in orderly rows covered by protective sheathes.

"There's a fine view of the rear garden from the window," Rufford was saying, encouraging him to venture further into the room.

The door did not open fully, coming up against something solid on the other side. Pushed up against the adjacent wall, Tom discovered, was a single divan with a simple white duvet neatly pulled up onto the pillow.

Rufford must have seen his puzzlement at finding this: he looked embarrassed. "Sometimes I lose track of time," he said, as if this explained everything.

Tom nodded, pretending this was entirely understandable, except it threw a new light on Rufford as a man with the outward show of someone comfortable in society – affable and sociable – but whose inner life had shrunk to a small attic room, little more than a monk's cell where he could keep the outside world at bay. There was something terrible about it. Yet from the tiny dormer window, as Rufford had said, the view was lovely: inspirational. The golden cast of the late afternoon sunlight filled the garden with colour and light, and reflected it back into the little room.

"Would you like to see the garden?" Rufford offered, checking his watch. "There's just enough time before it goes dark."

Tom followed him down the stairs and outside through the back door onto a raised terrace with a low wall and curving stone steps leading down into the garden. From here a stone path curved between the lawn and an area of small shrubs protected by a brick boundary wall where orange-berried firethorn and japonica flourished. On the other side of the lawn, a shingled summer house of cedar wood faced the afternoon sun, and beyond this, situated at the bottom of the garden, with its backdrop of natural woodland, an old stone wall covered in lichen provided shelter to an ornamental pond fringed with exotic grasses, ferns and hostas, past their best now, but no doubt beautiful at the height of summer.

Strolling back along the path towards the house, they paused to sit for a while by the summer house on a sandstone bench warmed by the afternoon sun.

It was pleasant there: peaceful and well-ordered.

"Was it like this when you came?" Tom asked.

Rufford shook his head. "No," he said with a rueful smile. "It was – how shall I put it? – a jungle? Everyone thought I was mad. 'You won't know where to start,' they said." He paused, adding with evident pleasure, "At least I had the satisfaction of proving them wrong."

"Did it take long?" Tom asked, suspecting it had.

"Three or four years," Rufford said, leaning forward and resting his elbows on his knees as he surveyed his handiwork. He turned suddenly, asking, "Do you think it was worth it?"

"A job worth doing is worth doing well."

Rufford smiled expansively. "That's exactly what I told them," he said. "But," he added with a small frown, "I don't think they understood how much I needed to do something creative at the time – I still do."

Tom nodded sensing the long hours spent in toil were more about the means to ease a broken heart than the self-congratulation that sprang from a job well done.

The sun began flirting with the tops of the trees, lacing the garden with shadows, and a hint of chill crept into the air.

As the shadows grew longer, Rufford's mood changed: he was suddenly withdrawn; remote; his outward cheerfulness sinking with the sun. His face had grown solemn. "Strange," he said at last, his voice catching slightly as he spoke, "I always imagined that some day ..." There was a long pause. "Some day, she'd come ... and we'd sit – here on this bench, and I'd show her the garden ... " He turned away, unable to say anything more.

Tom leaned forward and touched Rufford's arm. "I came," he said, hoping this might be enough.

Rufford brushed a hand across his face. "Yes!" he said, hastily mastering his self-control. "Yes – you have!" And he stood up, in command of himself once more. "Come indoors. It's going cold."

They went in through the french windows that led from the terrace into a pleasant oak-beamed sitting room that extended to the front of the house. It was filled with a comfortable blend of traditional and modern furniture. On either side of the tall cream stone fireplace, the alcoves were filled with books, neatly arranged in order of height on the shelves. And above the fireplace itself hung a solitary work of art in an elegant frame. The subject was unmistakeable.

Rothwell Mere.

If Tom never saw the piece again, he knew he would recall every minute detail of that scene: the late spring evening with its cloudless sky; the golden sunlight etched on every ripple, every blade of grass; the myriad colours captured in the zig-zag patterns of the wake behind the duckling brood; the shimmering green and bronze of the reeds. And behind the brilliance, beyond the mere, something that could not fail to draw the eye and hold it – the impenetrable darkness of the shadows in the trees: advancing; menacing and unstoppable – like Death itself.

Rufford was standing back, watching him.

At first, Tom did not know what to say: he understood the power of images too well. The painting of Brack, waiting in the yard could still catch him unawares some days and leave him choked. "My mother's sketch," he said, hearing his voice breaking as he spoke.

"Yes," Rufford said, and with almost religious reverence, he lifted the picture off the wall. "I've not shown this to anyone," he said, turning it over.

On the back, instead of a simple piece of hardboard – was a second sheet of glass. Beneath it, clearly visible, Tom could make out the words written in his mother's hand: the bold, defiant message. 'To John. A memento of an enchanted place. May 1963. From Laura – with love.'

Tom studied the hastily written words, coming to terms with the potency of them reaching out to him from the past. Here was the proof, if ever he had doubted it, of the love that had bound his mother to this man. The words written by Rufford on his photograph had been a single strand, insubstantial in itself perhaps and easily broken, but the message on the sketch, brief as it was, was the missing thread. The one intertwined with the other, giving the whole an unbreakable strength. Robert had been right to fear this bond.

Rufford took the picture from him. "Do you think she

loved me, Thomas?" he was asking as he returned it to its pride of place, adjusting its position slightly, ensuring it was straight. "I tell myself she did."

Tom did not know what to say.

Rufford turned, smiling apologetically. "I'm sorry, you can't possibly answer that. Do you want to see the rest of the collection?" And he led the way across the hallway and into another room – and another world. He put on the lights and stood back to let Tom go through first. "This is my gallery," he said quietly.

In a large room devoid of furniture, the windows shuttered against unwanted light and the walls heavily painted a deep terracotta, was the Rufford Collection, individually lit with loving care – upward of thirty or more paintings and other works of art by Laura Douglas. It was an astonishing display.

Tom stood in the doorway, rooted to the spot.

"Please – do look round," Rufford was urging him.

In something of a dream, Tom stepped into the room. The picture nearest the door was entitled *Snow on Larches* – a study of a group of trees behind Rigg End.

"This was the first painting I ever bought," Rufford was telling him. "It reminded me of the pieces she showed me one day at the Lodge. Only practice pieces," he said, still clearly in awe of them, "exploring the different colours hidden in snow. But they struck me as quite remarkable – even then."

Tom moved on, still in something of a dream. On the same wall was a quartet of smaller water colours with a single theme – a tumbled stone wall in a woodland clearing reflecting the seasonal changes of a year. Elsewhere, there were studies of wild flowers, some in oils, others in pastels or watercolours; intricate close-ups of tree bark, fissured and flaking; mosses and lichen on stone walls; studies of trees in summer and winter, several in pen and ink; and finally – and most poignantly of all to Tom – a watercolour – the view across the valley from Rigg End, executed, he guessed from the cast of the light, early one January morning when the sky was intensely blue above the silver mist along the river, and the air crystal clear, rime clinging to the grass stems in the shade. It was a work dedicated to a landscape she had grown to love. Maybe it reminded her of somewhere else.

"I never understood why she never came back," Rufford was saying. "Until I saw this."

"She loved the view."

"Yes," he said sadly. "I could tell."

They stayed for some time in the gallery, Tom struggling to remember if he could recall any of these works before. A handful perhaps – no more. He felt ashamed at his lack of interest in so much of her work. He had been blind to her success: the well-respected courses that she ran; the creativity and laughter filling the studio; the pleasure she had found in encouraging others to touch the world as she had done. He felt diminished by the knowledge of his ignorance. It hurt him to know Rufford had seen what he had so signally failed to recognise – her brilliance.

"She was my Muse," he heard Rufford say. "Perhaps you'd noticed. I learned to look at the world through her eyes."

His expression was filled with a sense of mystery that such a thing should happen.

"She would've been pleased," Tom said, wondering if this was an adequate response under such circumstances.

Rufford smiled. Perhaps it was.

Later, back in the sitting room, Rufford put on the fire and closed the curtains against the onset of evening. He seemed keen now to pursue other matters, perhaps conscious time was pressing. "I've a favour to ask," he said out of the blue. "I wondered if you'd consider staying on a few more days? I'm going down to Shropshire tomorrow – to see my parents." He paused, implying his request had some significance. "I wondered if you might like to come? My mother already knows about you," he added, looking mildly embarrassed.

Faced with the unexpected, Tom floundered.

Rufford took his silence as reluctance. "You don't have to, if you feel you can't," he said, eager to reassure him. "I won't press you." And he promptly let the matter drop. "Would you like a drink? Coffee? Tea? Something else?"

Tom automatically chose tea and Rufford went into the kitchen to make it. A few minutes later he returned with two steaming mugs and handed one across to him. "Would you like to see the photographs I took of your mother?" he was asking, retrieving an album in a blue leather binding from the bookshelf.

Inside the album were half-a-dozen black-and-white photos of a young woman wrapped up against the cold, standing at the edge of the mere. She had turned to smile into the camera: happy, and visibly in love. Small wonder then that Rufford had believed she would return to him.

"Perhaps you should see these too," Rufford was saying, bringing other albums off the shelf, and selecting pages here and there he said might be of interest. It was a ploy of course, Tom knew, showing him the faces of people he should know and telling him their names: a sepia print of Rufford's parents on their wedding day; a studio portrait of Charles, straight-backed and proud in his Air Force uniform, and a much later colour photograph – Geraldine, as cheerful and as dimpled as when she was a bride – and Charles, bewildered now, a sad confusion in his eyes.

"My father's not the man he used to be," Rufford explained with heavy emphasis.

Tom understood.

There were other photographs: Michael, the Rufford uncle he never known; his wife, Caroline, elegant and beautiful; and their three pretty daughters – his cousins; Megan on the cusp of womanhood, wide-eyed and waiting for her life to start; Josie, a newly hatched teenager, growing fast and slightly gauche; and Daisy, still a child, mischievous and unafraid.

"I decided some time ago, they should know about you," Rufford said quietly, closing the albums and returning them to the shelves. "I hope you don't mind."

Although he did not ask, Tom knew what Rufford wanted most – Tom's willingness to be acknowledged as his son. Was it so hard to understand? Surely he was owed that much at least? So Tom had agreed – to this, and more – and later wondered if he might have gone too far too soon.

Back at The George, he went to the bar and ordered a straight whisky, needing a shot of Dutch courage before making his call. At the payphone in the hallway, he hesitated before dialling the number and waited anxiously for Robert to pick up the phone. It rang several times before he answered.

They exchanged the usual greetings, Tom aware his voice sounded taut and on edge. "Just a quick call," he said, wanting to get it over with as soon as possible.

"Anything wrong?" Robert asked.

There was no easy way to break the news. "I've met Rufford. He's asked me to stay on for a few days – and I said I would. Will that be okay?"

There was an aching silence down the phone.

"Of course," Robert said at last, apparently unwilling, or unable to say anything more on the topic. Maybe Sarah was in the hall. "Duncan's here if I need him."

"Tell him I owe him a pint if you do."

"I will," Robert said without any further comment. "Take care, Tom."

"And you, Dad," Tom said, suddenly uncomfortable after all those years using this familiar term. Things had changed.

He went up to his room and lay stretched out on the bed staring up at the ceiling, wondering if he had done the right thing. That morning, he had never seriously considered the possible outcome of meeting Rufford. Perhaps subconsciously, the prospect had been too daunting to give it more than a cursory thought before dismissing it. But they *had* met, and promises had been made he would have to keep.

He sat up, seeking some distraction and switched on the television.

On the screen, the newsreader sombrely announced that British Summer Time would end at 2.00 a.m. and advised viewers to turn back their clocks before they went to bed.

Tom felt a shiver running over him. Tomorrow, he realised with sudden clarity, he would turn his own clock back – not by just a single hour – but by a lifetime.

CHAPTER THIRTY-TWO

Geraldine was coming down the steps to greet them, her face glowing with undisguised pleasure. "Oh, John," she said, reaching up to kiss him on the cheek. "I can't tell you how much this means to me." She held him close for a moment. "And this is Thomas?" she asked, her eyes drawn inevitably in Thomas's direction. She was barely able to contain her excitement.

Thomas was holding back, standing awkwardly by the car, his hands plunged deep into the pockets of his jeans. He had not said as much, but John could sense his deep uncertainty. From the moment they had set off earlier that afternoon, it had lodged between them like a substantial ghost, an unseen but very tangible presence, filling the journey to Little Retton with strained silences and fragmented conversation. For most of the time, Thomas had chosen to concentrate on the shifting scene outside the car: the rolling landscape of small pastures and wooded hills; the grey-walled manor houses and abbeys set in parkland; and picturesque Shropshire towns with narrow streets and open market spaces flanked by black-and-white half-timbered buildings. But the closer they had come to Little Retton, the quieter he had become, until he barely spoke at all. And once they had arrived at Sylvans, his tenseness was plainly visible for all to see: the knitted brow; the tightness round the mouth pinching in his cheeks; and the strained, taut look about his eyes. Now, with Geraldine's attention fully on him, Thomas was trying hard to hide his uncertainty behind a mask of self-assurance and easy affability, smiling bravely as he stepped forward to meet her.

John introduced them, listening to his heart quicken as he spoke.

"Pleased to meet you," Thomas was saying as Geraldine captured both his hands in hers, her eyes searching his face, eager to take in everything about him.

"Oh, John," she said, with a brief glance in his direction, her eyes brimming with emotion. "He looks just like you did at his age."

There was a moment's awkwardness.

Geraldine shook her head, tutting softly to herself, patting Thomas's hands reassuringly. "Oh dear – how silly of me," she said, laughing nervously. "I'm so excited, you see. Do come on in, won't you? There's a nasty chill in the air today."

In the hallway, she took their coats while beyond the closed door of the sitting room, a cacophony of sound from the afternoon film on TV was making its presence felt.

"Have you told Charles?" John asked, raising his voice slightly to be heard above the din.

"Oh yes," she assured him, " – straight after you phoned," adding with another nervous smile, "I just said you were coming down to see us – and you were bringing someone I knew he'd love to meet." Under the barrage of noise from the sitting room, her anxiety visibly increased. "That was what we agreed, wasn't it?"

"No point in complicating things," John said, beginning to wish he had not been in such a hurry to arrange this visit. "We'll just have to take things as they come – one step at a time."

"Yes – as you say – one step at a time." She paused to put a tentative hand on his arm. "I'm afraid he's been a little difficult this week," she confessed. "Even Kenneth said so yesterday." She turned to Thomas, evidently picking her words with care. "Your grandfather has a few problems, I'm afraid," she explained with masterly understatement. "With his memory."

Thomas nodded, giving this his serious attention.

"He doesn't always understand, you see," Geraldine went on, evidently feeling it was necessary to explain things further. "He gets easily confused – and then I'm afraid he gets very cross indeed. Please don't let him upset you, will you?"

"No, I shan't."

She looked relieved.

For a moment, all three of them stood in the hallway, caught in a web of uncertainty while the sound of gunfire and explosions emanating from the sitting room swirled around them. It was difficult to ignore.

In that moment, the expression on Thomas's face said it all – Why did I agree to this?

John could feel his stomach curl itself into a very tight knot. He cursed his folly: he had been much too quick to seize the moment. Thomas was not ready for this – no one was. It would have been far kinder to arrange a meeting with Geraldine first – perhaps at Kinnerswood with Michael and Caroline. Thomas would have been less anxious, and Geraldine would have had the pleasure of meeting her grandson for the first time without having to tip-toe around Charles' fragile state of mind and uncertain temper. There would have been no unnecessary embarrassment; no anxiety; no potential for disaster; a good starting point. But for reasons John could no longer explain, even to himself, he had felt a compulsion to jump this major hurdle first: his father. It had been a bad idea. Too late now for regrets. Thomas, he realised with sudden blinding clarity, had agreed to come, not because he wanted to, but because he felt a sense of obligation. And Geraldine, usually so adept at taking things in her stride, was simply unprepared. Neither of them had been given sufficient time to make the necessary emotional adjustments. In wanting so much so quickly, John feared, he may have over-reached himself. Now, as he stood with the others in the hallway, Charles harrumphing and swearing above the din of celluloid warfare in the sitting room, he was convinced he had.

There was another loud harrumph followed by the gruff demand to know, "Who's there!"

Geraldine stiffened perceptibly. "We've got visitors, dear," she called back cheerfully. "Remember?"

"Bloody visitors! Tell them to go away!"

John saw Thomas swallow hard.

Geraldine opened the door into the battle-zone. "It's John, dear," she said, raising her voice above the rat-a-tat-tat of machine gun fire.

"Nonsense! He came yesterday," came the irritable reply.

John intervened, placing himself squarely between his father's chair and the television. "It's definitely me, Charles," he said, as he hunkered down in front of the old man, telling himself as he always did he must never lose his temper, whatever the provocation. "And I came to see you last week, if you remember," he added, just to set the record straight.

The old man waved him aside angrily. "Get out of the way, whoever you are! I'm watching this film!"

John reached out and took hold of the bony hand clutching the remote control. He stroked it gently, feeling the vice-like grip beginning to relax. "Charles," he said, gently prising open the fingers. "It's me – John." And with a little more effort, managed to retrieve the control and reduce the volume to a non-existent level.

Charles frowned ferociously, his concentration shifting from the screen he could no longer see, nor hear. From under beetled brows, he peered at him for some considerable time. "John?" he said at last.

John nodded.

The belligerence mellowed a little. "Had a good drive down?"

"Not bad," John said, conscious his tongue felt strangely thick and his mouth had gone dry. "I've brought someone to

365

see you." He glanced over to where Thomas was standing rock-like by the door.

Charles jerked round in his seat, rigidly alert, as if expecting an unprovoked attack from the rear. He frowned, trying to concentrate, and followed the young man's progress towards him with all the intensity of a watchful bird of prey.

John stood up and let Thomas have his place. In what was probably a few seconds, nothing more, although it felt like an eternity, there was a definite pause, before he gathered his wits enough to say without any ceremony whatsoever, "Thomas has come to see you, Charles. He's my son."

A much longer silence ensued, the old man glaring up at the much younger version of himself standing solidly in front of him.

Since Laura's funeral and the many months of wishful thinking in between, John had practised this announcement – or rather several versions of it – none of them as blunt as this. It had just come out: unadorned; naked; shocking. He heard the words and felt their impact, his heart slamming against his ribs with a frightening thud, then continuing to knock and pound as if it were trying to escape the confines of his chest. If there was one, absolutely wrong way to tell his father this momentous news, he told himself as he listened to the thunder echo in his head, then surely this was it. He surveyed the unfolding scene with a mixture of trepidation and mounting alarm.

Thomas was trying to smile as he leaned forward offering to shake the old man's hand, and John watched helplessly as his father's irritation slipped into deepening confusion. The old man's mouth fell open, bewildered and wordless. For a moment nothing happened, then slowly, the claw-like fingers with their paper-thin skin and staring veins reached out uncertainly and took hold of Thomas's strong, sun-tanned hand, shaking it – or rather flapping it – up and down in a mechanical, slow motion sort of way. And Thomas was saying, "Hello," and smiling hopefully, seeking reassurance all was well.

"Thomas, you say?" Charles said after mulling over the name for a moment, frowning again as the feeble processes of his mind wrestled with this bewildering piece of information. Finding no enlightenment, he said abruptly, "Sit down – sit down," and released his hold, waving impatiently in the direction of the adjacent chair. "Don't stand there like a stuffed dummy."

Thomas obliged, perching himself on the edge of the chair, his smile still firmly fixed in place.

"Come for tea, have you?" Charles demanded.

Thomas swallowed hard and nodded.

"So I should bloody think so!" Charles said. "Never see anyone these days." And he swivelled in his chair again, searching for the person he expected to be somewhere in the room. "What's-her-name over there will bring us some," he added, dismissing Geraldine with a peremptory wave of his hand.

She left quickly.

Charles' attention shifted back to Thomas. He leaned forward in his chair to study him more closely. "Thomas, you say," he repeated, still wrestling with the conundrum of who this person was. "John's boy."

Thomas nodded encouragingly.

The old man thought about this, frowning to himself. "I forget things now, you know. Not what I used to be," he added with a shake of his head. And suddenly, all belligerence was gone, like snow in summer. "It's my age, you know."

Thomas just nodded and kept on smiling.

"Mm ... Thomas," Charles repeated, sinking back into the empty chambers of his memory. "Had a brother once ... What happened to him?" he asked, looking around vaguely for some guidance. "Can't remember."

"He went to fight the Fascists – in Spain," John reminded him.

"Never came back?"

"No."

"Stupid bugger. What did he expect? Never join an army," Charles added with a flash of anger, a barb aimed straight at John, soon forgotten, his attention easily distracted. He fixed his unblinking gaze on the young man again. "You're very like your father. Have I told you that?"

Thomas glanced across at John, then shook his head.

Charles sank back in his seat, bewildered. "Can't think why not. Should have said so sooner." And after a moment's reflection, perked up noticeably, taking hold of Thomas's hand again and patting it affectionately. "Glad you came. Had a good drive down?"

John heard himself let out a very audible sigh of relief,

and realised he had been holding his breath for some considerable length of time.

It was dark when they returned to Westercot, the brief visit to Sylvans as much as Tom could bear. He had been relieved when John suggested it was getting late and they should take their leave. Even more relieved there was no suggestion they should divert to Kinnerswood to call in on Michael and his family. He felt drained. Too many conversations laced with muddled thoughts and random subjects; fragmented memories of the war; friends known and lost; hopes for the future shattered by the past.

Charles had frequently mistaken him for John. Sometimes, without warning, the old man had suddenly demanded, "Are you married yet?" his belligerence firmly back in place.

To which Tom had admitted, "Not yet," fearing this would trigger worse. And indeed it had.

"Why not?"

"I haven't found the right girl."

The old man had exploded with indignation. "Rubbish!" he had said. "When are you going to marry that girl you keep mooning over? What are you waiting for? – the Second Coming?"

At which point, Geraldine had tactfully intervened with a slice of sponge cake and cup of tea, and after a moment or two the old man had suddenly asked him what he was doing with himself these days. The notion of farming had produced a frown of incomprehension followed by an animated five minutes of curious questioning, the answers

Tom gave being filed away – or possibly lost – in the mish-mash of his grandfather's disordered thoughts. But in the final moment of parting, the old man had clung onto his hand and said pathetically, "You will come and see me again, won't you, my boy? Very much appreciate it if you did." And Tom had said he would, wondering if such a promise should ever have been made.

On the porch saying goodbye, Geraldine had looked tired. She had hugged him close, confiding in him while John was still in the hall, "You know, Thomas, John did love your mother – very much indeed. I'm glad you felt you could get in touch with him. I know this must have been very hard for you. Thank you so much for coming to see us. We do appreciate it." And she had reached up and planted a kiss on his cheek, hurriedly composing herself as John came out to join them.

The journey back had been largely in silence. Tom felt no compulsion to talk, and John, mercifully seemed prepared to accept his unwillingness.

Now, upstairs in the comfortably furnished guest room John had prepared for him, Tom felt drained. He unpacked his bag and stood staring out into the darkness for a while, seeing in his reflection caught in the diamond panes an image not just of himself, but of an older self in John; and then another, even older self in Charles, with his occasional tendency to cock his head when speaking. In Charles, with his steel-grey hair and flamboyant moustache, fraying jumper and tartan rug thrown over his knees despite a roaring fire in the hearth, he had seen his likeness stretching back into the past – and a glimpse of what he might become.

Exhaustion had left him strangely empty of emotion: there was only a bottomless well of tiredness and a sense he should have made more of his visit. Nothing else. He closed the curtains, shutting out the image in the panes.

A door opened. Downstairs John called up to him to join him for a drink.

The sitting room was comfortably warm, and a symphony he recognised but could not identify was playing softly from the hi-fi speakers somewhere in the room.

"Beer or whisky?" John was asking. There was a nervous edge to his voice.

Tom settled for whisky.

"Soda?"

"No thanks. Just straight." He need its potency.

They settled into their respective chairs under the gaze of the pastel sketch above the fireplace. Tom tried to avoid taking too much notice of it: he would have preferred the presence of another scene – the broad sweep of the valley below Rigg End; the track leading down to the lane; the stone wall and the trees. The image of Rothwell Mere left him uncomfortable, an awkward reminder he was growing in his mother's belly when she drew it, and she had gone out of John's life for ever that fine May evening, ignoring her true feelings for him, and his for her. She had left him, and deprived her son of his true inheritance. The more he pondered this, the more distressed he felt.

There was a physical pain now when he thought of

Robert's mother, Grace: her welcoming smile; his pleasure in her company. Even as age took its toll, her vivid stories of their Gillmuir and Douglas kin had filled his childhood visits with much wonder and delight. And later, when he returned to Rigg End, he would pour over the photographs in Robert's album, remembering the names and places she had told him of. So when she died, he had deeply mourned her loss, the only grandparent he had ever known – and cared for.

But now he knew – not just as a bald, stated fact – but as a tangible, living thing in the touch of a hand and warm embrace, this sense of kinship he had treasured was a lie. Until that afternoon, he had not truly faced this knowledge and accepted it – that Grace had never been his kin; that the link that once had been a source of pride and satisfaction – 'The Douglas Connection' – had never existed. He belonged to another tribe – and they had claimed him. Inside his head, a small but persistent voice whispered with a regular insistence, "You are not Thomas Moray. You are not Thomas Moray." And his thoughts would not stop their maddening circle, whirling round and round like a demented Catherine wheel, trying to escape its fixing pin.

"I'm sorry," John was saying, addressing the firelight. "I should never have asked you to go. It was too soon."

Tom pulled himself back into the present. He took a long draught of the fine malt, the sensation of it stinging in his throat jolting him back in time, to another conversation, after he had found the photograph and challenged Robert, seeking truth, and finding his life slipping into uncertainty instead. *Truth is not always plain or simple.*

Talking had become difficult.

John persisted. "It was selfish of me. I should have had more sense."

It would be better, Tom decided, to say nothing. Besides, words were refusing to form themselves into any sort of sentence that might serve a useful purpose. He gave up trying. Instead, he leaned back against the chair and closed his eyes, forcing himself to listen to the music, eager to blot out the insistent chanting in his head. After a while, he seemed to have succeeded: the music had gained the upper hand; he recognised the thread of melody and floated on it, content to let it buoy him up. He drifted, unaware for some time that Charles had crept back unbidden into his thoughts. Would they meet again? Perhaps. Perhaps not. If not, then so be it: he was content that he had known him.

The slow movement ended, and in the brief silence that followed, out of nowhere, he heard himself say, quite distinctly, "No – I'm glad we went. He's an old man." And a long-forgotten quatrain from the *Rubaiyat* sprang into his mind. *The Bird of Time has but a little way to fly – and lo! – the Bird is on the wing*. He opened his eyes.

John was studying him with an all-consuming gaze: the intense love of a father for his son.

Tom could feel its heat.

CHAPTER THIRTY-THREE

Sophie, in faded jeans and sporting a garish Peruvian poncho with matching knitted hat pulled down over her ears, came out of the shop on Lingford's busy high street and literally bumped into him. "Tom!" she said, throwing her arms round him to give him a quick peck on the cheek. "Oh – this is fantastic!" She was clutching a large, glossy green carrier bag which told the world she could afford to patronise Gerrards of Lingford – Purveyors of Fine Italian Footwear. "Snuggy boots – for winter," she explained, seeing him take notice of her purchase. "An absolute must. Look – what are you doing here? I thought you were going home at the weekend."

"I changed my mind," he hedged. "Anyway, I thought you said you were going back to college."

"Tomorrow," she said, linking her arm through his and propelling him down the street. "Shall we go for a coffee? Say you will."

Sophie was a chameleon, Tom decided: she dressed to match her mood. Today she was a dizzy carefree student. The stylish, more cautious Sophie who had entertained him at her brother's flat, and the equally anxious Sophie who had solemnly quizzed him on the possibility of improving her sex life the following morning, had been put aside. Clearly, from her general demeanour and non-stop chatter, he had managed to 'cheer her up'.

With time on his hands and nothing to lose, he found himself upstairs in Carters, an up-market independent department store, surrounded by small intimate groups of ladies of a certain age, with time and money to spend on morning coffee and a little gossip. There was an atmosphere of refined restraint and hushed conversation. He was the only man, a fact that registered on all the faces turned in his direction as he came through the door. Some, from the raised eyebrows and half-smiles, evidently thought they knew him.

"I love it here," Sophie was saying in a stage whisper as she dumped her expensive purchase unceremoniously on the floor under a vacant table in the corner. "You can spy on everyone without them knowing." She pulled off her hat, stuffing it down behind her on the seat, and raked her fingers through her hair. She looked wonderfully rumpled, just as she had the morning after they had spent the night together. Was it barely a week ago? It seemed much more.

When he came back with their coffee, she was engaged in her favourite sport, her chin propped on her hand, eyes darting from table to table. "They're bursting with curiosity," she said as he put down the cup in front of her. "They can't take their eyes off you. Can't think why," she added, teasing him.

Tom stirred his coffee and refused to rise to the bait.

In the absence of him making any comment, she set off on a new tack, beginning with what she had clearly decided was the purpose of detaining him. "So if you thought *I* wasn't around, what made *you* change *your* mind?" she asked, her expression implying this was just an innocent enquiry.

Tom was uncertain how to answer. Had Oliver mentioned the article in the *Herald*? Across the table, Sophie was studying him over her coffee cup, her hazel eyes betraying a delightful mischief.

"What do you want me to say?" he asked, deciding to play her at her own game.

She stifled a laugh. "Oh come on! – Tell me!"

He had no intention of saying anything that did not need to be said. John might have no qualms about introducing him as his son to all and sundry, but Tom was not about to take the initiative himself – particularly if there were no need to divulge anything. So he shrugged off her insistence and adopted an air of indifference. "Just a whim," he said, making light of it.

She leaned across the table. "You're a rotten liar," she said in a conspiratorial whisper. "I know all about you."

Tom found heat rushing up from under his collar and spreading over his face. He kept his head down, studying his coffee cup with exaggerated interest until the moment passed.

"I think it's fantastic," she was saying, still mercifully keeping her voice lowered. "My God – I wish I'd been someone's love-child." She was waving her cup around with a casual indifference to its contents. "When did you find out?"

"When did you?" he asked, determined to deflect her interest in precise particulars in such a public place.

"Yesterday. Uncle Julius couldn't help himself apparently. He let something slip to Daddy – about why he'd been in such a state when he'd met you over lunch last week." She paused, evidently wanting to probe deeper. "Have you met him yet? – John Rufford – I mean? He does know you're in Lingford, doesn't he? His studio's just around the corner – in Chester Place. Did you know that?" Too many questions. She was breathless, wanting answers, heedless of the discomfort she was causing.

His silence must have spoken for him. She sat back in her seat, biting her lip, suddenly contrite. "Oh God, Tom, *mi scusa*. Sometimes I really don't know when to stop." Her slipping into Italian was charming, but had the effect of undermining her sincerity. She smiled at him apologetically. "Tell me you don't mind me being curious."

Whether he did or not seemed immaterial.

"We met on Saturday," he said, unwilling to say too much with so many eyes on him. "He asked me to stay on for a few days, that's all." He checked his watch. Almost eleven thirty. "I'm having lunch with him at twelve."

"Well I think that's brilliant," she said defiantly, pausing before leaning forward and plunging into the fray again. "When did you find out about him? I mean – did you know – when we –?" and she feigned embarrassment at mentioning their one-night stand.

Realising there was going to be no stopping her, Tom decided to give in gracefully and keep it simple. "I found out last year," he said, " – after he came to my mother's funeral."

"My God!" she said, her eyes widening. "Didn't you know who he was?" She was clearly conjuring up the scene in her imagination.

"No, not then. I found his photo in one of my mother's poetry books."

"*Che romantico!*" she enthused, propping her chin back onto her hands, a dreamy look washing over her.

"I suppose you've told Gregory."

"Of course!"

"What did he say?"

She looked bemused. "He said, 'that explains everything' – whatever that means. Except he showed me the piece in the *Herald* – and I've got to admit, you really do look like him." She was gazing into his eyes in a decidedly meaningful way.

"So I believe," he said, pretending not to notice she was flirting with him.

"Is that so bad?" she asked archly. "I mean – he's pretty gorgeous – you've got to admit it. No wonder I fell for you." She was laughing softly, her attention deflected artfully into the task of scooping up the remnants of the undissolved sugar lump at the bottom of her cup with a teaspoon, and slowly putting the sweet brown mixture into her mouth.

Tom wondered if it were wise to dwell on this too much.

She was suddenly more serious again. "I don't suppose

you're free this afternoon, are you?" she asked giving him a brief tentative smile. "Gregory won't be back 'til after six."

The thought of repeating his interlude with Sophie had its attractions, but also the potential to draw him further into a relationship he had no great interest in fostering. He found himself relieved he could decline her offer without the need to lie. "Sorry," he said, making sure he smiled as he said it, "I'm going over to Netherton Hall with John. He's taking some photos for Bernard's next book."

She looked genuinely disappointed. "Some other time then?" she suggested.

It was almost noon. He stood up and leaned forward, kissing her lightly on the cheek, promising nothing.

At the door, he turned. She gave him a little wave, smiling coquettishly at him. He waved back.

Arriving at Chester Place, Tom had little idea of what to expect on meeting Gemma Mortimer – beyond John's brief run-through of her history, and the observation that she was thoroughly reliable. "Runs everything like clockwork," he had said with evident satisfaction. With this in mind, Tom imagined her as 'a useful person', pleasant enough perhaps, but nothing out of the ordinary: a divorcée whose short marriage implied she might not have much going for her. Stepping through the door into the smart reception area with its stylish seating and decor and copious examples of John's photographic work mounted on the walls, it came as something of a shock to discover she was nothing short of glamorous; glamorous without being flashy, which made her doubly attractive. His immediate reaction to this vision of loveliness, with immaculate make-up, ash-blond hair and pale grey-blue eyes, not to mention a figure that ignited more than curiosity, was that John must be out of his mind overlooking her possibilities for so long. Was he totally blind? No red-blooded male could possibly be *that* blind, surely? There was something perverse about such self-imposed celibacy when there was no longer any reason for restraint. What a waste of a good woman!

Gemma for her part, had clearly been briefed on who he was before he arrived. She smiled up at him, her professional receptionist's smile perfectly in place. She invited him to take a seat, her voice honey-rich, and like its owner, beguiling. Tom could not get it out of his head that she and John would make the perfect pair.

"Would you like a coffee?" she was asking. "I'm afraid this morning's session's taken a little longer than Mr Rufford expected."

He declined, admitting to having just come from coffee at Carters. She smiled faintly at this intelligence, one eyebrow slightly raised, evidently *au fait* with the age, gender and social status of the clientele who frequented the store.

The telephone rang and she answered it, offering alternative times and dates for an appointment to whoever was calling. The negotiations continued for some time. Tom selected one of the magazines from the coffee table next to him and flicked idly through the pages. From the room upstairs, the wail of a small child could be heard, growing louder until it became an inconsolable howl, stifled at last into spasmodic exclamations of protest followed by silence.

Gemma smiled at him reassuringly. "First birthday photographs," she explained. "They're always a little troublesome." Any further conversation was halted by the telephone ringing again, and a protracted discussion followed on the existing commitments in Mr Rufford's diary over the coming fortnight. "I'm afraid he won't be able to set aside a whole day until the following week, Mrs Fullerton. His schedule was already quite full before ... yes, the Award has made a difference. Would Tuesday, the fourteenth be any use to you?" It seemed that it would. "Can I suggest ten o'clock – if that would suit? ... No, that's perfectly acceptable. I'll ask him to give you a call to confirm final arrangements ... yes, I'll make a note for him. Thank you."

There was still no sign of the session upstairs coming to an end. Gemma smiled at him again, wordlessly acknowledging his patience.

Against all his inclinations to remain silent on the subject, Tom found himself suddenly blurting out, "I'm John's son, by the way."

Gemma tried to appear preoccupied for a moment with the necessity of bringing John's appointments diary up-to-date. She glanced up, apparently unfazed by this information. "Yes – he said you'd be calling in." She paused, apparently wondering if it were appropriate for her to make any further comment before saying with well-practised politeness, "Mr Rufford mentioned you were staying with him at Lower Chursley."

"A nice part of the world."

"Yes. Do you know it well?"

"No, not really. My mother used to live in Meeston. I've been down to see her house a couple of times."

Mention of his mother produced an awkward silence for a moment before Gemma recovered her equilibrium sufficiently to enquire, "Will you be staying long?"

"A few days. I'm hoping to see more of the area. John's offered to take me on a couple of assignments."

"Are you going to Netherton Hall this afternoon?"

Tom confirmed he was.

At which point the door opened at the top of the stairs and a bespectacled young mother appeared clutching in her arms a small girl dressed in a frilly pink frock. This bundle of misery with a halo of golden curls had thrust one small fist into its mouth and was sucking on it vigorously. "She's teething," explained her mother, visibly flustered, and feeling it was necessary to explain the behaviour of her offspring to those present. Turning to John, she added with heartfelt gratitude, "Thank you so much for being so patient with her."

John smiled indulgently while the small child with red-rimmed eyes stared at him, suddenly fascinated. "I can assure you, Mrs Hall, I've seen it all before," he said, his voice radiating warmth and understanding. "The bright lights can be very unsettling for little ones."

The woman thanked him effusively, and he insisted for the second time there was nothing to apologise for; the photographs would be fine and she could collect them the following week. The child's gaze remained riveted on him:

hypnotised. When he smiled at her, she turned coyly and buried her face into her mother's shoulder.

Tom saw Gemma look away, apparently preoccupied by the need to note down details of Mrs Hall's next visit. He was curious. Was she so indifferent to John's capacity to charm? – he wondered. Had she seen him exercise this ability once too often and was totally unmoved by it? Or was there the smallest possibility she had learned to hide her interest, and perhaps she really harboured a deep and abiding longing he chose to ignore?

That afternoon, as John drove them out to Netherton Hall, Tom broached the possibility without making anything too obvious. "Gemma wasn't how I'd imagined her," he began, " – from what you'd said."

John raised an eyebrow, his concentration on the road.

"A good-looking woman," Tom observed.

"Yes."

"Is she going out with anyone?"

"A land agent, I think. Why? Are you interested?"

Tom ignored this. "You weren't tempted then? – when you first took her on?"

"My mind was on other things."

"My mother?"

"Yes."

Tom let this hang in the air for a moment before he asked, "Don't you think it's time you let my mother go?"

John frowned.

"You're wasting your life."

"I can't just forget her, Thomas."

"I didn't ask you to. I just want you to know I don't expect you to shut yourself away for ever." He was thinking of Robert seeking solace with Sarah to fill the dreadful void in his life. John could do the same: he could still attract women, and if not Gemma, there would be any number of others who might suit his needs. "Why don't you find someone else to love?"

"Why should I?"

"Life can get lonely, that's all." The image of Robert again: bereft; solitary. "You shouldn't close your mind to finding happiness," Tom persisted, finding Janet suddenly springing into his thoughts: he could see her smile; hear her laughter; remember the warm glow of comfortable ease he felt in her company, with nothing forced or strained. And with these memories came the inevitable palpable thud of his heart. Sophie was lovely, but lacked that indefinable 'something'. Janet was different. Janet *moved* him.

"I don't hear you telling me anything about *your* love life," John was observing caustically.

Convoluted explanations were not on Tom's agenda. He wanted to stick to the point. "I'll get over my spilt milk," he said. "All I'm saying is it's time you did the same. Take a good look at what you're missing. Someone to care for. Someone to have children with. I wouldn't want you to miss out on that second chance."

"I don't need a second chance, Thomas. I've got you. That's enough."

"Is it? – when I'm back at Rigg End, and you're at Westercot all on your own – brooding?"

"I don't brood," John objected. "I'm not a hen. I'll be content if you visit when you can."

"Well, I'd like to think you'd got someone else in your life, that's all."

"Anyone in mind?" John asked, openly mocking him.

Tom did not reply. Maybe he just wanted John to take up with Gemma so he could feel better about Robert taking up with Sarah. It was an uncomfortable thought.

CHAPTER THIRTY-FOUR

Tom stared out of the window of his room at Westercot watching the rain bleach against the panes, running in steady rivulets over the sill. It was November, and another week had passed. He should be going home: there was a farm to run; stock to tend. But he lacked any motivation to pack his bags and leave: he wanted to stay.

He made the call, in no doubt Robert could hear him stumble over his words, trying to excuse his absence.

How could he tell Robert he was tired of living the lie? – of pretending to be someone he was not? He felt safe at Westercot. He could be who he really was – John Rufford's son – surrounded by the warmth of family and friends and their unquestioning acceptance of him. He had stepped out of one world and into another, and it felt good.

But, if he were honest with himself, deep down, he could not shake off his other life so easily. Rigg End was his past, and what it meant to him: Robert; the Robsons; the camaraderie of the mart; walking The Rigg with Brack; the satisfactions from the farming year; and the wilderness beyond the Wall. He did not care to dwell on this: it troubled him.

Instead, he learned to savour the moment, and the more adept he became at this new skill, the easier it became to put his sense of disquiet aside. And why not? His days were full: a weekend at Kinnerswood with Michael and Caroline – Megan hanging onto his every word; sessions with John learning the art of the photographer – a wholly new adventure; and excursions to medieval manor houses – Bernard chattering like a magpie from the back seat of the car. He could be content.

But as the days became weeks, Tom wondered how Robert explained away his absence from the farm: he had never asked, and Robert had never said. If Sarah did not find it strange, Tom knew others would. They would draw their own conclusions. Up at The Gate or down at the mart, no one would be short of an opinion or two.

"Ay, well, ah canna blame the lad..."

"Who'd wanna be in the hoose with a new wife that he shoulda married hi'sel?"

And at the Tuesday Luncheon Club in the village hall, the local biddies would be leaning across the tables, nodding their heads wisely and whispering to one another.

"Yuh'd think Robert Moray woulda had more sense..."

"A man his age..."

"Drivin' the lad away like that."

Explanations were impossible, and silence damning. Tom's absence was enough: it spoke volumes.

And what was worse, Tom knew that much of what was said was true: he disliked the thought of Sarah in his mother's place. He might say otherwise to stem the tide of gossip, but it would not stop him feeling it was wrong. It still hurt. Robert had put the past behind him and chosen someone else. John had not. That was the difference.

Another week went by and Tom could no longer close his mind to the inevitable – the anniversary of his mother's death in four days' time. It was a nettle he would have to grasp. No one had mentioned it: not John – whose thoughtful silences were often more eloquent than words; nor Robert – perhaps because he expected Tom to raise the subject first.

That Monday afternoon, while John was in his studio taking portrait photographs of Davina Huntingdon and William Parker-Forbes to mark the occasion of their engagement, Tom made his call.

There was a momentary pause before Robert said, "Don't feel you have to come back for her anniversary, Tom. Let's not make a big thing of it. Better that way. It makes it harder. Besides," he added as an afterthought, not knowing the disquiet he would cause, "Sarah's here to help me through."

The king is dead, long live the king – or in this case the queen, Tom thought, a chill running through him. "Won't Jamie and Flora think it's odd if we don't?"

There was another pause. "They've not phoned," Robert said, a small but evident hint of sadness in his tone.

"So they still don't know about you and Sarah? Dad – you've got to tell them!"

The same response as always. "I'll tell them when they phone."

Nothing good would come of this, Tom could feel it in his bones.

"Sarah's just come in," Robert was saying, and the conversation was abruptly cut short.

Tom replaced the receiver, his hands cold and clammy; his blood pounding in his ears; and a voice in his head repeating over and over again that Robert Moray was a fool.

He returned to the sitting room seeking some diversion and stood by the bookshelves, his eyes skimming over the titles of the tidy rows of books. He remembered other times when Robert would read to them as children while a fire crackled in the grate: Sir Walter Scott with heroes' deeds of derring-do and desperate dangers overcome at last; and Dickens's memorable characters illuminated by extravagant descriptions that conjured up another time and place. Old memories. Good memories. In front of him, he noted casually, were poetry anthologies of Keats and Tennyson, books his mother loved – and there, between Lord Byron's *Don Juan* – and *Childe Harold's Pilgrimage*, he discovered what he half-expected to find – a slender volume of Khayyam's *Rubaiyat*.

He reached up and took it down from the shelf, the binding and exotic title script familiar, a reminder of his mother's treasured secret. He had found its twin, and when he turned the pages, he was not surprised when it fell open at the quatrain *'Ah, fill the Cup: – what boots it to repeat ...'* Nor to find a copy of the much-cherished black-and-white photograph of his mother John used to mark the poem: it seemed its natural home.

Casually, he turned the pages, its familiar illustrations strangely comforting: the young woman in diaphanous robes handing a nobleman his cup of wine; the sages arguing philosophy seated on their tasselled cushions; the gorgeous palaces and gardens. He dipped into other poems, recalling half-remembered lines.

> *Ah, Love! could thou and I*
> *with Fate conspire*
> *To grasp this sorry Scheme of*
> *Things entire,*
> *Would not we shatter it to bits –*
> *and then*
> *Remould it nearer to the Heart's*
> *Desire?*

A sadness crept over him. Its words left a melancholy echo, and he felt its poignancy reach down into his soul.

Janet filled his mind again. Like a phantom, she would do this when he least expected it – come out of nowhere, naked and beautiful, leaving him breathless and amazed at his sudden need for her. His heart would give a jolt, as it did then – like an electric shock passing through his frame – and a quiet dread would settle in its wake.

Was this his fate? Would he become a carbon copy of his father? – succumb as he had done? – possessed by a woman he had barely known, whose absence left an ache that seemed to grow with time – not lessen? Perhaps it was. But perhaps, he told himself, unwilling to go down without a fight, it was nothing to fear. Perhaps he should embrace it, not regard it as a curse. Could he do that? – shake off the affliction of the 'Pale Knight' of Keats' poem and become Tennyson's battle-hardened 'Ulysses', determined to take life by the throat and shake it? – *To strive, to seek, to find, and not to yield*? He wished he knew.

Outside, it had gone dark. The sweep of headlights skimming across the windows and briefly lighting up the room told him John was home. He went out into the unexpected warmth of the November evening to meet him, his mood strangely calm; accepting. He watched the tall figure emerging from the car, walking towards him down the pathway through the twilight; watched the easy movement of his gait; the tilt of his head as he looked up, calling his name to greet him; hearing the warmth in the voice.

I love this man, Tom thought, feeling it intensely in every fibre of his being. I love him beyond words. I am his son, and I am proud of him. Nothing could untie that knot, although soon, very soon, he must leave him here. Duty would call him home. If not this week, then the next. There was a farm to run.

John was taking off his jacket in the hall. "Bernard's been in touch. The visit to Hallam's all set for tomorrow. Should be a good day." He was smiling broadly at the prospect.

Tom put aside his gloomy thoughts and made no mention of his call to Robert.

Bernard was waiting for them outside his gate at Castors Green, dressed as usual in outlandish mode, his steady stream of interesting facts delivered over Tom's shoulder in the car, a welcome distraction.

"Plenty to photograph," Bernard informed them enthusiastically. "Built by Richard Devereux in 1472. A staunch Yorkist. Ruthless, mind – quite ruthless. Knew which side his bread was buttered on. Defected to Henry Tudor in 1485 ..."

They arrived at Hallam Manor to an effusive welcome from their hosts, Margaret and Sebastian Moorville-Smythe. Their dogs, a brown Labrador and Jack Russell attached themselves to Tom, bounding along beside him much to their hosts' embarrassment and his quiet satisfaction: he was missing Brack.

"Toby! Ben! Come here! Now! Oh dear. I'm so sorry. They're not usually so boisterous." Mrs Moorville-Smythe dragged them away, calling over her shoulder, "There's tea and biscuits in the conservatory ... We thought you might like some sandwiches for lunch ... Do help yourselves ..."

The day passed quickly in a cavalcade of striking images and scenery at every turn, to the accompaniment of Bernard's frequent forays into the minutiae of historical fact and anecdotal evidence.

It was growing dark when they left, and gone six when they dropped off Bernard and returned to Lower Chursley.

As they got out of the car, they could hear the phone ringing in the hall.

John hurried to answer it. Tom, in no particular rush and enjoying the scents of the evening air, sauntered after him. In the hallway, John had turned to meet him, his face pale and suddenly drawn. "It's for you, Thomas," he said sombrely, handing over the phone.

Tom felt a shiver running down his spine.

Ian's voice was cracking under the strain. "Thank God, Tom," he said. "Been trying to get you all day. There's been an accident. It's Rob. He's in Newcastle General."

Tom listened to himself ask, "What's happened?" as a void opened up inside him and all the pleasure of the day was swallowed up leaving nothing behind.

"He got trampled, Tom. A dog was running loose. It spooked the beasts."

"Is he bad?"

"They've had to operate."

From somewhere far away, Tom was asking about Sarah.

"She went over with him in the ambulance. Jamie's come down. He's picked up Flora from the station. They're at the hospital now."

Tom heard the silence in his head. There could be no more delay; no prevarication. He had to leave. "I'll pack now," he said.

"Duncan and me'll hang on here 'til you get back."

Tom put down the phone, his old world closing in on him: suffocating. "I have to go," he said.

John was nodding. "Of course. I understand."

Tom went up to his room and began to pack, a robot functioning because it must. John kept his distance, watching in silence, his face a mask. There were hasty goodbyes and a desperate embrace. Then the car door was slamming, the engine revving; a brief wave to the solitary figure by the gate; the long drive north, a bright full moon lighting up the road ahead.

It was almost ten when he reached the farm, lights blazing from its windows.

The yard was full of vehicles parked at random and in haste. The night air was sharp and cold, filled with the smell of cows and woodsmoke. Meg and Tod came creeping out from the barn and sat down on the cobbles, looking anxiously around.

Someone must have heard his car arrive. The light above the porch came on, flickering fitfully. The back door opened and Ian came out to meet him, striding across the yard. Duncan followed a little way behind.

"Any news?" Tom asked.

Ian embraced him, something he had never done before. "He's out of theatre, Tom. That's all we know."

Duncan was standing back, a bundle of reined-in agitation.

"What happened?" Tom asked.

"A damned dog happened!" Duncan said, unable to contain his rage. "Running loose like – all over the bloody place! And this woman's just standing there – shouting at it! Didn't take a blind bit of notice, did it? Just kept on barking and snapping at the cows' legs. Then there was no stopping them." He looked desperate. "I couldn't head them off, Tom. Honestly," he said. "Rob was trapped up by the gate. Brack did his best..." He trailed off, too upset to go on.

"I should've been here."

Ian shook his head. "Would've made no difference, Tom."

Tom was not so sure. He suddenly felt useless and very tired. "I'd better get myself over to the General."

Ian's hand stayed him. "Not much point, Tom. Sarah's there – and you look whacked out. Go over first thing tomorrow. Maybe there'll be more news then."

Ian's hand remained on his shoulder. Something else was wrong.

Tom scanned the yard. "Where's Brack?" he asked.

Ian's hold tightened a little. "I'm sorry, Tom," he said quietly. "Munro couldn't save him."

Tom was dimly aware he had not needed to be told. "Where is he?"

"In the shed. We tidied him up as best we could."

A band of iron tightened round Tom's chest. "Thanks," he said.

Ian patted his shoulder, letting him go. "Tom," he said, calling after him, a note of caution in his voice. "Jamie and Flora are inside with Bridie." He paused, frowning over what he was about to say. "They didn't know, did they? About Rob and Sarah?"

"No."

Ian nodded slowly to himself. "Thought not."

"Tell them I'll be in shortly, will you?"

"Aye, I'll do that."

But Tom knew it was a lie. He would be gone for a while.

Inside the shed, he closed the door behind him and knelt down on the floor, feeling the unyielding surface hard against his knees. A pool of blue light shone through the window onto the rough wooden boards.

The dog was stretched out stiff and broken on a bed of straw, head thrown back, teeth bared, his coat matted and mired, tinged with red. Tom leaned forward to stroke the head, running his fingers tenderly through the soft black hair behind the ears. The flesh was cold.

He sat back on his heels, listening to his breath catching in his chest. His vision blurred. He clenched his teeth, fighting against the rising urge to lift his head and howl.

It was some time before he left the shed.

CHAPTER THIRTY-FIVE

The kitchen was stiflingly hot. The atmosphere Arctic.

Bridie, with a smile fixed to her face, offered Tom a mug of piping hot tea. "I thought you'd be needing this," she said, looking anxiously in the direction of Jamie who was standing rigidly by the door into the hall. Ian and Duncan had retreated to lean against the sink, hands in their pockets, heads down studying their stockinged feet.

"Jamie," Tom said, acknowledging his presence with a cursory nod, noting his transformation was complete: hair neatly cropped; immaculate dark-grey suit and tie; and the adoption of the expression he no doubt used when reprimanding irresponsible behaviour by a member of the Lower Sixth.

Jamie responded with an equally cursory nod, but was evidently constrained by the presence of the Robsons from making any further comment.

Ian glanced up and disengaged himself from the sink. "Well," he said, "now you're all here, I think we'll be off," adding, not without some irony, "No doubt you'll have a lot to talk about." With a slight motion of the head, he indicated to Bridie they should remove themselves.

Bridie took the hint, collecting her coat from the back of a chair and patting Tom's arm as she left. "Rob's in good hands," she said encouragingly. "Coming, Duncan?"

Tom followed them into the yard, wanting to say he was grateful for their help, wondering after they had gone if he had thanked them enough.

He stayed outside for a while afterwards watching the scudding clouds lit up by the moon. He was under no illusions: Jamie was angry; Flora's absence from the kitchen was equally as ominous. Reluctantly, he collected his bags from the car and lugged them into the house. Jamie was still standing guard at the hall door.

"Where's Flora?" Tom asked.

"Upstairs," Jamie said icily.

Tom suspected she had removed herself until the Robsons had gone. "How was he? – when you left?" he asked, more interested in Robert than in Flora taking umbrage.

"Not good."

"Did you see him?"

"From a distance." Jamie paused to let this sink in. "But I suppose," he added, heavily underscoring his observation with a bitterness Tom had never heard him use before, "if Sarah hadn't been there, we *might* have been able to spend some time with him."

Tom put down his bags, easing himself onto a kitchen chair, and took refuge behind the mug of tea Bridie had made for him.

Jamie wasted no time in giving him a piece of his mind. He leaned heavily on the table, his face thrust forward.

"Why the hell didn't you tell us, Tom?" he blazed. "We were made to look complete idiots at the hospital."

Tom tried to remain calm. Their discomfort was perfectly understandable, he thought, except Jamie seemed to be laying the blame for their lack of knowledge entirely at his door.

Jamie's interrogation of him was interrupted by Flora's somewhat dramatic entrance. She flung open the door. "Well?" she demanded, striding into the room, "What have you got to say for yourself?"

For a moment, Tom was more shocked by her appearance than her outrage. She was dressed in a studded black leather biker jacket with a T-shirt and slashed black jeans stuffed into combat boots. Her hair had been cut short into a jet-black bob with a pink neon fringe covering half her face, her features plastered in thick pallid make-up, charcoal eye-shadow and bramble-coloured lipstick; several gold rings perforated one ear, and a gold stud was embedded in the side of her nose.

"I can't believe you didn't tell us!" she was saying, standing with her hands on her hips, every inch a Fury.

"It wasn't my place, was it?"

"It was your place to stop it!" she argued, the inflection of her words sounding different to his ears: metropolitan.

"Really?" he heard himself say, exactly as John Rufford might have said.

She paused in her attack, perhaps seeing in him someone different too. Whatever she was going to say was entirely forgotten. She just glared at him instead.

"And how was I supposed to stop it, Flora?" Tom asked, taking advantage of her confusion.

"You could have told him he was being a fool!"

"And that would have stopped him?"

"He'd have listened to you."

Tom gave a dismissive shrug.

"It's *obscene!*" Flora persisted, not prepared to let the matter drop so easily. "Mum's not been dead a year!" she added, screwing up what was visible of her face in disgust.

Mum, Tom noticed, not *Mam*. He no longer thought of her as 'Mam' either, which made him just as culpable. "It's been a long year for him," he said, knowing this at least was true.

"Not long enough obviously!"

"He was lonely, Flora."

"Lonely!" Her voice had risen to new heights of indignation.

"Yes – lonely."

"Christ, Tom! I can't believe I'm hearing this! She's less than half his age!"

"Does that matter?"

Jamie intervened. "He's an old man, Tom."

"Not that old," Tom heard himself insisting. Why was he defending him?

Flora took up the baton once again. "Old enough. He should have had more sense. What's got into him, for God's sake?"

Tom lacked both the will and stamina for this pointless argument. What had happened had happened. It couldn't be undone just because they objected. It was too late. Much too late. Couldn't they see that? Why were they taking their anger out on him? A deep and urgent need to demolish their self-righteousness suddenly overwhelmed him. "He needs someone to love, Flora. And if Sarah loves him –"

"How can she possibly *love* him?"

"Christ, Flora! I don't know! She says she does. We have to accept it."

"Oh – have we?" she said, pausing briefly to catch her breath. "She's nothing but a scheming little bitch. You didn't want her, so she went for the next best thing."

"What are you saying?"

"I'm saying she's a gold-digger, Tom. She wants the farm."

"No – you're wrong – "

"Am I?" she asked with a toss of her head, challenging him to contradict her. "This is *our* home, Tom. Just think about it – what happens if he dies?"

"What!"

Jamie was visibly upset. "Not now, Flora!" he insisted.

Tom suddenly felt his patience snap. "I can't believe I'm hearing this!"

"Well someone has to say it."

"No – they don't," Tom retaliated. "You stand there – the pair of you – deciding what's best for him. What right have you to do that?"

"He's our father!" Flora objected.

Tom choked off a bitter laugh. "Oh – I see. Suddenly you've remembered. Well – we must all sit up and take notice then." He was really angry with her now. "Where've you been, Flora? – since July? All wrapped up in your own little world with your arty friends – too 'busy' to come and see him." He was aware he was gesticulating in the way he had seen John elaborating on something he felt particularly strongly about.

Flora looked peeved. "That's not fair," she said. "I can't just drop everything – just like that."

Jamie sprang to her defence. "And it's a long way, Tom."

"Oh – it's a long way," Tom said with heavy sarcasm, mocking them both. "Almost as far as Ibiza, Flora?" he asked, taunting her. "Or was it somewhere else you managed to drag yourself off to in August? You can't even be bothered to phone him any more."

Jamie raised his hands, suddenly feeling the need to act the mediator. "Tom, please – this isn't helpful."

"Isn't it? Well – you're not much better, are you?" he said caustically. "When was the last time you picked up the phone?"

Jamie looked down, suddenly embarrassed.

"He was hurt, you know – when you didn't bother to keep in touch – both of you. He'd have told you – about the marriage, if you had. That's what he said anyway."

Silence descended, no one willing to say anything.

Eventually, Flora recovered herself sufficiently to fight back. "It's all very well for you to get on your high horse, Tom Moray, but where've *you* been these last three weeks? Let's face it, if you'd been here – doing your job – this accident wouldn't have happened, would it?"

It was a poisonous thing to say, because it struck home: it was the single, most dreadful thought that had dogged his conscience. His mind raced, searching for an acceptable answer. God knows what reason Robert had given Sarah, or Duncan, for his absence, but it would not have been the truth. "I can't believe you're asking me that question, Flora," he said, hoping he sounded suitably exasperated. "I wanted to let them have the place to themselves for a while. Can't you understand that?"

"For *three* weeks?" Flora said, utterly incredulous.

"Yes, what's wrong with that?"

"Nothing's *wrong* with it, Tom Moray, except you've never been away from the farm longer than a week since you came back from college! What it comes down to is you were just as mad at him as we are – only you just don't want to admit it." She looked triumphant.

For a brief moment, Tom almost hated her. She had touched a raw nerve, and he could sense danger. Once Flora had got the bit firmly between her teeth, it was better to give her something rather than nothing, however wide of the mark. Maybe, just maybe, he could deflect her from probing any deeper into where he had been, and why. "If you must know," he said, implying he was pained by the need to elaborate further, "I decided to meet up with Sophie Gorst again. Satisfied? Or do you want me to go into some of the details of what we got up to?" He listened to himself, almost as surprised by what he said as she was. But at least it silenced her. "Now, if you don't mind," he said, getting to his feet, "I've got an early start tomorrow if I'm going over to the hospital first thing."

Flora shrugged, folding her arms defensively in front of her. "You're probably wasting your time if Sarah's there," she said petulantly, determined not to give up the fight so easily.

"She's his wife, Flora – she takes precedence," Tom said, trying hard to keep a lid on his anger. "We have to live with it," and shooting a withering look in her direction, picked up his bags and hauled them off up to his room.

But for all his weariness, he could not sleep: he could hear their voices talking in the kitchen for some time afterwards. He stared up at the ceiling, just as he had the night after the funeral: tense; his heart knocking against his rib cage with a terrible ferocity, refusing to settle; his head full of unanswerable questions. What if Robert did not make it? Where would they all stand then? – Sarah? Flora? Jamie? Himself? And if Robert did survive – damaged and broken – what then?

He fell into a fitful sleep, and awoke suddenly, his heart still juddering inside him.

He reached out for the bedside clock. Nearly five-thirty. He got up, dressed and went downstairs to make himself some breakfast. A round of toast would do. There was unfinished business with Brack.

Outside, in the dark hour before dawn, a strained silence hung like a pall over everything. Nothing stirred.

Spade in hand, Tom chose a spot just outside the wall at the top of the track. It was a good spot, facing south. Every spring, purple and yellow crocus would flower at Brack's head, he thought, and a drift of daffodils behind his back. He dug the hole deep, the physical effort a welcome distraction.

He returned to the shed and tenderly wrapped the shattered remains of his dog in an old blanket and brought him out into the cold of the morning. By the grave, he knelt down, placing him carefully in the ground with all the reverence due to an old friend who would be sorely missed.

He knelt there for some time before shovelling the earth back into place.

The first glimmers of daylight were filtering through a thick mist above the river when Ian drove up the track and found him, spade in hand, standing over the fresh mound of earth. "He was a grand dog, Tom," he said quietly, putting a sympathetic arm around his shoulders.

Tom nodded. "The best," he said.

CHAPTER THIRTY-SIX

John leaned against the hall table and picked up the phone. It took a supreme effort to concentrate on what he had to say. "Gemma – has Bernard been in yet?" His voice seemed to be bottled up inside his head.

"No. Are you all right?"

"Queasy stomach. Must be something I ate yesterday at the Moorville-Smythes." Better not to mention the ridiculous amount of whisky he had consumed afterwards. He had never been in this state for years, in fact since he was dragged out of a bar in Germany by a couple of burly MPs and hauled back to barracks. "Tell him I'll have to give this afternoon a miss, will you?"

"Yes, of course. Hope you feel better soon."

He put down the phone and inched his way back to the sitting room. He wanted to lie down and preferably keep very still. He made it back to the recliner, lowered himself onto it and closed his eyes, listening to the silence in the house.

Westercot had been plunged back into its long familiar emptiness. Thomas had gone. John had always known he would have to leave – but not like this: not so suddenly.

Neither of them had raised the subject of Laura's anniversary, and half-formed plans of how and when to keep in touch had never been discussed. Suddenly, harsh reality had intervened.

They had embraced before he left, and Thomas had said, "Don't phone me, John. I'll phone you when I can."

John understood why this was the way things had to be, but it did not stop him feeling raw and vulnerable, as if someone had just turned him inside out and left every nerve exposed. He was like a snail with a cracked shell, his life falling apart with no idea how to put it together again.

The car door had slammed, Thomas had driven into the night and the tentacles of silence had invaded every room. John had roamed the house aimlessly. For a while he had sat on the bed in the guest room, heart-sick and despondent. On the chest of drawers by the bed was the camera Thomas had borrowed, its film half-used, and by it, the book on Rothwell Mere, the photograph on its back cover likely to raise awkward questions. Thomas had judged it better to leave it behind.

Later, John had retreated to the gallery armed with a very large whisky and a dining chair, and planted himself in front of Laura's painting, staring abstractedly at the view across the valley from Rigg End. He had lost track of time until something stirred him and he found it was gone ten o'clock. Thomas would have arrived at the farm by then, driving up that track, sucked back into his former life with friends and family around him. Out of reach.

Returning to the sitting room, he had poured himself

another drink and become maudlin, harbouring a dark resentment in his soul. How many times can a heart break? Robert Moray had snatched Thomas from him once again. An uncharitable thought, John knew. Unworthy. The man might die. It was no small thing, dying. He should have felt some pity, or sympathy at least, but in truth, he had felt nothing but a quiet rage.

After that he had worked his way through the whisky until the bottle was empty and at some point in the small hours, he had fallen into a drunken stupor. He had woken with a thick head, and the sudden recollection Bernard expected him that afternoon. He was in no state to do anything.

A light rain was beginning to patter against the windows, breaking the dreadful silence. He listened to it behind closed eyes. Was it raining at Rigg End? He tried to remember how it felt to stand at the top of the track, the chill November wind in his face; the strong, acrid smell of woodsmoke and cows in his nostrils; and the sound of dogs barking in the yard. Almost a year ago.

He should pull himself out of this torpor, he told himself, but he lacked the will. The rain, lisping softly against the panes lulled his brain, and he felt himself drifting off again, content to let sleep take its hold.

In a dream, he heard a phone ringing and an answerphone click in. Gemma's voice said, "Sorry to call, John. The proofs you wanted from Hadley's have arrived. Do you want to send Thomas down to collect them? Let me know, will you?" It was no dream.

John pulled himself awake and struggled to his feet, but she had rung off before he reached the door to the hall. And when he tried to ring her back, he managed to mis-dial twice before he finally got through.

His tongue was thick when he spoke, and his mouth tasted vile. "Gemma," he said, wrestling each word into place with considerable effort. "I'll have to leave the proofs for now. Thomas isn't here. He's had to go back – an accident on the farm. His father – Robert's been injured."

There was a moment's pause before she said, "Oh – I'm sorry. I could bring them over if you like? Would that help? The studio answerphone will pick up any calls."

Through the fog in his brain, he was asking himself – had she bought another car? She must have done. No doubt he had forgotten.

She took his hesitation as reluctance. "I don't have to if you don't feel up to bothering with them," she was saying.

"No – I'd be very grateful if you would. They might take my mind off things."

He put down the phone, his image in the hall mirror staring back at him. He was a mess: unshaven, hair awry, red-eyed and bleary. He must sober up. He had half-an-hour at most to pull himself together. He put on the kettle and made a strong black coffee.

He had just showered and changed when the doorbell rang. He was still bedraggled and unshaven when he answered it.

Gemma's expression betrayed her thoughts.

He felt uncomfortable under her critical gaze. Good grooming mattered.

She stood back, offering him the package with a strained smile.

"I'm sorry," he said, feeling the need to apologise. "Not at my best this morning."

She nodded, smiling awkwardly. "This afternoon," she said, quietly correcting him.

"Of course – do come in."

"No – it's all right. I won't stop," she said, starting to back away. "Not a good time – obviously – if you're not feeling well."

"No, please, come in. I'm glad you came."

Reluctantly, she took up his offer.

He closed the door behind her and showed her into the sitting room.

Gemma had never been to Westercot before. She was mildly curious, her eyes skimming lightly over the contents of the room, the most obvious of which, he realised too late, was the glass and empty whisky bottle on the floor next to the recliner. He had forgotten to remove them. Their presence had been noted.

"Would you like a drink?" he asked, adding before she misunderstood what he meant, "I've just made a coffee for myself." There was little point pretending he had no need of it: she had just seen the evidence.

"A coffee would be nice," she said, taking off her coat and leaving it over an arm of the sofa.

He was embarrassed he had to ask her whether she took

sugar: he had never made her a coffee in all the time he had known her.

When he returned, she was standing in front of the fireplace studying the picture.

"It's Rothwell Mere, isn't it?" she said, turning briefly to relieve him of the mug he was offering. "I recognise it – from Bernard's book."

"Yes," he said, deciding to leave it at that. Laura, Rothwell Mere and herons had not been part of his conversations with Gemma since the spring.

"It's her pastel sketch, isn't it?" she persisted.

He nodded.

She sipped at the coffee, still engrossed in the picture. "It's very beautiful," she said with a sad smile.

He sat down on the recliner unwilling to be drawn on the topic, concentrating instead on his much-needed coffee, its bitter taste a penance for his sins.

Finding him uncommunicative, she retreated to the sofa, and sat somewhat stiffly on the edge of her seat, hugging her mug in both hands. There was a long pause before she said very quietly, "It's a year ago tomorrow, isn't it? Since she died?"

It took all his willpower just to say, "Yes." And when she did not answer, he looked up.

There was pity in her eyes. "Not a good time for Thomas to go," she observed quietly.

"No," he said, feeling his heart stumble. Any more sympathy and he would lose his self-control. "Was Bernard all right? – about this afternoon?" he asked, determined to master himself as quickly as possible.

Mercifully, she took the hint. "He was sorry you weren't well," she said, her eyes briefly drawn back to the empty whisky bottle. "He thought it might have been the chicken sandwiches." She paused before adding, without any note of sarcasm, "He did comment the conservatory was very warm at the Manor."

He sighed. Why pretend? "It wasn't the chicken sandwiches," he said, hiding his embarrassment by draining the last dregs of his coffee from the bottom of the mug.

"I know," she said, looking him straight in the eyes, "but there's no harm in letting him think it was, is there? – I mean from a professional point of view?"

He was grateful for her discretion. "I suppose not."

She finished her coffee and put the empty mug on the floor by her feet. "Would you like me to look through the Hadley proofs with you?" she offered. "Or would you prefer me to go?"

He hesitated, unsure of what he wanted.

"I won't be offended if you want me to go," she was saying. "It's obviously been a difficult day for you."

If he were honest with himself, he needed company. "I'd prefer you to stay," he said, " – if you want to, of course."

"I'm offering."

"Then I'm grateful."

She got up from the sofa, collecting their mugs. "Do you want another coffee?" she was asking as she headed for the kitchen, " – or something more substantial in the food line?"

"Coffee would be fine for the moment – thank you."

"Black?"

"Yes – probably a good idea."

He heard her filling the kettle and rinsing out the mugs. "You need to keep yourself occupied, John," she was saying, adopting the tone he was well used to hearing. "It's the only way when your life get's turned upside down."

He pondered the wisdom of this. "Well," he said, attempting to pass off his foolishness as a light-hearted matter of little importance, "I've tried getting drunk and that doesn't seem to work."

"It never does," he heard her say. "I've tried that too."

He joined her in the kitchen, retrieving the proofs from the table where he had left them. The kettle had boiled and she was busily making their coffee, as she always did, every day at the studio.

Efficient, organised Gemma, he thought. Older and wiser than her years. Always there when she's needed.

"Why don't you take the day off tomorrow?" she suggested. "Ask Bernard to come over? He'll be dying to tell you what you've missed today."

He shook his head. "I don't think so," he said. "Not tomorrow."

She passed him his mug. "Tomorrow's just another day, John," she said solemnly, leaning back against the sink, challenging him to say otherwise. "It'll pass, you know," she insisted. "It's twenty-four hours – like every other day. It'll come – it'll go."

"I can't forget."

"I'm not suggesting that you should. All I'm saying is you

can't change what's happened, and tearing yourself apart like this isn't helping, is it?"

He could not argue with her logic.

"Besides, you've still got Thomas, haven't you?" she pointed out. "Nothing can change that, can it? – even if he can't be here." She reached out and put her hand on his shoulder, her eyes filled with compassion. "He'll come back, you know – when he can," she said with absolute conviction in her voice. "I'm sure of it."

CHAPTER THIRTY-SEVEN

Jamie and Flora left the hospital at lunch time. Access to Robert had been brief, and Flora visibly resented it: it was the anniversary of her mother's death and she was emotionally fragile.

Tom sat quietly with Sarah in the visitors' room during their visit, acting as her bodyguard. She was a shadow of herself: pale, tired and red-eyed. There, in the overheated atmosphere, with the distinctive aromas of laundry and disinfectant mingling with less definable smells, he had taken on his shoulders all her hopes and fears – and there were many. It was a burden he felt ill-equipped to bear, and he left wondering if he had been of any help at all.

As he swung the car into the yard, Ian came out of the hemmel to meet him with Meg and Tod in tow. "Any news?" he asked.

Tom shook his head. Meg came over to lean against him. Automatically, he ruffled the soft hair behind her ears. "There's a hell of a lot of damage," he said, not wanting to think about this too much.

"Aye," Ian said. "He looked in a bad way when the ambulance came."

An understatement, Tom thought. "It'll be a long haul," he said, not adding what was more to the point – if he pulls through.

"Next spring then?"

"I wouldn't like to say."

Ian scuffed the cobbles. "Changes here then?" he said, glancing over his shoulder at the hemmel where the cows were lowing and moving around, impatient for their feed.

Tom nodded.

"You'd not consider keeping them?"

Tom shook his head. "I'm a sheep man, Ian, you know that."

"Aye – well, you always were."

Meg continued leaning heavily against Tom, the warmth of her body reminding him of Brack. She whined softly, licking her lips and gazing up at him mournfully as if she understood his loss. "Duncan up at Willie's place?" he asked, wanting to turn his mind to something else. Duncan's old blue Land Rover was missing from the yard.

Ian stuffed his hands in his jacket pockets and frowned. "He's down in Wallbridge," he said, studying his boots. "Had some chairs to deliver," adding with an awkward smile, "Flora asked him to drop her off at the station."

"The station?"

"She said she had to get back."

Tom could not make head nor tail of this. "Has Jamie gone too?" he asked.

Ian shook his head. "No – he's inside." He paused. "Sarah coming back tonight?"

"No. She's staying over at her auntie's place in Gateshead. It's easier to travel from there."

"Aye. Poor lass. Holding up, is she?"

Tom nodded. What was the point of telling him the truth?

Ian seemed satisfied with this. "Well – better get on. Do you want me to go up The Rigg later?"

"No, I'll get changed and do it now. Want some fresh air. Thanks anyway."

Jamie was waiting for him in the kitchen.

"I hear Flora's gone," Tom said, rinsing his face with cold water: he wanted the stench of the hospital out of his nostrils. "Did she say why?"

"On the way back, she just got into her head she wanted to go. I couldn't talk her out of it, Tom. I said – today of all days – we need to be together. She just lost her temper and that was it. The next thing I know, she's packed her bag and asking Duncan to take her down to Wallbridge."

Tom folded the towel and hung it on the rail by the range. "Was she upset over Sarah again? – or something else this time?" He would have liked to have given his sister a piece of his mind: she had been almost impossible to talk to since he got back.

"She was in a queer mood," was all Jamie said.

"We'll talk about it later. I've got to get feed up to the sheep before it goes dark."

Up in his room, Tom changed into his work clothes, a familiar ritual he rarely thought about. Today was different. Today, as he watched himself in the mirror buttoning up his shirt, he felt a heavy weight settle round his heart. On this day of all days, Jamie had said, and he was right – the three of them should have spent a little time together. That's all that was needed – a little time – to remember.

He went over to the window and watched the shifting patterns of light across the valley. For a moment, he was back at Westercot, studying his mother's painting of the scene. What would she make of the year just gone? He hardly knew. Everything had changed. His mind wandered, conjuring up the memory of his sudden leave-taking and the desolation on John Rufford's face. He thought of Charles and Geraldine, hoping to see him before he left; and the half-promised time with Michael, Caroline and the girls. His other life. All snatched away in a moment. He felt the weight of its loss crush him, leaving an ache behind.

Downstairs, the kitchen door opened and Jamie called up to him. "I've made you a brew, if you want it."

"Thanks," he called back. "I'll be down in a minute."

For a few moments he stood, pulling himself together, then went downstairs and drank the tea, downing it quickly, retrieving his thick woollen socks from his wellingtons and pulling them on while Jamie watched him, looking lost for something to do.

Outside, the light was fading. Ian's Land Rover had gone and the dogs were shut up for the night. Tom heard Meg bark a greeting as he passed the shed door, but he wanted no one's company up on The Rigg. Brack's ghost would be companionship enough.

He piled a couple of hay bales into the tractor bucket

and climbed up into the cab. Memories of Brack were everywhere: tufts of black and white hair from his last moult trapped in odd corners; the smell of wet dog, strong and persistent on the old waterproof slung over the seat, and the muddy paw marks on the window sill. He turned on the ignition and the engine rumbled into life.

Driving up the track, his thoughts drifted back to Sarah, her face drawn, all trace of the happy young bride a distant memory.

Her voice had been barely a whisper. She had looked up at him, her eyes filled with misery and stifled panic. "Tom, what am I going to do?" she had asked, struggling with her news. "I'm pregnant."

He had said nothing at first: the shock had knocked him sideways.

She had waited for him to answer, still looking up into his eyes, seeking help he did not know how to give.

"Does he know?" was all he had thought to ask.

She had shaken her head. "I was going to tell him – today. I thought it might – you know – be a good time. Help him think about the future – not the past – but he can't hear me." She had been fighting back tears.

"You don't know that," he had said, hoping she would believe him. "Just keep telling him."

The tears had begun to stream down her cheeks and he had wiped them away with his hand, not knowing what else to do. She had nodded, trying to be brave, and gone back into the room where monitors bleeped, and the wreckage of a man lay beneath the blue and white coverlet.

He had wanted to sound so positive, for her sake, while his own thoughts were running amok. He had sat in the visitors' room, studying his hands, letting time drift by, existing in the here and now: breathing in the stifling air he hated; listening to the sudden clatter of activity and the casual chatter of people passing by – the hustle and bustle of staff and visitors ignoring his presence. Until at last Sarah had called him in, and Robert had stirred slightly, mouthing soundless words, before slipping back into unconsciousness again. He had sat beside him for a while, then left, his mind strangely separate from any need to think at all. Just to exist.

Up on The Rigg the sheep were gathered by the feeding troughs, their charcoal faces turned towards him, waiting patiently. When he climbed down from the cab, they came to meet him, pushing and shoving against his legs. They were silent for the most part, as they always were at this time of year, their lambs long gone and new ones growing in their bellies. Like Sarah's child, Tom thought. Brack had gone but life went on.

He watched them feed, listening to them shuffle and butt against the troughs, the smell of them coming on the wind, familiar and warm. But he felt no sense of being there, high up on the breast of the hill above the sweep of the valley floor. He was somewhere else, empty and alone. He turned away and climbed into the cab. The last of the light faded. He switched on the headlights and made his way back down the track to the house.

He soaked in the bath for a while, in no hurry to escape

the solitude it offered him, until Jamie called up from the kitchen. "Ready in five minutes!"

He towelled himself dry with no sense of purpose, the fresh vest and underpants he had left warming on the rail, clinging to his skin as he struggled into them. He went downstairs, the aroma of smoked bacon greeting him half-way.

Jamie was serving up an all-day-breakfast, heaping generous portions onto plates.

"What is it with Flora?" Tom asked.

Jamie shook his head, bewildered. "You know I'm not thrilled about what's happened, Tom," he said. "But Flora? – you can't talk to Flora."

"I'd noticed."

"Most of the way back in the car today, she was ranting – about the accident – the marriage – Mum's anniversary. Everything. I couldn't get a sensible word out of her."

Tom stabbed his fried egg with a sausage, watching the yolk ooze out onto the plate, and wondered what reaction the news of Sarah's pregnancy would have provoked. It was not too hard to imagine.

"Frankly, Tom, she was – I don't know – hysterical. Heard her throwing up in the bathroom afterwards," he added. "Sorry – you're eating."

Tom took a bite of the egg-soaked sausage and ignored what had been said.

"I've never seen her act that way before."

Tom carried on eating, deciding he could add nothing to Jamie's observations. It would be easy to be angry with

Flora's histrionics, but perhaps she was more fragile than she seemed. Maybe her outward show was just that – show, and underneath her resilience was wafer-thin. If she were struggling to come to terms with her father's marriage, how much more difficult would it be for her to cope with the new reality of Sarah's child?

"Tom?" Jamie was frowning at him.

"Sorry, I was miles away."

"I could see that. I said there's a letter for you – arrived this morning. Found it in the hall when we got back. Probably from Sophie," he added with a tentative smile. "I popped it behind the clock. Should have mentioned it before – completely forgot about it with all Flora's nonsense. Sorry."

Tom glanced across at the dresser. A sliver of white envelope was just visible behind the clock.

"She must have heard about Robert," Jamie was saying, adding in his ignorance, "Any chance of it getting serious? – between the two of you?"

"A bit too early for that," Tom said, not wanting to dwell too long on the subject.

"But you like her?"

Tom agreed, not proud of himself for making out his interest was more than it was. But already he could see his sham romance might prove useful in the future: visiting Sophie could provide him with a convenient excuse for seeing John. He needed to know he could do that: he did not want to become a prisoner at Rigg End. Not now.

But there was a price to pay for his duplicity. Jamie's

curiosity was not easily stifled. Sophie was his relation too, and Tom found himself becoming ever more entangled in a web of his own making. He escaped only by asking Jamie about Lesley, and mercifully, Jamie was only too happy to spend considerable time expanding on that subject.

It was almost eleven o'clock before Tom could excuse himself and retrieve Sophie's letter from behind the clock. He sat on his bed, exhausted, knowing what he had known for some time – that he was no good at lying, not on a long-term basis at least – and he must try to avoid it in future if at all possible.

The envelope lay face down in his hand and he slipped his thumb under the flap to open it. The sharp edge sliced through his skin, making it bleed. He sucked the cut, irritated by his carelessness.

Inside the envelope, there was a solitary sheet of paper. It was this singularity that struck him first: Sophie would never restrict herself to a single sheet of paper, she always had so much to say. Then there was the letter itself, written in blue ink; a neat, rounded hand – not Sophie's. And at the top of the page – no address.

His eyes skipped to the greeting. 'Dear Tom,' it began.

'Forgive me for not writing sooner – but I had my reasons.'

His attention shifted to the bottom of the page, his heart beginning to pound.

'Fondly remembering the good times that we had together –

'Jan' with three kisses after her name.

His eyes scanned over the remaining words, unwilling to accept their meaning.

'I thought I should tell you I'm back with Geoffrey,' she wrote. 'He got in touch again shortly after I moved down here in March, and we've managed to patch things up. No one knows back home and I think it's better that way. I know you'll understand. You have your own secrets.

'Don't be angry with me, Tom, but I don't think giving you my address would be a good idea. I'd rather you didn't write, and this way you can honestly say you don't know where I am.

'Look after yourself – whatever you decide to do.'

He read it again, as if by doing so, he could wave a magic wand and somehow alter what was written there. He had waited so long to hear from her; wanted this letter to arrive; lived quietly in the hope that they would meet again. But now it was not to be. He could not quite believe it. The writing blurred before his eyes and he heard his breath catch awkwardly in his throat.

He got up, leaving the note on the coverlet, and leaned against the window frame staring out into the dark. He could see nothing, just his own reflection gazing back at him – the image of John Rufford. Was this what *he* endured? – the great emptiness within?

He lay back on the bed, clutching the letter to his chest, his heart's pathetic thumping marking out the passing minutes with a steady leaden beat. Jan had made her choice, as his mother had made hers. He must accept it and not cling on to an impossible dream as John had done.

He steeled himself to read the letter one last time, noticing he had somehow streaked the page with blood.

CHAPTER THIRTY-EIGHT

The November days merged seamlessly together slipping towards December, Robert's condition a rollercoaster ride of ups and downs. He was conscious, but heavily sedated, and sometimes old memories resurfaced, alarmingly real to him. Once, he confused Sarah with Ruth, babbling incoherently and crying over their dead child.

Sarah came home shaken and frightened, unable to get it out of her head that this was some dreadful omen, and begged Tom not to tell anyone she was expecting in case she miscarried. She did not even tell her mother. Nothing would convince her these fears were groundless.

Sworn to silence on the subject, Tom called Mary Armstrong and asked her to stay over a few days. "Sarah's feeling the strain," he said but left at that.

With Mary around for a while, Sarah had less time to herself and her fears subsided.

Tom heaved a sigh of relief and got on with his life. He had lost all sense of time. There was nothing beyond what was immediate or necessary. The farm was everything: Ian came when needed; Duncan leant a hand. His life shrank to the daily round of Rigg End and hospital visiting hours.

The rest? – just background noise, momentous events abroad barely touching the numbness of his consciousness: images of Gorbachev and Bush shaking hands; a Romanian dictator overthrown.

Sometimes, he felt weary beyond words: hollowed out; emotionless; unable or unwilling to think of what might lie ahead. When Jamie rang on Friday evenings, there was little he could tell him, and Flora never rang at all.

Opportunities to speak to John were few and far between, and he did not know what to say. He had no energy to raise the subject of Robert's hasty marriage – and that now a child was on the way. He put this aside. Nor could he give John any hope of an early return to Westercot. Nothing was certain, or settled, and his other life began to slip into the backwaters of the daily round like the fading recollection of a pleasant dream.

Another week passed.

Sarah, determined and devoted, maintained her daily visits to the hospital. Tom could not do the same: the basic demands of the farm kept him away more often than he would have wished. But when he could not spare the time, she would go anyway, her little car clocking up the miles while the wearisome drive began to take its toll. In an evening, Tom would come home after a day of hedge cutting or clearing ditches to find her asleep by the range in the kitchen, exhausted, and he would set about making supper pretending it was no trouble at all.

With another week came better news. Tom took a batch of empty Mules down to the mart to sell on for fattening at the Wednesday sale. Jonty Tait was there. "How's he doin' then?" he asked, and later that evening, Dougie Watson called, eager to know more. "I heard it from Jonty Tait, like," he said, "an' I thought to masel' – as it's the Young Farmers' annual quiz on Saturday like, I could let folks know that Rob was pickin' up." He paused before asking tentatively, "Are yuh not thinkin' of tekkin' part this year then, Tom?"

It was a strange sensation, hearing Robert's warning from the year before – *You don't always get a second chance*. "Not in the mood for it, Dougie," he said.

"Ah well, that's understandable. But it's a shame like. It'll be yer last chance to pick up the cup."

But it no longer mattered: he was a different person now and Tom could not explain that half himself was permanently elsewhere – or why, and his excuses sounded lame and less than honest, which of course they were.

The week before Christmas Jamie arranged to come down to Rigg End for a couple of days once Gowrie Academy had broken up for the holidays. He was not intending to stay for Christmas itself: he had been invited to join his Uncle Sandy and Auntie Mary for the festivities in Edinburgh. "Lesley and I are getting engaged," he explained enthusiastically.

Having offered his congratulations, Tom was informed they were planning an early wedding. "No point in waiting, is there – if that's what we both want?"

"None at all," Tom heard himself say while he mused on the rapidly growing similarity between Robert and Jamie's approach to life: when opportunity knocked, they seized the moment. *Carpe diem* – as Jamie would have said.

Still in high spirits when he arrived at Rigg End, Jamie was keen to give Robert the news. He offered to take Sarah with him to the hospital.

Sarah was uncertain. "I can go later on my own, if you like," she said, clearly uncomfortable at the prospect of having to make one-to-one conversation during the journey with someone she suspected was not exactly over the moon about her marriage.

But Jamie would not hear of it. "Nonsense!" he said. "You look like you need a break." Which was true.

When they returned, Jamie was noticeably more reflective.

"What did he say?" Tom asked him over supper, wondering if Robert's reaction had dampened Jamie's spirits.

Jamie looked up suddenly and brightened considerably. "Oh – he was very pleased," he said, adding with a wry smile, "But he did ask if Lesley knew what she was taking on."

There was the sound of laughter in the house for the first time in several weeks.

Not long after supper, Sarah excused herself and went upstairs, leaving Jamie and Tom together in the sitting room sharing a bottle of whisky by the fire.

Jamie had slipped back into thoughtfulness. "I was wrong," he said, frowning a little over this observation, the image of Robert for the moment. "Sarah really cares for him, doesn't she?"

"He cares for her too."

"I could see that." He smiled awkwardly, his serious expression dissolving for the moment. "Pity Flora can't. Does she ever get in touch?"

Tom shook his head. "Has she said anything to you?"

"Not directly. I think she's embarrassed, Tom. She said some pretty terrible things that night – about Sarah. She knows she can't unsay them. Saying 'sorry' isn't always enough, is it?" He looked pained at having to admit this. "And maybe that's the problem – she's crossed the Rubicon and there's no going back for her."

"Maybe."

They both fell silent for a while watching the firelight, lulled by the warmth of the whisky and the crackling logs in the grate.

Jamie sighed. "Is there something you're not telling me, Tom?" he asked quietly.

"Mm?"

"About Sarah?"

Tom's inattention evaporated, half-expecting what was coming next.

"Is she pregnant?"

"What?" Tom said, implying this was a ridiculous thing to say. "Has she said anything?"

"No – just something about her," Jamie said thoughtfully. "Can't quite put my finger on it. She's not like she used to be. Haven't you noticed?"

"She's worried about Robert, that's all," Tom insisted, sensing he was losing ground.

Jamie was giving him a long hard look, the sort of look he used to give him when they were boys, and Tom had tried to keep a secret – and failed. "She is, isn't she?" he persisted.

It was pointless to lie. Tom drained his glass and confessed. "It's early days, Jamie. She doesn't want folk to know until she's at least three months gone – not even her mother."

Jamie nodded and considered the implications. "Better not tell Flora then?"

Tom agreed and Jamie returned to Leith with silence as his watchword.

The morning before Christmas, Sarah was unwell. Tom came in for his mid-morning break and found her slumped on a kitchen chair, her head in her hands on the table.

"I feel a bit faint," she said, as white as a sheet when she looked up.

Tom could only persuade her back to bed by promising to visit Robert himself that afternoon. Reluctantly, she agreed.

At the hospital, Tom found Robert had been moved into a larger ward, a measure of his continuing physical improvement, if nothing else. He was propped up on his bed in his striped pyjamas surrounded by bulky pillows, his head and chest still swathed in bandages, his left arm in a sling, and his injured leg encased in a fresh plaster from the knee down to the toes. His appearance reminded Tom of a grotesque cartoon character from some child's comic book – a badly wrapped Egyptian mummy – or a monstrous creation of Doctor Frankenstein. Except there was nothing funny here – just a man trapped inside his own infirmity, irritated by the well-meant heartiness of those around him – the nurses in their jolly Father Christmas hats, the local choir singing lively carols down the corridor. He was tetchy, fighting down pain, and in no mood for levity. "Where's Sarah?" he asked, his breath wheezing out of him like rusty bellows as he spoke.

"She needed to rest," Tom tried to reassure him.

"But she's all right, is she?"

"She tires easily, that's all."

Robert frowned, not easily convinced. "She needs to look after herself – and the baby."

"I've told her that."

"Well, tell her from me I won't have her wearing herself into a shadow coming here every day." His breathing became laboured and Tom tried to readjust the pillows at his back. But moving him, even a little, racked him. His jaw clenched as pain etched deep into his face until the spasm passed. When his breathing finally eased he seemed unwilling to talk for a while. Finally he said, "Do you think I've taken leave of my senses, Tom? – getting her pregnant so soon? You've never said anything."

"Not my place, is it?"

"Which means you think I have."

"No – just wondered if you'd thought things through enough." He was thinking of Jamie and Flora, and where they stood in all of this. "Jamie's guessed, by the way," he added. "But he's promised not to mention it to Flora."

Robert just nodded.

"Has she been up to visit? – We see nothing of her at Rigg End these days."

"No – but she's sent a card," Robert said, trying to smile. "Nicely done. Designed it herself," he added with a nod in the direction of the cabinet beside his bed. On top, vying for space behind the water jug and plastic tumbler was a striking 'Get Well' card: the image of a scarlet poinsettia in a dark blue pot standing on an lacy tablecloth.

Tom picked it up and studied it. It was exquisite and must have taken many hours of patient effort to complete. Maybe, he thought, this said more about Flora than the simple message she had written inside – 'Hope you soon feel better, Dad. Love Flora.' There were three kisses very precisely executed underneath. He put the card back on the cabinet in pride of place in front of the water jug.

"She's still upset, isn't she?" Robert was saying, " – about me and Sarah?"

"She doesn't understand."

Robert looked sad. "And how can I explain how I feel in a letter, Tom? It needs to be said face-to-face."

Tom said nothing, wishing there were easy answers to difficult questions.

A flurry of visitors arriving with presents for the old man in the next bed cut across their conversation. They were oblivious to the disruption they were causing, talking too loudly and making a fuss over finding enough chairs to sit on.

Their closeness irritated Robert. For a while, his attention was fixed on their unwelcome presence until they settled down, their chatter melting into the general hubbub around them in the ward. "I want to thank you," he said at last, reaching out to hold Tom's arm. "For coming back after the accident."

"What do you mean?"

"I mean I don't want you thinking I take you for granted – not now. Do you understand?" He was deadly serious.

"I think when you banged your head, you lost your marbles."

Robert was trying to smile. "I'm not blind, Tom," he said. "Sometimes you're like an open book, did you know that? It's in your eyes. And I can see it. Deep down, you're somewhere else, and I know where. It's as plain as day."

Tom looked away.

"You miss them, don't you?" Robert was saying. "Your family? And while I'm stuck in here, I'm keeping you from them." The words seemed oddly out of place. But it was true. "I'll try not to keep you waiting too long," he added, forcing a smile.

Somewhere down the corridor, a choir began to sing "The First Noel" and everyone fell silent, listening.

The carol ended. There was appreciative applause and the chatter sprang up again around them.

Robert said suddenly, "It was my fault, you know – what happened to Brack."

"Don't be daft. It was that woman and her damned dog."

"No," Robert insisted. "It wasn't just the dog, Tom." He shook his head, frowning at his recollection of events. "I was miles away. Not concentrating. Thinking about your mother – her anniversary – hoping she'd understand – about Sarah and me. I was in a kind of dream just standing there – by the wall – watching this dog down the other end of the field dancing round the cows – barking – jumping up at them setting them off. The woman was screaming at it. Duncan was waving his arms, yelling at me to get out the way. Brack was trying to head them off ..." He looked up, bewildered by his reaction. "I didn't move, Tom. Not an inch. Not a damned inch. Maybe I couldn't get my head around what was happening. I don't know. They've always been such gentle beasts ..."

The cheerful carolling came between them once again: this time a small group of children singing in the doorway: childish voices, high and piping; innocence itself.

"The cattle are lowing ..."

The carol ended. Robert sighed. "I know they'll have to go, Tom," he said with tears in his eyes. "I'll never have the strength to handle them again, will I?"

There was no point in saying otherwise.

"Ask Jarred Liddel if he wants to buy them, will you? He always said he would – if I sold up."

"He'll give you a fair price."

Robert nodded, and looked away.

CHAPTER THIRTY-NINE

Tom stacked the breakfast plates in the sink, his mind preoccupied on what else needed to be done that morning. Sarah was being obstinate and he was getting cross.

"But I *want* to visit him," she was insisting.

"He knows that."

"I could drive myself over if you're too busy."

"Christ, Sarah! It's not about me being too busy. It's about you – going over to Newcastle every day – tiring yourself out." He could have added she looked dreadful: her face haggard; dark rings around her eyes; her skin losing its lustre. "He's worried about you – about the baby."

She watched him zipping up his jacket getting ready to go out and said nothing. The new-found confidence of those early weeks after her marriage seemed to have drained right out of her.

"I'll be off then. See you around twelve."

"I'm not going to the Robsons," she said stubbornly. "If I'm not well enough to go to Newcastle, I'm not well enough to go to a party."

"Don't talk rot," Tom said irritably: he had planned his day around this New Year's party. He had even set his alarm an hour earlier to get through his chores, and give himself time enough to spruce up afterwards. "It's five minutes in the car and the change will do you good," he added, shoving his feet into his wellingtons. It would do him good too. He was becoming morose.

High Oakbank was bright with festive lights strung around the door twinkling their welcome through the half-light of the January afternoon. From the number of cars already at the farm, it seemed most of Stanegate and Liz's crowd from Drumlinfield were there to celebrate. Tom found a space further down the track and parked up. For the first time he noticed Sarah was finding it difficult to get out of the car. She looked up, smiling her gratitude when he offered her his hand.

Inside, there was a crush of folk spilling out into the hall from the downstairs rooms. They were already in the party mood, laughing and joking, drowning out the toe-tapping rhythms of old Abba hits playing from the hi-fi somewhere in the background. By the stairs, a large spruce, laden with lights, baubles and tinsel, filled the stairwell as far as the landing. The atmosphere was warm and welcoming.

Ian and Bridie pushed through the crowd to greet them.

"Come on in. Come on in – if you can," Ian said ushering them inside. "Ross and Liz have left us in charge of greeting folk. Good to be back in the old place again." He beamed broadly. "Happy New Year – to both of you. And a healthy one too," he added. "How is he?" Always Ian's first question these days.

"Making progress," Tom said, regardless of whether this

was true or not. He had learnt sympathy wore thin after a while, and everything that could be said on the subject had already been said.

"There's some food in the kitchen," Bridie said. "Help yourselves when you want some, won't you? You all right, Sarah lass? It's a bit stuffy in here, isn't it?"

Sarah nodded, looking anxiously at the press of people crushing up against her. She looked fragile, and the cheerful crimson dress she was wearing, perhaps hoping to put some colour in her cheeks, served only to emphasise how pale she was.

Bridie must have thought so too without knowing why. She guided her through to the sitting room with Tom in tow. "There's a space on the sofa next to Dana. Go and sit yourself down." She glanced up at Tom, all concern. "Poor lass. She looks a bit peaky, doesn't she? Good thing she came over. Help her take her mind off things."

Tom nodded.

Sarah sat down gratefully.

Dana, pregnant the last time Tom had seen her, was dandling a pretty little girl in pink and blue checked dungarees on her lap.

Sarah's face softened as she looked at the child. The little girl beamed up at her, then giggled, pretending to be shy. "What's her name?" she asked.

"Suzie Jane," Dana said, her rich Canadian accent stronger than Tom remembered. "Craig just adores her."

Ian returned, manoeuvring through the crowd with brimming glasses of rich mulled wine in each hand. "Here, set yourselves up with this," he said. "I've made it extra strong."

Tom was happy to oblige.

"Maybe I won't," Sarah said with an embarrassed smile.

"Too much of the good stuff over Christmas?" Ian said, hopelessly wide of the mark. "How about some sparkling apple juice?"

"Thank you."

"I'll get it sorted for you."

Suzie Jane tilted her head to look up at Tom. She stopped giggling, her rosebud mouth falling open in surprise, revealing small white baby teeth. Her large blue eyes widened.

"I can see you've won her heart already, Tom Moray," Dana said with an indulgent smile. "Don't you think so, Sarah?"

Sarah nodded, still watching the child.

Dana's smile suddenly froze. "Oh, you really must think badly of me, Sarah – I've not asked how Robert is. Craig and I – we were both so sorry to hear about his accident. So soon after your wedding too. He's such a lovely man. How is he?"

Tom left Sarah in Dana's capable hands: he wanted other company, other topics of conversation. But it seemed Robert was uppermost in everyone's mind.

"Aye – we miss his crack down the mart ..."

"Give him our best wishes will yer, lad?"

He moved on through the throng, seeking out friends, nodding in passing to old Harry and Maggie Fenwick from

Aitket Bank sitting in the corner with well-filled glasses of punch. They looked not a day older than they did a year ago, he thought, when Janet had brought them up to the Boxing Day party at Rigg End in her car ...

"You made it then," Duncan's familiar voice boomed in his ear above the music. "There's a load of food in the kitchen if you fancy some." He was waving a paper plate piled high with pork pie, scotch eggs and several sausage rolls under Tom's nose.

Food was not uppermost in Tom's mind. His thoughts were with Janet, remembering the pale-green scooped-necked jumper she had worn; the string of amber beads against the soft curve of her breasts; her scent when he was close to her; his fingers running down her neck. He took a long draught of mulled wine. It nearly took his breath away. "Sorry – I was thinking."

Duncan pulled a face. "I can see that, man," he said, his attention shifting to Sarah as she sat passively listening to Dana's animated conversation. "Things can change in a year, can't they?" he mused, trying to smile but not succeeding very well. Sarah's marriage had left its mark. "Are you sorry now you missed your chance?"

Tom drained his glass as if it were water. "No – are you?" he said, immediately regretting such a barbed retort.

Duncan shrugged, trying to make light of his frustrated hopes. "Not much point – is there?" he said. "I mean – crying over spilt milk like."

"Not much."

"Heard you'd got someone down in Cheshire."

"Who told you that?"

"Flora – that day ..." Duncan clammed up, embarrassed at having raised the subject. "Is it true then? You've got a lass down in Cheshire?"

"Maybe," Tom said, accepting another glass from Ian as he passed.

"Dark horse," Duncan said thoughtfully. "You always were."

For a moment, Tom wondered if Duncan had ever given credence to the rumours about Janet and himself, but the arrival of Ross with another tray of punch proved a useful distraction.

"Happy New Year, Tom," Ross said.

Tom drained his second glass and helped himself to a third. "How's Liz?" he asked.

"Having a rest. She'll be down later."

"Not long now?"

"A couple of weeks." Ross looked well-pleased at the prospect of becoming a father again. "They've told us it's a girl," he said confidentially.

"Got a name yet?"

"Keeping it a secret. Haven't told the boys yet – not sure they want a little sister." He was amused by this.

"Where are they, Ross?" There was no sign of Scott or Adam anywhere.

"Upstairs – playing video games with Grandpa Lowther. He bought them those console things for Christmas. Said it would keep them from getting under our feet over the next few weeks. Great idea."

Small talk. Irrelevant. The insubstantial glue of everyday life that filled so many conversations. Tom realised he wanted something more. He wanted to be bold. He wanted to ask awkward questions. He wanted to come right out with it and raise the subject of Ross and Duncan's wayward sister. Where was Janet these days? How was she? What was she doing with herself? A different kind of small talk. Useful. Informative. But he was aware that since the spring, her name had been absent from every Robson conversation – as if it were taboo. Perhaps it was. Perhaps they suspected what was true – that she was back with Geoffrey Frayling – and therefore quite beyond the pale.

Ross moved on, called upon to provide refreshment elsewhere and Tom had missed his chance. Somewhere beyond the heightened level of conversation and raucous laughter, he could hear Ross' favourite country singer, James Taylor, singing 'Fire and Rain'. It brought back the bitter sweet memories of that wonderful February evening in Janet's bed. All too brief. He felt the stabbing at his heart.

'...I've seen lonely days that I thought would never end ...'

"How's Janet these days?" he asked, the words out of his mouth before he could stop them.

Duncan frowned, eyeing him warily.

'...but I always thought that I'd see you again ...'

"I was just thinking," Tom went on, feeling bravado setting in under the influence of too much mulled wine on an empty stomach, "she was at our 'do' last Boxing Day. Brought up Harry and Maggie from Aitket Bank. Do you remember?" On reflection, he was pleased how easily he passed this off. A casual observation. Nothing more.

Duncan seemed reluctant to be drawn. He looked away, giving a polite nod in the direction of Harry Fenwick who had caught his eye and was raising his glass to him.

"Is she still down in Hampshire then?" Tom persisted.

Duncan cupped a hand to his ear, pretending not to hear so well over the din of the music.

"She went for that job at that veterinary centre, didn't she? Where was it again?" Tom feigned forgetting the name, clicking his fingers as if it were on the tip of his tongue. "Somewhere in the New Forest, wasn't it?" He had got the bit between his teeth now. Nothing was going to stop him.

'...Oh I've seen fire and I've seen rain ...'

Duncan was visibly struggling with what he could or should say. "Buckhurst," he said finally, providing Tom with the information he really wanted.

Tom smiled broadly. "That's it – Buckhurst!" he said, implying he knew it all the time.

Duncan was becoming agitated. "Look – Tom," he said sombrely drawing him to one side. "There's no easy way to say this – but there was an almighty row at home before she left see. Things were said like – and we don't keep in touch any more."

Tom put on an expression implying profound ignorance. "Christ, I'm sorry, Duncan. I – I wouldn't have mentioned it if I'd known."

Duncan shrugged this off, but not without scrutinising him more closely. Under his watchful gaze, Tom drank back the third glass, feeling a warm glow of triumph spreading over him. If nothing else he had something to go on.

'... *but I always thought I'd see you – one more time again* ...'

What he might do – or could do – with this intelligence, seemed irrelevant at that moment. Just having the information was enough. Except he was already playing with the idea he might follow it up. Contact the veterinary centre perhaps. See if she were there. It mattered not one jot that she did not want to hear from him.

Somewhere in the background, filtering through the rising tide of good-natured revelry and boisterousness, James Taylor began singing 'You've got a friend'.

Tom felt positively buoyant.

CHAPTER FORTY

At the time, Tom reflected later, his idea, fuelled by copious amounts of alcohol, had seemed perfectly reasonable. Totally logical in fact. When reality finally struck however, the cracks in his intoxicated logic inevitably began to show.

For several days, fired by the notion he should contact Janet – by phone or letter – it mattered not which, he remained convinced this was the right thing to do. On the first Wednesday of the New Year, he drove down to Wallbridge, ostensibly to do some shopping for Sarah. In the teeth of a gale and horizontal rain, he bought the vegetables she wanted at her favourite stall on the market, and on the way back to the car diverted down St Edward's Street to the main Post Office. There, on the side wall in its allotted space, he found the Hampshire Phone Book. He scribbled down the number of the Buckhurst Veterinary Centre together with its address on the back of a till receipt, stuffed this into his inside pocket to keep it dry, and plunged out again into the pouring rain, head down, ignoring the rivulets making progress down his neck. What did he care? He was on a mission. He was going to contact Janet.

At the first opportunity he would phone the Centre, he

told himself. Or at least that was the idea, except Sarah, under orders from Robert to visit only twice a week, now seemed to be permanently around the house. And when she was absent, Tom found himself occupied elsewhere, either bogged down by the everyday demands of running the farm, or helping Ross out dyking at High Oakbank, when the latest addition to the family, baby Polly, arrived unexpectedly and threw everyone's plans into chaos, including Tom's night out to celebrate his twenty-sixth birthday.

One afternoon a week later, when he finally had the house to himself, with Sarah up at Rattling Gate, he stood in the hall, poised with receiver in hand, only to discover he was beset by uncertainty. Beyond the act of making the call itself, he had never given any thought to what he would say when someone answered. On the face of it, all he had to do was to ask if Janet Robson were there – except – and here his confidence began to drain away – what if she were known as Janet Frayling? – or by any other name? What if *she* answered the phone? She had been quite explicit she did not want to hear from him. What would he say to her? What *could* he say to her? His mind was a perfect blank. He could think of absolutely nothing that might be regarded as appropriate under the circumstances, not least because what he really wanted to say was probably completely unacceptable – that he could not get her out of his head these days, and perhaps he was in love with her. At which point, he realised making the call was out of the question. He put down the phone, went out into the yard, loaded feed into the tractor bucket and took it up on The Rigg.

His alternative course of action – to write to her instead, c/o Buckhurst Veterinary Centre, threw up the same problems. Only this time, there was the added disquiet that, if for some reason she no longer worked at the Centre, anyone might open the letter. Writing 'Personal' in large capitals on the envelope was no guarantee against this possibility. And, as he knew only too well from a letter he received from Sophie earlier that week, the written word has a permanence that could be discovered by others if not carefully secreted out of harm's way. What if his letter were forwarded to Janet and then Geoffrey got sight of it? He had no way of knowing how much damage that might cause, but a fairly shrewd idea it would place the cat firmly amongst the pigeons. So with pen poised and a pristine sheet of paper in front of him, he faced the cold fact there was absolutely no way he could contact Janet, no matter how much he might want to.

Sophie's letter, he reflected, like Sophie herself, lacked discretion. She was back in 'student mode' after the Christmas holidays, full of bravado and bubbling over with her news.

'Mio caro Tommaso', she began enthusiastically, going on to express the right amount of concern for Robert in the next paragraph, and hoping he was continuing to improve.

'When are you coming to see us again?' she continued. 'Will you be down at Easter? I'll be back at Gregory's from 5th April. He's planning to go to Cannes with his latest girlfriend – Tanya – on the 12th for a long Easter weekend – so I'll have the place all to myself.' At which point, she had thrown caution to the wind. 'If you could come, that would mean I could have *you* all to myself! *Fantastico*! We could spend all our time in bed, couldn't we? Would you like that? I would!' Sophie liked exclamation marks almost as much as she liked being outrageous. 'Just think,' she went on, 'you could give me those lessons you promised – *come fare l'amore!*' And if this was not embarrassing enough, she was agog to tell him in the next paragraph, 'Tom – guess who I bumped into after Christmas – in Lingford. Yes – John Rufford! I suppose I shouldn't have been surprised – I was in Chester Place at the time after all – but I literally bumped into him. So I couldn't resist it! I introduced myself! Was that very naughty of me? I said, "Hi – I'm Sophie Gorst," and we shook hands, and then I said, "I know your son Tom Moray. We went out a couple of times when he was down in October." Oh Tom – he's really *gorgeous* – totally *stupendissimo* – just like you!' She continued in this vein for some time.

Tom's interest in Sophie's subsequent paragraphs describing in detail her plans to return to Callistini with her Aunt Rosemary during her summer vacation, was overshadowed entirely by the more pressing concern about what to do with her letter: should he burn it? – tear it into infinitesimally small pieces? – or bury it under lock and key in the bottom drawer? He certainly could not leave it lying around. He chose to lock it away, uncertain how he would answer it. ✦

The one positive aspect to receiving her letter was that Duncan was with him when the postman's van swept into the yard, and he had been witness to the envelope being handed over.

"From your girlfriend?" he had asked, perhaps because Tom had recognised the handwriting, and for no reason he could account for, had felt himself go hot under the collar when he looked at it. A premonition of its contents perhaps, he thought later.

It had been useful to say, "Yes," and to let the subject continue to be the source of amusement for Duncan when they went up to The Gate for a pint the same evening.

"Looks like she's really keen on you then."

"I wouldn't mind going down to see her again," he had said, knowing perfectly well this was at best a shameless excuse for a trip to Cheshire, but adding for good effect, "if I ever get the time."

"Never let it be said that Duncan Robson stood in the way of true love, Tom Moray. It's a bit quiet on the furniture front just now. I could help you out, if you like. Just say the word."

"Might take you up on that," Tom had said.

Towards closing time, there had been an awkward moment which revived Tom's concerns over his continued presence at the farm. News of Sarah's pregnancy had finally leaked out a few days before, Wallace unable to maintain his promise of secrecy under the influence of one strong ale too many. A group of local lads from Stanegate on a stag night were already well oiled when Tom and Duncan arrived. Tom knew most of them from school days. Rough lads who enjoyed their reputation, as long as they had the rest of the gang to rely on. Two of them – Ryan Bell and Jackson Cox – were always in trouble, not serious trouble, but trouble nonetheless. "Daft buggers," someone once called them – a description that always sprang to mind whenever Tom saw them – acting tough – acting the fool. Tom had scrapped with both of them over the years – and got the better of them. It had been worth the skinned knuckles at the time, but a fair bit of animosity still existed between them.

"Ah hear tell Sal Moray's got hersel' in the family way," Ryan had bawled out across the bar that evening.

"Aye – good goin' for a lass wi' her man laid up in hospital," Jackson had added with a grin on his face. There had been raucous laughter all round.

Tom had kept his concentration on his pint. Not his problem, he kept telling himself. Let them roar. Empty vessels make the most noise.

Which would have been fine except Ryan had added for good measure, "Well o' course, she mighta got a good tuppin' from someone else like." And there had been no mistaking who he was talking about from the meaningful nods and winks in Tom's direction. More laughter.

Tom had felt the old urge rising in him to floor Ryan on the spot with a neat cross-buttock, but Duncan, ever the knight in shining armour as far as Sarah was concerned, had been quicker off the mark. He had left his pint on the bar and strolled across to confront the pair of them. Over in the corner, a figure had risen, shadow-like from the semi-darkness, and sauntered over to join him: Willie

Robertson. All Willie had to do was stand there, hands on hips, eye-balling them: that was enough.

Behind the bar, Archie Ramsey had put down the glass he was polishing and reckoned it was time to intervene. "You'd like me to tell Wallace Armstrong what you'd just said, Ryan?" he asked casually raising his voice a little. "– next time I see him, like? Just to keep him informed?"

Ryan had pulled a face and shrugged. "Oh – away wi' yer, Archie. Only havin' a bit o' fun. Didn't mean anythin' by it, man."

"Well, just in case I let it slip, like – to Wallace – by mistake – maybe you'd better drink somewhere else for a while – the pair o' you."

They had backed off with a show of bravado that looked a little thin, avoiding Willie as they went, and everyone had settled down.

With a brief nod in Tom's direction, Willie had returned to his quiet corner to continue dealing with whatever business occupied him there. Something to his advantage, no doubt. Duncan had come back to retrieve his pint.

"You don't have to fight my battles for me," Tom had said.

Duncan had thumped him on the shoulder, good-naturedly. "I wouldn't lift a finger for you, Tom Moray. But I'll not have Sarah's name blackened hereabouts."

But the damage had been done, and Tom could see himself trapped at the farm until Robert was back and the baby was born. With luck, he told himself, it would be a red-head, and any notion it was someone else's child and not Robert's would be quashed for good. But in the meantime, any absences on his part would of necessity have to be short, or the rumour-mongers would be in full flow suggesting he had left because he had had no alternative – because Sarah's child was really his and either Robert had thrown him out, or worse, he had done a runner.

The following weekend, he decided to tell Robert. He would pick his moment.

At the hospital, Tom was pleased to find Robert much improved, even if visibly less robust than he used to be. He was sitting in a wheelchair stationed next to his immaculately tidy bed wearing his striped pyjamas and checked dressing gown. His progress was marked by the presence of two elbow crutches propped up beside him leaning against the bed. And for the first time since the accident, Tom thought, he looked almost like Robert Moray and not some oddly disfigured replica pretending to be him.

"You're looking better, Rob," he said, hoping he sounded sincere enough: Robert had developed an unerring ability to detect even the whitest lie.

Robert grimaced. "Wheel me out into the Day Room, will you? I'm sick of this place."

"What about the crutches?"

Robert glared at them impatiently. "Can hardly keep myself up on them, Tom, never mind walk."

"It takes time."

"It takes too long. I want to be home – with Sarah."

With its reluctant passenger, Tom manoeuvred the cumbersome chair out of the ward and down the shiny linoleum in the corridor, trying not to look at the scar still showing on the back of Robert's head where the hair was beginning to grow again at last. "Have they said when they'll be moving you over to the Memorial Hospital?" he asked.

"Maybe next week."

"It'll be better for Sarah – having you nearer home. She can get down to see you more often in Wallbridge."

"I keep fretting over not being with her when she needs me."

They had reached the Day Room, empty apart from its functional furniture and overheated atmosphere. Tom parked the chair by one of the windows. The view was not very inspiring: a vista filled with rooftops of other buildings in the hospital complex; the higgledy-piggledy skyline of shops and offices across the city; and a reluctant January sun occasionally bursting through the clouds to add a dash of colour to the afternoon.

Robert was staring out of the window, his eyes fixed on the horizon: home; Sarah; familiar places and faces.

"I spoke to Jarred – about the cows," Tom said.

"Is he interested?"

"Says he might be. Wants to think on it."

"Any mention of a price?"

"I said you'd be looking for at least the going rate at the mart – seven-hundred-and-fifty or thereabouts for most of them – more for Rosie of course, 'cos she's worth more."

"What did he say?"

"You know Jarred. Doesn't give much away. Said he'd speak to you first."

Robert smiled to himself. "Always was a cautious man, Jarred Liddel," he said. "Has Munro looked them over yet?"

"Came yesterday. Should see the first calves in about six weeks."

Robert eased himself into a more comfortable position and became lost in thought again. "You should get yourself away for a few days, Tom," he said at last, his concentration still fixed on the scene beyond the window. The sky was beginning to darken, the street lights flickering into life. He did not mention John Rufford by name, but his meaning was clear enough. "Get Mary down again to keep an eye on Sarah. Ian and Duncan will be happy enough to look after the stock."

"It's not that easy."

"Why not?"

"Gossip," Tom said, and told him about the incident up at The Gate.

Robert listened grim-faced, the muscles in his jaw clenched tight, his eyes blazing. "I wish to God I could get out of here," he said, and turned his attention once more to the view beyond the window as the darkness took hold. After a while, his anger seemed to subside.

Tom hesitated before asking, "Did Flora answer your letter?"

Robert merely nodded.

"How's she taken it – about the baby?"

Robert's attention remained fixed on the view. Almost casually, he pulled out a letter from his dressing gown pocket and handed it over. "You'd better read it," he said, forcing a tight smile. "She has some good news."

Tom read the letter twice. It was difficult to concentrate

on what Flora had written: it had been dashed off in considerable haste by the look of it, her handwriting, usually so neat and precise, little more than a barely legible scrawl.

"She's done well." Robert was saying, his rigid smile still firmly in place. "Her mother would've been proud of her."

"Yes," Tom agreed, his mind still badly disengaged. Flora had won a prestigious design award. She was justifiably cock-a-hoop about it. But her success had been casually linked to something far more important from a father's point of view.

"What do you think, Tom?" he was being asked.

Tom struggled to find the right words. "I don't know what to say," he admitted, letting his eyes skim over the letter once again.

Almost as an afterthought, and with casual indifference, Flora had announced she had married an American – a Harvey Mortlake – from New York. "Just a registry office 'do' after New Year – nothing fancy," she said. "A few friends that was all." She and Harvey were planning to start up their own design studio over there – leaving at the beginning of March. It was all terribly exciting. She was sorry she couldn't come up before they left – there was so much to do. But she was sure that with the baby on the way, he would have enough on his mind, apart from getting back on his feet again, of course. She hoped he was making good progress, and promised to write as soon as she was settled.

Flora, it seemed, had removed herself as far as possible from a situation she could no longer handle. Perhaps it revealed her vulnerability – and possibly something else – her immaturity.

Tom folded the letter and handed it back.

"Has she ever mentioned this Harvey Mortlake to you?" Robert was asking.

"No – I think I'd have remembered the name."

Robert stuffed the letter back into his pocket. "I never meant to hurt her you know," he said bitterly, "by marrying Sarah."

"She never understood."

"All the same ..."

There was an aching silence, each staring abstractedly out of the window into the night, their reflections staring back at them. Tom could feel another door closing, shutting him off from his once familiar world.

CHAPTER FORTY-ONE

The tanker driver was new. He had never reversed into the yard before. "More to the right," Tom was yelling at him above the din of the engine and beep-beeping of the warning signal. "Keep going. Keep going. Stop."

"Thanks mate."

Sarah was standing at the back porch watching them. "Tom," she called out. "That art collector's on the phone again. Mr Rufford, isn't it?"

"Tell him I'll ring back, will you?" Tom said, feigning indifference.

Sarah stood her ground. "It sounds a bit urgent, Tom," she said, frowning over the conundrum as to why an art collector should be so insistent.

She had taken John's first call a couple of days before, and Tom had come up with the half-truth that Mr Rufford's interest lay in the remaining unsold artworks of Laura Douglas. Whether she accepted this or not, at the time, the fact John had needed to call at all was uppermost in Tom's mind, and this excuse was the best he could come up with. John, it turned out, had a very good reason to make the call: Charles was unwell – a chest infection that seemed to be taking hold. Geraldine was worried.

With Sarah able to overhear his side of the conversation, Tom had struggled to get the message across that if Charles' condition took a turn for the worse, then he very much wanted to be kept informed. It appeared from Sarah's lack of curiosity afterwards that he had managed to pass this off reasonably well. The necessity of keeping the truth hidden from her, however, was beginning to wear him down, and what was worse from his perspective, was the lack of courage on his part to explain to John that the young woman who had answered the phone was in fact Robert's new wife – and a child was on the way.

And now John had called again. There could only be one reason: Charles was worse. Trying to remain unfazed by this required a considerable feat of self-control. In the face of Sarah's obvious unwillingness to relay his message, Tom was more insistent. "I'll ring him back," he repeated, trying to stay calm and concentrating on how many gallons of diesel were needed to fill the tank. "I've got his number."

Manoeuvring the tanker out of the yard, took almost as long as getting it in. The minutes were ticking by and Tom could feel the tension twisting his stomach into a tightening knot. His mind was already leaping ahead to the outcome of the call and how best to deal with it.

When he finally came into the house, Sarah was busy in the kitchen making breakfast. The frown on her forehead seemed to have deepened. "Mr Rufford asked me to make sure you called him straightaway," she said, turning the bacon over in the pan and giving Tom one of her 'what's-this-all-about' looks.

Tom ignored her, abandoning his wellingtons in the porch and padding through into the hall.

Somewhat too obviously, he thought, he decided to close the door behind him and waited a moment before he dialled John's number.

John was full of apologies. "I'm sorry," he said. "Obviously not a good time."

Tom kept his voice low. "Is it Charles?" he asked.

"Yes. He's been admitted to Retton Cottage Hospital. I'm afraid it's not looking good."

"I'll come down."

"We'd understand if you can't, Thomas. Don't feel you have to. You've got your hands full on the farm, we know that."

"I'll sort something out."

There was a noticeable pause on the other end of the line. "I'll be glad to see you."

When Tom put down the phone, it was noticeably quiet in the kitchen. There was a definite pause for a moment followed by the sound of sudden activity and a tap being run in the sink. He wondered if Sarah had been listening. If she had, she was now well and truly preoccupied pretending she had been busy all the time. Taking advantage of this Tom rang the Percy Elliott Memorial Hospital and asked for Ward Four. When he replaced the receiver, the signs of activity in the kitchen were still very audible.

"Sarah?" he called.

She appeared at the door drying her hands. "Breakfast's on the table," she said in that tone he recognised as signalling she would like to know why Mr Rufford was being so insistent.

He pretended to be unaware of this. "Sorry," he said, wanting to escape any interrogation as soon as possible. "I need to pack. Is Duncan around?"

The familiar little frown of puzzlement and irritation established itself on her brow. "He's just come into the yard," she said, visibly cross at having both her cooking and curiosity ignored.

Duncan, whistling tunelessly to a Whitney Houston song on the radio in the workshop, was unloading a fresh supply of sawn timber from his trailer.

Don't make it complicated, Tom thought, running through a string of possible excuses he could use. "Just need to go down to Cheshire for a bit," he said, avoiding a specific time-scale. "Can you and Ian hold the fort 'til I get back?"

"No problem, Tom," Duncan said, cheerfully prepared to do anything to help. "Off to see Sophie Gorst then?"

Tom slapped him on the back in a good-natured fashion. "If I get the chance," he lied, surprised how easy it was to pass this off as any sort of acceptable excuse to abandon his responsibilities on the farm at such short notice. But if it kept Duncan happy, why not?

Oblivious of the deception being worked on him, Duncan rattled on. "Dad'll be glad to have something to do," he was saying, manhandling a particularly large plank through the doorway. "Mam's always telling him he gets under her feet. Get yerself off, man." And with that, he resumed his tuneless whistling, concentrating on the job in hand.

In the kitchen, Sarah was waiting, arms folded.

Tom grabbed a round of toast from his plate, and tried to evade becoming embroiled in any further conversation.

Sarah was having none of it. She caught him by the sleeve. "What's going on, Tom?" she demanded.

He frowned at her, wanting her to see he was in no mood for a protracted discussion. "Not now, Sarah," he insisted. "I need to pack."

"And what am I supposed to tell Rob when I see him this afternoon?"

"You don't need to tell him anything," he said, perhaps a little too offhandedly. "I've left a message at the Percy Elliott. He'll understand. Don't worry about it."

She would not let go of his sleeve. "Tom," she said, becoming increasingly agitated, "there's something wrong. Why can't you tell me?"

He had no intention of losing his temper with her: he just wanted her to let him go. But her determination to know more was becoming an obstacle he could no longer afford to ignore: there was the potential for his silence to inflame her curiosity rather than stifle it. And what if she chose to share her bewilderment with Duncan?

She was still waiting for his reply.

So this was it, Tom thought – the moment he had dreaded, and there was no way round it. *The truth will come to light in the end.*

He sat her down at the kitchen table. "Listen, Sarah," he said, taking hold of her hand and hoping he sounded serious enough to engage her attention fully. "If I tell you what this is all about, you have to keep it to yourself. It's a secret. Do you understand?"

She nodded, giving him a little smile to reassure him. "Yes," she said, perhaps a little too readily.

"Listen to me, Sarah. I mean it," he said, desperate to hammer home the importance of this. "Because it's not just my secret – it's Robert's as well."

Her smile faded.

"You can't talk about it to anyone. Do you understand what I'm saying? You can't tell Duncan – your mam or dad, or any of your friends. Do you understand?" he repeated.

Her eyes widened like a small child's. "Yes," she whispered.

He tried not to rush things: he wanted her to appreciate the gravity of what he was about to say and take it in slowly, bit by bit. "Last year," he began, hearing his voice betraying his nervousness, and almost glad it did, "after Mam died, I discovered something." He paused to let this sink in. "Robert's not my father, Sarah," he confessed at last, and the rest of the story followed.

Her earlier eagerness to know his secret vanished as she digested the implications.

"Maybe, after today, you can guess who my father really is?" he said.

She nodded slowly. "Mr Rufford?"

"Yes."

She considered this for some time, biting her lip thoughtfully. Perhaps all the small changes she had noticed in him, and found so bewildering over the past year, now made sense to her. "He was upset, Tom," she said at last. "Why did he phone?"

He could tell her now, and the freedom to speak openly left him strangely elated; a guilty pleasure under such terrible circumstances.

She listened earnestly, nodding every once in a while to indicate she understood.

" ... So I want to see my granddad again – while I can," he explained.

She patted his hand. "Of course you do," she said solemnly. "Go on – you'd better get yourself packed and on your way. And Tom," she called after him. "I promise – I won't say a word – to anyone."

"Tell Robert I've told you, will you?"

She was biting her lip again. "Will he be upset?" she asked.

Tom shook his head. "No, I don't think so – not now."

From the expression on her face, he did not think she was entirely convinced.

He reached Lower Chursley just before noon and after a brief emotional reunion, John drove them down to Retton. He was wearing the strain of the last few days on his face for anyone to see, much as he had looked the first time they had met.

During the journey, little was said. There was little to say.

Charles was an old man. He was dying. That was all. Tom understood: John was facing what he himself had learned to face the year before. It was hard to talk at such a time, with nothing to do but wait for the inevitable. Sometimes the minutes seemed like hours, and every beat of the heart became a leaden pendulum marking out the slow and ponderous passage of time.

There would be days and weeks later to mull over the old man's life and legacy; to reflect on the good times rather than the bad; and to help Geraldine cope with the loss of the man she had loved so devotedly for so long.

It was a day for quiet fortitude, Tom thought – and for honesty as well. He had confessed one secret. Now he should confess another. Wipe the slate clean. He cleared his throat, feeling it tighten a little as he spoke. "John," he said, "I need to tell you something."

John just nodded, his eyes fixed on the road.

"About Sarah."

"Sarah?"

"She answered the phone when you called," Tom explained. "I had to tell her who you were – why you'd called. She'd not have understood why I'd got to come away if I hadn't."

John smiled faintly. "I suppose it had to come out sometime," he said quietly. And without any suspicion of the consequences of his question asked, "Who is she?"

Tom felt the all too familiar panic of knowing he was probably about to do something he might regret. "She's Robert's wife," he said, wishing there was an easier way to say this. "They got wed last October. She's expecting – sometime this summer."

His words hung in the air. At first there was no reaction: nothing, as if he had thought the words, not spoken them. Then John shot him a glance of such penetrating intensity he felt its full force strike him squarely in the chest. The next moment, the car was swerving into the side of the road and coming to a sudden and violent halt. Tom's head rebounded off the head rest with a jerk, and the car travelling behind them roared passed, horn blaring, the driver angrily gesticulating at the lack of any warning.

John's expression had frozen, his eyes riveting Tom to his seat. "He's *married?*" he said, his voice a potent mixture of incomprehension and anger Tom had never witnessed before.

A wave of guilt swept over him. He felt cold inside. He had never intended to break the news this way: he had planned to pick his moment with care. But Sarah's insistence to learn the truth, and his own urgent desire to rid himself of the burden of carrying too many secrets had overridden caution. He had done something terrible and he had no idea how to salvage anything from the wreckage. "I'm sorry," he managed at last, feeling the inadequacy of this apology sting his conscience. "I'm really sorry."

John was struck dumb. His breath, harsh and grating, came in fits and starts as he sat, just staring at him, disbelief chiselled into every line that furrowed his brow.

"I should have told you sooner," Tom confessed,

floundering under the weight of such a monumental miscalculation. "I just couldn't. I didn't know how."

There was still no response.

Tom stumbled on. "John," he said, desperate to explain himself, "I was pretty upset myself about things last October. I came down to Weaversham just to get away – to try and sort myself out. I wasn't thinking straight. I never expected that we'd meet up. It just happened. And when we did, there never seemed a right time to tell you."

There was a long pause before John asked, "Why did he do it, Thomas?" His expression betrayed a desperate need to understand. "Was it because I'd turned up at the funeral? Did that change the way he felt about her?"

Tom shook his head. "No, John, nothing like that. He still loved her. Maybe too much. She left a hole in his life he needed to fill."

John looked bewildered, the notion beyond his comprehension.

"It was a bad time to tell you," Tom said at last. "I'm sorry."

John looked away. "There would never have been a good time to tell me, Thomas," he said and they drove the rest of the way in silence.

It was mid-afternoon when they reached Retton Cottage Hospital. Charles was in a small side ward on his own, an oxygen supply by his bed to help him breathe. Geraldine was sitting beside him holding his hand: composed; dignified; stoic. She rose to greet them.

"Thank you for coming, Thomas," she said, holding him close for a moment.

"I wanted to see him."

She smiled up at him, pleased to see he meant it.

John leaned forward and kissed her. "How is he?"

"They say it's just a matter of time," she said, forcing a smile. "It could be hours. It could be days."

Charles lay with his eyes closed, wheezing as his chest rose and fell, all the bluster and bombast gone. All that was left was the dry husk of an old man: thinner, fragile, barely there.

John stood at the bottom of the bed, solemn and withdrawn, his thoughts held close, his eyes fixed on the old man.

Geraldine held Charles' hand again and leaned forward so he could hear her more easily. "Charles," she said encouragingly. "Thomas has come to see you."

"Hello, Granddad. I said I'd come."

There was a moment of unexpected clarity. Charles opened his eyes, turning his head slowly to look at him. Recognition flickered briefly into life, and a bony hand reached out to grasp his wrist. "Thomas?" the old man said, a faint smile quivering on his lips.

"Yes, I'm here."

"Had a good trip down?"

"Yes, thank you."

"Good. Good."

A few minutes later, the old man slipped back into semi-consciousness, drifting away from them all. There was just the sound of his laboured breathing and little else.

They stayed for more than hour. When there was no

change, Geraldine said, "John, come back tomorrow. Thomas has had a long journey and I'm perfectly all right here on my own. Michael said he'd call in later when he comes off duty. He'll let you know if there's any change."

They arrived back at Westercot to a full moon rising above the trees behind the house. It hung in the darkness, its disc a strangely copper hue.

John stopped and stood on the path for a moment staring up at it. "An eclipse," he said quietly, turning to Tom. "Do you think it's an omen?"

It seemed unnecessary to say the obvious.

They went inside and waited for a call that might not come.

It was almost midnight and still no word. John stretched and got up from his chair for the umpteenth time to wander round the room. "I've been thinking," he said, "about what you said – last year. About letting go of your mother. Was that because Robert had?"

"Probably."

"Well, I think you're right. I've made a New Year's resolution. I've decided to sell up – find somewhere else in the village perhaps – somewhere not filled with my impossible dreams. What do you think?"

"I think you'd miss the place."

John shook his head. "Not now," he said. "The future looks different to me now. I want to have the courage to embrace it – to leave the past behind – like Robert."

"What about her pictures? Would you sell those too?" It seemed unlikely.

"No. I could never do that. But maybe I shouldn't hide them away. I've made my collection a shrine, haven't I?" he said, almost apologising for cherishing them. "Not very sensible, is it?" A ghost of a smile flickered briefly into life. He checked his watch for the umpteenth time. "Want a nightcap?" he suggested.

Tom wished the phone would ring, and the difficult, but inevitable process of grieving could begin – and they could do it together: father and son. But the phone was silent, and John was trying to fill the void with plans for the future that needed the present to become the past. Nothing could be resolved till then.

"What about you?" John was asking as he poured them both a generous tumbler of whisky each. "Will you stay on at Rigg End?"

Tom took a long, slow draught, giving the matter some thought. "I don't know," he said at last, because it was true.

CHAPTER FORTY-TWO

It was almost two weeks before Tom returned to the farm. Spring was blowing in on a fresh wind: the crocus blooms beginning to fade; daffodil spears thrusting upwards in their place; Brack's grave surrounded by colour.

Robert, looking stronger and less haggard, with Sarah's arm around his waist, hobbled out on his crutches to greet Tom in the yard.

"Didn't expect to find you here," Tom said, pleased to see him.

"They let me out early, for good behaviour, Tom. Couldn't get back here fast enough," he added, smiling fondly down at Sarah. "Missed her cooking."

She was noticeably pregnant now. Tom could feel the curve of her belly against him when she reached up to kiss him on the cheek. "Sorry about your granddad," she said quietly.

He nodded his thanks, and turned to happier thoughts. "Have to say you're looking grand," he said, which she was: there were dimples in her cheeks again and the old sparkle in her eyes.

She smiled, clearly thrilled he thought so.

"Come on in, Tom," Robert was urging him. "Not a day for me to stand around for long without a coat."

The kitchen was warm and welcoming, filled with the aroma of a Sunday roast. Home, Tom thought, but strangely alien.

"Dinner's ready," Sarah said. "You'll be ready for something warming, Tom."

Robert lowered himself gingerly into his usual chair at the table and leaned the crutches up against the dresser while Sarah served up the meal. "Getting the hang of these damned things at last," he said triumphantly. "But I'll be glad to be rid of them."

"Will it be long?"

"Not so good with the stairs just yet," he confessed.

"He's very good at going up and down on his bottom," Sarah said mischievously, ruffling Robert's hair and leaning over to kiss him playfully.

Tom concentrated hard on his food finding their closeness still an embarrassment he found difficult to hide.

Robert was oblivious. "Jarred came over a couple of days ago and took the cows," he said. "Made a good offer, so there didn't seem much point waiting 'til they'd calved." There was a hint of regret in his voice.

Tom had not noticed they were gone. His thoughts had been elsewhere.

"Couldn't expect Ian to put his life on hold for ever, could I?" Robert was saying.

"Craig and Dana have invited Bridie and Ian over to

Alberta for Easter," Sarah explained. "So it's for the best. And Duncan – " She stifled a laugh. "You won't believe it!"

"Duncan's got other things on mind these days," Robert said solemnly.

"He's got a girlfriend, Tom. Beth Liddel! Jarred let it slip when he came over." She could barely contain herself. "Duncan goes red every time I mention it," she added, evidently enjoying teasing him.

Poor Duncan. No doubt Jarred Liddel, with his prize Limousins and five-hundred acres, would be no more enthusiastic about Duncan Robson for a son-in-law than Wallace Armstrong would have been.

There was chocolate sponge pudding and custard to follow, which Tom dutifully ate, although he was beginning to feel the effects of a large meal without the hunger that hard physical work could raise in a man. He was the last to finish.

Robert waited patiently.

Sarah cleared away the dishes with noisy efficiency. "Why don't you two go into the sitting room?" she suggested, artlessly organising their removal from her realm. "I've set up a lovely fire – and you'll have plenty to talk about."

"We'll get out of your way then," Robert said, struggling to his feet and refusing Tom's help when he offered it. "Have to do this on my own if I can," he said with a grimness that contradicted his apparent cheerful determination to succeed. He wrestled the crutches into place and extricated himself from the confines of the kitchen in a series of cumbersome manoeuvres.

Watching his painfully slow progress, Tom wondered if Robert's dedication outweighed his genuine ability. Rather than embarrass him by waiting, he went ahead to bank up the fire.

There were subtle changes to the room, he noticed: new soft cushions on the sofa and easy chairs; the hearth rug put out of harm's way in case Robert caught his crutches on it; and a low footstool rescued from the attic for him to rest his foot. Sarah was cherishing her man.

With a deep frown of concentration, Robert finally overcame the challenge of easing himself into the fireside chair. It took him a moment or two to recover himself, and he made no attempt to stop Tom relieving him of the crutches, or from making sure the cushions were supporting him in the right place. "Thanks Tom. I try not to make a fuss," he said. "It's just sometimes, if I move too fast, I get a bit of a pain here – under the ribs." He pointed to the offending spot. "The scar still pulls a bit. Shouldn't complain, should I?" he added. "I'm lucky to be here."

"You can't run before you walk," Tom said.

Robert looked up at him. "I like your humour, Tom," he said with a grim smile. "I'll be fine in a couple of months, you'll see."

"I'm sure you will."

Robert finally settled himself in his chair, in no hurry it seemed to broach the topic Tom felt certain was uppermost in his mind: the future. Instead, after a moment's reflection, Robert said, "Duncan was saying you've been seeing Sophie Gorst while you were away."

Tom smiled. "What do you think?"

"I think it made a good tale."

"It was all I could come with at the time. Felt a bit of a heel lying to him."

"You did what you thought best."

"Maybe." Tom paused, feeling he had to say something about the secret he had so signally failed to keep. "Look – Rob, I'm sorry I had to tell Sarah – you know – about you and me – without letting you know first."

"I don't think you had much choice, Tom. Fudging it would've made things worse. And maybe it's better this way. There should be no secrets between a man and wife, should there?"

It was a comment filled with pathos.

"What about Jamie and Flora? Shouldn't we be telling them now?"

"No, Tom," Robert said, absolutely set against the idea. "Let's leave things as they are at the moment. Do you mind?"

"No. I suppose there's no point muddying a pool if you don't have to."

"That's what I thought."

The room was warm, and Tom found himself slipping effortlessly into that comfortable state that can overtake anyone in mid-afternoon after a hearty meal. He was mulling over how his life was changing when Robert suddenly asked him, "So there's nothing between you and Sophie Gorst then?"

"No – nothing."

Robert smiled. "It was always Janet Robson for you, wasn't it?" he said, conjuring her out of nowhere.

Tom's comfortable languor evaporated. He could feel himself blush.

"Do you ever hear from her?" Robert was asking. "Ian says they don't keep in touch any more."

Tom decided against lying. "She sent me a letter back in November," he said casually. "There was no address," he added, not wanting to go too far down that particular road, because one afternoon at Westercot, he had done precisely what he had decided he would never do – in an act of sheer madness, he had picked up the phone and dialled the Buckhurst Veterinary Centre.

"Hello, I'm trying to get in touch with Janet Robson," he had said.

"Janet?" answered a bright young thing on the other end of the phone. "Oh, she doesn't work here any more. She was only here for a couple of months last year. Short-term contract."

"Do you know where she is now?"

"No, I'm sorry. She moved to Farnhamhurst, I think. Just hold on, I'll ask around." He had heard a muffled conversation before he was told, "Amy says she isn't there now. Sorry, but they might be able to help. I'll give you their number." And she had. He had phoned them, picking up very quickly that no one was willing, or able to oblige him with further information. The trail had gone dead.

Robert was evidently curious, waiting to see if he was going to expand on what Janet had written.

Tom shrugged off the notion there was anything to tell. "She's made a new life for herself," he said simply.

Robert just smiled. "Why is it I get the feeling you're still sweet on her?" he said with unerring insight.

"Not much point if I was. She's got someone else," Tom said, trying to draw a line under the subject.

Robert frowned. "Ah – I didn't know that." It seemed to trouble him. "Well, let's get down to business, Tom," he said with a sigh, shifting subjects once again. "In your letter, you said you'd been thinking things over."

"I'm not sure where to start."

"At the beginning, Tom. It's always the best."

Tom hesitated. There was no easy way to say what he had decided to do, and he knew Robert would find some of his decisions hard to take. "I need to strike out on my own, Rob," he began. "Best thing all round. Give you and Sarah some space. You'll be able to run this place on your own now the cows have gone."

Robert nodded slowly, his expression unchanged. Perhaps he had expected this for some time. "Another farm?" he asked.

"No – I want to start again – go back to college – take a degree in animal management."

Robert gave him a very old-fashioned look. "That's exactly what Mr Laidlaw advised you to do, isn't it?" he said. "At Hawkrigg – way back when?"

Tom was embarrassed to admit it.

"There was no telling you then, was there?"

"No – I didn't see the need."

"But you do now?"

"Yes. I want to make the most of what I've learned here at Rigg End, but do something different. Get my degree – sign up for a further education qualification and then aim for a lectureship somewhere."

"Any ideas where?"

"Not yet. Want to see how things work out."

Robert mulled this over. "I'm impressed," he said quietly. "I think your mother would've been too. She always hoped you'd aim for something a bit more – intellectually challenging."

"I shouldn't have been so stubborn."

"Well, I'm glad you were. We made a good team here you and I. Built the place up together." There was a note of pride in his voice.

Tom remembered feeling that same pride himself. "It was a good apprenticeship," he said.

"Nice of you to say so." Robert eased himself into another position on the chair, wincing slightly. "Can you just wedge the cushion a bit more to the right, Tom? I can't quite reach it."

Tom obliged, taking the opportunity to put a couple of extra logs on the fire.

"I take it you've found a college on your travels?"

"Yes. Alderheath – on the north side of Lingford. They run a two-year course. I went over to see them. There's no problem with funding – and I've got the qualifications – so I've enrolled as a mature student starting in September. I'll stay on to help at Rigg End 'til then."

Robert nodded.

There was no need for Tom to elaborate further on arrangements after that: Robert had already made the connection between Alderheath's location and its proximity to Lower Chursley. "Will you be staying at John's during term-time?" he asked, probably knowing the answer already.

"He asked if I'd like to consider it – doesn't want to stifle me, he says. He's looking for a new place himself this summer. Wants me to go down when he finds one – give it my blessing," he added, aware this was probably unnecessary information as far as Robert was concerned, but feeling compelled to tell him anyway.

"You will still come and visit us won't you, Tom?" Robert was asking, a nervous smile tugging at the corners of his mouth. "You'll always be welcome you know. Rigg End's been your home for twenty-six years. Nothing can change that."

It was an easy promise to make, but beyond it lay a harder task. Tom paused, knowing what he was going to say would be less welcome. He cleared his throat, feeling his mouth go dry. "Rob, I know you meant well, but I don't want to hold you to your promise – about the farm."

Robert frowned, not understanding fully what he meant.

Tom tried again. "I don't want you to think I'm ungrateful – but –" The words were jumbling in his head and he was afraid they were going to come out all wrong.

Robert was waiting.

"What I'm trying to say, Rob, is – I don't expect you to leave Rigg End to me. I know you said you would because we built up the place together, but it's Sarah's home now. And what happens if the baby turns out to be a boy and he grows up wanting to run the farm? Why shouldn't he? He'll be *your* son ..." He ran out of words.

Robert was having none of it. "No – no!" he said emphatically, shaking his head at the very suggestion. "It's your inheritance, Tom. I *want* you to have it."

"I know – you've always said so. But it's not the right thing to do, Rob – not now." Tom did not want to add what was so blindingly obvious – that the ties that had once bound him to Rigg End had irretrievably broken; his mother was dead; Brack was gone; and the bonds of his true father were drawing him away. He reached out and took hold of Robert's hand, finding its once calloused roughness strangely smooth to the touch. "You don't owe me anything, Rob," he insisted. "You've nurtured me – supported me in everything I've done – given me a solid grounding to build on for the future. What else could I ask for?"

Robert's face wore its familiar expression of locked-in emotion hiding the pain beneath. "If that's what you want," he said.

"Yes, that's what I want."

There was a moment of deep impenetrable silence, their hands still locked together.

"I wish you'd been mine, Tom," Robert said fiercely. "You should have been. You were everything I ever wanted from a son."

Tom stood up, trying to smile. It was impossible.

CHAPTER FORTY-THREE

August 1994

Janet brushed back her hair and bullied it into a restraining band at the nape of her neck. It would be another hot summer's day. She chose her light muslin skirt with its green and gold swirls, and the long-sleeved cream over-blouse to keep off the sun. She needed to feel cool and comfortable. Staring at her image in the mirror, she felt anything but.

Downstairs, Tabitha was patiently sitting on the kitchen window sill, cleaning her paws, waiting to be let in.

Janet opened the door and abstractedly began to make breakfast. The cat, purring loudly, weaved itself against her legs until she was fed, then quietly slipped away again through the open door into the garden.

"Come on, lazy bones," Janet called upstairs. "Breakfast's ready."

It was going to be a long morning she would find difficult to fill. Perhaps they should go for a walk in the forest.

They set off after breakfast following the winding sandy track through the scrub and young birch saplings, into the plantation where tall pines offered shade from the intense heat.

There was not a breath of wind. Nothing stirred, not even a cricket in the long grasses. There was just absolute silence, and the strong heady scent of resin filling the air.

She walked with her mind disengaged, aware she was trying not to think too deeply. Ahead of her, Gina, in her new green gingham birthday frock, was skipping along the track, her bunches of bright hair bobbing in the sunlight as she went – in a world of her own. Every now and then she would stop suddenly to study something that had caught her five-year-old's attention.

Janet followed her into a clearing of grass and fern shimmering in the heat. Gina had crouched down studying the ground intently, a chubby finger delicately following an outline in the silver sand. Janet hunkered down beside her. "Deer," she said. "See – they went that way."

Gina's eyes were wide with excitement. "Can we follow them?"

Janet shook her head. "They'll be hiding in the forest now."

Gina looked disappointed.

"Never mind. We've got to go home anyway. We've got someone coming to see us this afternoon." There – she had said it. Was that so difficult?

Gina frowned, unimpressed by the prospect of a visitor. "Who?" she asked, giving a very audible sigh of disapproval.

"A Mr Rufford."

"Has he come here before?"

"No."

Gina considered this for a moment. "Oh," she said,

looking suddenly very serious. "So I'll have to put my toys away."

"Yes, please."

A little after one-thirty, there was the sound of a car pulling off the road at Frith's End and proceeding at a slow pace down the dusty track leading to the cottage. Janet watched its progress from the kitchen window, wishing she could control the butterflies dancing in her stomach.

The car stopped in front of the gate and the dust settled to reveal a dark-blue 4x4. Its driver seemed in no hurry to get out: she could see him removing his sun glasses to read the name on the gatepost, and having satisfied himself he was at the right place, proceeded to complete other, unspecific tasks before opening the door.

He came through the gate, his jacket casually slung over one shoulder. He was smart, dressed in navy chinos and open-necked cream shirt, the sleeves rolled back to the elbow in the heat. The sight of him was heart-stopping.

With Gina in tow, she went out to meet him, Gina wrapping her small arms around her protectively. "Is that Mr Rufford, Mummy?" she asked in a whisper, watching him approach from behind her mother's skirt.

Janet heard her voice catch in her throat as she said, "Yes, it's Mr Rufford."

He looked up and waved as he came down the path. "Janet," he said smiling broadly.

He would have come closer, she was sure of it, except he had suddenly noticed Gina. He held back, his smile fading into uncertainty, the unspoken question clearly written in his eyes.

Her heart was hammering. "Tom," she said, trying to sound perfectly relaxed. "This is Gina."

Gina extricated herself and stood in front of him, looking up at him as a queen might receive an ambassador from a far-off foreign land.

His smile re-established itself. "Hello, Gina," he said graciously, stooping slightly to offer her a sun-tanned hand to shake, which she did with some vigour.

"Hello," she replied, putting on her best manners. "I was five yesterday."

A small frown of regret furrowed his brow. "Oh – I'm sorry – I didn't know. I'd have brought you a present."

"It doesn't matter," Gina informed him solemnly, and having satisfied herself as to what manner of man he was, she skipped off to sit on her swing under the trees from where she could watch the two of them with impunity as they stood, somewhat awkwardly facing one another, with some distance between them on the path.

Tom was apparently waiting for some guidance, his concentration divided between his loafers and Gina on her swing.

"She's Geoffrey's," Janet said quietly. She wanted there to be no doubt in his mind.

"Ah," he said, glancing briefly in Gina's direction again. She giggled and waved to him. He waved back. "She's very like her mother," he added, with a faint smile. "She has your eyes."

She wondered if he were already beginning to regret his decision to visit. Perhaps she should have been more honest with him when he phoned, but her head had been clamouring with the shock of hearing him again, and her desire to see him had overridden caution. Too late now. Perhaps he would stay awhile then politely take his leave. Yes, he would do that. "Did it take long from Hayscombe?" she asked casually, leading the way down the path towards the cottage.

"Only a couple of hours," he said, dismissing what must have been a wearisome journey in such heat. "Missed the turning to Frithwood. Had to go back to Woodstead and ask at the Post Office." His voice implied mild amusement. "Caused a bit of stir asking for Frith Cottage," he added.

"I remain something of a local curiosity," she explained. "Even after three years." Did she need to say more? Probably not. "I've made some lemonade. Would you like some?"

He said he would.

"You can sit out in the garden, if you like. It's cooler under the trees."

From the kitchen window, she watched him make himself comfortable on one of the cushioned garden seats, his jacket abandoned over the arm of another. He had changed into the man she had glimpsed during their brief interlude together: his face had filled out a little; his features subtly enhanced; and the rolling gait from years walking The Rigg had gone. Now he moved with an easy grace that drew the eye. It hurt her just to look at him, and in her heart she wished she had not let him come. Better to fondly remember old times than destroy them on a sudden whim. She poured out the freshly made lemonade into tall glasses and placed them on a tray. Taking a deep breath, she went out into the garden.

Gina bounded off her swing. "Can I have the one with the bendy straw?" she asked, and having secured possession of it, perched herself on another seat and continued studying their visitor with undisguised interest. In Gina's presence, conversation drifted into small talk restricted to observations on the garden and the pleasant location of the cottage, sheltered as it was by the cluster of mature pines that separated it from the open heath beyond. Eventually, Gina got bored with their talk, and leaving her empty glass on the tray, went back to her swing to watch them from this vantage point.

Tabitha emerged from the depths of a heather bed and crossed the lawn with evident intent, tail erect. She paused in front of this stranger, then curled herself up at his feet, resting her head on his shoe. He leaned forward to stroke her behind the ears. She purred appreciatively, looking up adoringly into his eyes. He turned his attention from the cat. "What happened, Jan?" he asked, giving her the benefit of his intense gaze.

"Gina happened," she said, realising this would never be enough for him.

"Did you know? – when we ...?" He was searching for the right words.

She shook her head. "Not at first. But that's why I had to leave. I'm sorry I couldn't tell you."

He said nothing, leaning down again to fuss the cat.

She wished she knew what he was thinking. "I didn't want to get you tangled up in my mess, Tom. You'd got enough to deal with at the time."

He nodded, sitting back and finishing his lemonade with deliberate slowness. "Where's Geoffrey these days?" he asked, catching her off-guard.

Her mouth went dry. "I don't know," she said, deciding to tell him the truth.

He raised an eyebrow but said nothing.

"We were never actually a couple," she confessed. "I was just a casual affair to him – one of many apparently. He said the baby probably wasn't his anyway." She turned to look away for a moment: he had said a great many other things besides – offensive and cruel.

Tom was frowning. "Then why tell me you'd got together again?"

"I needed to cut myself off, Tom – from everyone – once Gina was born. Ian and Bridie would have died of shame if they'd known the truth." She could hear herself sounding strangely petulant.

Tabitha jumped up onto the seat next to Tom and lay down, resting her head on his thigh, a tentative paw dabbing at his hand seeking more attention. He obliged, lost in thought for a moment. "Then what made you tell Duncan?" he asked.

"I ran out of money. It was as simple as that." What else could she say? "I lived with Amy rent-free 'til Gina was born – then I had to move out. I found a flat with another single mum and paid her to look after Gina while I was working at Farnhamhurst. Then things fell apart. She moved out, the temporary contract at Farnhamhurst came to an end and I couldn't find another job – so I couldn't pay the rent. I was desperate." It was an understatement, but it was all he needed to know.

He made no comment.

His silence made her feel defensive.

He looked up from the cat, his expression betraying his thoughts. "He always said he didn't know where you were," he said, a note of accusation in his voice.

"Don't be cross with him, Tom. He was keeping my secret."

He smiled apologetically and looked away. "Like you kept mine," he said, shifting his attention to the cat again. Tabitha's purring grew louder and more insistent. Eventually he said, "He used to call me 'a dark horse'. Takes one to know one, I suppose."

Janet studied her hands in her lap.

"Why did he tell me in the end?"

She concentrated on her hands. "I asked him to," she confessed. "Once it all came out ... about you." She dropped the subject quickly.

Tabitha rolled onto her back, demanding more attention. Tom stroked her under her chin and she closed her eyes in pure ecstasy.

Janet could feel herself shrinking inside. He would go soon, she decided. He was thinking how best to extricate himself from this awkward situation, and she turned her attention to Gina to mask her disquiet.

Gina was still happily occupied on the swing. "Look, Mummy!" she called out, seeing Janet take notice of her. And she urged the swing higher, laughing mischievously.

"Careful, Gina! Not too high."

With an expertise born of practice, Gina hopped effortlessly off the swing and bounded across the lawn to lean over the arm of Tom's chair with an air of self-importance. "I'm starting school soon," she said in all seriousness.

He was polite enough to look suitably impressed.

Gina began tugging at Janet's sleeve. "Can we show Mr Rufford where the deer hide at night?" she asked, putting on her most appealing smile.

Janet glanced across at him. "Maybe Mr Rufford has other plans," she said, giving him the chance to say he had, and take his leave.

He shrugged. "Not that I know of," he said, apparently prepared to stay a little longer.

"Will you come then?" Gina persisted.

"Why not?" he said, carefully extricating himself from a disappointed Tabitha and getting to his feet. "A walk would do me good after the drive." He stretched, enjoying the pleasure of it, unaware of Janet watching him. She could remember how he looked at other times.

Gina was clapping her hands in delight. "Come on then!"

They walked silently following the firebreak through the plantation, Gina dancing ahead of them, Tom in no hurry to restart a conversation. Away from the shade, the afternoon sun was searingly hot against Janet's skin. She should have brought her straw hat. Tom seemed unaware of its intensity, sauntering through the sunlight, jacket casually thrown over his shoulder.

"You know," she said, feeling she should make an effort to re-establish some rapport, "I always thought you and Sarah would get together again – once you'd got me out of your system." It was side-stepping another issue she would like to raise – but not yet. Maybe not at all.

He shook his head, glancing in her direction. "I meant what I said – we never clicked."

Without Gina there, she wondered, would he have added, "Not like us"? "Yes – well, I wasn't sure," she said. "It was quite a shock – when Duncan told me – about her and Robert."

"Yes – well, it was a shock to all of us." He pondered this for a moment. "But they were happy together, Jan – very happy."

"How is she?" It was a difficult topic to raise.

"Keeping busy," he said. "She's opened the bunkhouse again for the summer. Mary comes down from Rattling Gate pretty regularly to look after Robbie and Lauren. They're quite a handful," he added with a fleeting smile.

"Duncan said Rob wasn't well over Christmas."

"He never really got over the accident. Went downhill quite quickly in the spring."

They had arrived at the clearing and Gina was calling to them to hurry up, impatient to show the deer prints in the sand. Tom sauntered over and hunkered down beside her to inspect them.

"Do you think they'll come back tonight? – when it's gone dark?" Gina was asking him, making it sound mysterious and exciting all at once.

"Very likely," he said, keeping his voice low to chime with hers. "See – over there?" And he pointed to the spot. "Where the ferns are all trampled behind the tall grass? That's their secret hiding place."

Gina's eyes widened, delighted by this intelligence. "Do you know a lot about animals?" she whispered.

"Yes – but mainly farm animals," he said as if imparting a state secret. "I teach other people how to look after them."

"Mummy helps mend sick ones," Gina confided in him. "She's a senior veterinary nurse." She was immensely proud she knew how to pronounce this.

"So I believe," he said with great seriousness.

In the blink of an eye, Gina was her boisterous self again. She jumped up and pulled him to his feet. "Mummy," she called back. "Can Mr Rufford stay to tea?" And as if to confirm her invitation, added, "He can have some of my cake."

Tom turned, looking back to where Janet stood, a quizzical expression on his face.

She wondered what he was thinking. "Can you stay?" she asked, making the enquiry as undemanding as possible. "There's nothing special, I'm afraid. Just egg sandwiches and what's left of Gina's birthday cake."

"I didn't give you much warning," he said, apparently prepared to take full responsibility for her lack of adequate catering. "Sandwiches and birthday cake sound pretty good to me." And he engaged Gina with a knowing smile, accepting he was a willing accomplice to her plan.

They began to head back towards the cottage, Gina still skipping ahead of them.

"Where are you teaching?" Janet asked.

He seemed pleased she had overheard his conversation with Gina. "Abbotscombe College – Lecturer in Animal Management," he said with a touch of pride in his voice. "Just finished my first year – enjoying it."

"Abbotscombe's got a good reputation."

"I was lucky to get the post."

"I doubt luck had much to do with it."

"I'm flattered," he said, accepting her praise with a wry smile.

She would have liked to ask him something else.

Tea was monopolised by Gina's ceaseless chatter, and afterwards the evening sun tempted them back out into the garden. They sat on the bench seat by the kitchen wall, where the rough cottage bricks reflected the warmth of the day. The heat was less intense now, and a light breeze whispered in the tops of the pines wafting resin scent across the garden.

They were a comfortable foursome, Janet thought: Tom sitting next to her; Gina, tired after so much excitement and cake, falling into a light doze by her side; and Tabitha, not to be outdone, curled up against Tom.

He seemed in no hurry to leave, his concentration fixed on the horizon where the sun was beginning to sink towards the skyline of ragged pines across the heath.

"Do you miss Rigg End?" she asked.

"Sometimes."

"Duncan still feels bad about it – about the farm."

He looked surprised. "Really? Rob knew that all I ever wanted was a few things of my mother's – her old desk – the painting of Brack. Duncan was pretty much running the place over those last six months anyway."

"But giving him a half share, Tom – it just seemed – well, wrong."

He had tilted his head slightly to smile at her. "We all know which way the wind will blow," he said, " – eventually."

"Do you think so?"

"Robert knew what he was doing, Jan. He always did."

"Duncan is very fond of the children," she said.

"Do you think Robert didn't know that?"

On the far side of the heath, the sun finally slipped below the tops of the pines. Tabitha yawned and curled herself into a tighter ball snuggling closer to Tom for warmth.

"It must have been hard for Jamie and Flora – coming to terms with everything – what happened over the farm – you ..."

He was thoughtful for a moment. "I owed it to John to change my name," he said. "Robert knew I would. But it's all water under the bridge now. Jamie and I had a heart-to-heart about it afterwards." He laughed. "A half-brother is better than no brother, he says."

"What about Flora? Duncan said she'd changed."

"She's grown up, Jan, that's all. Like we all do when we

find out we can't run away from life." He was looking at her very intently now.

She turned away, finding his gaze too much to bear.

"Did you know she'd married again," he was saying. "In June? Kieran Grogan – someone from her London days. Nice guy."

"Yes. Duncan mentioned it."

"Did he tell you they've got five children between them?" He seemed bemused by this. "Five!"

"He said they're living at Meeston Lodge – your mother's place."

"Mm. I always knew there was a reason not to sell it – just never knew what it was." He was evidently pleased with his decision.

In the west, the sky was beginning to turn a liquid turquoise. The breeze had dropped and the first bats came out from their roosts in the eaves to flit silently and erratically above their heads between the house and trees.

"Do you see much of your family, Tom?" she asked. She wondered if he did: there were times she missed the once familiar closeness of High Oakbank Farm.

"Mm. Quite a lot. We're making up for lost time," he added.

"What about your father? Do you really believe he's a confirmed bachelor?"

"I don't think he'll ever change, Jan. Not now. He has this very intense platonic relationship with his astonishingly attractive receptionist." He frowned, passing off his inability to understand this incomprehensible arrangement with a casual shrug. "Still, he seems happy enough ferrying Bernard Makepeace round the countryside taking photographs of crumbling castles and majestic manors. Their third book comes out next month. I said I'd go up to Lingford for the official launch."

"Does he come down to Hayscombe often?"

"Usually a couple of times a month. He likes to sit in the garden."

She was suddenly aware of him withdrawing into himself, becoming remote: of a stillness about him that sent a shiver through her.

He turned suddenly to look at her, pausing before he said, "If I asked you, Jan, would you and Gina come to stay sometime – at Hayscombe? It's a pretty place – all honey-coloured Cotswold stone. We've a village green with a duck pond – and a children's playground. Gina would love it." His voice had taken on an unsettling husky quality.

"It's a nice thought, Tom," she said, betraying her reticence. She did not want to be drawn back into an relationship that had nowhere to go.

"No, I'm serious, Jan," he said, unexpectedly reaching out to take her hand. "Would you come? I'd love you to."

"There's Tabitha to think of –"

"Bring her with you. Why not? I'm sure I've got room for a cat." He was joking, of course, trying to get her to say 'yes'.

"What about Sophie?" she heard herself ask. Yes, what about Sophie Gorst? Where did she fit into his life?

"Sophie?" He sounded surprised by her question. "Did Duncan mention her?"

"In passing."

He laughed softly. "I was staying with John – not Sophie. I needed an excuse at the time, but I should have told him afterwards."

She was vexed with herself for asking.

He had begun to lightly thread his fingers through hers; a slow progression of infinite tenderness. "She's never been a part of my life, Jan. She married a handsome Italian three years ago and lives in Milan. We exchange Christmas cards, that's all."

She was watching his hands weave their magic against hers: his touch exquisite; delicate. And dangerous.

"What about you, Jan?" he was asking. "Anyone in your life?"

In the deepening twilight, she could barely see him, but she could imagine the look in his eyes as he spoke. "No," she said, aware he was leaning closer and she could feel his breath brushing lightly against her neck, reminding her of other times. She moved away a little, trying not to waken Gina. "Why did you come, Tom?" she asked, wishing she had kept him away.

He was puzzled. "You know why. I wanted to see you again. I've been wanting to see you for five years."

"But we can't turn the clock back. It's too late for that."

"No it's not, Jan," he insisted gently, raising her hand to his lips and kissing the tips of her fingers with a deliberate gentleness. "And this isn't about turning the clock back, is it? It's about you – and me – and what we've always known. That we belong together."

"Things have changed, Tom."

"Not the things that matter."

"You can't say that. I've got Gina now."

"Yes, you have," he said, and she could hear him smile. "And she's lovely. And so are you."